The Godfather
and
American Culture

SUNY series in Italian/American Culture
Fred L. Gardaphe, editor

The Godfather
and
American Culture

How the Corleones
Became "Our Gang"

Chris Messenger

State University of New York Press

Published by
State University of New York Press, Albany

For information, address the State University of New York Press,
90 State Street, Suite 700, Albany, NY 12207

Production by Marilyn P. Semerad
Marketing by Patrick Durocher

Library of Congress Cataloging-in-Publication Data

Messenger, Christian K., 1943–
   The Godfather and American culture : how the Corleones became
"Our Gang" / Chris Messenger.
      p. cm. — (SUNY series in Italian/American culture)
   Includes bibliographical references and index.
   ISBN 0-7914-5357-X (alk. paper) — ISBN 0-7914-5358-8 (pbk. : alk. paper)
   1. Puzo, Mario, 1920– Godfather.   2. Corleone family (Fictitious
characters)   3. Italian Americans in literature.   4. Criminals in literature.
5. Family in literature.   6. Mafia in literature.   I. Title.   II. Series.

PS3566.U9 G63 2002
813'.54—dc21   2001049424

10   9   8   7   6   5   4   3   2   1

Contents

Acknowledgments

The Godfather has been with us in America for a long time, and my interest has been germinating for what seems like decades as well. Puzo's and Coppola's texts have been important to my teaching about popular narrative at the University of Illinois at Chicago for fifteen years. I've taught *The Godfather* in many contexts in literature courses to everyone from initially dubious freshmen who thought the university was for other pursuits to Ph.D. candidates who became willing accomplices in critical heists of theories and reading agendas. Thanks also goes to several critical reading friends: Marsha Cassidy, Gloria Nardini, Dina Bozicas, Marina Lewis, and Gina Frangello. Special thanks to John Huntington whose standards dictate that his good estimate of my prose is a sign that I might have nailed it. I benefited from the State University of New York Press readings of Frank Lentricchia and Anthony J. Tamburri. I've come full circle with Fred Gardaphe through our mutual interests and manuscripts; having been called upon to perform a major service for each other, we've formed a critical family of two.

My first pass at the Roland Barthes material in chapter 5 was facilitated by a Humanities Institute Fellowship at UIC. At State University of New York Press, I would like to thank my acquisitions editor, James Peltz, production editor Marilyn Semerad, marketing manager Patrick Durocher, and freelance copyeditor Camille Hale. I am grateful to Donadio & Olson, Inc. for permission to quote from the works of Mario Puzo.

I've been surrounded at home by *Godfather* aficionados. A part of the Messenger family business has always been good reading, writing, and editing, and I hope I've been more benign paterfamilias than Corleone. Thanks, Carrie, Luke, and Ellie. Finally, no book would ever get done without Janet, editor and compass down all the years, who, when I made the offer, did not refuse, and thereby hangs the tale of our life.

Introduction

The Critic's Voice in Popular Fiction Study

Several years ago I became captivated by two scenes in *The Godfather,* which both fascinated and repelled me. The first is the deathbed scene between Vito Corleone and his dying *consigliere* Genco Abbandando on Connie Corleone's wedding day; the narrative voice concludes, "as if the Don could truly snatch the life of Genco Abbandando back from that most foul and criminal traitor to man" (48). The second scene shows Hollywood producer Jack Woltz in shock to find the severed head of his stallion, Khartoum, bleeding at the foot of his bed; after he stops screaming, he thinks that "there couldn't be any kind of world if people acted this way" (69). Everything about the two scenes is visceral and immediate, yet their respective conclusions seemed to me oddly ameliorating under strange circumstances of narrative agency. In the Genco scene, Mario Puzo ended with the blandest of universals about the power of death. The Woltz scene ended in either a great hypocrisy or a weak irony or both. I was unable to account for the scenes' undeniable power, which culminated in capitulation to slack moralizing about "death" or "capitalism." How *about* a popular writer who could get me going that way! I found myself writing "Puzo" or "Michael" or "Don C" in the margins of critical pieces I read. Everything I was absorbing about history, ideology, aesthetics, the family, dialogue, monologue, best sellers, elite fiction moved me to wander back to *The Godfather* as site.

Some day—and I knew that day might never come—I would be called upon to perform a service, to explain to myself and to a readership the full range of this American popular classic and the contradictions in the long career of its author. The challenge to get *The Godfather* and Puzo done right became the offer I couldn't refuse. Just like Don Corleone's family and its power, *The Godfather* appeared to take root in my critical consciousness. If I had indeed been colonized, like any aware colonial subject, I wanted to convert the language of domination into my own rhetorical capital. In short, I wanted to explain how the Corleones had become "Our Gang" in America, in as complete a takeover as any popular narrative had achieved in the late twentieth century.

Certain subjects kept posing themselves as questions to me: how were readers to grieve for the novel's real victims of the Corleones who

1

are never mentioned in the novel? I numbered these to be the drug addicts and runners; the victims of bookmakers, prostitution, and loan sharking; those who provided kickbacks for protection; and the honest members of labor unions. How could readers break into Puzo's monologic approval of his "good" murderers when he gives us little choice but to root for them to kill his "bad" murderers? How could I talk of these subjects without losing my objectivity, my critical "distance"? For I didn't feel distanced. At times, I was mad as hell at Puzo's text and wanted him/it to suffer critically for every morally equivocating, prurient, sensationalized piece of literature or film that I'd had put up with, ranging back to early childhood. At other moments, I thrilled to the Corleone victories over their enemies. After all, as a reader I had gone to their children's weddings, watched them cook pasta, and suffered the repeated injustices inflicted on them. When Michael Corleone orchestrated the deaths of the heads of the Five Families, I had to admit they got exactly what they deserved.

In this book I want to reproduce in criticism precisely this swing between the critical reader who disapproves of Puzo's rhetorical maneuvering and the reader in myself who as a child eagerly joined the Saturday matinee crowd cheering as the villains on screen finally bought it in their climactic battle with the white hats. But in this case the white hats had become the Corleones. Both readers, the moral scold and the cheerleader for the plot victories, lived inside my literary-critical self, which purported to or who was told to know better. "Know better" contains in its elite caution everything the trained literary critic knows about advocacy, ethical argument, and evaluation, which the critic is taught belongs to the discourses of law, philosophy, and religion. Such concepts lie behind any possible renderings we can make as critics, but since the New Criticism, they remain in prewriting, to be mined or ground into rational and finally theoretical arguments far from the level of the text or its engendered responses. The injustices done to and by the Corleones were finally matched by my readerly sense of injustice, what I might call "crimes against the narrative" committed by the author for my pleasure and instruction.

Pierre Bourdieu in his postscript to *Distinction* (1979, trans. 1984) summarizes Kant's principle of pure taste as "nothing other than a refusal, a disgust—a disgust for objects which impose enjoyment." Bourdieu adds that "disgust is the paradoxical experience of enjoyment extorted by violence, an enjoyment which arouses horror. This horror, *unknown to those who surrender to sensation* [emphasis mine] results fundamentally from the removal of distance, in which freedom is asserted, between the representation and the thing represented" (488), causing an alienation from the artifact but providing its own peculiar definition of enjoyment, which only the trained critic can truly savor. However, what happens when the critic wants to retain a relation with the large readership of a best seller such as

The Godfather, who wants to retain both a membership in those "attracted" and those "repelled" and needs to sustain this split personality while discussing a work, any work? I was not above surrendering to sensation but, like most readers and viewers, I wanted to pick my spots, script my own pleasures insofar as possible, and take offense when I wanted to. I supposedly knew how to be disinterested in the highest Kantian sense, to make disgust my hidden friend, to eschew sensation and sentiment when necessary, to refuse the "easy" insight and conclusion. Yet I didn't want to become some version of the critical police and live constantly with the fear that somewhere some reader or viewer is enjoying *The Godfather*. Well, I thought, Don Corleone knows how to practice this elite distancing. He knows how to serve up revenge, a dish best served cold, he tells us (404). Was there a riddle here? Could the vaunted modernist distancing, the view from "the tower," the historically conditioned great-grandchild of "emotion recollected in tranquility" be akin to the great calm from which the Don acted in the affairs of men? I presumed I had become somewhat desperate in crafting my critical strategies by analogy to the career of the protagonist whom I wished to explain by the criticism itself. Yet how could I keep my distance from *The Godfather* and mime the way in which Don Corleone keeps his distance from his victims?

I could attempt to kill Puzo with traditional elite critical strategies. However, that was not a very surgical gangland hit. What would I gain by demonstrating that he wasn't Balzac or Hemingway or Mailer (although he was trying to be all three at different times)? No one was likely to give me an argument there. Then, in an alternate move more in the contemporary critical climate, I could excoriate Puzo as caught in classic false consciousness, a writer purporting to create an ethnic hero, a modern Robin Hood, but a hero who was really the worst that the capitalist system could muster, a murderer who accumulated an excess capital, a fund of trust and obligation that masqueraded as Old World fealty but also had everything to do with corruption of institutions in an open society. Such an analysis seemed overly shrill and not revelatory of *The Godfather*'s power and popular acceptance.

I needed a key to what had always troubled me about popular fiction: its way of speaking about everything that is important in ways that prematurely recontain the subjects in some way or another. Popular literature's "escape" wasn't simple as a category. This escape came in a complex series of evasions and deflections about "Freedom," "America," and "Destiny" that often appeared to affirm on the level of a novel's symbolization precisely what I had wished to deny at the level of critique. I had the perennial precritical misgiving about popular literature criticism: how to transfer what I considered an ethical position or an aesthetic quarrel into a critical lingua franca that neither overtly privileged my sympathetic outrage from a secure bourgeois and academic position nor underscored my negative appraisal of what I considered to be an "inferior" literary product.

So, how to talk about a book and an author that I couldn't find the rhetoric to talk about? I could tell *why* I as a trained critic could not abide some of Puzo's novelistic choices. His text often seemed out of his control, both internally chaotic and contradictory. Yet thirty million copies of *The Godfather* were sold in the 1970s, making it by far the best-selling American novel of the decade. *The Godfather* films were stunningly powerful for audiences all over the world. People loved these movies and repeated their lines, until they entered the language ("I'll make him an offer he can't refuse"; "he sleeps with the fishes"; "leave the gun—take the cannoli"; "go to the mattresses"). The Corleones, the violent, immoral, misogynist Corleones, were a proto-family for our time, the tightly-knit unit, the family that murdered together stayed together. *The Godfather* posited a truly complete American fantasy, that of New World mobility and power within an Old World identity. The family ventured out into a larger America that it controlled in the hidden *name* of family. Even the morality play of Michael's dissolution as a melancholy, patriarchal murderer by the end of the second *Godfather* film did nothing to cut the fascination with the Corleone hegemony. Here was an American melodrama that took root in the national imagination as it did on the charts. The Corleone family takeover was both psychic and economic in the American culture. They had in fundamental ways become us. They were "Our Gang."

Then again, who comprises Puzo's readership? Surely it cuts and cross-cuts among critically trained readers and consumers who only read best sellers. Many of us consume fiction as a commodity across a wide spectrum of simplicity and difficulty and are capable of appreciating and discriminating between artifacts and their affects without having a crisis of readerly or professional conscience every time we convert our response from, say, Faulkner's *Absalom, Absalom!* to Mitchell's *Gone with the Wind*, two novels of 1936 which should have a miscegenated congress between them. Puzo himself has shown how rigidly he segregated his views of art from the marketplace. Before writing *The Godfather*, Puzo experienced twenty years as a "failed" or "undiscovered" novelist and later wrote that he felt he had been "a true believer in art": "I didn't believe in religion or love or women or men. I didn't believe in society or philosophy. But I believed in art for forty-five years. It gave me a comfort I found in no other place" ("The Making of *The Godfather*" 34). He also admitted he'd written "below his gifts in *The Godfather*" and then made a fortune. Yet his almost totally reified view of art as a godlike force and his immediate negation of all subjects that such art might portray perfectly mirrored the frustrations a reader might have in following out such concepts in his fiction. Puzo's rhetoric includes large abstractions that contain even greater suggestiveness, but then he prematurely hurls thunderbolts such as "love" and "philosophy" only to crash them back into place as they relate to his own personal melancholy and "comfort." Such a grandiose obsessiveness with the inflated led him finally, unerringly, to popular success.

Viewed another way, Puzo's belief in art and subsequent crisis of belief is revealing on several levels. First, he reproduces the popular readership's reverence for elite fiction it doesn't truly understand or even like but to which it is told to aspire. Second, his belief in art can mirror the critic's belief in criticism, a belief "shaken" when confronting precisely the fiction that Puzo finally produces. The critic has been trained to transact ambiguous, complex, ironic business through in-depth study and ever more philosophical and intellectual tools, rather than assess across a more horizontal field of surfaces the intent and impact that a work such as *The Godfather* has on American culture that converts its literary capital through film and television into language, style, and ideology. As *The Godfather* becomes pervasive on many fronts, it threatens not only to dwarf Puzo himself, who tends to fall away in studies of the films, for example, but it frustrates any critic who would see the works whole, the traditional humanist legacy for contemporary criticism from a critical godfather such as Lionel Trilling.

Thus I write here about an author, a novel, three films, a cultural text, and a set of critical questions. My work will be eclectic, embodying many approaches—structural, dialogic, new historicist, pragmatic, myth-critical, multiethnic—with a considerable degree of critical self-consciousness in the contemporary mode. I want to enter into dialogue what was facing Puzo as a writer after World War II with what facing Puzo causes me to notice in critical revolutions after the New Criticism in my reading choices as critic.

I do not render judgments on Puzo and *The Godfather* as much as situate him and his text, as I attempt to situate myself on several levels of American literary discussion. To decide finally on ways Puzo and *The Godfather* can be approached is to grant the author and his text a different sort of complexity than is usually called for in critical study. It's not a problem of worrying about Puzo and his novel not being complex enough; it's making the acknowledgment that *writing about popular authors and their fictions is complex.* The level of difficulty is complicated by the popular writer's strengths and weaknesses, the culture's rewards and neglect, the critic's training and goals. Thus levels of contradiction and irony resurface at the level of a metacriticism that necessarily will be about "critical thinking on popular phenomena." For the critic to earn that role, he must bring emotion, reason, and training but also admit his insecurities about illicit reading pleasures as well as his yearnings for wholeness, justice, and closure. I come to Puzo in writerly sympathy but scrutinize his career by critiquing the legend of the Corleones that America has wholeheartedly consumed for decades. I want to bring forth as much as

I can about what the Corleone hegemony reveals about Puzo's fiction, the *Godfather* films, and, by extension, American popular texts, their critics, and general readers.

Siting *"The Godfather"*

Siting *The Godfather* involves displaying its text in different semantic arguments. I place Puzo's novel in comparison with an elite novel, Doctorow's *Ragtime* (chapter 7), discuss it as fostering a tradition of mob narrative that presently culminates in *The Sopranos* (chapter 9), and hypothesize it as a Cold War text, a mega best-seller, a social melodrama, an ethnic novel, a popular novel. At all times, I'm aware of how the three *Godfather* films became the *Godfather* text for millions. Each such siting changes *The Godfather*'s configuration and adds to its status as a narrative phenomenon. Leslie Fiedler comments that a key facet of a true popular narrative is its "transparency," the ease at which it can be transferred from fiction to film (*What Was Literature* 122). A significant popular narrative generally does not have the originality or complexity to master or cover other texts with its uniqueness but instead takes on within its conventionality something of the site in which it is described. *The Godfather* is not a strong text but one that accrues meanings to it. Within this concept is a kind of antidiversity, a magnetizing site that absorbs, much as does Corleone power itself.

Such meanings, cultural formations, and vehicles sited by interaction with *The Godfather* include the concept of the family itself in America, both traditional and contemporary, the social entity with the largest signification; the best-selling novel read by millions, which affirms certain values within both sensational and sentimental frames; film and television in its adaptations; and an ethnic *habitare* or sociological *habitus* that can tell us about a novel or its characters' geographical place or the writer's place within a system of cultural capital. Sites can be social formations (Business, Family, the Mob, Crime); historical and cultural formations (Immigration, Cold War, Self-Made, Success, Pluralism, Isolation, "Old World," "New World," Destiny, Manifest Destiny); as well as literary genres and forms (popular, elite, myth, epic, melodrama, sentiment). A variety of critical paradigms can offer different sitings: New Historicism, Ethnic Criticism, Marxist Criticism, Myth Criticism, Literary Sociology, Cultural Studies, and Reader Response Criticism. Finally, *The Godfather* can now be sited as product and as part of the language. No current American fictional and film text is more quoted in films, television, books, advertising, and through brand names. *The Godfather* is mimed, mined, and strip-mined for its meanings in what has become "Godfather America."

Why *The Godfather* and why now, given the huge plurality of popular narratives extant at any moment? Historically, *The Godfather* is fundamentally a Cold War text about post–World War II with Michael Corleone as the soldier-son coming home first to wage war and then to keep the peace through threat and massive deterrence while presiding over a wary détente with his enemies (the other Families). No other American best seller mythically deals with this tense American period as does *The Godfather*; film counterparts in this vein may be *The Best Years of Our Lives* (1946) and *It's a Wonderful Life* (1946), affirmative American visions with hysteric edginess. *The Godfather* narrative is also an uncomplicated ethnic novel, not really dialogized in relation to Italian America as much as it is in thrall to popular melodrama; immigration and urban ethnicity go down easy in its text. When the novel appears in 1969, it does so at a time of enormous stress for the American father and family, at the end of a decade when the Vietnam war split countless fathers and sons and the country itself in debates over patriotism and duty. When the Civil Rights movement had in the 1960s begun to educate Americans in dramatic fashion about the right to claim what is justly yours in the name of oppressed identity on the one hand and American ideals on the other. Vito and Michael Corleone do not grow apart: they unite to kill the bastards and proclaim their family's rights. *The Godfather* may be the very expression of American capitalism with money and murder as constants, with the attendant ironies surrounding the Corleone isolation from or participation in pluralism, the economy, American systems of justice, and politics. Even after three decades, *The Godfather*'s continuing reception occurs in a climate of its own powerful shaping, as well as in a critical and social climate of multiethnic consciousness, identity politics, and an ongoing debate about the differences underlying both essentialism and its opposite. *The Godfather* has become a popular classic, exhibiting features of American social life that transcend the era of its writing, filming, and initial reception, as well as deeply situated in an American dialogue that continues to evolve through fresh vehicles such as *The Sopranos*. The constants firmly mixed in *The Godfather* continue to enthrall: America. Citizenship. Family. Ethnicity. Identity. Business. Reason. Murder.

Novels, Films, and Product Disclaimers

I'm not talking in this book about Coppola's three *Godfather* films as separate from Puzo's novel, nor am I particularly interested here in the critical issue of "book into film." Coppola is on record as stating that *The Godfather* was to him an initially unpromising vehicle for adaptation: "I was desperate to give the film class. I felt the book was cheap and sensational" (*New York* 52). Although Puzo shared screenwriting credits with

Coppola, it was Coppola who tightened the family melodrama, straightened out the narrative's chronology, removed some of Puzo's more egregiously sensational moments, such as Lucy Mancini's operation or the satirical brothel of over-aged stars in Hollywood.[1] When Coppola assumed artistic control over *Godfather II* and *Godfather III*, the Corleone saga became ever darker and more melancholy, exceedingly formal in its composition. After completing *Godfather I*, Coppola commented that "it's not really about the Mafia. It could just as well be about the Kennedys or the Rothschilds, about a dynasty which demands personal allegiance to a family that transcends even one's obligations to one's country" (52). Coppola's broad thematizing is much in evidence here. He surpasses in scope anything that Puzo claimed for his novel but actually was quite faithful in transposing Puzo's novel to the screen; there's less disconnect between book and movie than in most such adaptations. For one thing, *The Godfather* as novel was quite free of exposition, character reflection, and subjectivizing. With no novel sequel by Puzo, the saga passed more exclusively into film, to be copied repeatedly by cinema and television in the succeeding decades. No doubt the mob narrative comes down to us visually. Melodrama in its broad strokes and emotional tenor is very vivid in drama, opera, and film. Gangster melodramas have been a staple in film since the earliest days of silent film. In a narrative obsessed with "destiny," it may be that *The Godfather* was destined to leave the page for large and small screens.

Some ground rules should be mentioned about the countless references to *The Godfather* in the succeeding chapters. I will refer to Puzo's novel as *The Godfather* and to the three films as *Godfather I*, *Godfather II*, and *Godfather III*. When I refer to Puzo's novel and Coppola's films as a unit, I'll designate them as *Godfather narrative*. When I want to talk about the entire production of books, films, and their adaptations and spin-offs, I am designating this generic product as *mob narrative*. Beyond such definite namings, *The Godfather* is a site of a heterogeneous pluralism of meanings that has established itself in a culture's styles, language, and advertising; it has become what is marketed and what markets other products and images. Such will be referenced when necessary but a full-field description of this phenomenon is not attempted here. I will have much to say in this book about a "popular narrative," most often in the guise of *The Godfather* but often denoting a text of wide readership and acceptance that flies below the radar screen of the academy and literary criticism but that attracts a huge audience. Some of its properties can be sketched here prefatory to extended discussion.

Fiedler in *What Was Literature* provides perhaps the most pointed descriptions of popular narrative. He finds the narrative residing in the public domain, dealing more in images than words, and capable of passing easily into powerful (if not complex) film. Fiedler—whose prose is always naughty and overheated where pop is concerned—describes popular narrative's messages as more transparent, not meeting aesthetic or ethical standards beneath their "pious veneer," but rather "pandering to desires and lusts" (122). I would add that popular narrative also works in hallowed visuals of family and through family rites of passage. To gauge such power, I will repeatedly consider *The Godfather*'s mixture of extreme violence and domestic warmth, again and again the most powerful visual images in *Godfather* narrative. Such is also the most powerful expression of popular narrative, and mob families present it in a most inclusive form.

Some firm product disclaimers are in order in the wake of *The Godfather*'s enormous popularity as novel and films and the resultant penetration into audience consciousness of countless millions:

- The position of "godfather" in traditional religious and family structure is not coextensive with *The Godfather* or invented by Puzo but is a deeply traditional, hallowed, and serious part of extended family and community life. Godparents are not only Catholic and not only Italian.

- Mob narrative is not coextensive with Italian American narrative. The full richness of Italian American life is presented in a literature that is now in full flowering, both in fiction and in criticism (see chapter 4). Without becoming some sort of literary-critical action wing of the anti-defamation police, be it here said that mob narrative is only my copyright and is not code for "Italian American" in its fullness but will have reference to ethnic criticism as well as a host of other criticisms.

- *The Godfather* is not the first or final word on the presence of the Mafia in Italian or Italian American culture and life. Consciousness of the Mafia did not begin in Italian America because of Puzo; rather, Puzo's writing reflects aspects of Italian America, and he disseminates his interpretation to millions. Italian Americans don't need to read or view *Godfather* texts to know their heritage or condition, and *The Godfather* did not create any value system that was news to American immigrants from Sicily and southern Italy. Furthermore, I respect Italian American reactions to *Godfather* narrative in their full complexity, whether they secretly admire or openly loathe *The Godfather* or feel a complex mixture of pride, identification, and frustration in its stereotyping. It's a curious fate to be an "unprotected" ethnic minority where all bets are off in contemporary politically correct discourse.

The Common Languages of Mob Narrative

Remarkable visual examples of the mixture of violence and domestic warmth stud *The Godfather* films. In *Godfather II*, after young Vito

Corleone kills Fanucci, the minor neighborhood "Black Hand" mafioso on the Lower West Side of New York City, he returns home through the busy streets to his own front stoop, where his wife sits with their three small sons, in the midst of other bustling families and lives. The scene is an ethnic tableau; an old grandmother sits on a higher stoop; a man with a mandolin is visible right above Vito's shoulder. Mother holds toddler Fredo. Above her sits three-year-old Sonny dressed in an outfit that looks like soldier's garb; he waves a toy American flag, and Fredo holds another flag in his chubby fist. Vito takes infant Michael still wrapped in his baby blankets and says to him in Italian, "Michael, your father loves you very much, very much." He holds Michael's tiny fingers almost in wonder at such perfection.

Such a scene is a seamless mixture of family love, ethnic type-scene nostalgia, and melodramatic presentation. The young "Mama" Corleone looks off to the side, heedless of the camera. The very young children are fidgeting in anticipatory blankness. The shot almost becomes an extended still photograph in an album of ethnic urban immigration. The scene is evocative of the great photographs of New York tenement life dating back to Jacob Riis. Vito has done his day's work by killing Fanucci, and his family may now prosper. Something amazing has occurred, but it is portrayed in the mundanity of the street. Such a scene takes place in the public domain and is transmitted through the powerful images of patriotism, ethnic richness, family solidarity, and maternal and paternal love. Any ethical imperative against murder is canceled by Vito's strong presence. Here is where his power begins.

Beneath the piety of the young family man with his brood is a killer. Vito steps into full American adulthood by killing a man as will his son Michael. By 2000, Tony Soprano, the struggling inheritor of Vito's tale and responsibilities, kills a mob informant while taking his daughter on a college tour, a new rite of the American upper middle class (*Sopranos* 1, 5). During her admissions interview at Bowdoin, Tony gazes at a wall with an inscription from Nathaniel Hawthorne (Bowdoin 1825): "No Man Can Wear One Face to Himself and Another to the Multitude without Finally Getting Bewhildered as to Which May Be True." The path from that stoop in Little Italy where the Corleones sit to Tony in the anteroom at Bowdoin is three generations and, *pace* Hawthorne, the Corleones and the Sopranos are getting on rather well in their contradictions. Tony, bewhildered, has been "true" in his fashion. In the narrative of manners that *The Sopranos* can become, Tony also makes a belated "moral" decision not to order a hit on his daughter's sexually compromised high school soccer coach, thus intertwining the mob's reach with the suburbs' most upscale current family reality. He tumbles drunkenly into his own living room late at night, mumbling, "I didn't hurt nobody. Call the shrink. Town oughta give her a fuckin' bonus" (*Sopranos* 1, 9). The constants in mob narrative are murder and family; the frames are updated in middle-class scenarios. Film and television provide such vividness, while the visual images move to fill the silences that *omerta* dictates.

One issue to place under extended discussion is the Amerian audience's extension of sympathy to killer families, to bring them into *our* gang. Family bonds appear to innoculate mob murder against any moral constraints. Once a character is a "made" man, anything is possible in the range of human conduct. The aura of the kill hangs over every human action. Fisher in *Hard Facts* writes of nineteenth-century sentimentality's "experimental extension of humanity" to "prisoners, slaves, madmen, children, and animals" (100), to which we can now add murdering families. Cross DeLena in Puzo's *The Last Don* observes that once he "made his bones," "he should never be subject to the fates of ordinary men" (175), almost as if he becomes another species. Indeed, mob narrative authorized by Puzo is joined by the vampire narratives of Anne Rice to provide nuclear families who live with murder every day, who have it as a necessity, the constant transformative power of murder's violence. Vampire and Mafia families have murder as their "nature," grounding a popular exceptionalism that leads to an extraordinarily unstable moral landscape for the audience. How authors, books, and films negotiate this terrain of killer families will be the business of this book to describe and unpack. What Fisher sees as the "central psychological and social evil" of slavery in family in the nineteenth-century domestic novel (101) becomes the evil of murder for the sake of money in contemporary mob narrative. Murder or its threat keeps the money coming. The Corleone and Soprano destruction of family itself is the primary result of the lives of the murderers themselves and the consequences for the women and children they purport to protect.

The silences of *The Godfather* far outweigh its disclosures and provide a throwback text to Hemingwayesque silent heroism without Hemingway's evoked tension. Jewish American fiction hasn't stopped talking since Saul Bellow announced early in *Dangling Man* (1944), "If you have difficulties, grapple with them silently, goes one of their commandments. To hell with that! I intend to talk about mine, and if I had as many mouths as Siva has arms and kept them going all the time, I still could not do myself justice" (9), and Philip Roth's Alexander Portnoy in 1969, the year of *The Godfather*'s publication, took the impulse about as far as he could. By the 1960s, the confessional mode had fundamentally taken root in both American fiction and American poetry. Since 1969, most contemporary multiethnicity is also about claiming one's own voice and announcing self through becoming a speaking subject. This insurgent view of power/knowledge also belongs to a fictional revolution of women and gays, to move from being border citizens to the center of fiction. Italian American male silence was one prominent hold-out against the powerful trend and in Puzo, remained inherently conservative simply by its reticence, in the refusal to join in narcissistic subjectivity.[2]

The Mob has become a region that is a serious sensationalizing and distilling of a larger Italian American experience and culture. Inevitably in this book *The Godfather* rises to dominate both considerations of the serious religious and cultural institution of godparents, as well as a larger Italian American culture that so very clearly is not contained by the boundaries of mob narrative. At the same time, Puzo did not invent out of whole cloth the myth of the Mafia in Italian American life. It's culturally and historically grounded and already glorified and romanticized on a smaller, less mainstream scale over decades and even centuries. An initially excluded and wary immigrant population did not need Puzo to become the fictional laureate of ethnic Robin Hoods. The Corleones may have been introduced to American culture at large via the novel and films. Such minor neighborhood figures were always in the generic Italian American culture, outwitting an inscrutable distant system, doing "what everyone else does," according to their own lights, getting by, getting over, getting on with the business of family and life, and providing *respect*, a commodity in short supply among the urban poor. *The Godfather* creates a common language for America out of this more localized culture; it did not inaugurate the culture itself.[3]

This common language of mob narrative can be situated in various ways. The history of American fiction also moves beyond the obvious formal categories of Realism, Naturalism, and the Sentimental Novel and becomes the history of various regionalisms that can be broadly defined as that of the "New England Mind," or the "Southern Way of Life" or the "Frontier" (Fisher 241). I want to suggest that mob narrative itself can become a region, one with its own rituals of family marriage and death, ethnic and religious observance, customs in everything from food to conduct, and a world view that is strongly conditioned by both the pre-immigrant experience of oppression in the descent country and the consciousness that must adapt that prior experience in America. Mob narrative is not coextensive with Italian American narrative but is rather an offshoot from it, hybridized by the experience of many ethnic and/or oppressed groups that are suspicious of the law. Mobsters have everything you don't: power, money, women, cars, security, and most of all, a certain leverage. Mob narrative then seeks to link systems of power and authority in the "Old Countr[ies]" with what is perceived in the American social and legal system with the goal of finding out how to survive economically and culturally in a "New World."

Alan Greenspan and George Bailey: "Doing It for Strangers"

An alternative to this parochial, wary, and cautious ethnic narrative does exist. Fisher also conceives of a powerful core culture of American-

ization comprised of public education, economic advancement, and democratic civic culture (241) that provides both an alternative to the regionalisms and an effective absorption of them in what authorizes participation
in a public sphere.[4] Puzo makes some scant obeisances toward this other
America when Michael Corleone talks about his family joining the "general American destiny," but for the most part, mob narrative refuses to
believe that things as they are will be changed when played upon
America's schoolrooms, offices, military barracks, and suburbs. Mob
narrative usually treats these strong American determinants as inert
opposing environments, rather than the coopting forces, the "melting
pots" that need to consume the "regions" of anti-American resistance
in order to function in power. Mob narrative in general refuses to
dialogize with this idealized core America. Whatever else mob narrative accomplishes, it has few illusions about an American business culture that rather piously refuses to see mob narrative's predations as its
own mirror self.

American economic and family culture constantly seeks narratives
and heroes to regulate and explain our national life. The culture is constantly engaged in discourses about home, family, money, greed, and
security and does not only search for reinforcement and insight through
the extreme violence and sensation of mob narrative but also in other
more benign and constrained forms. Vito and Michael Corleone are not
the only fantasy figures who embody American hopes and economic
dreams. Briefly consider two other American heroes: Wall Street's Alan
Greenspan as all-powerful father and Bedford Falls' George Bailey in *It's
a Wonderful Life* as redeeming son.

Greenspan, the longtime chairman of the Federal Reserve Bank, is
the most frequently cited patriarchal overseer of the incredible American
boom economy and stock market run-up of the 1990s, the man who has
unequaled power to keep the American economy on course. Greenspan
is a father who will keep his children from being too indulgent, whose
job is to calm financial markets and maintain their stability. He's a
publically appointed official operating in the lifeworld at the highest
level of government power, which has voluntarily ceded control of the
financial system to him. In the early 1960s, Greenspan wrote that "capitalism holds integrity and trustworthiness as cardinal virtues and makes
them pay off in the marketplace" (*New Yorker*, 168). Greenspan becomes
a benign patriarch of an eagerly acquisitive national family prospering
unimaginably under his rule. Greenspan has been candid about his intellectual debt to Ayn Rand with whom he studied as a young man: "What
she did . . . was to make me think about why capitalism is not only effi-
cient and practical, but also moral," he told the *New York Times* in 1974
(Cassidy, *New Yorker* 167). Rand's long novels such as *Atlas Shrugged*
(1943) and *The Fountainhead* (1957) provided a popular fictional account
of American capitalism and the priorities of the truly strong men in its

system, matched only by the Corleones. The irony is that Greenspan works for all America. Rand and Puzo's heroes work for themselves and for family, respectively.

George Bailey is the small-town hero of Frank Capra's *It's a Wonderful Life*, who stays at home after his father's death and heroically navigates his struggling savings and loan company against the evil Mr. Potter and his big bank on behalf of the "little people" who need affordable housing during the Great Depression and World War II. George can never break away from Bedford Falls; it's his brother, Harry, who goes off to be a war hero like Michael Corleone. George becomes, by the end of Capra's tale, "the richest man in town" emotionally, one who overcomes a real hysteria about not breaking away from family and home to build and finance homes, to become a hero to people in a nascent melting pot. Finally he is recalled to life after despair, is "touched by an angel" and restored to family, which includes an extended grateful American public. Here is Fisher's dream of an American core culture triumphing since George sacrifices himself for "the people" who are outside any family or specific ethnic group. They are transferred from "customers" into working-class Americans who trust him and redeem him. George Bailey—always about to leave home and always turned back to it—does everything "for strangers," as Don Corleone would say.

This public ethic of sacrifice and service in *It's a Wonderful Life*, a "family classic," a film largely igonored and forgotten after World War II, becomes a television phenomenon in the early 1970s about the time of the *Godfather* takeover of economic life through mob narrative on film. George Bailey, however, is a *benign* capitalist hero. His demons are his own, and his violence is often inner-directed. The hard-working families on whose behalf George Bailey struggles take on a different caste in Italian American culture and narrative. It's crucial to recognize that Puzo hardly invented the hierarchical narrative of Old World suspicion of American life and promises and that the entire system of a "godfather" made perfect sense to immigrant families who were looking for any sort of protection against an American world that was arrayed against their survival. What mob narrative has converted into something sensational and ominous is a traditional serious aspect of Italian and then Italian American social cohesion. How to convert the clannishness of family unity into real power to control the vagaries of life in a new country? Gardaphe cites Richard Gambino's portrayal of that hierarchical Italian American family order:

> From top to bottom : 1. family members, "blood of my blood,"
> 2. *compari* and *padrini* and their female equivalents, *commare*
> and *madrine* ("godparents," a relationship that was by no means
> limited to those who were godparents in the Catholic religious

rites . . . and which would better translate as "intimate friends" and "venerated elders"), 3. *amici* or *amici di cappello* (friends to whom one tipped one's hat or said "hello"), meaning those whose family status demanded respect, and 4. *stranieri* (strangers), a designation for all others." (Gambino, *Blood of My Blood*, in Gardaphe, *Italian Signs, American Streets* 86)

The concept of a 'godfather' has been seriously chosen by vulnerable people for protection down through the centuries. Gardaphe conceives it as embracing the nuclear family, that the order of the family works like the walls around a castle (86). This feudal imagery is apt to describe what looks like an archaic structure pragmatically implanted within a modern democratic capitalist society. Thus assumptions about the communal life of a shared American society are nonexistent within this system. Equality is a fiction, consensual law would not protect anyone sufficiently. The differences are stunning.

None of the architecture of this Italian family order would yield any part of its network of relations to a public sphere of institutions and keepers of the public order and law. The one part of a shared sense of liberal freedom that the Italian American family and the American civic family might share would be the ideal of the strong and benevolent father to take care of both family and an unimpeded business life. This common bond cements the huge acceptance of the Corleone and Soprano families by the American readership and viewing audience. By audience vote, they have become Our Gangs.

A Chapter Preview

This book is divided into three parts. Part 1 of *"The Godfather" and American Culture* attempts to understand the issues and stakes involved in popular fiction study in the realm of aesthetics and morals and to chronicle and align Puzo's career with these issues and stakes to establish the critical and authorial backgrounds for reading *The Godfather*. Chapter 1 introduces the major questions to be asked in a study of popular fiction and of *The Godfather* in particular with relation to the history of "taste" and the power of sentiment in moral criticism. Chapter 2 works through Puzo's long career to gauge his ambitions and achievements. For a writer who became famous depicting the Italian American subject in *The Godfather*, Puzo actually devoted a considerable part of his writing career to avoid being defined by that subject or by popular success itself.

Part 2 of *"The Godfather" and American Culture* works through reading paradigms for *The Godfather* that also are models for further criticism of popular fiction. Chapter 3 reads key scenes of confrontation in the novel by way of Bakhtinian dialogics to ascertain the dynamic of authority and internal persuasion that Puzo nervously allows to surface from time to time in a challenge to the Corleone hegemony. Chapter 4 subjects the Bakhtinian model to criticism by ethnic ensemble to find how the specifically Italian and Sicilian backgrounds and rhetorical language troping as well as cultural analysis can account for facets of the text that seem either underdeveloped or contradictory according to more universal paradigms. Chapter 5 tries by way of reference to Barthes's *Mythologies* to account for the investiture of some loaded ideological messages within specific character zones in *The Godfather*. Part 2 of this book suggests that a critical reader can approach *The Godfather* armed with the most cogent of contemporary critical theories but must be ready to find how these theories illuminate the text and also create problems that place the entire project of reading popular fiction into subjective and intertextual relation.

Part 3 of this study concentrates on positioning *The Godfather* in relation to both elite and popular American fiction and to film and television. Fiction and films that engage countless millions of readers and viewers for decades do so not only by catching the *zeitgeist*, or by their intrinsic properties, however conceived by whatever critical paradigms, but also by existing in a literary-historical era, narrative tradition, and a field of texts. Most important, *The Godfather* exists within structures of feeling, with particular reference to melodrama, sentiment, and American history. I test the potential of *The Godfather* to enter certain established American literary conversations and chart the sustaining course of mob narrative in language, literature, and media. Chapter 6 begins by considering *The Godfather* as the last twentieth-century entry in an American business saga dating to the early 1900s; it looks at *The Godfather* as a late inheritor of a compelling success narrative that America always stands ready to read through melodrama at the level of the popular novel, particularly through the mutation and absorption of traditional female roles by men who do prove able to have it all in the family and in the murderous, perfidious workplace, which become and occupy the same space and entity. Chapter 7 performs a specifically comparative study of *The Godfather* with Doctorow's *Ragtime*, its elite literature twin in many respects. Chapter 8 defines *The Godfather* within Fiedler's concept of the American "inadvertent epic" and surveys how the epic subject informs the novel that has now entered our language, dreams, and culture in many media forms. Chapter 9 concludes the book with an analysis of *The Sopranos* as the most suggestive contemporary inheritor of *The Godfather*'s conventions and premises.

Part I

Popular Fiction Criticism and American Careers

chapter one

Popular Fiction:
Taste, Sentiment, and the
Culture of Criticism

Taste is basically an ability to judge the [way in which] moral ideas are made sensible ([it judges this] by means of a certain analogy in our reflection about [these ideas and their renderings in sensibility]); the pleasure that taste declares valid for mankind as such and not just for each person's private feeling must indeed derive from this [link] and from the resulting increase in our receptivity for the feeling that arises from moral ideas (and is called moral feeling).

—Immanuel Kant, "On Methodology Concerning Taste"
in *Critique of Aesthetic Judgment*

It is natural for us to seek a standard of taste; a rule by which the various sentiments of men may be reconciled; at least a decision afforded, confirming one sentiment, and condemning another.

—David Hume, "Of the Standard of Taste"

Our interpretation of a work and our experience of its value are mutually dependent, and each depends upon what might be called the psychological "set" of our encounter with it: not the "setting" of the work, or in the narrow sense, its context, but rather the nature and potency of our own assumptions, expectations, capacities, and interest in respect to it—our "prejudices" if you like, but hardly to be distinguished from our identity (or who, in fact we are) at the time of the encounter.

—Barbara Herrnstein Smith, *Contingencies of Value*

I begin by establishing certain questions to be asked of Puzo's incredible success in *The Godfather* and, by extension, that of any phenomenal best seller. What draws me as critic to this popular writer and to this narrative phenomenon? What training and praxis inform both the way I frame my questions and the evidence I choose to examine? I want to chart the inevitable questions and false starts that face the literary critic when confronting a work of such massive popularity as *The Godfather* with the goal of beginning to outline my rationale for a particular set of readings at a number of sites. The largest questions about these issues have everything to do with establishing a rationale for moral criticism in a pluralist culture that enables sentiment to be a powerful arbiter of judgment without completely privileging its contingent quality.

To set the issues in their purest form, I return briefly to the eighteenth-century debate over reason and sentiment as they inform judgments of taste in moral philosophy. The two most cogent figures must be Kant and Hume, the prominent architects of our modern view of feelings and judgments and the ways in which they form our concepts of the beautiful, the moral, and the ethical. Kant credits Hume with his awakening to the primacy of the world of experience over the world of ideas. Much of what would underwrite the authority of criticism in our time takes its shape through Kant's majestic formulations of the aesthetic, the beautiful, and the sublime and how the critic is vested or "disinterested" in the judgments. Such maxims in Kant's Critiques have licensed a twentieth-century pursuit of "art for art's sake," a denial of historicizing, a formalization of the critical power, an austerity beyond the sensible into a realm where art is perceived as higher and higher. No elite judgment of critical consistency can be truly made without Kantian underwriting. Yet Kant also provides the strongest basis for our inquiry into moral judgments that cohere within and without the aesthetic impulse.

Hume's more visceral and hedonistic embracing of the sentimental as a basis for moral apprehensions and evaluations is where Kant and Hume part company in the extreme. Hume calls for a more subjective and capacious view of the human responding imagination, one that reflects a "broader discipline of reflection on human nature" (Baier *Progress* 25) In an appendix to *An Enquiry concerning the Principles of Morals* entitled "Concerning Moral Sentiment," Hume wrote, "But though reason, when fully assisted and improved, be sufficient to instruct us in the pernicious or useful tendency of qualities and actions; it is not alone sufficient to produce any moral blame or approbation. . . . It is requisite a *sentiment* [italics Hume] should here display itself, in order to give a preference to the useful above the pernicious tendencies. This sentiment can be no other than a feeling for the happiness of mankind, and a resentment of their misery" (125). For writers who are conscious advocates, either moral or ethical about justice, equality, and freedom within society, Hume gives great cause. The credo about sentiments as moral guides leads not only to the ideals of a document such as the American Declaration of Independence ("happiness of mankind" / "*pursuit of happi-*

ness") but to an identification with society and its social arrangements and inequities ("resentment of their misery").

Hume is willing to undertake a dangerous tacking amidst issues, scenes, and effects. The critic's lot is always to feel he is overstepping emotional bounds and to pull back in this or that stay against his full range of feeling. Hume knew this when he wrote, "I am uneasy to think that I approve of one object and disapprove of another; call one thing beautiful, and another deform'd; decide concerning truth and falsehood, reason and folly, without knowing upon what principles I proceed" (Baier 22). Although it is impossible to graft fully the sentiments of a great eighteenth-century philosopher onto a current debate about the uses and modes of literary criticism, it's the methodological "uneasiness" Hume knew as he constructed his case for sentiment that is fully repeated in the contemporary critical establishment and was a staple of largely negative comment throughout the twentieth century. Modernism's brilliant refashioning of historical, moral, and social chaos in the church of its literature in the first half of the twentieth century was met and often influenced and enhanced by an equally powerful and austere set of formalisms led by the Anglo-American New Criticism as well as by various avant garde manifestos in Dada, Futurism, and Surrealism. Modernism canceled sentiment by rigor, formalism, and experimentalism both in succession and in concert. Postmodernism tends to treat Hume's "uneasiness" in a more relaxed pluralism of canonical and popular and refrains from judgment when it can in favor of flattening out questions of the "moral" and the "true" into equilibrated images and icons in fractured response.

Another powerful initiative in our critical climate is a committed social and gender-based multicultural fiction and criticism that counters postmodernism's more easily won pluralism with an instinctive commitment to diversity. No period since the midnineteenth century is producing fiction or criticism of sentiment to a wider acclaim. In allied initiatives, feminist criticism, New Historicism, and multiethnic criticism rise to suggest that we re-read the last century and a half to find countermovements in fiction through feeling as well as reason. Literary and culture critics resurrect women's domestic texts, slave narratives, and long forgotten best sellers, and attempt to chart the feelings of the reading public as exhibited in what they wholly embraced as consumers. As critics we may read in an attempt to find out what moves us, often not in a fiction of great depth but rather in a fiction of varied surfaces where we attempt to ascertain how our critical responses themselves can be considered complex across a breadth of literary forms, social issues, and moral imaginings. Therefore we constantly seek ways to integrate our reading selves in differing contexts in which we confront our most elite and popular texts. Hume conceived the two areas of sentiment and reason as they might work together uneasily in our critical imaginings: "What is honourable, what is fair, what is becoming, what is noble, what is generous, takes possession of the heart, and animates us to embrace and maintain it. What is intelligible, what is evident, what is probable, what is true, procures only the cool assent of the understanding; and gratifying a speculative curiosity, puts an end to our researches" (Hume 15). Hume anticipates, albeit pejoratively, Kant's "disinterestedness" in which such judgment shall not function beyond the identification of beauty or the sublime. To Hume, a "speculative" inquiry is not enough; the "end to our researches" cannot be allowed to forget what our "heart" tells us is "true."

To apply this maxim to a contemporary reading of *The Godfather*, it's therefore not enough to count the novel's sales, label its genres, talk about its myths, and carve its niche in a postmodern set of images, language, gestures, and copies. Puzo's novel, the three *Godfather* films, and the numerous extensions of mob narrative speak to a wide range of moral issues, chaotically raising vexing questions in our society about what are "honor," "fairness," and "generosity": our heart, as Hume knows, is fully engaged by such material. Is Vito Corleone justified in taking that first life on the Lower East Side of New York City? After the first Sicilian American death, is there no other? Does all justification, all blessing flow from this initial action? Yet, doesn't Vito Corleone's "generous heart" come from his power and authority? Is this power not authorized by the fact that he will take your life, demand, as Michael so indelicately relates it, your "brains or [your] signature on that paper"? Finally, isn't the Don acting for one of the most noble of reasons, the familial? We inquire into the nature of these arrangements and respond not only with our reason but our visceral reaction to what we believe is happening in such a powerful narrative transaction as *The Godfather*, one that is compelling not because of its symbolic intricacy or ironic commentary but because questions about our sympathies and affiliations are put so directly to us and by us as readers that we cannot deny the challenge to our public morality and private identities as parents, children, and family members in a plurality of roles. Should fiction, particularly popular fiction, be held to account for its commentary on such matters, and what would this account have to do with literary criticism?

Hume shows wit as well as a philosopher's courage in commenting on such dilemmas. He states that, "in many orders of beauty, particularly those of the finer arts, it is requisite to employ much reasoning, in order to feel the proper sentiment" (15). As critics, we can almost always find a formalist rhetoric to demonstrate what affect we need to find. As teachers, we can and do tell fiction and film classes words to the effect that "you'll notice when Sonny Corleone died in a hail of bullets at the toll booth (or when Fredo was shot to death on Lake Tahoe), how Coppola and Puzo achieved effects by depicting the scene as 'caught in the middle,' paying and paying, 'taking its toll,' between Long Island and New York City, neither here nor there (or died saying 'Hail Marys,' as a fisher of men, with Michael looking on 'through a glass darkly')," how an author or director achieved distancing by depicting a scene (in a flashback, in a dream sequence, stream-of-consciousness, through the music, through a first-person narration, in slow motion). We call such motions establishing a critical perspective as we perform the repertoire of critical rhetoric's power to demonstrate the aesthetics of any work over and above what shatters us in the scene's content and context. However, suppose we want to stop and ask about agency. Who killed these Corleone sons, and what will flow from that action? Who is guilty of what in this family, and how does it relate to our lives? What are the consequences for the novel and films and for society? Often the goal here in recounting such examples will be to describe fully the art of rendering the patterns of death in *The Godfather* to show how Puzo imaginatively and rhetorically attempts to make us understand and feel those patterns. How does the understanding connect to the feeling? What do both have to do with the reader-viewer's pleasure and instruction?

Once again, Hume to the front. His hypothesis is "that morality is determined by sentiment. It defines virtue to be *whatever mental action or quality gives to a spectator the pleasing sentiment of approbation*" (italics Hume) (85). Sentiment itself is directly linked to the proving of the good and the true, nor can there be any way to achieve the perception of these ends without feeling. Hume continues: "it appears evident, that the ultimate ends of human actions can never, in any case, be accounted for by *reason* [emphasis Hume], but recommend themselves entirely to the sentiments and affections of mankind, without any dependence on the intellectual faculties" (87). Morality and sentiment cannot be severed, and it follows that if sentiment is discounted or discredited, any moral statement in a critical judgment will be very hard to mount or sustain before the disinterestedness that is seen to be proper when appraising art for its beauty and truth. Therefore, not only might it traditionally be seen as bad form to respond critically to *The Godfather* in the first place as a questionable artifact, but it would also be a compounded crime to take seriously its moral imaginings when sentiment is cancelled and morality is out of bounds for criticism.

The sheer breadth of individual response through sentiment is potentially limitless. Kant quotes Hume in the *Critique of Aesthetic Judgment*, specifically in book 2, "Analytic of the Sublime," in a note observing that "there is a considerable diversity in the sentiments of beauty and worth, and that education, custom, prejudice, caprice, and humour frequently vary our taste of this kind" and that "beauty and worth are merely of a relative nature and consist in an agreeable sentiment, produced by an object in a particular mind, according to the peculiar structure and constitution of that mind" (Hume in Kant 149). This extended note on Hume's more relaxed and expansive view of sentiment appears to open a space for Kant through structures of feeling that allow a critic to retain sentiments within aesthetic judgments. However, Kant is actually more interested in demonstrating his seconding of Hume regarding the absolute difference between each and every subject's responding imagination.

Moreover, Kant's one extended passage on "sentimentality" in the *Critique of Aesthetic Judgment* is a strongly negative attack on its excesses and one that sets a strong precedent for later criticism. Although Kant acknowledges that "affects" are beautiful and sensible, he delineates them into categories of the "vigorous" and the "languorous." Two centuries later it is difficult not to code these affects immediately into male and female, respectively, and to gauge the power and damage that such bifurcation has caused and continues to cause in the appraisal of feelings. According to Kant, "vigorous affects" make us conscious that "we have forces to overcome any resistance" and are "aesthetically sublime," even those of "desperation," as long as that desperation is "indignant" rather than "despondent." However, an affect of the "languid kind," which never resists, "has nothing noble about it." A further distinction between "spirited emotions" and "tender ones" yields Kant's view that when the tender increases to the level of affects, "they are utterly useless: and a propensity toward them is called *sentimentality*" (italics Kant) (Kant 133). Kant thus installs a test of intensity for emotions. When that intensity gives rise to an imbalance of feeling over reason, it is dangerously enervating. *Sentimentality* will become the "bad" noun, triumphing over its more respectable male parent *sentiment* and always associated with overindulgence, lassitude, and superficiality.

Kant immediately tells his readers where to look for such a syndrome: where emotion as affect "creates a soul that is gentle but also weak and that shows a beautiful side," "fanciful" but not "enthusiastic." Such souls are addicted to "romances and maudlin plays; insipid moral precepts that dally with (falsely) so-called noble attitudes but that in fact make the heart languid and insensitive to the stern precept of duty." (133). Kant could here be describing Emma Bovary's reading program or that of Rousseau. Popular fiction in its highest form or on its best day could never rise to Kant's occasion, certainly no fiction that evinced any passivity or tender openness, that by extension was written for and by women. Kant in his Puritanism reads out any passionately personal enjoyment: we'll have none of that being carried away by heroes and heroines here. Kant's suspicions go as far back as Plato's rhetorical conceit in the *Republic* of banishing poets from his ideal Republic on account of their imitation of virtue and their stirring up of the citizenry to no good purpose.

Kant continues with criticisms that the sentimental is harmful to our self-reliance and leads to a false humility, a sort of craven Christianity (anticipating Nietzschean discontents). Such "impetuous agitations" must lead to a "pure intellectual purposiveness," or else we are merely aroused gratuitously; sentimentality may be bad foreplay indeed. Thus Kant's own doctrine of "disinterestedness" when applied to taste and beauty will not be allowed to apply to affects. To signify, such affects must be placed in a purposive economy. Any sort of strong feeling of the sublime must have reference "to our *way of thinking*" (italics Kant), to "maxims directed to providing the intellectual [side in us] and our rational ideas with supremacy over sensibility" (134–35). It's difficult to overestimate the influence of Kantian philosophy on all aspects of judgment and taste in the literary culture of the twentieth century. Not only did Kant call for the suppression of unregulated feeling in any system of judgment, he also cast into sharp distinction the aesthetic power of judgment set against the intellectual power of judgment, while again stressing the need for both judgments to be rooted in "disinterest." Kant wrote, "And hence it seems not only that the feeling for the beautiful is distinct in kind from moral feeling (as it indeed actually is), but also that it is difficult to reconcile the interest which can be connected with the beautiful with the moral interest, and that it is impossible to do this by an alleged intrinsic affinity between the two" ("On Intellectual Interest in the Beautiful" 165).

Such a summary judgment on these two forms of judgment inheres in the critical presuppositions and operational stances of some of the most brilliant culture critics of the late twentieth century. For example, Roland Barthes at the conclusion of *Mythologies* concludes that we are doomed to speak "excessively" about reality, that the critic of culture must either "poetize" or "ideologize" (158), must either work in aesthetics or the political. Bourdieu after heroic labor through the intricate sociological cataloguing of capital in *Distinction*, admits to a methodological necessity in his "Postscript: Towards a 'Vulgar' Critique of 'Pure' Critiques" when he quotes Proust to stand for his own choices: "I have had to struggle here with my dearest aesthetic impressions, endeavoring to push intellectual honesty to to its ultimate cruelest limits" (485). Bourdieu practices an austerity to match that of Kant on a different plane with different goals. He refuses to believe in art even as Kant had crafted a sensationless pleasure and writes of having to cultivate a "deliberate amnesia," a "readiness to renounce the whole corpus of cultivated discourse on culture" (485). Even though Bourdieu's "Postscript" is a critique of Kantian critique, it is nonetheless caught in the terms that Kant had set forth, in the perceptual "distinctions" that enable *Distinction* as a text and theoretical program to come into being. Bourdieu defines the "aesthetic disposition" as "a generalized capacity to neutralize ordinary agencies and to bracket off particular ends" (54), and such would appear to be a widely accepted estimate of Kantian critique in our time. Bourdieu understands the "aesthetic sense as the sense of distinction itself" (56), the ensemble of the various ways in which literature study validates its discipline and takes to a high ground that knows not its own designation but that moves surely to expunge any taint of historicizing or politicizing on behalf of any critical rhetoric that would open new texts or new spaces in canonical texts.

Reading the Popular: Aesthetics, Morals, Taste

In the arsenal of elite critical tools descended from Kant and invigorated by Hume, what can be of practical use in approaching Puzo's novel? Defiantly materialistic, melodramatic rather than ironic, sensational rather than realistic, pedestrian in style rather than intricate, often sexist, parochial, vulgar—*The Godfather* resists traditional critical overtures and attempts to speak of its power and value. Perhaps its "distinction" lies precisely in having reached so many varied audiences without any of the approved modes of distinction through literary capital, without an approved "poetizing" critique. Yet the narrative of *The Godfather* in novel and films remains as an extraordinary fact and influence on millions of readers and viewers all over the world. What is needed in its study is to seek a supple "standard of taste," in which the "various sentiments of men may be reconciled" (Hume "Of the Standard of Taste" 309), and the "propadeutic," which Kant called for "that will truly establish our taste" and aid in "developing our moral ideas and in cultivating moral feeling" (232). Such a challenge in popular fiction criticism means nothing less than striving for a re-association of sensibility between reason and feeling in the service of raising issues about the moral transactions of mob narrative in the life world of *The Godfather*.

Kantian aesthetic value is phenomenologicially quite thin as opposed to the Humean account of aesthetics, which casts the formation in this more social realm (Railton 88–90). Barbara Herrnstein Smith puts it best when she comments, "As Hume's detailing of the conditions affecting human performance becomes richer and more subtle, his claim that there is an objective standard of taste grounded in nature becomes weaker. As Kant's speculations of what would make a judgment of taste totally objective becomes tighter, purer, and more foolproof, his demonstration becomes more remote from conditions of any sublunary world" (70). For the most part, I too will cast my vote with the party of Hume as realizing more of taste and sentiment's subjectivities in the belief that narratives crucially depend on eliciting our moral beliefs and feelings to reach us as readers (Carroll 141). Such activation of feelings will not yield a criticism that is tidy or conclusive. This criticism will involve coming to understand that the interrogation of a work such as *The Godfather* is perhaps to question the very base of our moral understanding in the way fiction plays us as readers. Noel Carroll identifies a class of narratives "that pervert and confuse moral understanding by connecting moral principles, concepts, and emotions to dubious particulars" (150). Hume himself had been troubled by works "where vicious manners are described, without being marked with the proper characters of blame and disapprobation;" he said that "we are displeased to find the limits of vice and virtue so much confused" (315). *The Godfather* is a laboratory for such moral conflicts in reader identification, with so much mayhem from the heroes while readers' concepts of the larger society and citizenship are overturned, crime inscribed as business and vice versa, and the hallowed and universal signification of family invoked whenever necessary. The catalogue of what the Family can become in *The Godfather* is almost endless in its slippage: justification for any action, security for its members, outlaw band, prison house, immigrant cadre, heroic American business, murderous corporation, fulfillment of the American Dream, myth of a "Founding Father" and descendants.

Carroll cites Martha Nussbaum who contends of the novel genre that it "generally constructs empathy and compassion in ways highly relevant to citizenship," yet Carroll knows that the novel is not always "beneficent" (156), that as an inclusive narrative of society, there are moments in novels that trouble us greatly even as we are absorbed and carried along by the plot and identification with the characters. Beryl Gaut tries to relativize aesthetics when she writes, "A work of art may be judged to be aesthetically good *insofar* as it's beautiful, is formally unified and strongly expressive, but aesthetically bad *insofar* as it trivializes the issues with which it deals and manifests ethically reprehensible attitudes" (184). To adapt this maxim to *The Godfather* is complicated for the novel's melodramatic form is always overexpressive; the family is formally unified, but the text is sprawling. Unity often becomes repetition in which the same speeches on "destiny" or "cunning" are given indiscriminately to different characters in a tedium of resemblances rather than a delight of recognitions for the reader desiring to synthesize judgments and make them whole. To show the relative trivializing of the moral and ethical in *The Godfather* will be the business of chapters 3 and 5 here but in the context of attempting to account for such inscription in any novel and how we make sense of it, according to a host of factors. I don't want to jettison aesthetics in this study but to make moral judgments part of the judging of aesthetic judgment, to suggest that our "distaste" may arise from a palpable sense that the form of the text through its language can, in ways often hard to identify with precision, abuse our view of the rightness of the sentiments expressed, the reasons posited in the life-world of the novel.

Hume would caution at the outset of such an errand that "taste is not able to distinguish all the particular flavors amidst the disorder in which they are presented" (311) and the continuum of taste would run from its delicacy in the work of a master through the most sensational and vacuous production of popular literature. *Approbation* is Hume's hardworking noun. Over and over again, he shows us *the act of proving true*:

true to the lifeworld of the characters, the sentiments of the author, the shape of their civil society. All is played against and through the emotional mindset of the reader, the genre in which it is cast, the times in which it is read, and the critical sign under which it resides in a particular commentary. Hume observes the sheer diversity of taste and why we almost always choose "a predilection for that which suits our particular turn and disposition," but his conclusion that "such preferences are innocent and unavoidable and can never reasonably be the object of dispute" (314) is absolutely contested in the dialogues that comprise the critical discourse in the ideological climate in which we now read and write at the beginning of the twenty-first century. No ethical judgment of literature is currently seen to be innocent, and our narcissistic critical meditations on our "dispositions" most often rise to eclipse the primary text that nominally spurred us into song, Positioning our identity becomes more important than establishing our viewpoint.

Kant traditionally staves off such performative anxiety. The ethical and the aesthetic are woven together into the moral judgment, nor can residual Kantian legerdemain render them separate in our time. Kant's weapons remain formidable, and we yearn toward them as powerful traditional magic, even as we subvert their tenets. Kant's "aesthetic power of judgment," the "ability to judge forms without using concepts" and to make a "judgment . . . not based on an interest and also gives rise to none" is a perfect double *cordon sanitaire,* absolving a critic from having any ideologically formed positions or presuppositions. Why would he need them since only beauty, perfectly apprehensible and of-and-for-itself is the goal that further absolves the judgment of consequences or agendas, as if the "judgers" did not come marked in so many ways by living in the world. Such license to describe the aesthetic is of course the heritage of Romanticism throughout the variety of heroic artistic individualisms down through the modernists, cohering in every sort of artistic product from Byron's poetry to the alienated refrains of rock lyricists. Yet the ways in which the aesthetic "covers" life and becomes a substitute for it yields some very strange adherents. Puzo's earnest statement that "I believed in art for twenty five years. It gave me a comfort I could find in no other place" suggests the fix that aesthetics was and was in by the late twentieth century, a falsely sealed corner where any perception could be indulged without consequence and with enormous formations of exile, self-pity, isolation, and reflexive commentary. Bourdieu writes, "The aestheticism which makes the artistic intention the basis of the 'art of living' implies a sort of moral agnosticism, the perfect antithesis of the ethical disposition which subordinates art to the values of the art of living" (47). Bourdieu sentimentally sees that subordination as the empirical wisdom of the working classes who cannot, for example see the artful construction of a prize-winning photograph on poverty but instead shudder at the plight of the human subject as "there but for certain minor moves in the economy or the grace of God go I" or who just have instinctive sympathy for another human being, not mediated by art.[1] The "moral agnosticism" of aesthetics is of little use when a critic of popular fiction wants to confront Puzo or any popular writer who through sensational and melodramatic action elides the victims of history or confers magically their ability to fly by all nets of social constraint and law to "take vengeance" to "save [my] family."[2] Thus Kantian aesthetics confers something of the same sense of being above the law as the Corleone "family business" in *The Godfather*. In each case, both in high art and high crime, the gesture is toward an absolution, a motion that does not recognize laws or morality and considers itself above spatial and temporal constraints as well as dialogue with other forces or constituted collectivities. "Disinterestedness" is inimical to any protest against the morality of fiction. Although Bourdieu writes that morality and agreeableness are the explicit norms of the working class, it must also be the base of the popular readership, what he calls the "popular aesthetic" (41). Yet just as surely, these norms are expressed in a false consciousness. "Disinterestedness" is never an option for the popular readership or for moral or ethical critics, and this, at least, is what they share. Bourdieu writes that "nothing is more alien to popular consciousness than the idea of an aesthetic pleasure that . . . is independent of the charming of the senses," which challenges Kant, who had said that taste that needed "charm" and "emotion" had not emerged from "barbarism" (42).

Therefore popular fiction and the taste culture confront each other over what looks like insurmountable barriers to accommodation and dialogue, complicated by the critic's uneasy relation to assumed identities. I want to call on sentiment to reintroduce feeling into a discussion of Puzo's popular fiction, to become a bit melodramatic myself when need be, to perhaps draw on sentiment as the very tool of the readership itself, and to try to speak through that mask. The only way perhaps to match Puzo's impact is provisionally to mime his effects. If he opts out of the system of elite fiction's creation after *The Fortunate Pilgrim*, why should I hold my ground there as critic since Puzo is talking about the whole host of life-world issues that make me uneasy about my own stubborn residence in formalist criticism? I meet him on the grounds of his fiction when I wish to remain "interested" rather than "disinterested." Writing about morality and ethics is worth doing in relation to *The Godfather* because Puzo himself is raising such issues all the time in this popular narrative. To abandon the search for his meanings because such errands do not fit the historical caste of critical debate or are in debt to the emotions and the sympathies would then suggest that we have no way to engage this writer and fiction in dialogue. To refuse to meet seriously a vastly popular text such as *The Godfather* on the grounds of its largely pedestrian pronouncements about family, destiny, and immigration is to forego an opportunity to understand where millions of people have had their emotional and rational responses to these huge cultural formations both confirmed and challenged. We cannot afford to wave off *The Godfather's* take on the subjects of American civil society, capitalism, and its arrangements and say that they are all just manifestations of some false consciousness or the "unconscious," political or otherwise, or to be degraded appetites or simplifications. Such is to do violence to the study of this phenomenon. There will be moments when, unavoidably, I will want to describe *The Godfather* in terms of something else, to void its content and replace it with my own, to "expose" its gaps or inconsistencies, but these rhetorical acts need not be primary or definitive. Just as often, I will say that *The Godfather* is about exactly what it appears to be about: Money, Family, Business, Immigrants. Negations and refusals are never the whole story in complex response to popular fiction.

Such a range of critical motion on taste allows for freer speculations on its mediating power. Kant, Bourdieu, and Puzo are caught in varying refusals. Kant demands "sensationless" pleasure. Bourdieu denies himself any aesthetic pleasure and then grimly sets about contextualizing the sensible pleasures of the working class according to their being caught in an economy that rules their response even as it rules that of their critics. Puzo first flees his ethnic family, attempts an elite literature career, goes bad to write an enormous best seller, then dissolves into complacent reprise. In each case they are perhaps exemplifying a "fundamental refusal of the facile" (486), which Kant describes as "pure taste." The taste culture will always be at odds with the popular, and intellectuals and authors will warily affiliate with taste while just as warily maintaining an attraction-repulsion to the facile: Kant through male sentiment, Bourdieu through "rigor," yet sympathy for the consuming class, Puzo through his mystified worship of art where he might be Exhibit A in a Bourdieuian analysis (see chapter 2 in this volume).

Bourdieu is almost lyrical in his negativity and quite sensational when he describes Kant's taste that renounces the facile as "based on the disgust that is often called 'visceral' " (486). He evokes "easy virtue" and the "easy lay," and clearly the terms themselves when transcoded into popular fiction suggest a prostituted or an adulterated text, some betrayal or lie of art, perhaps incarnated through Puzo's declaration "I wrote below my gifts in [*The Godfather*]" or in Michael's famous kiss of death in *Godfather II* in Havana when he passionately declares "I know it was you, Fredo. You broke my heart." In effect, Michael tells him that he sold out the family for money and respect, got their brother Sonny killed, and was complicituous in the attempt on the life of Michael, Kay, and the children in the Lake Tahoe compound. Michael's disgust is visible, his dis-taste enormous. His judgment is that Fredo has broken the law, which is, in Kant's terms, a law for everyone in the family. Michael's "judgment" gives rise to an "interest," that Fredo must die; in the name of family, Michael must kill family. Within the contorted morality that

The Godfather posits, this is a moral choice, but one made out of disgust, passion, and the power of judgment.

Bourdieu leaves behind his "dearest aesthetic impressions" to practice sociology. Puzo practices popular literature by "writing below his gifts." Michael Corleone "goes bad" by killing Sollozzo and McCluskey and thereby truly joins the family for the first time. Further ironies crosscut among the critic, the author, and the characters. Don Corleone has "taste," which separates him from his murderous peers. He is strait-laced in matters of sex, and a man of reason, a statesman, full of disgust for the actions of both his supplicants and his headstrong oldest son. To turn the prism, critics know from their earliest training that to paraphrase and transpose Don Corleone, "revenge [interpretation, evaluation] is a dish best served cold." Within the taste culture of aesthetics, even in an era when aesthetics is in relative eclipse, the nominal critical act should not raise one's voice but reason, obfuscate, allude to, reformulate, and eviscerate taste-fully, armed with mighty weapons of philosophy, rhetoric, and language. Who are more mandarin, above the fray, and disinterested than Vito Corleone and his son, Michael? It's Michael who is the family inheritor, not Sonny, the violent, sexually potent son who brawls his way through sensational scenes, a Corleone seemingly on loan from 1930s Warner Brothers brash and visceral gangster epics. He is discredited through dis-taste, as is the Cold War weapons system brute known as Luca Brasi and the child seducer and horse lover Jack Woltz. *The Godfather* pronounces its own distasteful judgment on these figures.

There's no denying the fact that the critic would like to keep his distance from the Corleone empire and its workings analogous to the manner in which Don Corleone "launders" both his orders to kill and the money he amasses. American fiction criticism in general wants to stay away from the physical and material facts of murder and money. These hard facts are resistant to a sustained formalist or ideological criticism through any of the literary-critical tools in vogue at any time. The refusal of criticism to confront a moral and violent muddle has its fictional analogue in Michael Corleone's initial refusal, almost disgust, with his own family. Michael has to wean himself away from Dartmouth, his World War II heroism, and his romance with Kay Adams to get back to the family, where he becomes a success. There's a parable in Michael's trajectory and justifications in what might be called the "Popular Subversive." Kant's "Negative Magnitudes" in *Critique of Judgment* measure pure taste by the intensity of denied impulse, by the highest degree of tension (Bourdieu 490), and here we find something close to a principle of higher prurience, the abstraction of the sensible and the coarse into a more intellectual form. Such a ratcheting up of the emotional denial within the very figure of the example defines quite well the symbolic American Romance Paradigm, the inaugurating critical trope to canonize a run of writers and tropes in the American 1850s (Poe, Melville, Hawthorne, blackness, whiteness, redness, but no slaves, masters, or Indians) by a criticism taking dominion in the American 1950s. The genius of this intensity centers on the hidden meaning, the symbolic complexity, the ironic layering, the deflections from historical bodies onto "colors"—the move, in short, to taste. Bourdieu quotes Derrida on the "arid pleasure" of Kant's critique (494, 600), and such a pleasure becomes a cornerstone of the first generation of American Literature study in the academy after World War II. Tellingly, such aridity within a coldly chosen symbolic "pleasure" would make Michael Corleone the popular avatar of an abstract refusal to traffic in the sentimental but to become a mandarin "power of blackness" on his own, to abscond to a tower of his own creation, to deny a common humanity within the murderous family. Such would be an elite critical reading of Michael's passage with the potential result of making him a metacritical brooder over his inhabited mob narrative. However, Puzo gives scant evidence that such was his intention at all, and such a critical stance would tell us very little about the narrative's hold on its audience in American culture.

A more useful critical approach would be to attempt a full-field description of the various acts of Puzo and his Corleone family coordinated with readerly and critical acts. What might be the congress among these subjects? Everything about the family is concealed on the surface from America, yet nothing is concealed in Puzo's writing. The writing holds no secrets, yet the family business is an invisible empire. Within the "Popular Subversive" then would be a series of guilty pleasures that take dead aim at the taste culture and the hegemony of aesthetics, each transgression predicated on the necessity of an action that could be described as "going bad," which would include:

- Vito and Michael Corleone becoming murderers (Going Bad= Becoming the Godfather)

- Mario Puzo writing the novel (Going Bad=Writing *The Godfather*)

- Readership (Going Bad=Reading and Liking *The Godfather*)

- Critical Act (Going Bad=Writing on *The Godfather*).

In each case, "disinterest" and the "beautiful" are canceled. In the society in which he finds himself in New York around 1920, Vito Corleone cannot see a way to rise in the world. His first obstacle to autonomy and security is the "Black Hand" extortionist, Don Fanucci. Vito Corleone would establish himself as a "made man," something created or produced beyond natural law, a killer to be feared when he comes speaking reason in a soft voice. It will be in your best *interest* to hear his practical maxims and, upon reflection, to do his bidding. Puzo tries to "escape" his ethnicity in

World War II and during the first years of his writing career. When he writes *The Fortunate Pilgrim* to critical acclaim but little popular success, he says he feels betrayed and thus knows what he must do: "write below his gifts" in the next novel, which, in chronicling the descent into and growth of a great crime empire, is paralleled in the writing change from *The Fortunate Pilgrim* to *The Godfather* in characterization, tone, and complexity. Going bad is going away from the moral norms, the taste culture, ethnic realism, and the standards of critical judgment.

The Godfather counters all the authorities that function like the invisible government of literary culture to keep Puzo from validating his "belief in art" as a talisman to ward off any life-world interference. Puzo goes outside the debate to find his godfather. The Corleone historical situation is such that the "Family" replaces "Art" as the first principle, even as *The Godfather* replaces Puzo's earlier fiction. Puzo believes in Don Corleone as he had in art; he finds in *him* the protection that he could "find in no other place" (*The Godfather Papers* 34). *The Godfather* is Puzo's revision of the power of art to the popular realm where he as author cannot be touched by criticism and because of success.

The innocent or naive transgression in this Popular Subversive series would be that of the popular reader who is consuming the product according to the dictates of the author and can't put the book down or goes to see the films repeatedly. For that audience, "liking" *The Godfather* would include approving of the actions that the Corleones must take outside the law on behalf of the sanctioned family and its survival or simply not taking heed of the issues at all. For the critic going bad, the analysis of a popular work involves many issues that make *The Godfather* compelling. They include the critical positing of a metaphorical-hypothetical relation of author to work, author to character, and author to vocation that must be mediated not only by aesthetics (ironically conceived as the refuge from which Puzo decamps) but also by issues of the critic's choice of subject to study (popular fiction), author (a best-selling author), issues (morality of the text, ethical norms, taking form "seriously" in Puzo's text, history, elite and popular literary relations). Each of these choices, too, suggests a crisis of "belief" on the part of the critic, allowing that it might be outside traditional literary study that he might find the most interesting issues of fiction's rationale and praxis. To analyze *The Godfather* is to become something of a metaphorical Corleone family member, seeing from *cosa nostra* (reconfigured as popular fiction) just what that outside world of elite fiction and criticism looks like from different discriminations and considerations within popular fiction.[3] Once uneasily situated, the popular fiction critic is constantly adjusting what Smith in *Contingencies of Value* calls "prejudices" in the best sense ("assumptions, expectations, capacities") that determine critical "identity" during an informed reading (10). And then, having been sucked back in (to reverse Michael's intimation in *Godfather III*), how do I find my way back *out*, and why would I wish to do so? Within the Popular Subversive, every player becomes something of an outlaw, fostering a new identity.

Reading *The Godfather*: Liberal Pluralist Training and Praxis in the Bourgeois Sphere

Working against the traditional anathematization of the popular, the critic who wishes to confront it faces a complicated task. The two most prominent Anglo-American contemporary schools of criticism of the popular can generally be placed under the headings of the American popular culture movement and the British cultural studies group. These movements have been poles apart in genesis and influences. The American popular culture movement dates from the early 1970s and is an outgrowth of both the American studies content and artifact-based school of analysis and a more media-wise component comprising the study of, in addition to popular fiction, advertising, television, music, and video. The American study has been egalitarian and generally not theoretically based and has shown itself to be descriptive rather than analytical with an antipathy toward evaluation and moral judgment. The British Cultural Studies movement is largely rooted in a Marxist theoretical base that studies all aspects of media culture as revealing multiple false consciousnesses in a variety of rhetorics. The British critics tend to void or replace the content of the popular texts with their suggestive absences, to read affirmative narratives as documents of a hegemonic culture that practices its obfuscations and dominations through the culture industry. The godfathers of such a critical program would undoubtedly include Antonio Gramsci, Louis Althusser, and Raymond Williams, along with the austere works of Max Horkheimer and Theodor Adorno. The Cultural Studies movement's critical rhetoric routinely contains implicit moral criticism of the contemporary culture that spawns the popular works.

Along with these critical movements in popular culture study, the criticism of popular fiction has been enhanced by the major speculations on reader response across a range of imaginings from class-based readers to psychoanalytic studies of how we read and for what formations and to gender and race-based reading in the "multiples" that comprise the makeup of the contemporary reading audience. Critics from the more tropological Chicago school of the critical formalist tradition, who branch off from New Criticism toward Kenneth Burke but still honor the text for what it can yield to the responding reader, present a hybrid critical approach. One of the most interesting has been Peter Rabinowitz in *Before Reading* (1987). A critic trained by Wayne Booth to read for irony and figural density, Rabinowitz extends that skill into a set of reading precon-

ceptions held by readers from varying classes of training and professional interest. Rabinowitz is also influenced by the strong and continuing meditations on interpretive communities by writers such as Stanley
Fish and aims to understand, as carefully as possible, the ways in which
we model an array of preconceptions about a fictional text prior to the
act of assembling our judgments when we read the fiction.

One of Rabinowitz's opening observations is that the academy, site
of reader training for the American professionalized middle class, will
always value complexity over "more formulaic" literature, and, therefore, critics will only find the "formulaic" amidst the noncanonical texts.
To drive critics out to the formulaic without any map back to the main
line of elite literary criticism, to segregate elite from popular fiction in all
critical discourse is to inherently develop a rigid canonical economy, one
that in the past few decades has been greatly challenged and one for
which conservative critics mourn as they conceive of the decline in "reading standards" and choice of texts during the culture wars. Rabinowitz's
good sense yields a maxim that I fully endorse in this book: "It is impossible to examine the mechanism of literary evaluation itself without studying both texts that are highly regarded by our literary judges *and* texts
that are generally deemed inferior" (11). If *The Godfather* is to have the
range of reference that I hope it to have, I must demonstrate its relevance
on a number of fronts, to establish and sustain a dialogue with other
popular texts as well as with elite fiction, with other historical periods in
American fiction, with major formations in our history such as immigration and the constructed "melting pot" in their relation to the strong
American figures of family and business. I want to establish that *The
Godfather*'s nightmares belong to a national psyche consistently captured
by popular fiction but not often touched deeply by literary-critical debates over canonicity and one that rumbles on beneath the critical and
academic wars fought about interpretation. Thus I want to historicize
Rabinowitz's formalist rules for reading in order to drive down deeper
into America's story in mythic and historical imagining.

In his section on "Popular Fiction as a Genre," Rabinowitz examines at some length the problems and contradictions of an ironic mode
of interpretation. He knows that when, for example, we find inconsistencies in elite texts, we read them as intentionally crafted or at least coherent in their complexity, but when we find inconsistencies in popular
texts, we ignore them or read them as flaws (188). Certainly the popular
readership reads for the plot, according to the writer's intent to fill the
signifier. The trained critic will indeed arrest the text at any point he
chooses to intervene in the author's sequence with a reified excerpt that
takes on a life of its own as the critic's purloined text, which he then
covers with a meaning. Rabinowitz contends that a "basic rule of coherence" in popular literature is that the "ironic reading . . . whatever its
textual grounding, would be wrong as an interpretation of the author's

intentions" (190), adding that it's conceivable that popular and elite reading strategies are "not mutually exclusive," although he suspects "only
academics would actually read" a novel in this fashion. Yet it's clear that
when an "academic" reads *The Godfather*, he does so with many of the
same conflicts and social conditioning as that of a so-called popular reader.
He's subject to the same field imaginary of American values and notions
of "family" and "business." The academic reader is different in kind
rather than degree, as Bourdieu would tell us.

Rabinowitz is most concerned with the ultimate goal of achieving
the right or best reading and one that is a single critical act by a trained
professional. With a novel of such wide cultural dissemination as *The
Godfather*, into so many different areas of national life, it's difficult to
know what a "right" reading of it might be. If I acknowledge the fact that
I know the rules of the elite critical game, I believe I can and should read
against what I deem to be authorial intent for a number of reasons.
Rabinowitz suggests that this wouldn't be playing fair, a lingering bias
that comes closer to that of Booth and perhaps E. D. Hirsch. I freely
admit *The Godfather* fractures my reading responses into conflicting feelings and several judgments, which I continually want to place in an
"interested" rather than "disinterested" posture. I read the novel as an
American male academic of a certain age and training who believes the
comprehension of *The Godfather* is a very complex matter, which reaches
deep into the history of American fiction and American configuration of
the national errand and family. Although Rabinowitz states that "for any
actual act of reading, we must choose one genre or the other" (193), the
"actual act" must be qualified in criticism, often line-by-line and chapter-
by-chapter as texts and characters contradict themselves.

Such contradictions are apparent all through *The Godfather* and never
more prominent than in the Corleones' violent acts in the name of reason
and family. Surely a character such as Michael Corleone, his face fractured by Captain McCluskey's blow outside the hospital, his life similarly fractured among Sicilian/American, war hero, Ivy League college
boy and family avenger lives overtly under the sign of physical doubleness for much of the novel. The reader lives with Michael's hybridity all
the time; he's the ultimate outsider (brooding, isolated, half-assimilated)
who also becomes the ultimate insider, the son, the heir from whom all
power will flow. We may not always be comfortable when Puzo invokes
"Michael the killer" over "Michael the good son" or feel Puzo has artfully and meaningfully transitioned between them, but all readers, not
just critical academic ones, are capable of grasping the contradictions of
The Godfather's discourse. We are asked to accept non-assimilation over
the putative melting pot story, where our strong feelings are enlisted on
the side of the "good" murderers as they battle the "bad" murderers.
Such reading agility is not simply a critic's construct; it's required of all

Godfather readers to suppress parts of a reading self at the expense of others, to lose, for a while, a liberal pluralist view or a First World nonethnic view, to submit to the novel's way with us. I no longer know how to get to the point of a "right" reading without severe commentary on the intent of such a reading. I'm often constructing "a" reading to show a specific facet of *The Godfather's* range or authority within a *critical ensemble*, which might be defined as multiculturalism at its most inclusive at the critical level, not quite a melting pot but capable of a real suppleness. The Aristotelian urge to find *The Godfather's* proper cubbyhole and file it is what I want to resist in order to demonstrate that a novel of wide cultural acceptance as an instinctive "read" can be as interesting to write about as a novel of intellectual depth. To learn how to write on this phenomenon is to write a book on Puzo and *The Godfather*.

Part of that learning involves a nontheoretical attempt to face squarely my own reading temperament, insofar as I can, to know the fundamental predispositions and academic credentials that shape me as a liberal, pluralist, secular reader. My deep background through all pluralistic misgivings about *The Godfather's* hermeticism and conservative family isolation most likely springs from the ideals of the Enlightenment as articulated through a massive descriptive program of Western culture. The pluralist themes of what Richard Bernstein calls an "engaged fallible liberalism" include antifoundationalism, fallibilism, the social character of the self, contingency, and the regulative idea of a critical community (387–88). In their fierce identity, the Corleones believe themselves to be *the* foundation of any order. They are infallible and antisocial; they refuse to recognize that any outside community regulates their conduct or lives; and they guard against contingency, feeling it an insult to their control. It's clear from reading *The Godfather* and other documents that the Enlightenment appears to have missed Sicily.

Jurgen Habermas in the past several decades has defined the "bourgeois public sphere," a culture's common life that is defined and debated through a broadly conceived dialogue that buttresses and modulates legal, political, and economic institutions and their policies. A Corleone or Soprano will always disparage such a culture that they reduce to the "big shots" or the "Carnegies and Rockefellers" as Tony Soprano says, or the *pezzonovantis* and .90 calibers of *The Godfather*, while Michael abstracts the society he might someday join as "some country club crowd, the good simple life of well-to-do Americans" (363). Liberal theorists believe they move in a sphere elevated beyond such suspicion and cliché voiced by the ethnic outsiders. Theories of civil society value a shared code of human conduct and transaction beyond the family or clan and refer back to founding documents that authorize the American and French revolutions of the common man as well, such as Rousseau's "Social Contract" (1762), in which he wrote, "Each of us puts his person and all his power in common under the supreme direction of the general will, and in our corporate capacity, we receive each member as an indivisible part of the whole" (Miller 220). Here is a partial but crucial beginning of the Enlightenment road to both freedom and justice, says Habermas (Trey 24). John Gray has recently commented that the Enlightenment in America has achieved "the status of a civil religion," and he quotes Richard Rorty in his belief that America gives "democracy priority over philosophy" and that humanism puts "power in the service of love" held together "by nothing less fragile than social hope" (144, 170–71).

John Kekes flatly states that pluralism is a moral theory (12) and one that enlarges our view of justice. He also quotes Michael Sandel to the effect that "society being composed of a plurality of persons . . . is best arranged when it is governed by principles that do not *themselves* presuppose any particular conception of the good. . . . This is the liberalism of Kant" (200). Thus does disinterest as a harbinger of taste wind its way back into moral imagining. Such cultural armature and consensus from the bourgeois life world helps comprise the assumptions in American society that live within the reader who also turns pages of *The Godfather* to revel in the Corleones' sensational and bloody triumphs. This multifaceted reader of prejudices, allegiances, and conditioning is always potentially alive to the contradictions in Puzo's text. John Guillory in *Cultural Capital* defines several of these liberal assumptions, such as "competing interest groups," "balance of societal demands," "democratic civic culture," and "political participation and trust" (4). If I read *The Godfather* in the American society in which the Corleones move, I find most of pluralism's precepts to be antithetical to the ethics and world view of the Corleones.

Pluralism is built into liberalism "as it were on the ground floor" (Kekes 201). Pluralism appears as a more static theory of the tolerance of differences, while liberal influence would animate that tolerance toward a desirable end that liberalism could articulate in a social sphere. A short list of the resulting adversarial positions on major issues might be as follows:

1. Good and Evil

- **Corleones**: The nature of good and evil is universal and natural. Evil is lodged in authority or the state and must be opposed to get justice. The state is always inimical to its citizens [what might be called the "Sicilian world view" according to Puzo].

- **Liberal Pluralist** Reader (Me): Evil is socially and culturally based and can be, should be opposed in service of justice. Evil is not inherently coextensive with the state or with any satanic individual or ethnic group; it is not identified. Evil is, in fact, a hyperbolic embarrassment in sacred/profane rhetoric.

2. Business

• **Corleones**: The business of making money takes primacy. Nothing should be allowed to get in its way.

• **Liberal Pluralist**: Business is business but rapacious if unchecked since competing groups go out of balance. The Mob is its perfect lawless example, limiting freedom and assaulting human rights.

3. Ethnic Solidarity and Family

• **Corleones**: Ethnic identity and family unity are the only stays against disaster in America. The "common good" is a naive fantasy.

• **Liberal Pluralist**: Ethnic family identity is admirable but can and should be converted to a wider, shared Americanism that dissolves "hyphenated" identities when the "common good" is at stake.

4. Communication

• **Corleones**: Old World gestural forms (*bella figura*) constitute powerful weapons against the bareness of language not marked by identity.

• **Liberal Pluralist**: Old World gestural forms are quaint, melodramatic, and immature but should be nominally honored for their authenticity.

5. Destiny

• **Corleones:** Resignation to individual destiny is inevitable. Class and ethnic identity *are* destiny.

• **Liberal Pluralist**: Resignation to destiny is superstitious and fatalistic, unless it is couched in American collective terms of "Manifest Destiny."

6. Individual Responsibility

• **Corleones**: Belief in individual responsibility extends only to yourself and your identified and extended family.

• **Liberal Pluralist**: Belief in individual responsibility must be visionary and extend to everyone, for the health of the collective society depends on such duties taken seriously.

7. Women

• **Corleones**: Women must be kept out of the family business; yet women and children provide the moral rationale for any action the men may take in the name of family.

• **Liberal Pluralist**: Women should have equal opportunity to rights and privileges in society and should control their decisions about marriage and reproduction.

8. Death

• **Corleones**: "What can *we* do about death?" It comes to all people.

• **Liberal Pluralist**: "What can we *do* about death?" We have a social imperative to bring all people under the rule of law and work to eradicate hunger, disease, and poverty.

Not only do these opposed positions cohere "before reading," they also are extrinsic or beyond reading, as germane to reading a text as voting a party ticket, building a career, or constructing an emotional life. The liberal pluralist ethic is one of advocacy over resignation. Such a view descends in part from John Dewey's pragmatism at the turn of the twentieth century to the contemporary views of Rorty, essentially the capitalist version of "what is to be done?" in an engaged left pluralism. Rorty would call the human rights culture a positive outcome of a sentimental education (172). Rorty's squarely in the party of Hume: we train our feelings through texts such as *Uncle Tom's Cabin*, but, as Rorty knows, "sentimental education works only on people who can relax long enough to listen" (180); it becomes a class argument of whether the Corleones or any ethnic or historically or economically oppressed group can afford to move out from identity to a more universal humanism. This humanism possesses a view of agency and freedom, nurtured carefully through an American society that has developed along a line of sympathetic political development.[4] The liberal pluralist feels his communitarian ethic to be as natural, as "humanist," as Don Corleone feels his family-based business and Old World identitarian view to be. The temperamental shift in reading comes when the liberal pluralist reader, who, after all, is in some form of identity in *his* pluralism, can pull back to the intolerance of the one identity of the Corleones, turn off the hallowed differences of pluralism, and vote "Corleone" all the way. This reader can indeed also become part of an "Old World" imaginary, can take both the persecution of the peasant Corleones and the absolute baronial power of the dominant Corleones and negotiate a readerly way through a modern America in a tolerant fantasy of both power and freedom where the Corleones truly become "Our Gang."

Such a reader experiences both revulsion and exhilaration when drawn into the Corleone world, one capable of altering or suspending many beliefs. *The Godfather* and, by extension, popular fiction, licenses a terrific mobility and freedom. To live through a Don Corleone allows a reader to know both an avenging peasant and the wielder of enormous personal patriarchal power within a criminal empire and a man who goes home at night to an American family. Here is the freedom of popular fiction, which posits a fanciful crossing of generic lines in an imagined mobile society. In *Gone with the Wind*, Scarlett O'Hara is plantation ingenue, an Atlanta businesswoman and a suffering romantic heroine. In Judith Krantz's *Princess Daisy*, Daisy is a white Russian princess, a New York career woman, an incestuous rape victim—and a suffering romantic heroine. Within the elusive and cliché-ridden American Dream is the geography of *The Godfather* itself: that, in America, one can move outward in total freedom to follow an individual destiny, yet return to a rooted identity (the Family, Tara, Princess-hood). A Corleone can take the law into his own hands, transgress any bond with society in the name of family and its security. Here is the extremity of the "Freedom To," the radical sanction in a material and liberal culture acted out in a natural abundance where "making self" is a male identity kit, as American heroes from Huck to Gatsby to Holden to Michael Corleone have known.

In this vein, the liberal pluralist society appears paralyzed by tolerance, forms, and consensus in comparison with the the latent fury of Old World fatalism, which suddenly in paroxysms of violence can vanquish its foes like a slumbering beast awakening to feed. The liberal society with its balances, flexibility, and trust becomes the democratic, civic enemy for the Corleones to overcome or pay off as complicitous ally. Any critic of American popular fiction is writing from the political freedom of the liberal culture that sanctions the taste culture to operate in its restricted sphere of capital. As Puzo's characters know, it's the very tolerance of the American civic and judicial structures that allows their dreams to flourish. It's the very agreement by the pluralist culture that their differences are OK, indeed hallowed in principle. Thus the moral question of What if everyone acted this way? encircles everyone who has agreed to play by the rules as long as they are individual successes. This question comes to be the great challenge to the "ethic" of the Godfather himself. In the semantic domain of literary criticism, the question posed by the critic from the precincts of the taste culture is "what moral questions can be asked in and of popular fiction?" It's the critic's task to move through the thicket of prohibitions of (a) asking moral questions and (b) asking them of a popular text, to find the implications and connections between aesthetics and these questions. In Kant's terms, such would be to find ways to link the pleasure and displeasure we call "taste," as defined through our labeling the beautiful and the sublime, with the pleasure and displeasure we call "moral feeling" that always is enlisted when we are "judging for an interest."

Hume in "Of a Standard of Taste" in particular was very clear on what we ought to do with characters such as the Corleones when we encounter them in literature:

> But where the ideas of morality and decency alter from one age to another, and where vicious manners are described, without being marked with the proper characters of blame and disapprobation, they must be allowed to [i.e., we must agree that they] disfigure the poem, and to be a real deformity. I cannot, nor is it proper I should, enter into such sentiments, and however I may excuse the poet, on account of the manners of his age, I can never relish the composition. (315)

Hume practices moral criticism here after clearly stating that if the poet has not the proper awe and horror before the "vicious" scenes he imagines, then Hume will not accept the narrative as true or important. Thus, Hume would not want to identify with a Sicilian brigand or American robber baron if Puzo was not interested in tallying up the moral balance sheet in the fiction. Calling up these moral imperatives places Hume provisionally outside the "vicious manners" (of a mob family) in a privileged place, akin to that of aesthetics but actually informed almost exclusively by sentiments. Such personal and historically based reader projections usually occur within characteristic moves of trained readers and many different responses might influence our continuing struggles to link the aesthetic reading to the moral reading. A text such as *The Godfather* grounds our yearning signifieds and dreams in a life world of action and character choice. Hume in *A Treatise of Human Nature* has a reflection on our reflections on vice and virtue that takes as its example "wilful murder"; it states "the vice entirely escapes you as long as you consider the object" (468–69). Hume then changes the focus as he subjectifies the response to the "vice": "You never can find it, till you turn your reflexion into your own breast, and find a sentiment of disapprobation which arises in you toward the action. Here is a matter of fact: but 'tis the object of feeling, not of reason. It lies in yourself, not in the object. . . . Vice and virtue, therefore, may be compar'd to sounds, colors, heat and cold" (*Treatise* 468–69). Hume's view is that human motives are the only proper object of moral judgments and that actions undertaken on behalf of these motives are what we may judge.

In an altogether serendipitous way, Hume provides a structure whereby feeling is corrected by reason (Shaw 34). In *The Godfather*, murders are carried out within a structure of planning and justification that constitutes not only a Corleone *apologia* but something akin to a brief for the oppressed and powerless. The Corleones practice their own utilitarianism, reasoning their way to why a Fanucci must die, a McCluskey, a Paulie Gatto. At each point the murder carried out is reasonable and justified as necessary for the family's survival and prosperity.[5] When I make a moral judgment *against* such predation, I consider the Corleone rhetoric, their means/ends arguments, and their array of justifications. Within this consideration, I'm also writing a microcosmic abstract of my own liberal pluralist view, of my sense of the law and the social contract. These allegiances are in play prior to my aesthetic appraisal or my formalist interest, but they work to shape my critical operations, as Bourdieu knows. Reader-critics of *The Godfather* continually find themselves in the dynamic of moving back and forth in judgment amidst *The Godfather*'s signifieds: the family is compelling; the family is contemptible. Its solidarity is thrilling; its solidarity is hermetic and un-American. Terrific set-piece scenes in *The Godfather* are powerful and revealing on enormous questions of good versus evil, nature versus history, and myth versus fiction, but their logic is often rudimentary and morally chaotic. If I want to show Puzo prematurely affirming a universal signified in face of a strong historical or moral contradiction, I appraise a site where I demonstrate that the aesthetics of the scene dictates the fictional meaning through a mystification. The morality of the scene (its "message") is discussed through the morality of the fictional rhetoric (see chapter 5).

Booth in *The Company We Keep* (1988) writes of the disparate ways a text "deepened my experience, heightened my sensibilities, matured my judgement, consoled me, shocked me" (52). Such is a formidable list of emotional, civic, and sensational pleasures, pluralist to be sure. Yet what if *The Godfather* "deepened my experience" in dealing with and through popular fiction, if my experience was not necessarily some variant of cultural enlightenment but experience in writing on this structural form? Reading *The Godfather* then becomes my experiment in which I may shape the results. If I do not respect the text's conclusions and probe for the problem in authorial intent, some rough handling may be in order; an achieved moral reading must rise from the ruins of *The Godfather*. My "judgment" can "mature" only after I've taken *The Godfather* not as far as I can, the critic's normal Promethean impulse, but after I keep asking the text to formulate more cogent questions and choices for its characters and situations. Such is the inevitable critical and academic conversion of even plot-driven, goal-oriented action texts such as *The Godfather* to reflective ends. As Booth rather censoriously knows, we may ask the author in a moralistic moment, "Why have you failed in your inherent responsibility to give us, your readers, the ethical support we need?" (125). Booth goes on to cite Sartre in *What Is Literature* that the author demand more of the reader, that for Sartre, the ethical, ideological, and political judgments are made when we gauge "how well the fiction serves the reader's freedom" (127), a phrase that when unpacked might suffice for a modernist and existential credo on critical reading with freedom as the liberal pluralist end to be served.[6]

A more consistent postmodern view is to let all terminology coexist in a more relaxed tension where the inability to sharply distinguish popular from elite, moral from aesthetic might count as a creative first step. Elite and popular literature both evade the social, political, moral, and ethical. Elite literature drives the heroic figure upward into the tower where he becomes the heroic artist. Popular literature inflates the heroic figure into a man of mythic proportions. In each case, the ground of the fiction where moral and ethical choices are to be made in society is can-celed out, and fictional realism is no road home. Stephen Dedalus may awake from the nightmare of history by a rhetorical epiphany. Vito and Michael Corleone leave history behind and become gods in a parallel universe to America; they awaken to opportunity. In the case of both elite and popular fiction, the deep need is for control of the text and the life, a freedom not reinvested in the pluralism that recognizes society and other people. The bourgeois flees to become an artist, the immigrant flees oppression as well to become "author of his destiny," a capitalist stand-in for a creator, an author, a god. Don Corleone will make himself up as surely as Stephen Dedalus. What logically follows in dealing with Puzo and *The Godfather* is that if an author inscribes God in the very title, we as reader critics from a more prosaic universe are surely within our rights to mark well Puzo's appropriations in his/His name.

Jameson: Simultaneity and Reading the Popular

At its best, America in its ideals and the promises of its institutions may be so much more than the bleak Corleone vision of it. However, the Corleones may operate as rapaciously as the economic system itself and may, indeed, exemplify it. How does the reader process both the promise and the predation of the Corleones? Certainly Fredric Jameson in his commentary on *The Godfather* suggests that its true displaced or uncon-scious story is nothing less than the substitution of the myth of the Mafia for American business itself, the humming engine of late industrial capi-talism ("Reification" 32). Jameson believes that the substitution of the figure of "Crime" for "Business" deflects criticism of *The Godfather* to-ward a moral and ethical criticism that doesn't really penetrate to its economic subject. He asks that if the obfuscation of Business as Crime is the "ideological" function of *The Godfather* narrative, then what is its Utopian function? He finds that function to be the Family itself as a site of envy and longing for a solidarity over and against radical instabilities in a capitalist system. These twin functions of ideological critique and Utopian longing are fundamental to all Jamesonian study of popular forms and comprise the fullest response to thinking through the field of fictional meanings that a critical reader confronts in *The Godfather*.

Within Jameson's body of work is a strong yearning for a re-created wholeness of being. His is a powerful romantic sensibility shackled to a set of terrible truths about the forces that move human society. It's not only that he continually addresses *ideological function* and *Utopian fantasy* but that he consistently modifies these terms with *urgent* and *desperate* as modifiers, respectively. Jameson's critique of popular forms is charged and tense; he states that *The Godfather* activates "our deepest fantasies about the nature of social life" (34). Jameson sounds quite Humean in his reaching out to the widest possible sense of "rightness" that we can command and ask of ourselves as we read. *The Godfather* tells us not only about our society "as we live it now" but as we feel "in our bones" we ought to live it (34), a remarkably precritical and instinctual statement from a contemporary critic whose fascination with the popular has been conveyed through an austerity and rigor of critical formulation but who remains a passionate, primitive sensibility in relation to what he calls in *The Political Unconscious* (1981) the pull of "magical narratives."

Jameson believes the reader's task is, as in a fairy tale, "to reawaken in the midst of a privatizing and psychologizing society" to what a text can truly mean to us, to be critically aware of all the various obfuscations and elisions that a naive capitalist text might offer but to remain enchanted and enthralled, to mount a rhetorical unmasking in the service of a Utopian goal of reaching signifieds of promise: justice, tolerance, wholeness. Jameson cannot renounce an ethical quest even as he denounces ethicism as a premature complacency while he works "toward the light" while "falling into history" (33). For him, the critical act itself recapitulates biblical trajectory, for it is undertaken in the sadness of a fallen world amidst texts that wander and can never see the whole truth, that in some Hegelian riddle are always doomed to be sundered from themselves as they locally re-create the truths of the master narratives.[7] In the conceptual chaos and enormous signification of *The Godfather*, one can find critical melodramas aplenty transmuted into the actions of the Corleones. Jameson wants to retain a common subject and society, which is why he still respects the great realistic novels of the nineteenth century. Jameson is enormously inclusive, arguing that a popular narrative can account for everything if its surface meanings, psychic underside, and cultural significance are taken into account. Don Corleone would try to account for everything in the life of his family. No powerful event that happens in his world goes unnoticed or uncaused. He warns the other crime families that he will take it personally even if a bolt of lightning should strike Michael on his return from Sicily (293–94). The Corleones themselves "read" the totality that is America and extrapolate only what they need and try to control the rest. They are continually attempting to, in the classic Marxist formulation, "wrest a realm of Freedom from a realm of Necessity" (*The Political Unconscious* 19) but their localized self-mystification of this urgency is to accrue enough money, power, and influence through coercion and murder masked as reason to join that "general American family," a hollow yearning that commits them to an ever-darker and Sisyphean task, sundered from themselves.

In the rhetorically dramatic conclusion to *The Political Unconscious*, Jameson outlines a critical program for a popular literature study that would acknowledge all the potential power in the popular form as well as its potential abuse in false consciousness. He states, "If the ideological function of mass culture is understood as a process whereby otherwise dangerous and protopolitical impulses are 'managed' and defused, re-channeled and offered spurious objects, then some preliminary step must also be theorized in which these same impulses—the raw material upon which the process works—are initially awakened within the very text that seeks to still them" (287). In *The Godfather*, crime, violence, and narrow ethnicity are rechanneled and shown to produce unimaginable American wealth and power *within the very text of the family itself*, which *The Godfather* asks us to read as both the ground and reason any action is sanctioned. Within a false consciousness, the family provides *The Godfather* with "a reaffirmation of this or that legitimizing strategy" (287). A key concept for Jameson in his commitment to the dialectic is "simultaneity," the ability to think through all the contradictions of a text's production and reception at one and the same moment, to hold all findings in a true suspension, to never let the critical voice lapse into moralizing or ethical commentary without shoring up the opposite side of the argument. A criticism of the extended *Godfather* narrative must respect that simultaneous attraction and repulsion and must live the extreme contradictions of the Family. *The Godfather* at one and the same time describes the absolute power of the family to signify nurture, justice, and security, while at the same time the text displaces "family" to an extended obscene business entity. The family business is "protection"; the family business is "murder." The family business is an extreme example of ethnic identity; the Corleone desire to be legitimate, to "join" America, is in lip service to pluralism's wholeness and future promise.

Jameson often aims a backhanded blow at the traces of an ethical criticism in lines such as "Only an ethical politics, linked to those ethical categories we have often had occasion to criticize . . . will need to 'prove' that one of these forms of class consciousness is good or positive and the other reprehensible or wicked" (290). He prefers the imprint of the ethical and affirmative as long as it is in the deferred "hard saying" of a criticism that both humanizes Marxism and decries the facility of traditional humanism, that can bear the Utopian when it is seen to be an imaginative desperation and a necessity. Every popular novel yields up some part of this internal dynamic without theorizing it, eliding the negative hermeneutic of power and authority in the "going bad" or "vengeance" narrative that is made bearable by the positive signifieds that are called up in the name of "family," "country" or "survival." Two distinct moments of false consciousness may be identified. The first is a premature optimism and affirmation of a transcendental signified on the part of the reader (the "life is beautiful" syndrome uttered by Don Corleone at his death or by Roberto Benigni to a bemused and morally stunned Hollywood in 1999). The second moment of false consciousness is through a description of some precapitalist structure, either historical (feudal) or literary (epic) as the actual face of a modern social structure (business or the Family) or a literary form (the popular novel). This affirmation and description comprise the face of the popular narrative and the viewpoint of its implied author.

Jameson is confident that such simultaneous readings will transcend what we know as literary or even cultural criticism with an unceasing dialogue between the ideological and the Utopian, the instrumental and the communal reading of culture, and will be able to wed a functional method to an "anticipatory" one (296). Such a program yields the widest scope for reading popular fiction. A literary criticism that cannot grasp the Utopian appeal of best sellers can scarcely then appropriate their narrative energies and must doom itself to an elitist whining. In the succeeding chapters, I will stress that *The Godfather* is both a truth and a lie, its family the most rooted of American signifieds in ethnic identity and yet the most unstable compound of nurture, violence, and illegitimacy. The consequences of that doubleness in signification are what a multiple criticism of *The Godfather* is all about. What does it mean in our time to read this novel so redolent of past oppression and future promise, a novel that is visceral and immediate in calling on our readerly allegiances and American signifieds, a novel not well made but surely important? Clarifying responses to *The Godfather* does not entail a full-field theory or a final judgment of its power or worth but rather as careful and complete a bringing-forth of all the ways in which this family and this novel touch what is most vital to us in American culture through a vehicle that we may wish better (whatever that may come to mean) but that is never not powerful, compelling, full of precisely what engages our taste at long last.

Conclusion

In such varied acts of reading and criticism as I have posited in chapter 1, we come closer to more utilitarian definitions of taste, such as that of Bourdieu, who argues that taste is "the basis of the mutual adjustment of all the features associated with a person" and that "the idea of taste, typically bourgeois . . . presupposes absolute freedom of choice"

(*Distinction* 173, 177), in that taste is seemingly universal and without a firm basis of comparison from person to person.[8] Taste becomes the powerful critical wild card that can always be played as something else. Guillory believes in several stated equivalences that evaluation can always be called a judgment, that a theory of taste is the aesthetic itself, and that the act of judgment is the assignment or recognition of cultural capital, which is aesthetic value (306, 332), whereas Howard Caygill states that Hume's "Of the Standard of Taste" stipulated that "the standard of taste is recognized to be indeterminate: it has neither the understanding's concern with the universal nor sentiment's dispersal in particulars, yet possesses characteristics of both" (77). This capacious and fluid definition opens a space for taste to play with the paradoxes inherent in the continual movement from proof to emotional comprehension, from momentary apprehensions of truth in narrative balanced by questions about the rhetoric of the form or the architecture of the disclosure. Such an acknowledgment of the many bases of taste should not dictate that the aesthetic valuing or devaluing of a text or partial text be an endless series of occasions for metacritical inquiry on the valuation of making judgments at all. Such way paralysis lies and the endless solipsism of sad liberal misgivings. Rather the benefit of a book such as this one, I hope, will be to use taste and the aesthetic not as absolutes but as the traditional yet contested categories from which to argue for and model the criticism of popular texts and authors through focus on Puzo and *The Godfather*.

Pure taste in Kant's critique is a "fundamental refusal of the facile" (Bourdieu 486). Such is the power of that negation that no simple straightforward meaning of taste will ever be granted authority by critical method. The taste culture will always be at odds with the popular, especially in the sentimental and melodramatic narratives that comprise the form. However, Hume's more inclusive taste is an amalgam of sense and reason, which sentiment dominates. Contemporary critics of intellect and rhetorical power who are also moved by the social and historical ramifications of the literary act and the world thus illuminated are provoked into affiliation with sentiment and at the same time pulled away from its identification by instinctive mistrust. Jameson, Barthes, and Bourdieu and their readers have all come to know too much and too well how subjective judgments are constructed and what violence we tend to do to our best reading selves as we convict authors of premature affirmation or false consciousness, in all the bad faith webs we can name but can never truly step outside of in our writings. Such writers are all caught in contemporary criticism's most sentimental motion: the oxymoronic, deeply felt but austere refusal to take refuge and comfort in any particular critique but to believe passionately in the act itself. Barthes in *Mythologies* speaks of the melancholy role of the "mythologist" who attempts to probe language in popular culture. Barthes writes that "his speech is a metalanguage. . . . His task always remains ambiguous, hampered by its ethical origin" (156). Such a critic who wishes to confront "a myth [that] reaches the entire community. . . must become estranged if he wants to liberate the myth." Barthes creates a melodrama for the critic himself: "He must live this assignment without any hope of going back . . ." (157). Barthes's language is most passionate and incendiary when he confronts a paired linguistic and moral crisis, in this case, the critic living out an assignment as a spy or double consciousness in a country or role not conducive to bringing honor or joy to himself or to his readers. Such estrangement in the service of a moral errand is easier to contemplate heroically than to achieve in popular fiction criticism, where the critic so often finds himself outside the family of heroes, villains, authors, and readers.

The Godfather has real power. The novel and films live in our dreams, in our sense of origins and family as Americans, in our fantasies of social power and control over our lives. However, The Godfather also squarely asks us to choose a lawlessness that violates our shared democratic social space and the norms agreed upon to guide civilized conduct in a free society. When we choose to question Puzo, what sort of moral or ethical readers do we become, and how do we then relate to our sensational, sentimental, melodramatic reading selves? Such questions move past the disinterestedness of the taste culture that lives in the ruse that it is not part of an economy itself. The following chapters take The Godfather's pleasure and instruction seriously through both reason and feeling.

chapter two

Mario Puzo: An American Writer's Career

I had been a true believer in art. I didn't believe in religion or love or women or men. I didn't believe in society or philosophy. But I believed in art for forty-five years. It gave me a comfort I found in no other place.

—Puzo, "The Making of *The Godfather*"

Tried to write a trashy potboiler but had to give it up. Immoral and uninteresting, that's why.

—Puzo, "Notes from an Unsuccessful Writer's Diary"

I have written three novels. The Godfather is not as good as the preceding two. I wrote it to make money.

—Puzo, "The Making of *The Godfather*"

Finally, we must ask explicitly a question which is bound to be asked: what is the degree of conscious strategy, cynical calculation, in the objective strategies which observation brings to light and which ensure the correspondence between positions and dispositions?

—Bourdieu, *The Field of Cultural Production*

With the publication of *The Godfather* in 1969, Mario Puzo became the greatest multiethnic literary success in an American literary climate that had only begun to register such seismic changes in its critical mapping. He, however, took little solace in that achievement.

Puzo's career pre- and post-*Godfather* is revealing, both for what he writes and for what he doesn't, for the insights his earlier and later novels provide both on *The Godfather* but also on the writer himself as he struggles for a readership and toward a self-examination. The greatest of all popular immigrant sagas came from a failed elite author who had spent two decades avoiding Italian American subjects and refusing to chase a wide readership. I believe this irony stunned Puzo, never far from a pervasive and wary cynicism about human relations, to a series of revelations in *Fools Die* (1978) that might explain his writer's psyche to a public that had placed him on a pedestal. Rather than freeing Puzo to become the sort of writer he might want to be, one melancholy result of *The Godfather*'s extraordinary popularity is that it made him rueful at his success; he could not find ways to repeat a genre creation that he had never wanted to write in the first place. *The Godfather* did not authorize Puzo to become a genre industry himself such as a King, Clancy, or Rice.

Puzo's career is paradigmatic as he writes along the faultlines of ethnic, mainstream, elite, and popular fiction in the post–World War II era. I want to speculate on Puzo's *habitus* or social-cultural milieu and chart his hesitancies, gaps, and resentments, before and after his great success. Never in American literary history had the imperative to write the Great American Novel been so emblazoned on the horizon for a generation as it had for the male writers coming home after World War II. Puzo's first novel, *The Dark Arena* (1955), is a Hemingwayesque-novel of postwar Germany with tough guy veterans who could spring from *In Our Time*. *The Fortunate Pilgrim* (1964) is his best novel by all measures and comprises an excellent rendering of New York's Lower West Side Italian immigrant culture. *The Godfather* made Puzo a literary celebrity while Coppola's films largely superseded the novel's achievement. Yet in corners of *The Godfather*, Puzo questioned the very writer's enterprise that made his reputation. Puzo's sequel to *The Godfather* is hardly what might have been expected but rather the sprawling *Fools Die*, a novel very knowing about literary success and its ironies. At last Puzo hypothetically could be free of his author's dreams and humiliations, having "made his bones" with *The Godfather*. *Fools Die*'s hero is John Merlyn, a novelist, an orphan rather than an ethnic hero, and a self-proclaimed magician who is transfixed by gambling and knows fear and defeat through a long, unnoticed writer's career. Puzo evinced a great confusion as a writer in a literary marketplace whose negotiations had remained an economic and artistic riddle to him. Awash in money and novelistic capital after *The Godfather*, Puzo did not feel honored, nor could he honor the writer in himself. Thus we can see how, prior to specific considerations of *The Godfather*, Puzo's overall vision of fiction and the novelist's role needs to be explored.

Puzo: Choosing a Dream

Puzo's success with *The Godfather* removed the suffering identity that he had so carefully built up as a lonely outsider to his family, Italian American culture, and the literary establishment. In many respects, the developing figure of Michael Corleone is Puzo himself at his grandest and most morose. Michael is expelled into the larger American culture by service in World War II; an Ivy Leaguer for a semester at Dartmouth, he meets a New England daughter, Kay Adams. Michael is nonetheless "sucked back in," in Coppola/Puzo's memorable phrase in *Godfather III*, to salvage his family's honor and his own, to save his father, and, ultimately, to succeed him. He becomes Italian American with a vengeance. Likewise, success as the author of *The Godfather* moved Puzo away from his love affair with elite fiction. In many respects, writing about the Mafia for Puzo was equivalent to joining the Mafia, to doing its business. While such never occurred to Puzo on a fully conscious level in all his years and writings, I want to speculate that the intricacies of "going bad" on two levels (becoming the godfather instead of an "American Hero," writing *The Godfather* instead of an elite novel) are what compel Puzo to write what is surely in *Fools Die* the strangest sequel to an American popular classic.[1] In Puzo's case, escape and isolation, his great crutches painfully erected over two decades of a writing life in America, were always seductively calling him back from *The Godfather*'s pinnacle of success. The slack profligacy of *Fools Die* is Puzo's fictional *summa* on his writing life.

An earlier and even more curious text of clues than *Fools Die* exists in which to search for Puzo's views and writer's discontents. A volume of Puzoian miscellany entitled *The Godfather Papers and Other Confessions* (1972) provides Puzo's most detailed comments on his writing life. *The Godfather Papers*, however, is not a collection that centers on the writing of the novel or on the collaboration with Coppola on the screenplay for the first film. Instead, these are book reviews, magazine essays, a short story, pieces written and published between 1966 and 1968 for the most part, during *The Godfather*'s composition. It's the sort of slapped-together book that a writer can expect to publish only when he's "hot," when all his musings are seemingly relevant for a public that simply wants more. The heart of the collection was three new pieces: "Choosing a Dream: Italians in Hell's Kitchen," "The Making of *The Godfather*," and "Notes from an Unsuccessful Writer's Diary." Taken together, they form a picture of Puzo as ethnic subject/author and as a writer working through a long and wounding love-hate affair with ethnicity and fiction, as well as a malaise and discouragement at the moment of amazing success.

Puzo was the son of parents who had both grown up on barren, rocky, hillside farms outside Naples; he imagines that his direct ancestors had been illiterate for a thousand years. After emigration, Puzo's mother's first husband became a New York Central railroad laborer who died in a docks accident, leaving a wife and four young children in the Italian Lower West Side known as "Hell's Kitchen." Mario Puzo was born in 1920 after his mother remarried. His father (a "mystery," a "Southern Italian with blue eyes") disappeared when Puzo was twelve, and Puzo himself worked for the railroad from ages fifteen to twenty-one when he joined the army after Pearl Harbor (24). Puzo's use of this autobiographical Italian American material initially had been cautious and circuitous, not an unusual stance in modern American fiction for an ethnic writer. In his first novel, *The Dark Arena*, Walter Mosca can be intuited as Italian, but Puzo makes little of his specific ethnic background, either in the book's early New York family scenes or in the bulk of the novel set in a defeated postwar Germany. *The Fortunate Pilgrim* is Puzo's radical turn to the Italian American subject and a classic example of a second-generation ethnic novel rendered with great fidelity and care. Such tacking between subjects in successive novels earned Puzo in 1955 and 1964 good reviews and very little money or readership. In the wake of *The Godfather*, Puzo evinced a very harsh look at his ethnic roots:

> As a child and in my adolescence, living in the hell of New York's Neapolitan ghetto, I never heard an Italian singing. None of the grown-ups I knew were charming or loving or understanding. Rather they seemed coarse, vulgar, and insulting. And so later in my life when I was exposed to all the cliches about lovable Italians, singing Italians, happy-go-lucky Italians, I wondered where the hell the moviemakers and storywriters got all their ideas from. ("Choosing A Dream" 13)

Puzo rejected lyrical references to his past in favor of being an ethnic tough guy. Yet his primary images throughout "Choosing" are those of "Dreaming" and "Escape," and the way to "escape these uncongenial folk" was to "become an artist, a writer" (14). Even here, Puzo knows that in their hard work, the Italian Americans he describes were already "more American than [he] could ever become" (13), and he simulated the classic outsider's stance against work, love, and commitment. Although he married early and had five children, Puzo continually chafes against the domestic role in these essays, nowhere affirming the massive bonds of family and honor that shore up *The Godfather* against all Corleone enemies, internal and external. Instead, he knows that when he wrote about "these illiterate men and women, he "felt a condescending pity," for "I did not understand that they simply could not afford to dream." Puzo, however, wrote, "I would make my escape. . . . I would be rich, famous, happy. I would master my destiny" (14). The clash and dissonance in his lines between the realized Italian men and women present in real American time and his artist's thin cry for integrity and space already set Puzo's stance toward his lineage and writings. Rather than explore their richness, his first instincts were to flee into *bildungsroman/ kunstleroman*, the archetypal modernist flight for the young writer. The adjectives he uses, *rich, famous,* and *happy,* are generalized American Dream images from the "good life" that in Puzo remain stubbornly resistant to all specificity. What's crucial is how innocent his appraisals are, yet how they are also encased in an Old World and more mythic *"destino,"* a strongly fated, ingrained sense of the Italian immigrants: "To refuse to believe that an almighty force predetermined the fate of all people was to court disaster" (Gardaphe *Italian Signs* 81). Such a pattern is the cultural and instinctive source of Puzo's dominant vision of authority and of the negative cast to any personal freedom that the characters in *The Godfather* and, by extension, all his characters feel. The only escape is into arts and dreams, never into an America of diversity or heterogeneity. While Puzo rebelled against the *Italianita* of his life and putative destiny, he was most comfortable fleeing the social and cultural subject in the time-honored modernist renunciation of church, nation, and ethnicity.

It was in the library of the Hudson Guild settlement house that young Puzo devoured books, beginning with tales of Indian warfare on the American frontier, then up through the adventure novels of writers such as Rafael Sabatini, and culminating at age fourteen in the discovery of Dostoevsky's suffering heroes, whose tragic and egotistical centering on self in reflexivity captured Puzo's boy's heart and his writerly sense of a grand passionate way of being. After discovering Dostoevsky, Puzo writes, "I had always hated religion even as a child, but now I became a true believer. I believed in art. A belief that has helped me as well as any other" (24). In a gratuitous fashion, Puzo brings in his abhorrence of religion along with its replacement, in a familiar modernist mantra, but even the off-hand "as well as any other" suggests that he is referencing such stereotypical affiliations and shifts without being deeply held by any of them. Here is a common Puzo use of rhetoric. He often wishes to speak in abstractions (religion, art) that are lofty and potentially grand, but then to show his weariness, his mastery of the transcendence or abjection, he deflates the language into slackness ("as well as any other"). For example, he's bemused by his own "innocent getaway" from "baffled loved ones" and his girlfriend into World War II (28). Puzo as imagined criminal performs his "getaway" from the family he could not love and embrace. He's pleased that his country had "ordered" him to defend it, much as Michael Corleone had been ordered back into family service to avenge his father's shooting. His own chronological literary production follows the pattern of his life. *The Dark Arena* would become the postwar novel he lived in Germany, while *The Fortunate Pilgrim* is the novel of his childhood and family life before his first "escape" into military service in 1941. *The Godfather* becomes the dream, the mythical tale that partially came out of his roots or experiences or ambitions but provided him with a fictional father to revere, emulate, and finally supplant in power and love, as well as a son's destiny to both leave the family and return to it in heroic triumph. *Fools Die* then functions as the retrospective of both

Puzo's actual adult experience and his writing life, while creating his
first three novels.

Wondering in "Choosing a Dream" why he became a writer, Puzo
thinks, "Was it the poverty or the books I read? Who traumatized me, my
mother or the Brothers Karamazov? Being Italian? Or the girl sitting with
me on the bridge as the engine steam deliciously made us vanish? Did
it make any difference that I grew up Italian rather than Irish or black?"
(28) This series of questions is admirably comprehensive, referencing
class, reading, oedipal musing, early epiphany, ethnicity, and race. However, it comes in Puzo's usual off-hand listing with no attempt to integrate or oppose terms or states of being. While we might, in our current
overheated critical climate about identity, actually appreciate a veteran
professional writer who can so off-handedly mix and not match the fundamental content of fierce critical debates, we can also see why no one
would take Puzo very seriously as a writer through such cursory self-
examination; his self-scrutiny is broad but not deep. He won't go much
further than conclude with the fruits of his enormous success. Thus, to
the above questions, Puzo answers, "No matter. The good times are
beginning. I am another Italian success story. Not as great as DiMaggio
or Sinatra but quite enough. It will serve" (29). Puzo finally chooses to
dream of other things than *Italianita* or literary success. He's more ener-
gized by the synthetic pleasures of self-pity, male isolation, Hollywood,
Las Vegas, and gambling as *Fools Die* will show.

"The Making of *The Godfather*," the carrot essay in the collection, is
disappointingly scant on the writing of the novel or on the screenplay
collaboration with Coppola on the first film. The thirty-six-page essay is
divided into two parts, "The Book," (33–41) and "The Movie," (41–69),
already showing Puzo's 1972 awareness that *The Godfather*, soon to become the best-selling American novel of the 1970s, was destined to be
dwarfed and "covered" by the Academy Award–winning *Godfather* films
as had happened to *Gone with the Wind* and its epic screen adaptation
(1936, 1939). Puzo already knows what his audience wants to hear about
in "The Movie" section of the essay: Hollywood anecdotes about casting
the film, a confrontation with Frank Sinatra in a restaurant over the
character of Johnny Fontane in the novel, a depiction of the world of
producers and directors. Furthermore, in "The Book," Puzo just isn't
interested in sharing the secrets of his craft. He has no impulse at all to
emulate a James or Conrad in their prefaces or reflections. His first sentence sets the tone: "I have written three novels. *The Godfather* is not as
good as the preceding two. I wrote it to make money" (33). He continues
to describe the difference by stating, "I was forty-five years old and tired
of being an artist," owing twenty thousand dollars to relatives, finance
companies, bookmakers. He decided it was "time to grow up and sell
out" and agreed to do a book his editors had been urging him to develop
from the minor Mafia tales embedded in corners of *The Fortunate Pilgrim*;

"just give me enough money to get started," he told them (34). While Puzo always refuses to go into depth about his feelings, he's often admirable in his refusal to either self-aggrandize his successes or complain about his failures.

It's intriguing to note that Puzo welds together his weariness in maturity as "selling out," with money owed as the problem and money advanced as the solution. He's determined to ground *The Godfather* in material rather than aesthetic markers he had revered. Writing about the Mafia to get out of debt is equivalent to going to the Mafia to get the money needed to get out of debt. The writing thus becomes the localized move to "go bad" against the legitimate artistic currency of his first two novels. Immediately after providing the facts of the matter, Puzo repeats his most revealing statement about his writing: "I had been a true believer in art. I didn't believe in religion or love or women or men. I didn't believe in society or philosophy. But I believed in art for forty-five years. It gave me a comfort I found in no other place" (34). The decision to write *The Godfather* becomes a true leave-taking for him, a farewell to his author's dreams of becoming a high-culture success. However, what does the belief in art mean when all the subjects that art might address or that might comprise that art are negated or discounted? A bleak poverty to his renunciations of art strips the aesthetic of any of its subjects or emotional or rational contexts. Art is segmented off as a talisman, a religion in and of itself and one that has failed.

"The Book" section of "The Making of *The Godfather*" never does describe Puzo wrestling with the text of *The Godfather* but finishes with an extension of the money anxiety evinced in the decision to write the book at all. He recalls a cascade of financial haggling and windfalls, notes about advance payments, the sale of paperback rights, telling his family about the book deals, the sale of movie rights, his animus against book tours and interviews, statistics on various best-seller lists. and how long *The Godfather* stayed on top of the charts. Societal and class markers that changed his economic status and that of his family become the real story. Finally, a rueful short paragraph ends the section: "The book got much better reviews than I expected. I wished like hell I'd written it better. I like the book. It has energy and I lucked out by creating a central character that was popularly accepted as genuinely mythic. But I wrote below my gifts in that novel" (41). Puzo here hits two key points about his success. The novel's melodramatic "energy" keeps the Corleone family story hurtling forward, and the father and son team of Vito and Michael Corleone mythically encode Freudian, epic, ethnic, capitalist, self-made, and male literary images of enduring power. For millions of readers and viewers, such achievements by Puzo were plentiful and thrilling.

Such slash-and-burn rhetoric by Puzo immediately after *The Godfather*'s success as novel and film appeared to sever radically his actual career and professed fictional aspirations. Much of the following commentary will attempt to regain or reopen the dialogue between Puzo and the novelist's art, to not let his statement stand that *The Godfather* is such a decidedly inferior work. No author can will such a complete break from his past or future texts. *The Godfather* must stand in relation to other works in Puzo's very long career. To begin to place his veneration of and then denial of art in a series of contexts is to discover what forces Puzo sought to harness or control as well as the larger cultural and social climate that, in another critical trope, was in effect writing him.

The Writerly Politics of Choosing a Dream: Puzo and Bourdieu's *Habitus*

Bourdieu's *The Field of Cultural Production* is the most comprehensive theory of a sociology of culture to be presented in the West in the past several decades. He attempts to situate all cultural producers and consumers along a range of class distinctions, affiliations, and practices in order to understand a full field in which relations can be determined through both individual and class *habitus*, "the set of social conditions of the production, circulation, and consumption of symbolic goods" (9). Bourdieu would reject the direct relating of an author's individual biography to a specific work of literature; however, he would use that information extensively and break it down to show an author's examined and unexamined decisions, standards, and impulses to create what he or she would believe to be "art" or a "popular" work. He would, in his own terms, be interested in a Puzo, for example, as "social agent as producer" (11), as an author "who lends coherence to the 'mental structure' of [his] class" (13). Key for Bourdieu is that the cultural or literary field inhabited by any one author is naturally subordinate to the field of power relations in general in which art functions as a symbolic capital, more or less traded in a market in which the author has a stake and is a stake. An author creates within the ruse of imaginative creator, while he or she is played within a system of hierarchical representation that has already slotted that author as canonical or noncanonical, popular or elite, multiethnic or mainstream. Within the dominant class, one that acknowledges the role of symbolic artistic capital, the author always has a dominated role because of a low degree of economic capital (15).

How might Bourdieu explain a Puzo in the full curve of his writer's ambitions, long frustrations, great success, and drifting aftermath? One of Bourdieu's laws of capital is that within the dominant class, cultural capital decreases as one moves from the dominated to the dominant fractions of society (45), that in effect Puzo loses his stature (certainly in his own mind) when he writes *The Godfather*. The relationship of "mutual exclusion" between material gratification and the recognition by one's peers, the success of a huge best seller set against the recognition as a writer of the generation of Mailer, Vidal, and Styron that he would have craved—all coalesce in Puzo's *Godfather* crisis at age forty-five, which Bourdieu might explain thusly: "Aging, which dissolves the ambiguities, converting the elective, provisional refusals of adolescent bohemian life into the unrelieved privation of the aged, embittered bohemian, so often takes the form of an emotional crisis, marked by reversals and abjurations which often lead to the meanest tasks of industrial art..." (50). Thus Puzo's trajectory could be reinterpreted as a bad faith abjection, which from the depths of *Godfather* success, he could write "The Making of *The Godfather*" and *Fools Die* on his "own terms" as the newer, bigger, and more hollow success he felt himself to be after renouncing "art."

Bourdieu writes of the "eternally displaced writer," one who is "always out of step." His example is a French prose epic writer of the nineteenth century, Leon Cladel (1835–92) who resigned himself to a form of the rustic novel in which he self-indulgently depicted the peasantry, country life, and country people "without that holy roughness of touch which distinguishes the early manner of the master painters" (69–70). One can posit a Puzo who was driven to *The Godfather* by lack of commercial success and canonical notice, a Puzo who writes a more synthetic Mafia tale out of the headlines rather than a complex multiethnic treatment of the interlocking of family and business, American success myths, and Sicilian history. Bourdieu conceives of an "anti-intellectual populism, more or less conservative, in which 'the people' [in Puzo, read: "the Family"] are once again merely a projection in fantasy of relations internal to the intellectual field" (70). To cast *The Godfather* in such a dynamic, the family becomes the final arbiter and raison d'etre for any action, no matter how morally circumscribed. These actions are justified against a larger America identified with a naive and lumbering entity of good intentions and potential individual rights and freedoms that cannot be joined by the ethnic subject or overtly opposed by him.

One of Bourdieu's largest questions is to what extent an author caught in such a system can ever be completely aware of his socio-cultural *habitus*, given the author's traditional propensity for levels of meaning, self-scrutiny, and the self-reflexive nature of authorial production, whether overtly privileged in the text or simply inherent in it. Bourdieu's conclusion is that "lucidity is always partial" and is a matter "of position and trajectory within the field, so that it varies from one agent and one moment to another" (72). Clearly, Puzo in "Choosing a Dream" and "The Making of *The Godfather*" has a depressed grasp of his decades-long struggle to carve out a significant career, and it's precisely at the moment of *The Godfather*'s extraordinary success that he can more confidently renounce his belief in art shored up by economic rather than artistic capital. In his action, he writes backed by the Corleone family in a transmuted way, their powerful Italian and family identity conflated with his own, with the might of their reception behind him. The literary-cultural production of *The Godfather* is Puzo becoming Vito and Michael Corleone, to be reclaimed by an Old World network of assumptions and values. Puzo himself reverts back from the chase for high-culture recognition in the elite marketplace to becoming a writer of the people (those victim Corleones) for the people (a mass readership). The ironies surrounding his writing the blockbuster best seller are patterned out in the trajectory of the hero within that very text. Michael Corleone becomes ethnic in his identity again, becomes the avenging family hero, and leaves America, college, heroism, and "reputation"; Puzo follows close behind.

Yet Puzo has unfinished writerly business within his *habitus,* and to find his deepest hunches and wounds, one must track back through his renderings of the artist in *The Godfather* itself, specifically in the roles and relations of Johnny Fontane and Nino Valenti. For where Puzo described himself "writing below his gifts," he was very precisely writing about the use and abuse of such gifts through his two Italian crooners. This unremarked ongoing storyline in the novel sinks out of Coppola's movie and critical notice, but it has crucial points to make about Puzo's fictional ethic and ethics.

The Ballad of Nino and Johnny

Although Puzo begins "Choosing a Dream" in *The Godfather Papers* by announcing that when growing up, he'd never heard an Italian sing-ing, the characters of Johnny Fontane and Nino Valenti in *The Godfather* are expressly portrayed through their singing styles, audiences, and the way they use their talent. As is well known, Puzo's Johnny Fontane is loosely based on some major anecdotes of Frank Sinatra's career in his rise to Hollywood power, his early 1950s problems with his singing voice, and his reputed ties to the Mafia. Nino Valenti is Johnny's boyhood chum, a "big, muscular, snotty looking Italian guy" (316), a terrific but undeveloped singer whom Johnny finally coaxes to Hollywood where he briefly prospers but then spirals down into suicidal drinking and abuse. Nino has characteristics, physical and otherwise, that link him to Dean Martin, Sinatra's running mate in the "rat pack" beginning in the 1950s. Johnny and Nino are much favored by their Don, Vito Corleone, who can never resist doing them services. They are godsons, figuratively out of the family business and literally out of the line of fire. Johnny is central to the Jack Woltz Hollywood plot and reappears whenever the action shifts back to California and Las Vegas. He recovers his voice and singing career through throat surgery and solidifies his power in the movie business. Nino is the sidekick, the jokester, the unassimilated paisan whose death wish is not plumbed by Puzo and whose terminal depression is another loose end in the novel.

Such a summary of their roles in *The Godfather* does not address their position as artists, singers of both popular songs and traditional folk ballads in a number of styles. I want to suggest that Puzo in the crisis of writing *The Godfather* below his gifts created a bifurcated view of talent in its responsibilities, development, and use as popular art. Johnny and Nino at one level are a double meditation on art and more likely an expression of the various urges in one artist—their author Mario Puzo. Of all the major and minor Italian American characters in *The Godfather*, only Nino Valenti fails to make the cut in Coppola's and Puzo's screenplay for the first film. As Nino hovers around in *The Godfather* in his genial yet morose way, the screenplay has no place for him. He's a more raw and unconstructed Johnny Fontane, who himself is buffed by the record industry and Hollywood into a national sex symbol, while Nino stays home in the neighborhood. Johnny's restoration as godson and entertainment industry mogul is paralleled by Nino's Hollywood seduction and demise. No one and nothing can save Nino while Johnny's throat, career, and influence can be "fixed." What is the ballad of Nino and Johnny for Puzo?

During the band's refreshment break at Connie Corleone's wedding, "a young man named Nino Valenti picked up a discarded mandolin, put his left foot up on a chair and began to sing a coarse Sicilian love song. Nino Valenti's face was handsome though bloated by continual drinking. . . . He rolled his eyes as his tongue caressed the obscene lyrics. The women

Our Gang in full regalia at Connie Corleone's wedding (*Godfather I*). Courtesy Museum of Modern Art/Film Stills Archive.

shrieked with glee and the men shouted the last word of each stanza with the singer" (20). Nino spontaneously creates a bond with the whole audience, both men and women. His singing is bawdy and suggestive, with no attempt to package himself. His chosen instrument is charmingly archaic-ethnic. He's not hired; he plays in no one's band. As Johnny Fontane sweeps into the wedding garden, he instantly draws a crowd, both family members he knows and the guests who know him only by his records. When Nino calls to him from the bandstand, Johnny recalls their boyhood days, and they embrace. With Nino accompanying him on mandolin, Johnny is transformed back to his roots, and he too chants "the words to an obscene Sicilian love song," complete with suggestive body language by Nino, a song with a "sly, double-meaning tag line that finished each stanza." The wedding guests were all proud of Johnny for "he was of them and he had become a famous singer, a movie star who slept with the most desired women in the world" (34), yet he had come to pay his respects to his Godfather. Nino and Johnny's "set" concludes by lifting Connie up between them so that through a "mock battle and wooing," they use their "voices like swords" until Johnny "with the most delicate courtesy" allows Nino to take the bride from his arm (35).

Clearly this first scene between them establishes the power of the ethnic folk art that Nino practices; the people envelop Johnny, reputation and all, but he defers "with delicate courtesy" to Nino, an aesthetic choice. At this point, the art of the song is integrated for the occasion and sung to family by extended family. Nothing is produced or marketed for anyone beyond the moment. Johnny and Nino are equilibrated in their ritual love song to the bride. Yet the aura of Johnny's celebrity is everywhere—a movie star, seducer of world famous women, holding the "hearts of fifty million women in his hands" (35). In the Corleone compound, on this day of family celebration, Johnny, Nino, songs, their rendition, the audience, the venue are all organic and give pleasure as well as eager audience participation and response.

However, when Johnny and Nino are removed from the penumbra of Corleone environment and authority, their arts and lives begin to crumble. Despite being the hearthrob of a nation, Johnny in Hollywood is a "dumb romantic guinea" as his WASP movie star wife calls him and adds, "you still think screwing is really like those dopey songs you used to sing" (12). Johnny's voice has gone bad, and his sexual performance is affected as well. As a singer, he loved "clean phrasing. It was the only thing in life he really understood and he knew he understood it better than anyone else on earth" (160), but now he didn't dare sing for anyone, especially as part of a seduction, and he can't bear to listen to his records. In the depths of his insecurity, he summons Nino to Los Angeles for companionship and trust, and they begin to do studio work together. When Puzo in effect decides to become a "rackets guy" himself to write *The Godfather,* he renounces his belief in art. Nino never makes the leap to "crook" status and remains pure, on the outside of all corruption. Never having to make his bones in the Family or in Hollywood, Nino-Puzo is authentic, truth-telling, lovable, obscene, drunk, and a gambler—and thus himself pure. Nino's not constricted by any of the Family's murderous pressures or by any of Puzo's writing pressures and ambition. At other moments he functions as Johnny's conscience and takes him out of embarrassing situations. Always in the background is the unspoken truth or threat that Nino is the real artist, though it is Johnny who has the nostalgia for his own major period: "He had been good, damn good. He hadn't realized how good he was. . . . He had been a real artist and never knew it, and never knew how much he loved it" (190–91), the regret at his own naiveté somehow stamping him with the better part of himself, a Ninolike lack of self-knowledge.

Johnny is a Hollywood record company professional creation and Nino the coarse neighborhood mandolin player. Puzo is both figures and neither at the same time. He's amused by Nino and sentimental about Johnny. Taken together, the folk artist covered by the best-selling singer and movie star, no place of integrity is left for the serious artist (read novelist) to sing like Nino and succeed like Johnny. Puzo inscribes these emblems of art and an artist's craft in *The Godfather*. Johnny and Nino are minor notes strung through the family mayhem and the popular epic of immigration. Nino drinks himself to death without further explanation. What makes him so sad? He's fully sexual, talented, loved by the Family. Why can't he be saved or assimilated into some family arrangement? Why can't Nino "choose a dream?"

I'm tempted to the hyperbolic conclusion that Nino's death is that of the ethnic artist and Italian son in Puzo, twin identities that will not survive in him. Nino isn't a killer for the Don, can't be bought by Hollywood, loves his booze and gambling, and refuses to take seriously even the structure that writing *The Godfather* brings into being.[2] However, Puzo is clearly on point in *The Godfather*, never wishing to slow down the hurtling narrative self-reflection. *Fools Die* will be Puzo's lengthy text of lessons learned and tales to tell without a driving narrative. It's in the corners of the tangential sections of *The Godfather* where Nino and Johnny play, in Las Vegas and Hollywood, that Puzo reveals the most about negotiating his way through his *habitus* in scenes that end up on Coppola's cutting room floor as he made his film stay on course as a tight family melodrama of authority and its succession. Nino asks repeatedly in the novel, in every way possible, "[W]hat am I doing here? What is this life?" These are Puzo's questions as well.

One other major minor character is cut from the *Godfather* film. He is Jules Segal, a surgeon with skills to rival Johnny's in singing, Luca Brasi's in mayhem, and Bonasera's as undertaker using all his powers to make bodies "live." Although Nino fades out, Johnny Fontane has one more moment of drama in *The Godfather* when he has a throat operation to restore the full power of his singing voice. The operation is performed by Jules Segal, a renegade doctor, who describes himself as "the brightest young surgeon and diagnostician on the East Coast until they got me on an abortion rap" (318), who had been taken up by Don Corleone who was impressed with his courage. In keeping with the theme that everything can be fixed by Don Corleone, Jules Segal is also a miraculous artist as surgeon. His most famous operation in the novel is his tightening of Lucy Mancini's pelvic wall, which cures her vaginal "ugliness" (she can only be satisfied by Sonny Corleone's "blood-gorged pole" when the novel turns epic in size). Jules and a fellow surgeon work on poor Lucy's body in some of the novel's most repellent prose. In the end, Johnny's voice does equal Lucy's vagina as an organ of pleasure, and Jules can fix them both. But just when the male reader cringes or, if female, looks for revenge, Puzo himself seems to understand the nonsense, the sheer giddy oversexed and sexist prose. He has another doctor comment to Jules that "if society would only be realistic, people like you and I, really talented people, could do important work and leave this stuff for the hacks" (315) and "you're going to waste . . . Jules. Another couple of years and you can forget about serious surgery. You won't be up to it" (316).

Such arguments well describe an author such as Puzo in his quandaries about writing *The Godfather*. At the very moment of his most sexist trash in the text, Puzo summons one "surgeon" (read novelist) to tell another that this sensational stuff will kill ya' for serious work. Puzo in *The Godfather Papers* remarked that most critics have missed his casual irony, but this time he scores. Yet the symbolic critique is a mere footnote. Lucy and Jules live in Vegas in sexual bliss, and Nino passes away. Yet Puzo's intuition that after *The Godfather*, he wouldn't be "up to it" is borne out in *Fools Die*, at the end of a decade of complete and utter *Godfather* success.

Merlyn in *Fools Die*: "Going Under"

Puzo chooses to conclude *The Godfather Papers* with a sad little collection of diary excerpts from his early years as a writer. He tells his readers that the entries are to him now "embarrassingly egoistic" but that "now older and more cunning . . . I resist the temptation to cover my tracks" (233). "Notes From an Unsuccessful Writer's Diary" covers the years 1950–53, during the writing of *The Dark Arena* and concludes nine months before that novel's acceptance for publication in January 1954. Puzo takes us through his personal crises as a writer struggling to raise his family, carve out space for himself, and get his work done. He's full of rather conventional doubt and self-loathing and a defeatism that never rises above bourgeois anxiety about his chosen role and his ability to achieve success. Placing this piece at the end of *The Godfather Papers*, a volume in which he might have been expected to, if not give himself a *festschrift*, at least bask in the glow of his achievement, suggests that Puzo was in 1972 still possessed after *The Godfather* by the memories and demons of early humiliation and sustained failure.

Fools Die in effect is the extension of "Notes From an Unsuccessful Writer's Diary" into a very long book, the first half of which (to p. 283) concludes with the author hero John Merlyn becoming financially well-off through the sale of paperback and film rights to his new novel. Books 1 through 4 of *Fools Die* flesh out the thirteen pages of "Notes" with fidelity. Then the novel lumbers back and forth among New York, Hollywood, and Las Vegas through a number of movie, gambling, and literary characters and anecdotes before mercifully coming to an end at over five hundred pages. Though Puzo hoped to stitch *Fools Die* together through his focus on gambling and luck, to write a popular novel about the interlocking worlds of Hollywood and Las Vegas, his real subject here is his own writerly life. The obligatory trappings of a post-*Godfather* blockbuster never materialize. Puzo was rich in novelistic capital after *The Godfather* and could have written and published whatever he wished. That *Fools Die* often appears unedited, even in the rudimentary shifts in mood, tone, and voice, that it stalls and then lurches forward, suggests the editing-publishing confidence in Puzo's aura. He was not the first newly famous novelist or film director to receive carte blanche and then produce an indulgent botch of a work. Yet there's every reason to believe that this was the novel closest to his sensibilties and his quarrel with his universe, not the war novel (*The Dark Arena*), the ethnic family novel (*The Fortunate Pilgrim*), or the mob melodrama (*The Godfather*). Millions of *Godfather* aficionados were now ready in *Fools Die* to begin the long march of a serious writer in America, ready or not, and read about Puzo's passage, as he broke his decade-long silence in fiction.[3]

Puzo's writer, John Merlyn, comes to the reader as an orphan with no desire to find out anything about his origins: "I have no history. No remembered parents" (57). We hear nothing about a real last name, nothing about foster parents; he joined the army at fifteen, lying about his age. After the war, he enrolled in writing courses at the New School because "everybody wanted to be a writer" (57). And just like that, *Fools Die* inaugurates a hero both blank and an artist. Puzo astonishingly has distanced himself as far as possible from an Italian American identity in his famous best seller. *Fools Die*, in a stubborn defiance, will cancel his audience's expectations. This book will be about the writer, not immigrants, Italian Americans, or major social events. Since Puzo is hardly an experimentalist or a psychologizing novelist, *Fools Die* had to proceed by anecdote, the potentially self-conscious material of a novel about a novelist sunk in everydayness. Puzo writes about "love," "life," "men," and "women," all the subjects he tells us he didn't believe in any more in "The Making of *The Godfather*."

One early scene in *Fools Die* catches Merlyn's frustration and anger at his lot. Diagnosed with a diseased gallbladder at a veterns' hospital in Manhattan, he is hit by an enormous pain while working at his night job during Christmas week. He takes a cab to the hospital where he's left off a half block from the entrance. Another wracking seizure drops him to his knees in the street, and Merlyn writes, "I remember rolling over once to stop the pain and rolling off the ledge of the sidewalk and into the gutter. The edge of the curb was a pillow for my head" (62). He sees Christmas lights twinkling from a store: "I lay there thinking I was a fucking animal. Here I was an artist, a book published and the critic had called me a genius, one of the hopes of American literature, and I was dying like a dog in the gutter. . . . Just because I had no money in the bank. . . . That was the truth of the whole business. The self-pity was nearly as good as morphine" (62). The "dog in the gutter" simile is not original, of course, nor are the class resentments at his lot as an uncompensated writer. The injustice of it all is mainlined into self-pity. Art cannot stave off physical misery and social humbling, and Merlyn's no good to himself or his family when it's Christmas without any dough. Pointedly Puzo did not add to this scene in *Fools Die* his later statement: "that's when I decided to become rich and famous," as if that's a life choice. He did so in one of those public epiphanies after the fact so beloved by interviewers, in an anecdote about his Christmas agony recounted to *Time* about a 1955 gallbladder attack just after the publication of *The Dark Arena*.[4]

Puzo had already transmuted this material into *The Godfather* when Vito Corleone is shot in the street in an assassination attempt before Christmas while he is buying fruit from a stand: "The first bullet caught Don Corleone in the back. He felt the hammer shot of its impact. . . . The next two bullets hit him in the buttocks and sent him sprawling in the middle of the street. . . . The gunmen fired two more hasty shots at the Don lying in the gutter" (80). At no point in the novel is the Don in more dire peril or in a more exposed state. This shooting sets in motion all of the novel's major events, including Michael's revenge killings on Sollozzo and McCluskey and his eventual take-over as Don. Puzo made the immediate reaction to the Don's riddled body highly public as opposed to his own lonely crawling through the gutter to the hospital entrance. Police cars scream toward the site of the Don's shooting, and following *Daily News* photographers snap pictures of everything in sight. Michael, trysting with Kay in New York City, first learns of the shooting when he sees the front-page news photo "of his father lying in the street, his head in a pool of blood"; his first reaction is "cold rage" (79), a hint he has begun to metamorphose into an executioner and his father's true son.

Far from Merlyn (and Puzo's) lonely gallbladder attack, imprinted mostly on Puzo's dark sense of his own failure, the Don rises again from his pain to become himself, and Michael is his son in whom he will be well pleased. The family consequences, the miracle of recovery, and the notoriety given the shooting in *The Godfather* completely reverse Puzo/ Merlyn's sick anonymity in *Fools Die*. Puzo/Merlyn pays his debts to *The Godfather* scene when he lies to his gambler buddies in Vegas about his gallbladder scar: "I was in the war. I got hit by machine-gun bullets" (48). Within the nominal two novelistic scenes of Christmas, pain, the gutter, and the hospital, Puzo shows how the melodrama maximizes the effect of the image in several ways, while Merlyn's caviling enervates and is remarked but without energy for the rest of the novel. Generic in its self-pity, it's not used in genre.

"Going under" is Puzo's nightmare image in "Notes." He feels completely isolated from wife, children, and their emotional contact: "Everyday life has such poverty . . . with writing or another art you have a shield against life as well as an integrating force" (235). Gauging his impact, he writes, "I do not inspire confidence, or love, or trust, or faith, or respect" (245), a male crisis that allows him to constantly play the victim, not savagely or bitterly but rather doggedly in his refusal to give up the sad pleasures of artistic hermitage. In *Fools Die*, a decade after Vito and Michael Corleone have placed the identity of family and its security above every other human entity and goal for millions of readers and viewers to affirm, Merlyn turns on the family to reveal it as the accusing millstone from the larger society, the entity for which he feels most responsible yet is unable to provide for or truly give himself to. He hovers in his basement study, like some tinkerer at a hobby, year after year grinding out the precious pages, alternately taking several small jobs or quitting his jobs to get sustained writing time. *Fools Die* weirdly depicts a zone of noncontact with wife and children. They are markers by whom Merlyn can take his emotional temperature when he emerges from his creator's cave: "My wife put up with me for five years while I wrote a book, never complained. She wasn't too happy about it, but what the hell, I was home nights. When my first novel was turned down and I was heartbroken, she said bitterly, 'I knew you would never sell it' " (76). Merlyn feels stunned by this further rejection and retreats to his favorite locale to brood and think: "Gambling in Vegas, I figured it out. Why the hell should they be sympathetic? Why should they give a shit about this crazy eccentricity I had about creating art? . . . They were absolutely right. But I never felt the same about them again" (77).

Gambling and Las Vegas are magic for Merlyn, the self-proclaimed magician, who sees himself as a "degenerate gambler," one who can't always help himself. Merlyn (and Puzo) are most comfortable philosophizing from the gaming tables. In fact, Puzo wrote accompanying text to a picture book, *Inside Las Vegas* (1978), published the same year as *Fools Die*, in which Puzo suggests that "family and gambling could be equated as time-consuming vices" (20) but that gambling has "bettered" his character by forcing him to write more since gambling put him repeatedly in debt (8), and "I gave [gambling] all up because I had no time to write and I was trying to finish a novel" (165). For Puzo, nothing is privleged over gambling, certainly not writing and family. He knows they should be, but he's honest enough about his own character to admit that hasn't always been the case. He states that he knows "as a social human being" that it would have been better to earn his money by hard work, but the money he really loved came when he had no control, for "the whole magic power of gambling lies in its essential purity from endeavor, in its absence of guilt" (341). Merlyn would have liked his life and loves to run on an economy akin to that of gambling: "In short, how I would like to be loved in a way never earned so that I would never have to keep earning it or work for it. I love that love the way I love the money I win when I get lucky gambling" (65). Gambling is not work, and its purity is rather like art but doesn't require the long unrewarded years of discipline that writing does, whereas family is an instantaneous producer of guilt and is never not work.

Rather than write as an adversary to the middle class, Merlyn is more of a secretly discontented man to whom appearances are still important; he's careful rather than relentless. The "magical" part of Merlyn wants to feel "mystical" about "pure, untainted" art and write "universal characters," while he reserves his wife and children as an occasional sanctuary to which he could return "and all the pain would vanish because I'd have supper with my family" (68). Merlyn manipulates family as rationale for action, haven against the world, and as the millstone that makes freedom for any man impossible. A world of family pressure that was vividly brought to life in *The Godfather* is pallid and cramped in *Fools Die*.

Merlyn when not being "magical" in the service of fiction muses most about Las Vegas and big scores. Puzo's account of Merlyn's becoming a "crook" is instructive for the way criminality weaves its way into Puzo's consciousness as not just subject but almost precondition for fiction, especially popular fiction. Merlyn "became a crook" initially through his Civil Service job as administrative aide to army reserve units during the Korean War (94). Through the selection process of army reservists, Merlyn gets to play a complicated game of sheltering certain young men from service in return for laundered kickbacks and perks. Yet in the middle of his extended explanation of the genesis of his dealings, he writes that "the only thing I wanted to do was create a great work of art. But not the fame or money or power, or so I thought." The greatest influence on him was *The Brothers Karamazov*, which gave him strength and told him "about the vulnerable beauty of all people." Then he knew his calling: "And so all I wished for was to write a book that would make people feel as I felt that day. It was to me the ultimate exercise of power. And the purest." He works on his first novel for five years, and it makes very little money, while called "a genuine work of art" by some critics. When Merlyn cannot get a publisher's advance for his second novel, what he hopes would be his *Crime and Punishment*, he stops writing and flees to Vegas. On his return to New York City and family, "it became clear. To become the artist and good man I yearned to be, I had to take bribes for a little while. You can sell yourself anything" (98).

Once Merlyn gets into the swing of his crookedness, he is more at peace than he has been in years: "The truth was that I had become a happy man because I had become a traitor to society" (certainly the Corleone career trajectory), and "I figured out that I was getting my revenge for having been rejected as an artist. . . . For my complete lack of worldly success. And my general uselessness in the whole scheme of things" (106). Merlyn's reasoning is classic bourgeois artistic resentment portrayed openly and clumsily by Puzo. Nine years after publishing *The Godfather* and creating a monumental criminal in Vito Corleone, who has gone outside the law *not* because of minor family problems, money, or needing time to write, but for seeing his whole family destroyed in Sicily, Puzo takes the reader through Merlyn's tepid little staged confessional. *Fools Die* appears closer to Puzo's heart and gut, the contrived bourgeois thievery, the bribing and fixing. The Corleones were mythic self-justifying avatars of the process that drove a pinched and discouraged Puzo to the writing of *The Godfather* in the first place. *Fools Die* is Puzo's act of contrition whereby Merlyn's incentives to finally go bad and write for the big book are those realistically provided by very common class markers: lack of money, family needs, male humiliation.

Such incremental moments are best expressed when Merlyn takes on book reviews and magazine piece work once the bribes kick in: "I was a pure storyteller, a fiction writer. It seemed demeaning to me and my art to write anything else. But what the hell, I was a crook, nothing was beneath me now" (115). Criminality extends to going against literary potential as well. Merlyn writes pulps, war stories, soft-core porn, "flashy snotty film reviews," "sober snotty book reviews." He never signs his real name, knowing he is "an artist, but that's nothing to brag about. That's just a religion or a hobby. But now I really had a skill, I was an expert schlock writer," whereas he hadn't even been "a really first-rate bribe taker government clerk" (118–19). As Merlyn prepares for his second gambling trip to Vegas with all his bribe money in tow, he kisses his wife "partly out of affection but really to make sure she would not awaken when I dug out the hidden money." He tells his wife he must write before he leaves, edits for an hour while she sleeps, and then goes to the closet with the big trunk full of "all my old manuscripts" of the first novel. Forty thousand dollars is hidden under the manuscripts, carbons, and re-writes "of the book I had worked on for five years and had earned me three thousand dollars. It was a hell of a lot of paper" (131–32).

Merlyn carries the swag to the kitchen table, where he counts it, sipping
his coffee. He then zips the bills into his Vegas "winner's jacket" and tells
his wife in the morning that it's notes for the article he's writing on
Vegas, his "cover story," literally and figuratively.

Puzo writes a short deft scene here where instead of having Merlyn
whine or philosophize about his plight as artist, his manuscripts is converted into paper money at the bottom of the closet trunk, money not
earned by the artist but by the "crook," then reconverted back from
dollars into fraudulent notes for the article that sends him on his gambler's
way to Las Vegas. The illegal money is first "covered" by story (the old
manuscripts) and then the money is "covered" by more story (the bogus
article notes) for the Vegas trip. The double reconversion of the bills is
bound to writing, yet not earned by it, and implicated in Merlyn's writerly
and life decisions. An aura of timid, domestic hoarding is evident here—
hall closets, kitchen tables, kissing the wife good night, and pleading
work. Beneath pages and pages and years of hard work is the bribe
money, the printed bills—better than marital sex, better than writing, and
holding out the promise of a wondrous Las Vegas payoff. Merlyn's deep
structural identity is that of "artist as crook"; such is the sad fall created
by Puzo from the family power so identified with the Corleones in the
pages of *his* great success.

Puzo and Norman Mailer

Merlyn stubbornly refuses to go away but is weary of himself and
his labors. What ploy Puzo uses to flog himself and the reader through
the second half of *Fools Die* is to create Osano, an improbable Italian
American Norman Mailer as powerful literary success, goad, confessor,
role model, writing buddy, and cautionary tale. By doing so, Puzo signals that, in *Fools Die*, he's going the Mailer route. Of all the venues open
to Puzo in fiction after *The Godfather*, he chose to give us himself as
subject in *Fools Die*, his career as text, his gambling obsession as controlling metaphor for art and life. It wasn't really an act of *hubris* on his part.
He'd always been quite honest as a writer and refused the sort of self-
aggrandizing postures that might have helped make his way. His characters aren't wild egotists or particularly self-reflective. They don't analyze
self or the larger culture obsessively, nor do they sense they march in the
flow of history. In short, they don't fit the profile of Norman Mailer.
What caused Puzo to enter the fictional lists with a Mailer manque as
a character?

Puzo (b. 1920) and Mailer (b. 1923) are almost exact contemporaries
on different trajectories of striving and success. Both writers begin their
careers after World War II in an intensely ambitious male cohort that
returns home to launch writing lives in a literary climate that privileges

the American novel as a holy grail, a Great American Book that could be written about a society thrust onto a world stage as the victor in 1945 with a full half-century's legacy of both American expansion and modernist artistic growth. The preceding generation's careers of Hemingway, Faulkner, Thomas Wolfe, Steinbeck, and Fitzgerald provided varying fables of public-private success and visibility for writers such as Mailer, Saul Bellow, James Baldwin, Gore Vidal, and William Styron. By 1968 when Puzo writes a negative review of Mailer's *Armies of the Night* and scores him in a mock-*Paris Review* interview on his contemporaries, Mailer is America's foremost postwar man of letters with as many successes in nonfiction and essays (*The Armies of the Night, Of a Fire on the Moon, Advertisements for Myself, The Presidential Papers*, "The White Negro") as in eclectic, sporadic novels (*The Deer Park, An American Dream, Why Are We in Viet Nam?*). His early fame in 1948 with the publication of *The Naked and the Dead* coincides with the start of Puzo's work on *The Dark Arena*. Between *Naked* and *The Deer Park* (1955), published the same year as *The Dark Arena*, Mailer becomes more of an ideologue and flamboyant public intellectual, publishing only one short didactic novel, *(Barbary Shore)* but embroiling himself in left-wing politics, cultural criticism, and New York's bohemian and drug scene. In the same period as sketched out in *The Godfather Papers*, Puzo anonymously slugs it out in a series of low-paying Civil Service and other jobs, fitfully works on his first novel, and feels family and responsibilities for finances pushing him under. Mailer graduated from Harvard in 1943 and stated that after Pearl Harbor, he had already been "worrying darkly whether it would be more likely that a great war novel would be written about Europe or the Pacific" (*Advertisements for Myself* 10). On another front, Puzo "graduated" from his dead-end job on the railroad in NYC in 1941 at the time of Pearl Harbor and was liberated from family and ethnicity by the war.

Wanting to become a truly hybridized *American* writer, Puzo undoubtedly admired Mailer's freeing himself to be his own created persona. The one part of himself that Mailer most wanted to destroy was that of the "thoroughly nice Jewish boy," thereby expunging a hyphenated American identity as he pursued rather openly the myth of supplanting a Hemingway. Puzo had to admire this in Mailer, consciously or unconsciously. *The Dark Arena* is full of Hemingway accents and strips its Italian-American protagonist of much recognizable ethnic identity. Puzo's male characters are Hemingwayesque in their square-jawed stoic defeatism, and he ends the novel with a death reminiscent of that of Catherine in *A Farewell to Arms*. Then Puzo spent years writing *The Fortunate Pilgrim* and *The Godfather*. With these two novels, he became not only an Italian American writer for good, but then a best-selling writer through a novel that refused him critical capital. He had sought neither multiethnic distinction nor blockbuster status, and both placed him farther away than ever from a Mailer, who by 1969, in the year of *The Godfather*'s publication, was riding a wave of

critical and public acclaim for his powerful nonfiction about the
1960s American cataclysm and his visionary grasp of American history
and mythos.

I note these hypothetical parallels and differences between Mailer
and Puzo before looking at Osano in *Fools Die* to point out how large
Mailer must have loomed on Puzo's screen, how he had achieved everything an American ethnic writer of talent in Puzo's generation could have
achieved by age forty-five (the age Puzo had stopped believing in art as
he tells us). How does Puzo intuit the curve of Mailer's career in a way
that makes some sense of his own career and choices, as well as the critical
responses to his work? Puzo mentions Mailer in a witty little send-up of
the much-praised *Paris Review* writers' interview series; in a putative book
review in which he plays both subject and interviewer, he asks himself,
"[H]ow come you people never ask writers about money?"; instead the
questions are about pages written per day, pen versus typewriter, representations of sex but never "how much they got for their paperback rights?"
(82) Puzo asks Puzo, "Can Norman Mailer really scrounge a hundred
grand advance just by picking up the phone?" and implores the *Paris
Review* just once to "interview a guy like Harold Robbins. Then your col-
lections will really sell. And don't forget to ask how much he makes" (87).
When asked if he knows Mailer's work, Puzo replies, "I know that work
all right. He's a crook. He was an honest, believing writer until the publishers worked him over when he was trying to peddle *[The] Deer Park*.
Now he's a crook, his last two novels dastardly crimes committed in cold
blood and in full view of the public. . . . He should just scoop up his loot
and make his getaway fast" (85).

By the time of Mailer's *An American Dream* and *Why Are We in Viet
Nam?*, Puzo can only describe him and his work in terms of criminality
(crook, crimes, cold blood, loot, and getaway), basically the same rhetoric
he would use to cast himself in the decision to write *The Godfather* and
in Merlyn's views of his own descent into a literary "underworld" in
Fools Die. In 1968, Puzo was already "covering" Mailer's career in many
ways with his own, preparing for the psychic transfer to Osano a decade
later. His mention of Mailer's attack on other writers refers to Mailer's
continual habit of writing of his contemporaries, especially in Mailer's
notorious "Talent in the Room" essay in *Advertisements,* in which Mailer
comments on his generation of male writers in Olympian, instinctive
hunches about their work and weak points.[5] Of course, Puzo was beneath Mailer's written notice, circling in the outer reaches of the literary
universe in which his generational cohort was shaping the canon of
postwar American fiction to 1970. Mailer's sense that "the past did not
exist for us," that there was "a frontier for my generation of novelists"
after World War II conveys some of the heightened melodrama of the
novelist's role that sweeps Puzo along in its wake for decades. Other
Mailer pronouncements sound like anthems for Puzo from the stereo-

typical "now there are too many times when I no longer give a good goddam for most of the human race" and the ironically reversed "I had the freak of luck to start high on the mountain, and go down sharp while others were passing me" to, most tellingly for Puzo, "I have been a cheap gambler with [my talent]" (426). Everything about Puzo's 1950s in *The Godfather Papers* (perhaps akin in Puzo's mind to Mailer's *Advertisements*) suggests it was his true crisis decade, the racking self-doubt of whether the first novel could be completed, its sinking beneath public notice, the continuing humiliation of family handouts and low-level jobs, the anxiety of finding time to write balanced against family responsibilities. In so many ways, Mailer lives the high success version of the resentments and insecurities that Puzo lives below the bar. Mailer has to fight to keep himself raw enough to be the psychic outsider. Puzo merely lives on the edges looking in; he's a less flamboyant man and a tamer artist. Therefore, if Puzo really did feel himself shadowing Mailer in his writerly disaffections on the lower frequencies, it would make sense for him to finally create an imaginary Mailer for *Fools Die*.

Puzo's sympathetic mention of Mailer's publishing problems with *The Deer Park* suggests that somehow it was that novel—its writing, publishing, and reception—that made Mailer a "crook,"and *Fools Die* appears to be Puzo's *The Deer Park*. Merlyn and Osano in *Fools Die* appear to have real antecedents in Mailer's *The Deer Park* two decades earlier. Like Merlyn, Mailer's protagonist is also an orphan, one who never knew his mother, whose father gave him away at age five. Sergius O'Shaughnessy's own lineage is "mongrel"—mixed Welsh-English, Russian-Slovene—but he poses as an Irishman with all that implies in wit, romanticism, and literary talent. Also like Merlyn, Sergius comes out of the orphanage in his teens with only one ambition, "that some day I would be a brave writer" (25), for "I always thought there was going to be an extra destiny coming my direction. I knew I was more gifted than others" (23). Sergius swings in the novel's arc from Greenwich Village to Hollywood; with the mobility of a lover and artist, he lives on the fringe of both the New York literary world and the film capital. Even though the reader sees very little of his special gifts, his symbolic capital is high: he opens a bullfight academy in the Village (shades of Papa Hemingway) and begins a bullfighting novel. He can conclude, "I had the intolerable conviction that I could write about worlds I knew better than anyone alive" (303). Sergius is a vintage hipster, the fictionalized embodiment of Mailer's 1950s theorizing that culminated in the brilliance of "The White Negro" (1957). Mailer's best short story, "The Time of Her Time" (1959), placed in *Advertisements* after "The Talent in the Room," follows Sergius through sexual warfare, as a "messiah of the one-night stand" (434). Recasting Mailer as the Italian American writer Osano is a bit of cross-ethnic subconscious revenge, as if Puzo is saying, very well, if you wished to become Irish Catholic in persona for Sergius O'Shaughnessy, let's see if I can make you Italian American as well. If Mailer was willing to throw himself into an orphan-writer-assumed ethnic identity, Puzo would seem to say he'd be fair game for Puzo himself to go Mailer one better and disappear completely into the orphan identity of Merlyn, a character with no past, real or imagined, and a Mailer/Osano to scrutinize and watch self-destruct.

Merlyn's real sleight-of-hand is to begin his long account in *Fools Die* with a three-page fragment that the reader later learns is the only completed part of Osano's ambitious and long-promised manuscript, the novel he hoped would bring him the Nobel Prize. These first pages are a stream of largely self-referential maxims of fictional promises to be kept in what we are about to read, along with a list of subjects to be covered: "The poor struggling genius world, the crooked world, and the classy literary world. All this laced with plenty of sex, some complicated ideas you won't be hit over the head with . . ." (4). Puzo-Merlyn wants Mailer-Osano around so that he can show the rise and fall of talent in conflict with ambition and self-destructiveness. As he takes on a review assignment for a journal essay on Osano, Merlyn writes that Osano "didn't know I was out to kill him because I was an unsuccessful writer with one flop novel published and the second coming hard" (122). Puzo catches none of Mailer's language, intelligence, wit, or breadth of interest as he writes through Osano who's an obscene boor, full of blunt opinions about life, love, and literature, almost as if Sonny Corleone or Jack Woltz from *The Godfather* had been fitted with a muse and sensibility and had changed careers. Osano is raw sexuality and aggression with hardly enough rhetorical control to make us believe he could sign a piece under his own name. Indeed Merlyn begins to ghost-write material for him as confidante, editorial assistant, and finally literary executor. When Osano dies of advanced syphillis, Merlyn assumes control of Osano's last unpublished work and mistress but loses both. Rather than provide what a reader might expect—an *All About Eve* or *Misery* consuming the Osano figure in blind ambition or rage—Puzo settles for Merlyn's gloomy takeover of a largely empty Osano, whom he reduces even further. Thus a diminished great American writer confirms Merlyn's own defeatist view of literature.

What hanging with Osano provides for Merlyn is a way for Puzo to give his own views on art through analogies and then to critique his own character from the standpoint of a Mailer with some of the most insightful personal criticism Puzo ever allowed himself. Merlyn believes that an artist doesn't need sensitivity, intelligence, anguish, or ecstasy, but rather "the truth was you were like a safecracker fiddling with the dial and listening to the tumblers click into place and after a couple of years the door might swing open and you could start typing" (233). First, Merlyn transforms art and its inspiration into theft, patiently trying various combinations until he hits it with no volition or creative leap, but rather, the way is clear, and in the presence of the wealth of the safe, the words begin to flow. Only in the presence of the contents of the safe can he "start" writing, which is theft plus the presence of riches to be appropriated. This negative art writing is contrasted by Merlyn with what he learns writing for the pulps: "[I]t was a skill I had, finally a craft. I wasn't just a lousy fucking artist" but "Osano never understood that" (233). What Osano does understand, however, is Merlyn himself beyond all defenses, and in his criticism of Merlyn, we may come as close as we can to Puzo's self-estimate. As he names Merlyn his executor, Osano psychologizes Merlyn, notes his dependence on bourgeois security and family, and scores his lack of success with half his writing life gone: " 'You live in your own world, you do exactly what you want to do. You control your life. You never get into trouble and when you do, you don't panic; you get out of it. Well, I admire you but I don't envy you. I've never seen you do or say a really mean thing but I don't think you really give a shit about anybody. You're just steering your life" (243). On the one hand, many of these traits are those of the traditional American hero, a man questing for personal freedom, looking for autonomy, cool under fire. To live in his "own world" would also describe exactly the kind of environment that Vito and Michael Corleone try to build for the family, and their lack of panic is the stuff of legend. Yet Osano also pierces Merlyn's bleakness; much of his complacent decency and lack of aggressiveness is simply a hardness of heart. Merlyn emerges as a conflicted, not complex signifier: part existential male hero, part terminally depressed worker bee. What Osano's analysis means for *The Godfather*'s creator becomes clear. Puzo largely cashes in the dream of art to identify with the dream of Don Corleone, the father who will never fail his family or cease to control his life. Corleone power will thrill millions, but when the tumblers finally fell and the safe door swung open to great success, the safe was empty, as far as Puzo was concerned. Puzo had no identity after *The Godfather*.

Puzo cleverly weights the give and take of Osano and Merlyn to allow Osano to delineate Merlyn for the reader. Osano tells Merlyn that he just "tries to beat all the traps" and labels him "a safe magician," for "you just write and gamble and play the good father and husband" (264), as succinct a self-description of Puzo as one will find. Merlyn comes back at Osano with the tame brief that "in fact you could say that life itself wasn't a big deal, never mind his fucking literature" (265). Merlyn goes back to his own writing, and for two years he works twelve-to-fifteen-hour days, going all out to write a novel that he feels will give him great notoriety. He sells it to a paperback house for half-a-million dollars. Everyone had warned him that a novel about kidnapping a child where the kidnapper is the hero "would not appeal to a mass public," but his editor tells Merlyn, "You told such a great story that it doesn't matter" (280). This unpleasant subject carried through to great success in the face of moral objections is obviously Puzo's answer to those readers and critics who scored him a decade earlier for the immorality of the Corleone predators but whose criticisms had made no difference to the novel's reception whatsoever. The end of book 4 of *Fools Die* sends Merlyn to Hollywood to write the screenplay of his blockbuster, which is never named.

Fools Die really concludes here, but the novel cascades on for two hundred fifty more pages of Hollywood shenanigans, Las Vegas skullduggery and murder, and a major love affair by Merlyn with Janelle, a star-crossed Hollywood dream girl who, to his credit, Puzo writes as honestly and complexly as he ever wrote any female character.[6] She stands as another in the line of doomed Marilyn figures and also a copy of Mailer's Cherry Melanie in *An American Dream*. Somewhere along the way, Osano dies, largely forgotten after Merlyn's big score with his best seller. Merlyn in true fantasy fashion gets to finish Osano's last big book but knows, "I had tried to live without illusions and without risk. I had none of [Osano's] love for life and his faith in it" (499). *Fools Die* finally ends; it has stopped. Merlyn's family appears conveniently as foil, goad, problem, or sanctuary whenever Puzo needs them, but we hardly even learn the names of the children. The gambling material, the Hollywood characters, the New York scene, Merlyn's sporadic attempts to either write hard and long or tell the reader about why he can't write at all must be extracted from the tangle of prose. Nevertheless, taken in tandem with *The Godfather Papers* essays, Merlyn's attempt in *Fools Die* to interrogate Osano and have Osano/Mailer construct a doubly imaginary Merlyn/Puzo in return yields as much as we were ever to know about Puzo and his writerly temperament.

Puzo and James Jones

Almost any serious American reader in 1978 could have identified a reductive portrait of Norman Mailer in the outlines of Osano in *Fools Die*. Puzo had a much more straightforward and positive response to the work of another prominent contemporary, James Jones, who makes a brief and unnamed appearance in *The Godfather* that has gone undiscussed. However, the curve of Jones' career from the success of *From Here to Eternity* (1951) to the negative reception of his massive sequel *Some Came Running* (1957) and the literary problems it posited provide further speculation on what Puzo himself may have gleaned from the writerly odysseys of "the talent in the room."

When Johnny Fontane is bankrolled in Hollywood after Woltz gets the message, Johnny looks around for story properties to acquire for production or for his own future film roles. The upshot of Johnny's getting his plum film role from Woltz was, of course, Puzo's rendition of Frank Sinatra winning the role of Maggio in *From Here To Eternity* from Harry Cohn at Paramount and going on to win the 1953 Academy Award for Best Supporting Actor. Now Johnny's "brain was really whirring along. He called the author of the book, the best-selling novel on which his new film was based. The author was a guy his own age who had come up the hard way and was now a celebrity in the literary world." However, "he had come out to Hollywood and been treated like shit. . . . It didn't matter that his book had made him world famous" (175–76). Johnny thanks the author for the great part and asks him to send a copy of his next novel because "maybe I can get you a good deal for it, better than you got with Woltz" (176). The deal is made, and "the second book was perfect for what Johnny wanted. He wouldn't have to sing, it had a good, gutsy story with plenty of dames and sex and it had a part that Johnny instantly recognized as tailor-made for Nino. The character talked like Nino, acted like him, even looked like him" (189).

The "second book," Jones's *Some Came Running* ran to over twelve hundred pages and drove the critics to distraction. An eagerly awaited sequel to one of the biggest novels of the 1950s, *Some Came Running* failed to pick up on the action and romance of *Eternity*. Most readers became lost in the endless tale of a war veteran and author, Dave Hirsh, returning to his hometown of Parkman, Illinois, and struggling to find both a suitable literary subject and a place in middle-class, midwest America. *Some Came Running* was a book of a writer's frustration as Dave Hirsh endlessly parses out the meaning of art and life; in short, Jones eerily rendered the precise curve that Puzo would trace a decade and two decades later: a best-selling social melodrama followed by an Academy Award adaptation followed by a brooding and shapeless sequel that lacked narrative drive while penetrating deeper into the author's psyche. Puzo appeared to admire Jones's guts and honesty in *The Godfather*. By 1978 in *Fools Die*, he had written Jones's folly as well.

The roles that Johnny Fontane sees for himself and Nino Valenti in his nominal *Some Came Running* adaptation included what came to be Sinatra as Dave Hirsh and Dean Martin as 'Bama Dillert, working-class southern philosopher and professional gambler who is Dave Hirsh's best friend. A fairly complicated circuit is thus created by Puzo, who first introduces the reader to a Nino Valenti as a neighborhood guy, then posits him as a potential Dean Martin (tall, black curly hair, lethargic, alcoholic, instinctive ballad singer), then gets him his real-life part as Johnny sees how right his friend would be in the role. Just as Coppola pruned and shaped Puzo's vehicle for the *Godfather* films, *Some Came Running* was pulled together into a dramatic and often moving film by Vincente Minnelli and fueled by terrific performances from Sinatra, Martin, and Shirley MacLaine as Ginnie Moorhead, Dave Hirsh's working-class floozy girlfriend, sometime muse, and goad.

James Jones's career parallels those of Mailer and Puzo in its nominal American rites of passage for the generation of male writers born around 1920. After a troubled childhood in Robinson, Illinois, Jones enlisted in the army in 1939, was at Hickham Field in Hawaii on December 7, 1941, and was wounded at Guadalcanal. He worked consistently at his fiction before *Eternity* as the last prominent writing discovery of Maxwell Perkins, the fabled Scribner's editor. Jones always considered *Some Came Running* his best work, and Puzo may have recognized a familiar American stamp on Jones's career, early success and a long writing life stretching thereafter with critics waiting, knives out. Jones went to Hollywood to support himself with film scripts in the late 1950s, much as Puzo did in the 1970s. Never celebrated for his style or elegance, Jones at his best provided powerful scenes and characters and a deep ingrained honesty. Of *Some Came Running*, a Jones biographer wrote that it was "a very different book from what might have been expected, a difficult book about very unhappy people. What was original was easy to miss. What was admirable was easy to ignore" (Garrett 123). What was there in *Some Came Running* to capture Puzo's admiration? As Dave Hirsh slips back into his hometown and takes a hotel room, he pulls books from his army bag to set on the dresser: "there were five, all Viking Portables. Fitzgerald, Hemingway, Faulkner, Steinbeck, Wolfe," and "the sight of the five books there on the dresser, their pages swelled with too much reading, their covers dog eared and warped from too many barracks bags and afflicted with a rash of water and mold sports, really touched him deeply. He had dragged them half way across Europe, they had seen a lot of country with him" (12–13). Jones heralds the triumph of modern American fiction here in the texts of the major male authors Dave Hirsh has venerated but also has to beat, the ones whose humanistic values would be highlighted after the war as an antidote to political and historical novels, as a literature of values and the human condition. *Some Came Running*'s major battle will be not with Nazis or Japs but with finding and going with the proper muse in the midst of midwest and middle-class stasis.

Much in *Some Came Running* must have appealed to the Puzo writing *Fools Die*. Jones's largest subject is the writer's calling and craft; Dave Hirsh himself wants to create art, a universal story but one full of truth: "Day-to-day, hard, rigorous craftsmanlike writing, saying all those things he felt, and thought, and wondered.... And the sum, the upshot, the lump of what he wanted to get said was that each man was a Sacred Universe in himself and at the same time a noisome garbage pail whose bottom had rotted out.... And that therefore there was only growth, only change, and the pain of change, and the ecstasy of that pain ..." (756). Such are the Olympian coming-of-age thoughts of the American male writer, made elegant across the Atlantic by Joyce's Stephen Dedalus, hyperbolic by Wolfe's Eugene Gant, and coincident with every cry of a misunderstood and consciously aesthetic male modernist of large ambition in Jones and Puzo's time. Jones is more lyrical and intense than Puzo would ever be and had a greater interest in sexual energy and tension as the wellspring of characterization. Dave Hirsh's inspiration for his fiction swings in an arc between two women. The ice princess of a writer and critic, Gwen French, fears his rougher male side and wants to bring out the great artist in him rather than give him her body. The dim Ginnie Moorhead, whom he often excoriates, wants only to be with him and be loved, a people's heroine. 'Bama Dillert plays Nino to Dave Hirsh's Johnny, believing in the gambling life and making the link: "gambling was about the only profession left any more that had any individuality and freedom left at all. . . . 'Except for yore writin, of course, it has 'em' " (580). The discovery by Puzo in Jones of a fellow author who could make such an equation of Puzo's twin loves of gambling and writing must have been a revelation.

The inability of Dave Hirsh to seduce the elite muse of Gwen French or to craft a successful plot-line inspired by proletarian muse Ginnie Moorhead makes his own big book founder hopelessly. When Dave dies protecting Ginnie's life, Gwen and her father eerily do the posthumous editing on his manuscript, and the tender, sentimental chapters disappear.[7] Puzo was vitally interested in a twelve-hundred-page novel that could be sustained as a writer's meditation on fiction, and damn the Jones critics who said that the book had failed. I suggest that Puzo saw himself in the same position after *The Godfather* that Jones did after *From Here to Eternity*. He was overnight famous, made a huge movie sale, and had the chance to do screenplays for more and easier money. He came to Hollywood, felt worked over and more-or-less ignored, as Jones had done in Puzo's view, and Puzo writes that sleight into his Jones cameo in *The Godfather* ("he had come out to Hollywood expecting to be treated like a wheel and, like most authors, had been treated like shit" (*The Godfather* 175). In any event, Puzo doesn't create Jones in compromising dialogue in his Godfather cameo as he did with Mailer-Osano in *Fools Die*. He keeps him pure and honorable. The biggest tribute to Jones in *Fools Die* is in Merlyn's emulation of so many authorial traits from Dave Hirsh in *Some Came Running*: orphan, war veteran, writer who venerates the art, depressed center of creativity.

Nino and Johnny: Encore

Johnny Fontane and Nino Valenti spark the Jones connection in *The Godfather*. Their relation to their singing takes Puzo to Dave Hirsh and 'Bama Dillert, as 'Bama wonders how in hell Dave can be so tied up in knots over women and writing. *Some Came Running* as film makes an appearance in *The Godfather* as "the first movie [Johnny] had produced with himself as star and Nino in a featured part was making tons of money" (376). Johnny's sexual desire suffers as his singing voice comes back; his technique in the studio is better than ever before: "[T]he chords were true and rich, he didn't have to force it at all. Easy, easy, just pouring out. . . . And it didn't matter if he fell on his face with movies, it didn't matter if he couldn't get it up with Tina the night before" (382). Johnny has his art back, and Puzo's sad renunciation of art can be countered in a triumphant moment because Johnny's singing is better than acting, better than sex. In the next paragraph, Nino Valenti lies near death, not caring "enough about anything to make him want to stay alive" (382). At the end of Michael Corleone's last visit to Las Vegas, he comes to pay his respects to Nino on his deathbed and tells him the Don is always asking about him, to which Nino grins and responds, "Tell him I'm dying. Tell him show business is more dangerous than the olive oil business" (390). The "olive oil business" has always been the euphemism for murder throughout *The Godfather*, and Nino who "speaks death" with nothing to lose, gracefully references the family but suggests Hollywood is more treacherous in its blandishments than Corleone service. What's the parable here? Puzo knows that the Corleones are the most dangerous men alive, but in creating them, he has also gone back on his Ninos, on his real neighborhood guys from *The Fortunate Pilgrim*. Nino is beyond the Corleone family's help, as is Puzo, who sensationalized the Italian American life and immigrant passage a few short years after *The Fortunate Pilgrim*'s hard and rather austere treatment. Nino bows out literally and figuratively because there's no place for an honest paisan who wishes to remain uncommodified in both his art and his life. Neither Nino nor Puzo is in firm control of this intimation, to be sure, but somewhere among ethnic guilt, a writer's view that he is selling out, and Puzo's own need to squelch the "degenerate gambler" in himself lies the demise of Nino Valenti. The final note on Nino's passing might be that he disappeared completely out of the *Godfather* films, an extraneous figure alternately brooding and cracking wise (never a welcome part of popular action narrative) and therefore deemed invisible by Hollywood and known only residually to the novel's readers and not in the ongoing popular cinematic saga of Corleone hegemony and tragic fall. Puzo as Italian American writer and unreconstructed story-teller dies a little here, too, though beginning with *The Sicilian*, Puzo will reprise himself for the rest of his career. However, the exhaustion of *Fools Die* is in part Nino's eulogy, a novel where all the characters essentially make Nino's sad journey toward discouragement and unexplained silence.

Why does Johnny totally recover his powers while Nino dies? Johnny is the all-around popular success that *The Godfather* becomes as book and film. Must Johnny get stronger as Nino weakens? Must the Sicilian wedding singer fade in comparison to the studio-burnished and surgically repaired Johnny Fontane? Is the riddle of Nino's death bound up with his authenticity that no one really wants, including himself? Is Johnny's euphoria at his "comeback" hollow in the face of Nino's slow suicide? Such questions hang as loose connections in the novel where these two artistic neighborhood pals are decidedly minor figures, the lounge acts for the family orchestration of power and violence. Puzo could not high-light the theme of the legitimate and illegitimate artist in *The Godfather*. The popular vehicle about family identity was all wrong. Nor do I wish to claim that inside the blockbuster family saga was an intricate medita-tion on art and its costs and blandishments, some hidden meaning that would make *The Godfather*'s structure and thematics more complicated. I would suggest, however, that Puzo was never far from an inchoate dialogue with himself about art as a religion, family as a cross to bear, Italian identity as compromised, and writing and gambling as necessary to him as air.

Puzo's view in "Choosing a Dream" that he never heard an Italian singing when he was young because they couldn't afford to dream should put us on notice from the outset of *The Godfather* that Johnny and Nino as Italian singers will be figures of some importance to Puzo's sense of his rhetoric and its pitch. Puzo does not sing, he does not come in praise, he does not hope, in some deeply pessimistic and rather grave bow to both an Old World past and a temperamental disposition. He's an honest guy. Not all the magic surgery on Johnny's voice, a gift from best-seller heaven, can make Puzo forego the silencing of Nino Valenti, the unrecon-structed depressive part of himself, the gambler he most loves. Puzo even gets to take one last shot at his Godfather self when Johnny's saintly ex-wife, Virginia, turns on him at last at one point and says, "I never liked your singing anyway. Now that you've shown you can make movies, I'm glad you can't sing anymore" (378). Substitute "write" for "sing" here, and Puzo shows Virginia to be a prophet about the truth of his own career after *The Godfather* makes his bones.

Puzo dropped more clues about his alienation from his writing in the very last remarks excerpted from his writer's diary in *The Godfather Papers*. In March 1953 he noted, "tried to write a trashy potboiler but had to give it up. Immoral and uninteresting, that's why" (246). Could this abortive attempt have been the genesis of *The Godfather*? Was Puzo refer-ring to the subject matter or the characters' actions as immoral, or was the writing itself immoral? Did he find the text boring to work on, or was the writing an uninteresting task? As usual, he was not specific enough, but we may speculate. In April 1953, after not being able to sell the manuscript that became *The Dark Arena*, he writes, "I don't think I will ever be able to like anyone again. No matter how good things turn out later. And won't be able to think well of myself" (246). In *Fools Die*, Merlyn notes about his family that he "never felt the same about them again" (76–77) after they were angry at his failures to sell his work. Such turning on both the vehicles on which he was working, his own sense of self-worth, and his relation to the family estimating that worth show Puzo caught in early negatives that no amount of Godfather success could convert into a coherent sense of career. As much as he had been lionized, he was caught, early and late, in his bourgeois idealism about art, its overturning in his early sorrow, and in the appropriation of a rather stock and tame artist's revolt at being misunderstood and unappreciated. There are no incongruous or cautionary or ingratiating tales to tell about Puzo's writerly career. What is interesting is how tenaciously he held on to his hope of portraying his writer's disillusion, how honestly he wanted to share with a public hardly wanting to know about such stasis, how his antennae went out to the work and struggles of peers such as Mailer and Jones as they patterned out their own affairs with American success. In 1972 Puzo prefaces his 1950s diary with a post-*Godfather* disclaimer that the entries are painful to read, egoistic, naive about art and life, and "now older and more cunning, trickier with a sentence, slicker with a phrase, I resist the temptation to cover my tracks" (233). By 1978, *Fools Die* in five hundred pages expands on the fourteen pages of the diary printed here, when the resentment cloaked in the shards of a Hollywood and Las Vegas "potboiler" is finally the story he wanted to tell; he has reverted to his truth as he was given to know it. Whatever else *Fools Die* might be, it is not cunning, tricky, or slick.

Bourdieu wrote that "enrichment accompanies ageing when the work manages to enter the game, when it becomes a stake in the game and so incorporates some of the energy produced in the struggle of which it is the object" (*Field of Cultural Production* 111). Puzo might also be found concretely as "the experience of a life-condition occupying a particular position" "within the dispositions of the habitus" (*Distinction* 172). *The Godfather* became the stake in Puzo's career that turned his long fact of famelessness around but did not alter his fixed sense of himself as an early failure. He knew corners and intimations of himself as an economic marker in literary culture. The deformation of his writer's character is projected centrally in *Fools Die* and through moments of artistic misgiving in *The Godfather*. "I'm going down," says Johnny Fontane to his godfather. "I can't sing anymore," "I have to gamble" (31–33). Don Corleone rises to his most agitated state in the novel, furiously mimicking Johnny's weakness while telling him, " 'You can start by acting like a man.' Suddenly anger contorted his face. He shouted. 'LIKE A MAN!' " (37). Johnny's "womanly" cries are countered, salved, arrested in development, and the Don fixes everything for him in Hollywood, becoming the father to whom Puzo/Johnny confesses, the father who absolves him and sends him back into popular culture production armed with the family's trust and ability to strike fear into the industry. Puzo's own fatherlessness is assuaged in such moments, and in the "trashy potboiler" tradition, Johnny becomes a winning ticket, having confessed the weakness of his singing voice, the sin of gambling and letting women and family control his emotions. *The Godfather*, fittingly enough, is a text where all can be forgiven and a new start made for the writer and the pop star.

The ballad of Nino and Johnny folds into the best-selling melodrama of *The Godfather* while Merlyn's sad tune in *Fools Die* goes largely unheard. The wisdom of the literary transformation of a writer's capital and its debits into the roles of Nino and Johnny proves the readerly power of the best seller's mythical work, while *Fools Die* and its discontents are even more generic in the sense of familiar notes from Puzo's life and career, which write him as surely as he struggles to write within their generative fields without creating a real *Godfather* sequel in fiction. Few American blockbuster writers in Puzo's time came close to his desire to place his whole writerly life before the unwelcoming popular reader. That stubborn misplaced courage was Puzo's signing off on his own mythos, while the transforming powers of the *Godfather* novel and films and their dispersal into American language and culture remain what *The Godfather*'s audience knows and wants to know.

Part II

Reading *The Godfather*: Critical Strategies and Theoretical Models

chapter three

Bakhtin and Puzo:
Authority as the Family Business

The authoritative word demands that we acknowledge it, that we make it our own; it binds us, quite independent of any power it might have to persuade us internally; we encounter it with its authority already fused to it.

—Bakhtin, *The Dialogic Imagination*

Sonny grinned at him and said slyly, "I want to enter the family business." When he saw that the Don's face remained impassive, that he did not laugh at the joke, he added hastily, "I can learn to sell olive oil."

—Puzo, *The Godfather*

After *The Godfather* nominally changed everything in his writing life, Puzo considered his elite failure and his popular multiethnic block-buster success with bemused resignation. In his essays, he played the unassimilated ethnic son and the unassimilated unsuccessful novelist, as he moved rhetorically from margin to margin. But in the character of the godfather, in Don Corleone, Puzo finally found the true "comfort he could find in no other place." He came to believe in the Don as he had believed in art, finding in him the protection he had previously found in fiction. The Don's autonomy is Puzo's extension of the dream of the power of art, the realm where he can't be threatened. Art for art's sake mutates into the family for the family's sake. The family business comes to be the making of authority itself.

How does Puzo establish and maintain the enormous power of Don Corleone? My aim is to answer that question through Bakhtinian analysis. The fit between Bakhtin and Puzo is adversarial. Bakhtin is the champion of dialogue, growth, and learning from the answering voice. Puzo's novel is a text about power and its necessary monologues, stasis, secretiveness, and denial of the answering voice. I look at strategies of control in *The Godfather* and, by way of Bakhtin, at the forces that bid to break this control apart, both on the plane of Don Corleone's imperatives and Puzo's strategies. I conclude by speculating on the ways in which these authorial choices in dialogue are those of any novelist who must shape both novelistic design and characters' destiny. My view is that the "family business" in both mob rule and fiction is precisely that of making authority. I will examine three key scenes in detail: the deathbed exchange between the dying Genco Abbandando and Don Corleone, teenage Sonny Corleone's interview with his father after he commits a minor hold-up, and Kay Adams Corleone's exchange with her mother-in-law after her marriage. In each case, Don Corleone's edifice of belief and meaning is briefly exposed through questions about truth, morality, and the legitimacy of the Corleone family and enterprise. Genco as dying confederate, Sonny as the son who has witnessed his father kill a man, and Kay as the wife who knows her husband, Michael, is a murderer all threaten to speak politically.

M. M. Bakhtin's exhaustive attempts to describe the dynamics of language production have become central to much important contemporary theorizing on the novel and what Bakhtin calls the "novelistic."[1] *Dialogics, heteroglossia,* and *carnivalization* are now familiar signposts in critical debate where Bakhtin appears as a man for all current critical seasons. Derridean in his insistence on the play of language, he appears to have operated in the Lacanian certainty that language is most severely transacted in the language of another or the "other." Bakhtin reminds one of Foucault when he posits a teeming discourse full of accents without specific subjects. Yet he suggests that all language reflects and is the mediation of the social structures producing the speakers, a view closer to Marxist critical theory. His version of reader-response theory would place the response of the reader, listener, or dialogue participant as occurring almost *before* language production and dictated by the transaction in communication. Such a transaction belongs neither to writer nor reader nor to either participant but rather is a boundary event. Finally, Bakhtin's work is not limited to literary study; he is claimed by other disciplines as a linguist, philosopher, and sociohistorian of knowledge.

Bakhtin's central categories of *Authoritative Discourse* and *Internally Persuasive Discourse* in *The Dialogic Imagination* (1981) are expert tools to describe shifts and priorities in Puzo's structure of dialogue in *The Godfather*. Bakhtin defines the "authoritative word" as one that "demands we acknowledge it," "that we make it our own; it binds us, quite independent of any power it might have to persuade us internally; we encounter it with its authority already fused to it" (Bakhtin 342). Most relevant to *The Godfather*, Bakhtin's "authoritative word" is "the word of the fathers" (342). Within the "contact zone," the authoritative discourse confronts the potential and also the threat of internally persuasive discourse. The internally persuasive word "is, as it is affirmed through assimilation, tightly interwoven with 'one's own word' " (345). The internally persuasive word "enters into an intense interaction, a *struggle* with other internally persuasive discourses"; "it is *open*: in each of the new contexts which dialogize it, this discourse is able to reveal ever newer *ways to mean*" (346).

The struggles between internally persuasive discourses and with authoritative discourse describe *The Godfather*'s most interesting dialogues at points where Puzo and Don Corleone's edifice of belief and meaning is revealed in the exposure and recontainment of questions about the truth, morality, and legitimacy of the Corleone family and enterprise. Such questions in a general sense are always rising to the surface in any fictional text for, as Bakhtin points out, "the speaking person in the novel is always, to one degree or another, an *ideologue*, and his words are always *ideologemes*" (333). Bakhtin provides signposts to the Corleone language transactions, which allow us to find our way in the larger collective transactions in Puzo's world of murder, business, and family. The suppressions by characters in the text tell us a good deal about Puzo's crises of narrative authority and his resultant cover-ups. Bakhtin's maxim is that the "author is to be found at the center of organization where all levels intersect" (49). I want to meditate on Puzo by way of Bakhtin, on the author's duties as traffic cop at the intersection, where he manages free flow and collision, the very carnivalization of the life pulsing there in its regulation and anarchy.

Politicized and De-Politicized Speech

All authors manage all scenes in their novels; "manage" is not by definition pejorative and does not simply apply to best-selling fiction. However, Puzo's choices in *The Godfather* allow us to examine an author who "do" the voices in particularly vivid and segmented forms that raise more questions than they answer. Furthermore, Puzo evidences a principle of nervous confrontation of words in authoritative and internally persuasive discourse, of revelations and then seemingly a forgetting of the moment of revelation. Popular fiction appears to thrive on the authority of the monologue and its own forgetting. What happens when dialogue threatens the exposure of that authority in major characters and their authors?

Bakhtin's distinctions between authoritative discourse and internally persuasive discourse allow us to chart the feints and parries of characters as they fall in and out of various speech genres in *The Godfather*. The speech of Don Corleone is an example of what Roland Barthes in *Mythologies* labeled "de-politicized speech" (Barthes 142). Such speech is everywhere given an eternal justification. "*Myth is de-politicized speech*"; myth "purifies," "makes innocent," gives a "natural and eternal justification" and possesses a "clarity" (Barthes 143). Almost any address by Don Corleone may illustrate these characteristics, which are enhanced and performed through the ethnic signification which will be discussed in chapter 4. The counter to de-politicized speech is obviously politicized speech. Barthes describes it in "Myth on the Left" as speech in which language is operational and transitively linked to its object, where man is a producer and "speaks in order to transform reality and no longer to preserve it as an image" (Barthes 146).

Dialogics makes dynamic the political positions taken by characters and narrative voices within given novelistic scenes. Dialogics helps to identify the power relations within each speech act and what is to be gained, lost, retained, or overcome by participants in dialogue, including the voices of the author. In *The Godfather*, Don Corleone's rhetoric consistently counters any politicized speech because Puzo cannot often risk the devaluation of his ruling family's "natural" currency. Yet in extraordinary moments, Puzo allows a competing rhetoric to challenge Don Corleone's de-politicized speech. Puzo then orchestrates the crises in authority thus represented, in general recontaining the novel's most intriguing scenes and implications. Dialogue is overturned in favor of a monologic order in plot favored by Don Corleone and his author. My suggestion is that this orchestration and monologic order is emblematic of a general popular fiction strategy to both raise extremely important and emotional issues and then, having aroused reader interest and sympathy, "solve" the issues in a way that privileges power and narrative drive.

As his final act on his daughter's wedding day, Don Corleone visits the hospital in which his long-time subordinate, Genco Abbandando, lies in the last throes of a wasting cancer. The scene bears quoting in full and is numbered into numbered sections for reference below:

1. The Don bent closer. The others in the room were astonished to see tears running down Don Corleone's face as he shook his head. The quavering voice grew louder, filling the room. With a tortured superhuman effort, Abbandando lifted his head off his pillow, eyes unseeing, and pointed a skeletal forefinger at the Don. "Godfather, Godfather," he called out blindly, "save me from death, I beg of you. My flesh is burning off my bones and I can feel the worms eating away my brain. Godfather, cure me, you have the power, dry the tears of my poor wife. In Corleone we played together as children and now will you let me die when I fear hell for my sins?"

2. The Don was silent. Abbandando said, "It is your daughter's wedding day, you cannot refuse me."

   The Don spoke quietly, gravely to pierce through the blasphemous delirium.

3. "Old friend," he said, "I have no such powers. If I did I would be more merciful than God, believe me. But don't fear death and don't fear hell. I will have a mass said for your soul every night and every morning. Your wife and your children will pray for you. How can God punish you with so many pleas for mercy?"

4. The skeleton face took on a cunning expression that was obscene. Abbandando said slyly, "It's been arranged then?"

When the Don answered, his voice was cold, without comfort. "You blaspheme. Resign yourself."

5. Abbandando fell back on the pillow. His eyes lost their wild gleam of hope. The nurse came back into the room and started shooing them out in a very matter-of-fact way. The Don got up but Abbandando put out his hand. "Godfather," he said, "stay here with me and help me meet death. Perhaps if He sees you near me He will be frightened and leave me in peace. Or perhaps you can say a word, pull a few strings, eh?" The dying man winked as if he were mocking the Don, now not really serious. "You're brothers in blood after all." Then, as if fearing the Don would be offended, he clutched at his hand. "Stay with me, let me hold your hand. We'll outwit that bastard as we've outwitted others. Godfather, don't betray me."

6. The Don motioned the other people out of the room. They left. He took the withered claw of Genco Abbandando in his own two broad hands. Softly, reassuringly, he comforted his friend, as they waited for death together.

7. As if the Don could truly snatch the life of Genco Abbandando back

8. from that most foul and criminal traitor to man." (47–48)

1. The Don bent closer . . . for my sins

The first section of the dialogue is both formally framed and politically urgent.[2] The initial language of Don Corleone and Genco is marked by Genco's language of religious supplication as he pleads Lazaruslike for deliverance from death by the god figure.[3] Yet the formality is cut by internally persuasive images of human men in real time. Don Corleone weeps to the "astonishment" of people in the room; Genco invokes the equality of their childhood play. His last phrase, "will you let me die when I fear hell for my sins?" exposes his fear for his actions and changes the register of the dialogue. Now Genco has begun the attempt to drag the don into human time where they have been murderers together.

2. The Don was silent ... blasphemous delirium

Such silence precludes an answering word. Don Corleone does not wish to enter into this potentially truthful relation to his confederate. Genco then moves to restore formality as a way of reaching the Don. He retreats to the conventions of the wedding day supplicant. The Don bids reply in most formal terms ("quietly, gravely") "to pierce through the blasphemous delirium." Here is an authorial judgment on the danger inherent in Genco's speech, one not really intended to answer Genco's plea but rather to counter a dangerous precedent. "Blasphemous delirium" is Puzo's disparagement designed to contain Genco, to show him as a man out of control, a man about to speak politically. Any language that may be contained on the level of the sacred and the profane precludes a dialogue about secular good and evil.

3. Old friend ... pleas for mercy

The Don addresses Genco as "old friend," a knight to his squire. The ironies of his disclaimers about possessing powers stand in the face of orders he gave in the novel's first pages, orders to subordinates to brutally right the wrongs brought to him by wedding guests. Here death appears to be what Don Corleone cannot forestall. Such logic is irrefutable in this case but conceals in piety his other life-and-death roles and decisions. Consistent in his role, *he* will not intervene for Genco any more than he will personally break thumbs, but rather he will have mass said by someone else. Women and children will pray for Genco; it is not man's (or godfather's) work. The Don has kept the formal distance from Genco's urgency in the authority of de-politicized and highly stylized speech. Bakhtin writes of this battle to draw discourse "into the contact zone" where "there is a struggle constantly being waged to overcome the official line with its tendency to distance itself from the zone of contact . . ." (Bakhtin 345). Authoritative discourse withdraws into its solid mass of forms and refuses interaction. It is the language of godfathers but also of the bureaucracies and governments the family influences and the corporate world they often mime.

4. The skeleton face ... Resign yourself

Here is perhaps *The Godfather*'s most intriguing moment. The tenor of the dialogue shifts violently as Genco exposes their life-world relation. The skeleton is "cunning" and "obscene." It is death speaking, with no mediation of forms, "slyly," like a fool or rogue: "It's been arranged, then?" In Puzo's best line, the intransitive "it has been" searches for the "you" to complete its agency, to drag Don Corleone from myth into the light of common day. Such a move would call up the world of faceless capitalist deals and murders where Genco and the Don have been so effective. The business language of arrangements is the pivot between false and true consciousness about Don Corleone's role. "It's been arranged, then" also suggests Genco's firm belief in the Don's terrible earthly power. Once more, but more forcefully, Don Corleone denies the relation, their dialogue, and their potential sameness to label Genco as a blasphemer, an archaic trope from religious discourse.

Genco has "blasphemed," indeed. He has spoken from outside the naturalized terms of the Don's power. Without authority he has "spoken death" and fittingly so, since the shift to the political register of arrangements is where these two old partners-in-slaughter have truly lived their lives. Genco has no more stake in de-politicized speech; as the "oppressed," in Barthes' terms, "he has only an active, transitive (political) language" (Barthes 149). Genco speaks death, is death, and finally equates the Don *with* death. The Don is the death-bringer, not the life-saver. Such is the novel's potentially deepest moral consequence but one phrased to affirm the Don's power in plot logic for the popular reader.

5. Abbandando fell back . . . don't betray me

Genco is beyond verbal strategies after the Don commands, "Resign yourself." All his ploys in dialogue have been stymied by the Don who will not be reached by wedding-day convention, biblical language, business language, or, most daringly, urgent politicizing of their relationship in an attempt at internally persuasive discourse. Genco shifts to yet another register, that of old cronies or confederates. He parodies the high speech acts of supplication and the granting of favors. The "wink[ing]" and "mocking" suggest a carnivalization of forms, a dance of death by this skeleton-Genco. Genco reinstates his vision of their equality because he has nothing left to lose. As Barthes points out, in politicized speech, the oppressed is "quasi-unable to lie; lying is a richness, a lie presupposes property, truth and forms to spare" (148). For a terrible instant, Genco has abolished the Don Corleone myth and has correctly identified him as death. Genco drags the Don into one of his few exposures in the novel. Don Corleone is converted from universal to human: together, the henchmen will "outwit that bastard [death]."

6. The Don motioned . . . death together

However, Puzo is not to be outwitted. He swiftly reinstates the Don's authority in the last ameliorating sentences. The Don answers through body language and is tentatively drawn on a human scale. He takes Genco's "withered claw" in "his own two broad hands"; they are peasant boys together, no longer residing on different dialogic planes. Don Corleone is given a physical presence rather than a disembodied authoritative voice. The personal entreaty for the Don to act has been answered but only after such action has been voided of any consequence by Genco's parody of their previous speech acts.

7. As if the Don ... Abbandando back

Here is Puzo's most performative flourish in authorial voice in this passage. From the description of the two old blood brothers awaiting death, all dialogue spent, Puzo restores the novel's universal order. "As if the Don" is one of the novel's trickiest phrases. As Bakhtin writes, "authoritative discourse permits no play with the context framing it" (343). Yet here, it is framed as play, the Don sustaining Genco's fiction that together they may have some calming power in the face of death. This is the mimesis Genco believes in, the miming of mortal and immortal roles. If the voice of the phrase is meant to be ironic, it is Puzo's voice and said with annoyance, "as if" the old peasant is simply too credulous for words. Most likely, Genco and the Don are sustaining the fiction of the Don's mythic power, a relief to both of them for different reasons! Gods do not laugh at others or at themselves in Puzo, nor may they be laughed at. Popular fiction itself is noticeably humorless, except on "humor" shelves. The dangerous and insurgent god-play of American authors such as Melville, Twain, Faulkner, and Coover is anethema to the rigid authority of popular fiction.

8. From that most foul ... to man

The way for Puzo to relieve the vulnerability of the "as if" phrase is by the immediate invocation of the majesty of death as the "most foul and criminal traitor." To restore authoritative discourse, the new signification is Puzo asking, what can we do about death? Bakhtin refers to such a monologic author's statement as a detachable "semantic ornament" (*Problems of Dostoevsky's Poetics* 84). Puzo's authority is most contrived because least realized, a bad copy of the Don's "natural" language. Death is "foul and criminal," a traitor beyond humanity as Puzo indulges in what Bakhtin calls "hidden polemic."[4] The text which had briefly resided in a death scene of rich implication is restored to its sonorous, duplicitous normality. Puzo's authorial narration mimics the Don's initial reaction to Genco in the biblical and authoritative speech genres and conflates the Don's evasiveness with his own; he does not appear to understand the difference. "It's been arranged" refers to deals made by the author as well. Genco, the old murderer, dies with his insight and is absolved back into his "family."[5]

Puzo has briefly attempted to dialogize the Don's power but "foul" and "criminal" traitors are mythical villains to battle, seemingly from nowhere, with no network of causal elements. Don Corleone's speech picks up on the accents of death and urgency in Genco's voice and ritualizes the replies; to Bakhtin, this is "stylization."[6] As Bakhtin writes, "the word encounters an alien word and cannot help encountering it in a living, tension-filled interaction" (*The Dialogic Imagination* 279). Met on a human scale by Genco, Don Corleone becomes death. Genco calls on all their death-dealing understanding and on the richness of language forms shared between them. Sancho Panza has become the grinning skull who parodies the wedding-day world of favors. It's not the limits of power that have been exposed, as perhaps Puzo would like readers to believe. It's the *base* of power, the murderers' bond, the calling in of their whole long history. For Puzo and for the Don, it's not what they've done that's blasphemous, obscene, cunning, or sly but rather the dialogue about it. The mock-horror about blasphemy is really a horror of exposure, the threat of a non-Corleone victim to speak of lived relations. Such a scene exposes the authority of popular fiction-making through its drama of Genco's suppression.[7]

Genco is truly dead. He has fought to keep himself and dialogue alive within authoritative forms. He remains caught in authority's monologue about itself. Thus, ruptures often appear at a seam of myth and fiction in popular fiction, where myth threatens to break apart into truths about power. The aesthetic damage inflicted by Puzo's coda denotes his own fear of fiction. Such exposures of myth's artifice in monologics in popular fiction are revealing. They suggest a writer laboring in degrees of bondage to plot's monologic within melodrama and often incapable of sustaining the morality of fictional discourse, which must belong to dialogue and politicization. Bourdieu in *The Field of Cultural Production* calls such narrative acts "the deceptive satisfactions offered by the false philistine humanism of the sellers of illusion" and posits instead the massive asceticism of an author (Flaubert) who remains, "like Spinoza's god immanent and co-extensive with his creation" (210–11). Such rigor defines neither Puzo's intent nor his praxis and defines an alternate aesthetic of high realism.

The Family Business

A second powerful dialogue scene directly relates to the Don Corleone–Genco interview in its structure. When Sonny, the Don's impetuous oldest son, commits an amateur stick-up as a teenager, the Don evinces real frustration:

For the first time, the Don met defeat. Alone with his son, he gave full vent to his rage, cursing the hulking Sonny in Sicilian dialect, a language so much more satisfying than any other for expressing rage. He ended up with a question. "What gave you the right to commit such an act? What made you wish to commit such an act?"

Sonny stood there, angry, refusing to answer. The Don said with contempt, "And so stupid. What did you earn for that night's work? Fifty dollars each? Twenty dollars? You risked your life for twenty dollars, eh?"

As if he hadn't heard these last words, Sonny said defiantly, "I saw you kill Fanucci."

The Don said, "Ahhh," and sank back in his chair. He waited.

Sonny said, "When Fanucci left the building, Mama said I could go up the house. I saw you go up the roof and I followed you. I saw everything you did. I stayed up there and I saw you throw away the wallet and the gun."

The Don sighed. "Well, then I can't talk to you about how you should behave. Don't you want to finish school, don't you want to be a lawyer? Lawyers can steal more money with a briefcase than a thousand men with guns and masks."

Sonny grinned at him and said slyly, "I want to enter the family business." When he saw that the Don's face remained impassive, that he did not laugh at the joke, added hastily, "I can learn how to sell olive oil."

Still the Don did not answer. Finally he shrugged. "Every man has one destiny," he said. He did not add that the witnessing of Fanucci's murder had decided that of his son. He merely turned away and added quietly, "Come in tomorrow morning at nine o'clock. Genco will show you what to do." (220–21)

As with Genco, Puzo allows Sonny to pierce the official, powerful language of the Don with the reality that the Don is the death-bringer. Sonny grins "slyly" as had Genco; "slyly" becomes the signature for politicized speech, that the truth of the Don's historical reality is to be the issue. Sonny is the death's head, as Genco had been, a young executioner. Sonny also carnivalizes death-business as Don Corleone's real business. He earns his language because of his witnessing of the Don's first murder, that of a minor New York City neighborhood boss. Instantly, Don Corleone relinquishes the registers of authoritative speech for "[I] can't talk to you about how you should behave." Now the Don can speak to Sonny about a career in law, that he could "steal more money with a briefcase" than with guns. This deflection is not enough for Sonny, however; he presses the Don further through the parody of both father/son rites of passage and business discourses: "I want to enter the family business." When he receives no answer, like Genco in the "It's been arranged, then?" dialogue, Sonny realizes he has gone too far toward challenging authority. He mistakenly invokes the carnivalesque, believing he can be free to subvert the Don's authority, but he forgets that Dons do not laugh at themselves. Sonny then "hastily" extends the "olive oil" branch, and Don Corleone measures his answer before replying, "Every man has one destiny."

Destiny in *The Godfather* poses the highest authority, a concept that Puzo continually invokes and that, he would like us to believe, unites authority and internal persuasiveness. Puzo's next line after "destiny" is author-narrated: "He did not add that the witnessing of Fanucci's murder had decided that of his son" (221). Such an utterance is the equivocating deflection of the nervous author from the moral responsibility of the father-murderer to the son and witness: what can the Don do? It's out of his hands, as when death was claiming Genco. Destiny has decreed that Sonny *watch* his father murder a man. Such contorted, moral sleight-of-hand denies the Don's responsibility. The language itself denies agency as in the previous "It's been arranged" example: "He did not add that . . ." and "had decided that . . ." Finally, the whole passage is replete with halting attempts to counter dialogue: "refusing to answer," "as if he had not heard these last words," "I can't talk to you about how you should behave," "the Don's face remained impassive," "Still the Don did not answer." What is not spoken and only postscripted in conditional terms is Puzo's "blasphemy," all smoothed over in the restoration of father/son passage and economic security: "come in tomorrow, my boy, and start learning your trade."

Sonny does not respond but becomes an eager apprentice in the murderer's art. Two pages later he has "made a reputation" as a "most cunning executioner" (223); "cunning" was Genco's death-head expression as he spoke of "arrangements." Puzo's "he did not add" is his counterpart to the Genco scene's "most foul and criminal traitor." In each case, Puzo must miss the moral point of agency and personal responsibility to keep *The Godfather* on track as a family melodrama. In the Don Corleone–Sonny interview, moral agency is deflected onto the witness of murder; it's *his* destiny. In the Don Corleone–Genco interview, moral agency is irrelevant. Death purportedly is bigger than both of them, and they are helpless before it. This is undoubtedly true, yet Puzo's novel has not earned the statement on the page. Such refusal to parse out simple chains of motive and result, influence and implication, are symptomatic of popular fiction's general defective causality, one that readers can easily ignore in their march through the plot.

Puzo at his most distressingly cosmic suggests that Don Corleone helped people "not perhaps out of cunning [again . . .] or planning but because of his variety of interests or perhaps because of the nature of the universe, the interlinking of good and evil, natural of itself" (392). "Cunning" is rejected here in favor of a bizarre combination of business and philosophical language. The "nature of the universe" is about as far as a novel's rhetoric may go, and we thrill to the devastating and lasting effects that authors and characters can sometimes approximate as they perceive a glimpse of it. But Puzo is not that author. He wants the "interlinking" of good and evil to be "natural" as well because it relieves the pressure of censoriousness and judgment waiting to historicize the Don and his violence.

Popular fiction lives on the authority of such rhetoric in a literature of inflation. Characters are represented as monumental: their genitalia, fortunes, romances, histories, decadence. Melodrama itself depends on people defined by these massive determinants. In best sellers, which fixate on the one, the private, the "most beautiful," "most powerful," "wealthiest," "most evil," with whom can dialogue ever truly take place? Perhaps only with the critical reader confronting the author's design. That reader may stop and question the contingent moments, the anxious breaking and reinstating of authority as necessary to domination in both the Corleone empire and that of Puzo.

Bakhtin states that the "parodic stylization of generic, professional and other strata of language is sometimes interrupted by the direct authorial word (usually an expression of pathos, of Sentimental or idyllic sensibility), which directly embodies . . . semantic and axiological intentions of the author" (*The Dialogic Imagination* 301). Bakhtin is speaking of heteroglossia in the English comic novel. Yet his statement appears just as germane to the relentlessly vast summing up by Puzo in and around the Corleone melodrama, a world full of traitors and criminals who are more specific and locatable than death itself and who render values and value judgments moot. Bakhtin writes of novelists who achieve an "obtusely stubborn unity," who "simply [do] not listen to the fundamental heteroglossia inherent in actual language" (327). Puzo has this obtuse listener in the Don, who restores the correct monologue out of authority's necessity.

Puzo is tied to his own rigid center of authority in *The Godfather*. Bakhtin observes that once an author "has chosen a hero and the dominant of his hero's representation, the author is already bound by the inner logic of what he has chosen, and he must reveal it in his representation" (*Problems of Dostoevsky's Poetics* 65). Thus, Puzo is following a "destiny" determined by his design, one that is universally male, secretive, monologic, and dominant. Puzo's design presupposes inevitable clashes over narrative authority, the border skirmishes that Genco and Sonny represent, the sudden flaring up into dialogue that promises a different and revealing study of a heretofore unquestioned center. To drag *The Godfather* into dialogized relations is a victory, however brief, for fiction's democratizing powers. The continual return to the myth of unbroken power and domination is a lesser "destiny" for *The Godfather* with its many potentially insightful moments. The Don's interviews with Genco and Sonny are made more dramatic and pathetic by their isolation and defeat in the larger structure of "destined" authorial control.

The Women's Room

One direct cry against the Don's absolute authority and violence comes from Michael Corleone's wife, Kay. She asks him, "What if everybody felt the same way? How could society ever function, we'd be back in the times of the cavemen" (365). Michael's response is not really Bakhtin's "answering word" at all but rather exposes the limits beyond which Puzo cannot conceptualize, given the logic of his authorial choices. Michael invokes his father's "code of ethics"; he tells Kay the Don believed that society's "rules would have condemned him to a life not suitable to a man like himself, a man of extraordinary force and character" (365).[8]

To deflect Kay, Michael "grins," most unsual for him and the rare but telling signature of carnivalizing in *The Godfather*, even as Sonny "grins" in the "family business" interview. Then Michael equivocates, "I'm just telling you what my father believes," an evasion that signifies he has been speaking in another's discourse. Kay picks up on that and asks what *he* believes. Michael tells her he believes in his family but would like to join society after compiling enough money and power: "I'd like to make my children as secure as possible before they join that general destiny" (365). "Destiny" again is the conceptual bottom line in *The Godfather*, here the hazy American good-life future which could be referenced all the way back to the Declaration of Independence. To Puzo, destiny itself is his limit of conceptualization: it was the Don's "oft-repeated belief that every man has but one destiny" (201)—oft-repeated, indeed. Puzo writes that Sonny Corleone "had been truly tender-hearted" as a boy and "that he had become a murderer as a man was simply his destiny" (266), thus overturning any coherent theory of personality development advanced in this century, as well as articulating a complacent renunciation of ethics and free will. Destiny becomes a deep background historicization, a prior Sicilian historical moment that determines but is not present. Destiny inhabits a rigid plot and is nondialectical with no contingencies. No freedom can be defined from it, as it is curiously both cause and effect.[9] Michael will see to it that his children "joined the general family of humanity" (411), a neutralized group, an essence pulled out of time from the American Family itself and thus freed from any determinant contradictions. This "general family," existing everywhere and nowhere, is ornamental and prematurely Utopian. The general family denies the crimes of Corleone family business and is reductive and historically cynical, as well as hypocritical about an America that the larger novel argues again and again is not worth joining on its terms, neither its institutions nor its laws nor its morals.

Kay's interrogation extends to another family member, Mama Corleone. Part of Puzo's victimization of Kay is the way he places her in thrall as a convert to the Catholic church, the institution Puzo reserves for deathbeds and women but refuses to include in his network of corruptible cultural and social relations negotiated by men. Kay asks Mama, "[W]hy do you go [to church] every single morning?" (392).

> In a completely natural way, Mama Corleone said, "I go for my husband," she pointed down toward the floor, "so he don't go down there." She paused. "I say prayers for his soul every day so he go up there." She pointed heavenward. She said this with an impish smile, as if she were subverting her husband's will in some way, or as if it were a losing cause. It was said jokingly almost, in her grim, Italian, old crone fashion. And as always when her husband was not present, there was an attitude of disrespect to the great Don. (392–93)

All Puzo's cues toward politicized speech and carnivalization are here: the "natural" signature heralding Mama as beyond or beneath power's notice, the ascription of church power to non-males, the "so he don't go down there," an "impish" acknowledgment of the Don's evil, structurally similar to Sonny and Michael's "grinning" about the family business. With her "grim, Italian old crone" cast, she even resembles Genco on his deathbed and speaks tranquilly the lines he read desperately, from the start "subverting" the Don's worldly authority, as Genco had done with a wink only when he had given up hope. These key conversations between Mama and Kay, the Don and Genco, and the Don and Sonny all represent interviews of intense, if tentative, politicization and dialogue where Don Corleone and his empire might be historicized, where the web of death and mortal terror for souls, for human complicity and responsibility might be faced in real time. Kay, through Puzo's customary silence after politicized speech, does not interrogate her mother-in-law further. Mama Corleone's insight dies with her in another brief "attitude of disrespect to the great Don." Puzo works hardest to suppress these constructions.

Kay can hardly remember who she is or what she has been told, what cause-and-effect relations might apply in her life with Michael. Puzo constructs dialogue for her such as "You're really a gangster then, isn't that so? But I really don't care. What I care about is that you obviously don't love me. You didn't even call me up when you got back home" (361). Such a confused statement begins in moral questioning of a lover but immediately shifts into romance language (anything to be with you, and I was lonely). Kay as moral touchstone is unreliable at best—New England Adams or no Adams. She forgets several times that she has worked out for herself that Michael is, like his father, a murderer, (237, 360–65, 393). In her last attempt at the truth after Carlo Rizzi's murder, she still asks, "[I]s it true?"

Michael's reply is one final, duplicitous performance to deny the charge of being the death-bringer:

> Michael shook his head wearily. "Of course it's not. Just believe me, this one time I'm letting you ask about my affairs, and I'm giving you an answer. It is not true." He had never been more convincing. He looked directly into her eyes. He was using all the mutual trust they had built up in their married life to make her believe him. And she could not doubt any longer. She smiled at him ruefully and came into his arms for a kiss. (436–37)

Michael's speech is a one-man parody of dialogue. Not only is there no "answering word" or chance for one but also the language naming the moment is one of the granting *by his authority* of her rights.[10] The grant is similar to Genco's "rights" on his deathbed, Sonny's after witnessing his father as murderer, or Mama's duties as church "crone." Michael is "letting [her]," "giving [her], and "using" trust, all decisions made unilaterally at his behest and interspersed with the romantic cliché of gazing into her eyes followed by smiles and kisses. The woman has inarticulately been set right. Immediately thereafter, Puzo does give Kay the intuitive knowledge (coded female) of Michael's death-head power through the ritualistic body language of himself and his subordinates, signifying his utter dominance such as "Roman emperors of antiquity, who by divine right held the power of life and death over their fellow men" (437). Kay emerges in the novel's last lines as the new Mama Corleone, praying for the soul of *her* husband, a nice, safe irony, which compartmentalizes one final time Puzo's sharp segmenting of men and women, world and soul, heaven and hell, real authority and transcendant appeals.

In the novel's last paragraph, in almost a parody of powerlessness, of the inability to reach dialogue, Kay "empties" her mind of all she knows—family, anger, rebellion, questions—to become the perfect avatar of popular fiction's lack of memory and consequences. The emptying is actually one of both fiction and history, of dialogized relations and social crimes. Dialogue is driven down beneath or rises above the avenues of power toward prayers, the last transcendant ruse and deflection in Puzo's fiction. Kay ends "with a profound and deeply willed desire to believe, to be heard . . ." (446), but the making of belief has always been denied her in the fiction, and she will not be heard by an earthly power, at least not by this male dominant and its author who powerfully but almost surely accidentally has concluded with a paradigm of the fear of fiction: the chance for the answering word in a text of rich possibility. She is now in league with "the nature of the universe," sharply segregated from *The Godfather*'s historical unconscious, which might include institutions the Corleones buy off and into, such as the courts, the police, and the political structure.

Kay's "profound . . . desire . . . to be heard" is validated by Bakhtin's declaration that "every word is directed toward an *answer* and cannot escape the profound influence of the answering word it anticipates" (*The Dialogic Imagination* 280). Just so does Genco seek to know the "arrangements"; his survival depends on them. Just so must Sonny speak the "family business" of murder to be taken into the novel's authority. The "answering word[s]" demanded from Corleones must be about death and its agency.

- Kay to Michael: *Are you or aren't you a murderer?*

- Genco to the Don: *Can you save me from death?*

- Sonny to the Don: *May I kill for you?*

These questions about the actual powers and influences of the Corleone life-world slip in and around the cracks of the monolithic melodrama. They disturb; they intrigue; and finally, Puzo is not comfortable with them, any more than the Don or Michael. The questions are too sly, too cunning—they blaspheme in pronouncing the forbidden thoughts about the "family business" of "arranged" murders. They must be silenced.[11]

Destiny and Design

To a considerable degree, the value I find in what I consider Puzo's best scenes come from my application of second-order scrutiny to dialogue such as "it's been arranged then?" and "I want to enter the family business." I have become what Booth calls the "intending ironist" whose analysis "is part of the significance the text may acquire" (*The Company We Keep* 39). Dwelling in irony slows immensely the reader of a hurtling melodrama like *The Godfather*. Puzo needs these challenges to the Corleone life world of power and authority. Such subversions suggest power has a performance aspect, that it must be tested by what it is not in order to be power. Authority is created by its subversion, which allows authority to act in a full-blown manner.[12] Genco, Sonny, and Mama Corleone speak the Don's power tentatively, while the "intending ironist," the critic scanning the potential Corleone examples, sanctions irony to make sense of their scenes of power. The discrimination among irony's different levels and intensities always confers authority on the critic-reader and his readings.

Rabinowitz in *Before Reading* codifies this conferral in his categories of popular versus serious reading or, as he ascribes them, readings of *configuration* and readings of *signification*. With readings of configuration, Rabinowitz suggests we read expecting a less complex and ironic plot pattern (188). He stresses that we tend to hold popular and elite fiction up against different backgrounds. An example might be comparing *Princess Daisy* to the world of advertising or to a blockbuster historical romance rather than to *The Portrait of a Lady* or "Daisy Miller." Popular fiction narratives are "predominantly functional, plot-oriented, and metonymic" (Rabinowitz 184). Thus, if I were to read *The Godfather* as a "configurational" text, I would read the Don Corleone–Genco, Don Corleone–Sonny, Michael-Kay, and Kay-Mama scenes as examples of the Don's great power.[13] The specifics of moral judgment would be suspended or not called into play at all in favor of more functional questions such as: Are the Corleones powerful enough? Will the Corleones, especially the Don and Michael, defeat their enemies?

If we read *The Godfather*'s scenes to look for moments when power strains to remain in authority, when power is undercut, we are reading ironically for inconsistencies, for cracks in the Corleone edifice. At the same time, if we assume "popular text," we leap to the assumption that they are cracks in *Puzo*'s edifice as well, that it is not in his intent to stop here and ruminate on the ironies of power, its obfuscations and inhumanities.[14] To bore in so heavily on the ironic reading of these scenes is to perform an elite reading of a popular text, to hold that text accountable in every way to the moral implications of its own statements, either potential or written.

A more character-oriented novel text would focus on the psychological development of the characters in what Rabinowitz calls "operations of signification" (184). *The Godfather* ignores one marvelous opportunity for a dialogized characterization by providing no scenes of Michael Corleone becoming a decorated World War II hero. In the military, in the most traditional popular vision of the American melting pot, the reader could see Michael in the larger America as a peer in conflict and exchange. Yet, in the monologic of Puzo's design, such a scene or scenes would break the hermetic seal on Corleone solidarity and isolation. The reader knows nothing of what Michael learns in the larger historical frame experience. Presumably Puzo has a wary conception of its value,[15] but the ironic reader feels this lost opportunity, the absence and suppression. A life-world experience of great potential is shut down, due to Puzo's iron generic rules of configuration. A dialogue with America is denied as a threat. Michael will not be a Prince Hal among the common people on his way to the complex authority of kingship. Nor did Puzo mean him to be. Dialogizing is always inherently a humbling, a

ceding over, a giving up of essential control in the service of a reintegra-
tion, a further learning. The instrumentalization of this lesson is always
in the design of the author.

Similarly, other vivid scenes in *The Godfather* hang like oases, waiting for connection, in this novel so uninterested in psychological truth.
For example, Tom Hagen's recurring dream of his family and himself
tap-tapping as a group of blind beggars is introduced and then forgotten.
To the ironic reader on the watch for others, outsiders, and doubles, the
potentially rich metaphorical possibilities of Hagen pushing through his
"moral blindness" or coming to sense his guilt are frustrating—but only
if reading for ethical exploration. In popular novels, Rabinowitz writes,
we treat inconsistencies as flaws (188), turning back on their authors the
lack of memory and the "flow" of association. We as interpreters reserve
the right to call "inconsistency" either irony or bad art, and also we may
ironize the entire process at the expense of the author.[16]

At rare moments, authors can place the entire dialogized experience under a complex irony. Consider the plight of Nathaniel Hawthorne's
Goodman Brown, who at his story's end has constructed a belief that an
entire foul and evil dialogized world exists apart from his own consciousness. He feels he must live like a spy within it for the rest of his
days, carrying his own secret interpretation like a tumor on his brain and
his heart. Such a shattering conclusion has extreme reference to the
enchaining of dialogue, its brilliant placement in configuration, and its
emplotment from the realm of signification, its psychological resonance
in the psyche of the central character. Hawthorne complicates the
carnivalesque and achieves an overview through a metacommentary of
the varied levels in the curve of dialogue, the irony of association, and
unconscious thought. Or consider Thomas Pynchon's last rational woman,
Oedipa Maas, in *The Crying of Lot 49*. Her meditations turn entirely on
dialogue's efficacy or delusion, on the metaphors of "inside found" and
"outside lost," on the possibility that dialogue is babble without unity.
Pynchon, too, plays with configurations and signification, makes readers
believe "belief" with Oedipa about the importance of plot as good detective fiction must, and then cuts away any metonymic chain in favor of
reflexive meaning and hypothesis.

Such championing of the complex layering of Hawthorne and
Pynchon could stipulate a choice for an elite reading and for metaphysical speculation. No matter how expressed, in the service of no matter
what logic, an author always writes authoritative discourse in one way
or another. Authors have designs, and when they follow the logic of their
designs, their characters *may* have destinies. In reading popular authors
through elite critical rhetoric, we usually don't grant characters their
"destinies" but rather play devil's advocate and see how the authors
have persuaded us of the destinies set up for characters such as Vito and
Michael Corleone. In reading elite authors, we sometimes say that char-

acters who are caught in destinies are tragic. What is the difference between Design and Destiny in the roles of, for example, two prominent patriarchs, Thomas Sutpen in Faulkner's *Absalom, Absalom!* (1936) and Vito Corleone in *The Godfather*? Most fundamentally, Sutpen acknowledges a design, and Faulkner shows it to be blind, immoral, and wounding. Sutpen will not acknowledge women, children, or "others"; he is the "demon" (to Rosa Coldfield), brooding over his design, not helping anyone else, monomaniacally not a godfather. Faulkner is unrelenting on this score. Sutpen is as a bewildered author with a balky, unfinished text; he wonders aloud to General Compson where he made his mistake (263).

Puzo does not give Don Corleone the consciousness of a design; the Don "instinctively" makes correct choices. He responds at certain moments in his historical life to perceived class and economic oppression and thereby shapes his destiny; it is not a particular purpose held in planned intention. Everything about destiny suggests it gains power from an absent figure or figuration, one predetermined, fore-ordained, out of the province of human will. To get to this point, popular fiction launders design as plan or intention into destiny. Here is one reason why Sonny's death at the tollbooth in *The Godfather* carries no resonance, whereas, in *Absalom, Absalom!* Charles Bon's murder of Henry Sutpen before the gates of Sutpen's Hundred is shattering. Sutpen does not believe in destiny but in design; Don Corleone believes in destiny but takes no responsibility for design. In popular fiction, characters and authors do not speculate on interlocking roles of paternity and authorship. Such speculation would overturn configuration, of reading for the plot.

In *Absalom, Absalom!*, the magisterial demand by Bon, the son, is "Acknowledge me, Father." In *The Godfather*, the phantom collective demand from all the undialogized victims and chains of implication to the Corelones is never one of "acknowledge your historical reality, your crimes in America." The critic-reader of *Absalom, Absalom!* reads in line with what Bon asks as both son and victim, representing Sutpen's true American historical reality. However, the reader-critic of *The Godfather* is more like Bon before the gates, waiting for a sign, anything that will show Puzo aware of a moral dilemma of suffering caused, of havoc wreaked. Bon's cry "Acknowledge me" becomes the popular fiction critic's "acknowledge your progeny, your fiction." Such criticism calls for the sort of self-scrutiny, of *irony*, that authority in popular fiction never allows, that popular authors never undertake in their texts.

Fathers have designs, while sons have destinies. Authors have designs, while characters have destinies. Critics of moral persuasion want to refer characters' destinies back to novelistic designs. When an author in question appears to resist this probe in the fiction or to play dumb, the critic smells a rat and retaliates by ironizing the author's configuration process for his own ends of playing against the author for meaning rather than suggesting the author unfolds ever newer and widening meanings.

Without "inconsistencies as flaws" (Rabinowitz 188), the critic of popular fiction has no material to work with beyond the continual affirmation of characters' triumphs in the plot. The critic reader finds the author's pattern. The inconsistency is not "arranged, then" by the popular author, says the critic-reader but remains outside any pattern of unity in a chaos of signification.

Bakhtin again brings us back to fundamentals of our critical scrutiny: what does it mean to say what we mean in our collision of accents and voices—as authors, characters, readers, critics. Bakhtin writes of novelists who are "deaf to organic double-voicedness and to the internal dialogization of living and evolving discourse," that they will "never comprehend, or even realize, the actual possibilities and tasks of the novel as a genre" (327). He uses descriptions such as "naively self-confident," "obtusely stubborn unity," and "pure single-voiced language" to describe such novelistic language. These descriptions apply to characters within novels as well, especially to the Corleones and their mystique of the one, the powerful, the united—the father and the word of the father, the law.

The structures and conceptualizations of popular fiction are authoritarian and monologic. When we begin to speak of a politics of characterization, what system does an author choose for his autocratic state, his oligarchy, his novel? One voice? A confession? A few privileged voices? A polyphony? A complex frame? Even if characters are granted some sort of contingent freedom by an author, it is still the author's choice to do so with certain characters' destinies ensuing, if not recontained by irony. What Bakhtin wants to conceive is nothing less than the ultimate mimesis, the full field of social reality. Popular fiction shrinks from the task and is escaping the full description of reality's forces all the time. Analyzing the points of collision between key characters in the fiction often exposes the ideology of the text's production. If we find where myth collides with fiction, monologue with dialogue, that is where we will find popular fiction's management of narrative in the service of the unitary and the totalized description, explanation, or solution. We also find there the popular novel's power, but it may well be one that the critic labors into creation, demanding that the law judge the authorial design of a Mario Puzo in creating the destiny of the Corleones.

With such demands, the popular fiction critic cuts himself off from the popular readership and from a kinship with the author. Barthes in *Mythologies* concludes that the mythologist "attempts to find again under the assumed innocence of the most unsophisticated relationships, the profound alienation which this innocence is meant to make one accept" (156). Bakhtinian dialogic animates and forces this alienation into producing the evidence with which to confront the father, the author. Authority has its inevitable (but not inevitably evasive) design and destiny. The popular fiction critic's voice is always another authoritative voice that hopes to become an internally persuasive one.

chapter four

The Godfather and the Ethnic Ensemble

I'll tell you one thing you didn't learn from [Don Corleone]: talking the way you're talking now. There are things that have to be done and you do them and you never talk about them.

—Tom Hagen to Michael Corleone, *The Godfather*

I want them to grow up to be All-American kids, real All-American, the whole works.

—Michael Corleone, *The Godfather*

"I warned you, " Jules said.
"You didn't warn me right," Johnny said with cold anger.

—Jules Segal and Johnny Fontane, *The Godfather*

Gino turned his back to hide his face. "The Japs just attacked the United States," he said. He turned up the radio and drowned out all the voices in the room.

—Gino Corbo, *The Fortunate Pilgrim*

The Bakhtinian speech act analysis of key conversations in *The God-father* conducted in chapter 3 attempts to bring forth the principles of authority on which the Corleone *verbal* empire is founded. In the pronouncements and answering words of family members and outsiders, *The Godfather* charts a course in which the family triumphs in violence over its enemies. Yet such a formalist analysis, vital to the understanding of how moral issues are addressed by any author and any fiction, needs to be enhanced by reading Puzo as an Italian American author. Dialogics identifies the power relations within each speech act but does not, in and of itself, ethnically mark such relations. What happens if we expand our view to hypothesize reading Puzo ethnically according to gesture, language, and shared knowledge of intent between Italian American subjects? His ritualized scenes then take on different meanings. For example, if I state that Genco calls on their death-dealing past to make his pleas to the Don, the richness of the language and gestural forms they share must underwrite the praxis of the deathbed scene. Their base of power and their murderers' bond is strongly influenced by their boyhood friendship as well as by the long and terrible history of Sicily as the deep background historicization; how they articulate it is through an ethnic semiosis.

Thus a more universalizing critical approach such as Bakhtin's can be particularized by contemporary multiethnic concepts and applications. If Bakhtin's maxim is that the author is inevitably to be found at the center of organization in his novel, where all levels intersect, how can a reading of *The Godfather* be enhanced by opening Puzo's ethnic encyclopedia and reviewing the markers at his command and those that, in effect, write him as well? Ethnic semiosis can complement other models with an enriched description of speech acts and plot transactions that recast *The Godfather*'s major dialogic confrontations as ethnically "performed" within specific occasions, according to rules. To read *The Godfather* ethnically blind is to cast about for a more universal theoretical criterion, which Bakhtin satisfies. To read *The Godfather* through ethnic semiosis is to read partially through *bella figura*, an essentially unselfconscious genre of performance that does not yield to a literary criticism searching for characters' privileged individual consciousness but one that reveals the shape of narrative energies crucial to our understandings of the novel and *Godfather* films.

Part of the strategy of reading *The Godfather* ethnically is to counter those readings with Puzo's achievement in his critically acclaimed *Fortunate Pilgrim* (1964). What aspects of *The Fortunate Pilgrim* stand over and above *The Godfather* as in-depth explorations of ethnic passage in America in a commitment to realism? *The Fortunate Pilgrim*'s powerful ethnic semiosis proves Puzo is writing through his "gifts," not "below" them, and creating an ethnic novel of power. By reading some key scenes in *Pilgrim* against their possible counterpart scenes in *The Godfather*, we may note the closing down, the non-nuanced structural and sensible bareness of the blockbuster text. To explain the dialogic and ethnic power of *The Fortunate Pilgrim* is to focus quarrels with *The Godfather*'s lack of literariness on the one hand and to show other narrative roads taken by Puzo, other choices made.

A host of multiethnic strategies can make *The Godfather* resonate. The work of critics such as Werner Sollors and William Boelhower, for example, give us key concepts such as the difference between *consent* and *descent* narratives in ethnic literature (Sollors) and the importance of ethnically articulated type-scenes in American frame settings such as family weddings and traditional family dinners in an ethnic semiosis (Boelhower).[1] Furthermore, the entire repertoire of Italianita, including the gestural politics and social scripts of *bella figura* do much to explain in greater detail the verisimilitude that Puzo was striving for, a mimesis generally unavailable to the larger fictional audience as well as to the critical one without such specification. Thus chapters 3 and 4 together provide a full introduction to *The Godfather*'s language as performance. To grasp the ethnic semiosis of the novel is to be educated past high critical estrangement from the popular ethnic novel to something like a thick description of its aura. What appear to be the evasions practiced by Puzo and characters when seen through Bakhtin's categories can also be called perfectly pitched examples of Italian American voice and gesture when looked at as ethnic performance, no longer a segregated category but one more fully dialogic with moral consequence. To find out through ethnic analysis *how* power and authority are negotiated by Puzo does not explain his equivocations just because we may find them more culture-specific by casting them in a more dramatic light. Such would be another critical fallacy to let Puzo and the Corleones off the hook. Yet the contextualization provided by describing Puzo through the ethnic ensemble is an essential complement to dialogics.

Ethnic Semiosis

Puzo published his one really autobiographical essay "Choosing a Dream" in *The Godfather Papers* (1972) at the pinnacle of his success after the novel's best-selling ride and the emormous acclaim of the first *Godfather* film. In "Choosing," he admitted his great ambivalence about Italianita and an ethnic American identity, his bemused view of his own celebrity status, and his life-long infatuation with art. All his views were rendered in a literary and cultural climate that had not yet begun to codify and really celebrate multiethnic American fiction nor provide a critical climate within which a novelist might see him- or herself or take a stand. Given Puzo's subsequent indifference right up to the end of his life to scholars and critics conceptualizing his own ethnic writer's career or anyone else's, it's doubtful that his writing novels at a later juncture during the critical sanctioning and establishment of multiethnic or "border" literature would have made any impression on him or his work. Chapter 2 has chronicled Puzo's long love affair with art, the ways in which he believed his immersion in art might save his life and counter his poverties, both real and imagined. His ethnic identity as Italian American was encoded in overt and covert fashion in his novels for decades. No ethnic criticism clearly explains Puzo's work; however, we note some of its key precepts before reading selections from *The Godfather* and *The Fortunate Pilgrim* with the help of its corrective lenses.

Boelhower's *Through a Glass Darkly: Ethnic Semiosis in American Literature* (1987) remains the most provocative theorizing about the influence and different forms that the ethnic subject can take in American fiction. Boelhower argues that the ethnic sign is everywhere in American fiction and that ethnic writing is American writing (3). He conceives of an "inclusive transcontextuality . . . whereby to act as one of two terms (assimilation and Americanization versus pluralism and ethnification) . . . means immediately to summon the other term" (33). To be Italian American in America is to always contain within an action, utterance, or thought the interpenetration of the answering reality, either one of ethnic origin or American national environment. Both terms are fluid and ongoing, neither is inherently dominant. *Habitare* is the word Boelhower borrows from Gaston Bachelard to embody the concept of "the spatial unfolding of the proposition 'I Am' " (43). *Habitare* is born of national origin and geography and sites the clash and crisis of ethnic interaction. Boelhower's strongest oppositions within this unfolding are between the Native Americans and their Puritan European antagonists; the Puritan internal landscape was ruled by a literary-religious vision of a biblical new land and frames Boelhower's strongest intimation about the "Americans," their absolute dependence on a mapped and written narrative, whereas the Native Americans inhabit the land itself without an allegorical script.

Boelhower's sustained clash of perceptual and configuring sensibilities does not yield a "communicative exchange" as much as a juxtaposition of two opposing views of space, which can move out into oppositions on views of history, self-hood, community, and citizenship. The great European migration to America at the end of the nineteenth century places Boelhower's dynamic under reversed conditions from that of the Puritans and Native Americans. Now the Puritans have their national script firmly in place, and their first foes, the Native Americans, have "vanished" into convenient tales of "removal" and are praised in nostalgia for their "naturalness." Their literal threat as killer antagonists contesting for real land has been absorbed into the American narrative though they themselves have not assimilated. The *habitare* of the Sicilian and southern Italian immigrants in 1900 is then both similar and dissimilar to Boelhower's earlier colonial model. They flee after centuries of domination in a harsh and poor natural landscape where they are oppressed peasants, not mystical forest conservators. Illiterate, they possess no national script nor facility in the new land's language. They have no civil traditions, preserve a fierce family identity, and fear all central governments with their institutions of police and courts. The American *habitare* that they confront is an abstract land of rights, privileges, and freedoms underwriting a grid of mapped townships, constitutions, and bills of rights, subdivided into powers of state, city, and town governments. Immigrants are always expected to live up to the ideal construction of citizenship in this space, while the physical and demographic reality of the United States is precisely the constant historical arrival of disparate immigrant groups with their own *habitare*.

Thus the Italian or any immigrant advance into America is that of the oppressed, moving into the new land without maps, from subjugation to subjugation, from the bottom to the bottom. If the American Puritan colonist said, "[T]his is where my boundaries are," in a cognitive and historical-religious mapping of their interior-exterior landscapes, Boelhower conceives the Native American saying "[T]his is where my body is" (56). To enable themselves to reword their own narratives, the modern ethnic immigrants must become the new Native Americans, assumed to be "vanishing" into the national narrative and its subscribers as part of the American covenant with new arrivals. In a substitution, they must give up body for script, not as in aboriginal vanishing beyond both mapped territory and consciousness but vanishing into the national pool in a somewhat more complex and somber recasting of the melting pot. The question that so many ethnic narratives pose to the national story becomes, what is the relation of being doubly counted out (as peasants at home, as immigrants abroad) to being "Chosen?" For Puzo's Sicilian Americans in *The Godfather* are recalcitrant and obstinate "Injuns" with no urge to become part of America's fashioned tale and are resolved to grimly live out their own prior history within American borders and dispensations.

Puzo is Neapolitan, and such are the subject characters in *The Fortunate Pilgrim*. For *The Godfather*, Puzo chose to write about Sicilians, long burdened with a rich and dark history within Italian culture itself.[2] Indeed, *The Godfather*'s dominion over Italian American signification in American culture gave rise to the curious fact that after 1969, to the average American popular culture consumer, Italian Americans *are* Sicilians; they are represented by Mafia hoodlums and their enterprising murderous families to the exclusion of any other complex network of groups. If the Mafia and Sicily become convenient Others in American culture, a colorful lawless peasant population of violence and repressed passion within mainstream America, it appears that as literary or narrative subjects, these very Southern Italians now function as American southerners in the popular imagination, and Sicily perhaps becomes a geographical annex akin to signifiers such as Alabama or Mississippi. Sicily is symbolically akin to the American Deep South, a region traditionally scapegoated but also rendered earthier, more dramatic, and alive in its melodramatic representation. In the popular fantasy, lives there are more grotesque, poverty and illiteracy endemic, and fierce prejudices give rise to clan warfare. In literary terms, the Sicilians are positively Faulknerian in their mythic intransigence, patriarchal domination, and tragic, unyielding sense of honor. Luigi Barzini has observed that Italy is still somewhat of a pagan country, that religion spreads a thin veneer over older customs (45), and that "Sicily is the schoolroom model of Italy for beginners, with every Italian quality and defect magnified, exasperated, and brightly colored" (252) and thus perfect for popular fiction and melodrama.

A cursory look at Sicilian history proves that no other national group of early-twentieth-century American immigrants could possibly come from as deep a feudal past nor have such suggestive multiple lines to an American national script. Vito Andolini arrives at Ellis Island in 1901 and takes the name of Corleone, his native town in Sicily. He comes at the outset of the great Southern Italian migration to the United States. By 1924, 85 percent of the five million Italian immigrants arriving in the United States were from the South, and of those, the vast number were illiterate farm workers or laborers (Gambino 78, 114; Lopreato 103). Their social relationships in the new world were likely to be based almost entirely on kinship ties.[3] Education was mistrusted and the organs of government even more so. Sicily itself had been a colonized land, continually vulnerable to invasions from both Christian and Muslim North African worlds. Over the centuries from the Phoenicians, Crusaders, and Norsemen to the Habsburgs and Bourbons, all inhabitants of Europe's Mediterranean rim had their run at Sicily. Sicilians then are something like rugged rural Americans of many backgrounds with drops of racial and religious hybridizing. Such a historical reality might have yielded a first millennial pluralism or melting pot, but no such institutions were in store for Sicily, whose utter geographic vulnerability in the mid-Mediterranean never allowed the island to flourish in any isolation or idealism. The endless succession of governments in the major cities such as Palermo and Messina often made little difference in the interior of the island, which was seldom controlled by any legal or policing system (Smith xv). Indeed, Puzo appropriates Corleone, a rugged and isolated hillside town in the middle of empty western Sicily, the name of which becomes as famous in American popular literature as the fictional Peyton Place.

The Mafia itself is a very old institution in Sicily but most often loosely confederated within different regions as late as the midnineteenth century. The meanings of *mafia* are disparate, and while it has been used by Sicilians to refer to criminal organizations, it also has meant "good," "fine," and "admirable" (Gambino 268). Such range in meaning is almost inherently melodramatic in its potential for good versus evil within a mafia context. Furthermore, in the traditional interpretation of *mafia*, its criminal activity was only a means, never an end, because the chief object was to gain power and respect, with wealth merely an instrument. However, Barzini notes it's most likely that the trouble the Mafia defends one from is almost always controlled by the Mafia itself, that "such a rough and archaic form of justice" destroys all concepts of public virtue and state cohesion (255, 275). Faith in public authority did not increase in Sicily after Italian Unification in 1860 but actually decreased, and no sense of social obligation existed among Sicilians (D. Smith 466).

It is difficult to imagine an ethnic immigrant group more hostile to all forms of the American civil contract and promise than the Sicilians. To read *The Godfather* for American traces, for American influences and thematics, is heavy labor. The Corleones move through their isolated world according to their lights, with America remaining a deeply mistrusted territory. Most of the characters with whom they interact in the novel are also Sicilian in origin except for appointed outsiders (Tom Hagen, Kay Adams, Jack Woltz, Jules Segal, Moe Greene). Thus it's crucial for readers to crack the code of Italian American social exchange. To begin, almost all commentators on Italian life from sociologists to historians remark on its performative aspects in speech and gesture. Plain speaking without nuance is in itself a foreign language in Italy and one greatly derided at most junctures in *The Godfather* as well. *Bella figura* is the attention to form of presentation governing social situations and the code that expresses an individual's public utterance and social script (Nardini xiii; Gardaphe 20). *Bella figura* governs oral communication and shapes its social pragmatics while providing its theatre. Such presentation crucially stresses "being impeccable before the eyes of others" (Nardini 11), especially in public appearances where indirectness and forms rule over frank exchange. To know *bella figura* and observe its rules is to survive and prosper in *The Godfather*. For a Corleone to become impetuous, imprudent, impatient, to "not get the message," is to place the family at considerable risk and its enemies in real danger.

Such indirection in language and its interpretation comprises a "hidden meaning" not unlike the one in another semantic register posited by New Critical reading practices through veneration of Jamesian maxims such as "the figure in the carpet," the theme running through a narrative that suddenly is made visible through informed reading. Here the "figure" is kinetic and fluid, passing ephemerally from speaker to speaker, determined by the social setting, the power relations, the aims and goals of the participants, and, not least, by gender, race, class, and ethnicity. It's not just Italian and Italian American social presentation that is governed by conventions and rules but rather all praxis, yet literary criticism often reifies language itself at the expense of its setting and intent. Our modernist masters of Imagism and verbal precision decanted perhaps in Pound's "petals on a wet, black bough," or Williams's red wheelbarrow or Eliot's great fear of words that crack, slide, and will not hold their meanings still key elite readers to mistrust flourish and overdetermined gestural communication. It's too much altogether and not taste-ful at all. Figural indirection and a hidden ethnic narrative are not credited by elite literary criticism, which wants to elide a social situation as a mere surface phenomenon. However, in *The Godfather*, we must learn to read a euphemism as strategic and significant, not "imprecise," "slack," or "banal," some of the code words used to discredit the language of popular fiction.

Performing *The Godfather*

I would like ultimately to revisit Genco in the hospital during Don Corleone's final stop on Connie's wedding day to see if, armed with the precepts of *bella figura*, we might contextualize Puzo's equivocations as verisimilar cultural performance. Before such a visit, I want to look at other scenes in book 1 of *The Godfather*, which at times appears to be an etiquette manual for *bella figura* in which the family conducts business, feints and parries with an outside American world, marries off a daughter and loses a son (Michael) to exile in Sicily.

The Godfather begins in a New York criminal courtroom where Amerigo Bonasera, aspiring American, waits for sentence to be pronounced against the two young Anglo men who have savagely beaten his daughter. According to traditional Sicilian belief, such a civic environment of American law and order is precisely antithetical to any place where Puzo's Sicilian Americans can hope for justice. When the two men receive a suspended sentence because of their "fine families" (10), Bonasera knows "they have made fools of us" (11), and he must go to Don Corleone. The novel takes its leave of the American justice system immediately and plunges into the Corleone world where Bonasera is proven to be a Sicilian who has lost all his knowledge of how forms must be observed and ritualized in order to survive coherently. In short, he must be shorn of his "Amerigo" status, and his reeducation is a lesson that is taught through *bella figura*. In Bonasera's long interview with Don Corleone, he and the reader learn "how to read" the ethnic type-scene in its particular frame, that of a powerlessness asking power for vengeance against an external foe; Bonasera learns how to properly approach that court and judge.

Bonasera commits errors in both judgment and lack of supplication. He has gone to the police, believed in the courts, two decisions that deeply offend Don Corleone; however, he allows Bonasera to whisper to him his request, which is to kill the young men. When the Don replies, "That I cannot do. You are being carried away," Bonasera overturns all the delicacy of negotiation when he says "loudly, clearly, 'I will pay you anything you ask.' On hearing this, Hagen flinched, a nervous flick of his head. Sonny Corleone folded his arms, smiled sardonically as he turned from the window to watch the scene in the room for the first time" (31). Hagen's "flinch" establishes him as something like the bella figura parliamentarian for *The Godfather*, the one who knows and cites the Sicilian Rules of Order in performance. As the outsider turned passionate insider, Tom often corrects verbal conduct from Michael, Sonny, Jack Woltz, and Kay Adams Corleone. Bonasera has "blasphemed" like Genco, speaking of death without the proper euphemisms, calling into the open all the violence that the family has at its command. He is "being carried away" outside the proper forms. So egregious is his error that even the headstrong Sonny "sardonically" begins to listen intently to the performance. Such cues that draw Hagen and Sonny into scrutiny of the unfolding dialogue are strong hints to the reader that what is unfolding is both significant and heavily ritualized. The real unfolding of the plot (signification of the Don's power) is within the ethnic semiosis of their exchange, the aura that drives the scene.

Since Bonasera has broken the respectful frame of supplicant to the great Don on his daughter's wedding day, Don Corleone's "voice rang like cold death." Death is now in the room, and Bonasera will get a verbal lesson in what happens when *bella figura* is replaced by *brutta figura*. In the ensuing paragraph, the Don speaks through Bakhtinian authoritative discourse beginning with the classic powerful opening "No. Don't speak." He continues by using the pronoun *you* thirteen times to characterize Bonasera's "Americanization" and to distance himself from this hybridized creature ("you do not ask with respect," "you do not offer me your friendship," "you come into my home on the bridal day of my daughter and you ask me to do a murder"). Language is so powerful that "speaking death" is indeed bringing it into the home, especially obscene since the Corleone business *is* murder, and *bella figura* strives mightily to erase that fact. To fight Bonasera's breaking the frame, the Don responds in kind, even to the point of "scornful mimicry." To prove how stately performance has gone awry, the Don answers in mock performance, then modulates back into *bella figura* with "what have I ever done to make you treat me so disrespectfully?" (31). Bonasera's answer is a concise list of American "errors"—"America has been good to me. I wanted to be a good citizen. I wanted my child to be an American" (32)—that comprise good luck, civic duty, and assimilation, but such a profession of faith in the new land only raises the stakes as the Don in "cruel and contemptuous irony" rips his naive notions and then parodically tells him to forgive, to put away his un-American madness, for "life is full of misfortunes."

Bonasera's final desperate cry is "How much shall I pay you?" and the Don's decision is not further anger in mock dialogue but the "dismissal" one might give to an uncomprehending child. There's no way to bring Bonasera back within the forms the occasion demands. In another situation or set of circumstances, the feeling "but I cannot reason with this man" might bring death in *The Godfather* and often does. Here the Don wearily repeats the litany of "you" on the theme of "if you had come to me" your enemies "would fear you" (33). Finally Bonasera succumbs, bows his head, and proffers the correct ritualized response: "Be my friend. I accept." With verbal order restored at last after Bonasera's inchoate dismissal of the forms, the Don may conclude the interview with the famous words, "Some day, and that day may never come, I will call upon you to do me a service in return. Until that day, consider this justice a gift from my wife, your daughter's godmother" (33). The

Don has placed a premium on bringing Bonasera back within the ethnic world of speech forms after the failure of the petitioner's direct "American" approach.

Such a scene almost needs its visual recreation for full effect, which is why the *Godfather* films are so expressive of *bella figura* when the printed page may not as successfully convey the ethnically inflected transaction.[4] Coppola is crucially aware of the spatial positioning of Corleone power. The continuing image of the Godfather's chair threads its way through his *Godfather* trilogy. Beginning with the Don's greeting the wedding day guests in his darkened home office, the chair takes on grave significance: who will fill it after the Don is gone? Sonny dies violently, Fredo is incompetent, Michael ascends to the chair, and Coppola takes care to photograph him carefully from below as he spreads his arms out to cover the chair in *Godfather II*. Al Pacino as Michael is a compact young man, yet the camera angles make him massive in that chair where by the end of *Godfather I* he receives his subjects. The second film opens with the shot of the Don's empty chair, as if to stress the effort Michael must make to hold together the family's power in light of changing circumstances. The film concludes with Michael behind the darkened glass of his Tahoe window as Fredo is killed in the boat by Al Neri. Finally, in *Godfather III*, the last image of an aged, shrunken Michael is of him toppling off a bare chair into the Sicilian dust, having been stunned into catatonic old age by the murder of his daughter.

While Don Corleone must shift back and forth between correct form and his exasperation at form's breakdown, for an outsider such as Kay Adams, the Corleone environment is truly mysterious. As an emissary from nonethnic America, Kay's education in *bella figura* is of the longest standing in the novel. She begins by thinking her driver-escorts to her New York hotel (Clemenza and Paulie Gatto) were "wildly exotic. Their speech was movie Brooklynese and they treated her with exaggerated courtesy" (48). Kay begins as no more than a naive reader of the Family. She ends with the deepest knowledge as the woman prisoner in their myth. Jack Woltz, the Jewish American Hollywood movie producer (to be discussed at length in chapter 5) represents a different sort of "*Godfather* reader." He comes replete with his own power that is not family based but backed by the American government and system: he counts J. Edgar Hoover as a personal friend. When Tom Hagen goes to California to persuade Woltz to give Johnny Fontane a major role in an upcoming film, he and Woltz inhabit different worlds of dialogue. Woltz explodes in threats, making "his face a mask of anger," while Hagen "listened patiently." "Never make a threat," Hagen intones to himself, "never get angry." "The word 'reason' sounded so much better in Italian, *rajunah* [italics Puzo], to rejoin" (57). Puzo attempts to educate his readers to the full cultural meaning in the Italian language word choice. In this context, the Irish American adopted Italian American son goes back into the lists with the Jewish American movie mogul. He dangles possible financing of Woltz's film to give Woltz a graceful retreat into self-interest in order to justify a contract for Johnny. Woltz says "patronizingly," "this picture is budgeted at five million." Real money, like real death, is always in bad form within the Corleone speech acts, but Woltz presses his error, "what will it cost me to have that labor trouble cleared up? In cash. Right now?" (61). Hagen chooses his reply carefully. Since Woltz has broken through the delicate indirection of Corleone aid, Hagen says, "You are deliberately misunderstanding me. You are trying to make me an accomplice to extortion. Mr. Corleone promises only to speak in your favor on this labor trouble as a matter of friendship in return for your speaking on behalf of his client. A friendly exchange of influence, nothing more" (61).

Woltz calls this "the Mafia style. . . . All olive oil and sweet talk when what you're really doing is making threats" (62). However, as on the mark this statement is, Woltz as a critic of *bella figura* loses reader support when he continues with a harangue of sexual jealousy against Johnny Fontane who stole his starlet girlfriend. Woltz ends with his embarrassing admission that "a man in my position . . . can't afford to look ridiculous" (62). Like Johnny himself, Woltz is letting sex get in the way of business, and Hagen knows "in the Corleones' world, the physical beauty, the sexual power of women, carried not the slightest weight in worldly matters" (62). The interview collapses. Woltz calls the Corleones thugs; Hagen reminds him that Johnny is a godson; Woltz threatens to use influence at the White House. Hagen concludes much as Don Corleone had with Bonasera that "the guy was taking his words at their sentimental face value. He was not getting the message" (63).

The first seventy pages of *The Godfather* are obsessively about how to read the world of the Godfather, how to understand the Corleone initiatives, and what they care about but, most important, *how* they go about protecting and negotiating what they called "Cosa Nostra." This world is relentlessly made up of indirect speech forms in specific contexts. Boelhower suggests that ethnicity is the practice of "digging up cultural origins," a "way of staying behind," of "rediscovering place" (64). In the case of speech forms in *The Godfather*, such radical tracks cross the alignment of rhetoric and intent, with the map held by the Sicilian Americans. They force their more Americanized counterparts into these speech forms; judge them wanting in delicacy, morality, tact, strength; and conclude that they should lose their business, their racehorse, their lives. Such is the power of *bella figura* in *The Godfather*'s opening chapters that all characters, Sicilian and American, are reinvented through comprehension or miscomprehension of the language performance. As a rule-bound primer of the language and forms that cohere in the reasons and philosophy behind the carnage to come, *The Godfather*'s opening is as concise and meticulously presented as that in any Italian American fiction generally called its better.[5]

Michael's Gaze

Without question the *Godfather* films endorse the monolithic power so tightly constructed through *bella figura* and its forms. Yet the novel itself, a looser vehicle with conflicting impulses on Puzo's part (family melodrama, Hollywood novel, Las Vegas novel, Sicilian historical romance), breaks open *bella figura* from the inside at junctures where the Corleones argue and appraise each other from very different vantage points within the family. When they are off duty or not enlisted in a war, how do they see themselves and their rituals? Boelhower writes that ethnic semiotics is "nothing more or less than the interpretive gaze of the subject whose strategy of seeing is determined by the very ethno-symbolic space of the possible world he inhabits" (86). In looking at Michael Corleone's view of his own family *habitare*, we can see how he brings a hybridized perspective to Italianita.

Michael's ethnic passage in *The Godfather* is a complicated one. When the novel opens, he's the decorated war hero fresh from a semester at Dartmouth, bringing his New England girlfriend to a family wedding. We see no real internal battle in Michael, who has no reveries or impulses to break away from family into America. The reader is presented with Michael's heroic status as a given at the outset. Kay may have the presidential name of *Adams*, but Michael's war feats are presented with more than a little hint at John F. Kennedy and PT 109, an Irish American son with a true American father and godfather who wants to prove his courage equal to that of an older son and brother. To Sonny and the Don's surprise, Michael "enlisted and fought over the Pacific Ocean. He became a Captain and won medals. In 1944 his picture was printed in *Life* magazine with a photo layout of his deeds" (17). When Michael brings Kay to Connie's wedding, he's outside the ethnic scene, floating between his family and America. He's much more open and relaxed with her than he ever will be again. In telling her about Luca Brasi, his inflections and interior thoughts are reckless in light of *bella figura*: "[T]he hell with it, he thought. He said straight out . . ." (24). After regaling Kay with Luca's body count in the "famous olive oil war," "He smiled as if it were a joke" (24). Michael begins as a chronicler of local color, a commentator on the family. He tells of the Don's "reasoning" with a band leader to allow Johnny Fontane to be released from a personal services contract; the negotiations came down to "his signature or his brains . . . on that document" (42–43). Puzo stresses not so much the tale but its telling: Michael "told her. He told her without being funny. He told it without pride. He told her without any sort of explanation" (42). Michael is not invested, not Sicilian, not in performance. He could be a generic *Godfather* reader recalling a favorite anecdote.

On the day Vito Corleone is shot by Sollozzo, Michael and Kay make love in a New York hotel and then go to see *Carousel*, "and its sentimental story of a braggart thief made them smile at each other with amusement" (78). Puzo cites the American popular culture's most renowned melting pot entertainment, the American musical with its class, racial, and ethnic lines always highlighted, then recontained in moral statements.[6] More important, Michael and Kay share the cinematic referential joke to his family and knowledge of its reputation. Coming out of the play, Kay spots the screaming newspaper headline: VITO CORLEONE SHOT. ALLEGED RACKET CHIEF CRITICALLY WOUNDED (79), and Michael's world is "destined" to change more radically than his enlistment after Pearl Harbor. Yet the change is not a metamorphosis but a gradual "consent" to affirm his "descent." He begins by becoming the "go-fer" in the Corleone compound as Sonny tries to shield him from the violence to come, according to the Don's wishes. Michael is not to become part of the family business, which in the novel's logic means he must remain outside the ethnic frame as well. Sonny says, "You hang around me, Mike, you're gonna hear things you don't wanta hear" (92), again stressing the truth in language, the murderous orders about to be given. To break through Sonny's prohibitions, Michael stands up and yells, " 'You lousy bastard, he's my father. I'm not supposed to help him? . . . Stop treating me like a kid brother. I was in the war. I got shot, remember? I killed some Japs. What the hell do you think I'll do when you knock somebody off? Faint?' " (92–93). Michael's speech here contains several inflections: the chosen younger son, the American war veteran, the killer "for strangers" who now demands his manhood. He claims fitness for duty in the family war by what he has done in the American war, and he does so in an American exchange, equal to equal, no equivocation of embellishment, no delicacy of *bella figura*. What characterizes Michael's exchanges with Sonny and Tom Hagen, indeed with and among all the male Corleone conspirators and members of war councils, is the absolute dropping of masks when alone together, the jettisoning of *bella figura*. Even Sonny can enter into the carnivalization of the old Don when he's not present: "his voice held a faint trace of Italian accent. He was consciously mocking his father just to kid around" (131).

However, Michael remains outside the crisis emotionally, still identifying with Kay and doing bemused commentary on the family. When she asks if she can go with him to visit the Don in the hospital, he parries with a mock *Daily News* headline: "Girl from old Yankee family mixed up with son of big Mafia chief. How would your parents like that?" (113); Kay responds that her parents never read the *Daily News*. This exchange proves Michael is still in secondary sources, configuring the family legend from the outside as something he consumes rather than is consumed by. Kay also states her distance from the events by class commentary on reading tabloids, a Bourdieuian marker, to be sure, and one that, taken together with Michael's parody headline, buffers them from the business of this particular family business. Michael then attends a family council to discuss the status of the war in which all evidence of *bella figura* is completely down, all rhetorical flourish is missing from the dialogue of the insiders for themselves. Each sentence begins declaratively: "Hagen said quietly," "Sonny muttered," "Clemenza said slowly," "Sonny turned to Tessio" (116). As if finally remembering to ethnically mark the scene, Puzo has a button man bring a bowl of spaghetti and some wine. Suddenly Michael appears to scrutinize behavior: "They ate as they talked. Michael watched in amazement. He didn't eat and neither did Tom, but Sonny, Clemenza and Tessio dug in, mopping up sauce with crusts of bread. It was almost comical" (117). What to make of such nervous and awkward ethnic intervention? Puzo strains to keep Michael as commentator, strains too to drop an ethnic type-scene in the midst of a war council. His instincts tell him to find an intending ethnic subject to filter his gaze. The conspirators can't stop long enough to be ethnic. Michael with nothing to do can glimpse the eating, the taste-full afterthought to a Mafia meeting. As Boelhower says, the ethnic sign is often intermittent and weak (85), and Michael before he "makes his bones" functions more as an outsider to the ethnic world of the Corleones, reporting like an anthropologist on the local customs, this time as an informed reader of *The Godfather*. After his jaw is shattered by McCluskey outside the hospital, he loses his viewpoint, privilege, and American status. He's just another Corleone hood in the eyes of the police. He has become educated to his family role. Sonny is the reader's avatar when he explodes at Michael: "I've been sitting here waiting for the last three days, ever since the old man got shot, waiting for you to crack out of that Ivy League, war hero, bullshit character you've been wearing. I've been waiting for you to become my right arm so we can kill those fucks that are trying to destroy our father and our Family" (134).[7]

Sonny provides the signature of the raw primal family imperative, clanlike in its simplicity; it's coupled with the superhero break-out from what appears to Sonny as improbable working-class spokesman as silly, irrelevant American signifiers of education and heroism. When Michael convinces Sonny and Tom to let him avenge the Don, Hagen takes another tack and replies that he shouldn't let the broken jaw influence him, that it was business, not personal. Michael responds, "It's all personal, every bit of business. Every piece of shit every man has to eat every day of his life is personal" (146). Michael now articulates a very different line from that of his bemused spectator at the family window. He is male, visceral, individual, a class-bound action hero speaking for every oppressed man anywhere, refusing to be downtrodden.[8] Men must take things personally; there is no other recourse. Michael notes that his father took his going into the Marines personally. Speaking with all masks down, he asks Tom outright, "how many men do you figure the Don killed or had killed?" (146). Hagen tries to wrest control of the careening narrative back from the angry, converted American hero.[9] In shock, he restores the proper discourse: "I'll tell you one thing you didn't learn from him: talking the way you're talking now. There are things that have to be done and you do them and you never talk about them. You don't try to justify them. They can't be justified. You just do them. Then you forget it" (146–47). Michael is "talking" as an action hero, a loose-lipped champion of the underdog. Hagen favors silence, a man doing what he has to do, with no attempt at moral justification, and no memory. Michael now knows massive resentment; he has become a victim. Hagen tells him direct talk is unbecoming, not in line with Sicilian *omerta*. The two "brothers" provide the simplest rendition of *The Godfather's* ethic of conduct. Consider the scene before the reader in its ethnic hybridity: a Sicilian American war hero's son turned family avenger is upbraided by an Irish Corleone adopted son for not following the correct forms of Italianita. In essence, Tom has assimilated completely to becoming a Corleone, a "country" that he has embraced. All is written under the sign of a familiar popular fiction epiphany: that the hero is forced to go bad because of a wrong so intolerable that it would be unmanly not to take matters into his own hands.

Michael's conversion shows how Puzo neatly adjusts his time periods to counterpoint a world at war with the Corleone world at war. As peace breaks out over the globe in 1945, Michael's retaliatory killing of Sollozzo and McCluskey ushers in a new era of carnage for the Corleones. The last lines of book 1 are "The Five Families War of 1946 had begun" (153). This war sends Michael back overseas in exile, this time to the European theater (Sicily) to truly learn his origins. His second "wartime service," far from cementing his American identity as in the popular melting pot story for millions of American men in World War II, is to insert him firmly back into the Sicilian family cycle of violence in the name of "reason." Puzo un-Americanizes him in a reverse of assimilation or integration of ethnic and American identities. In 1946, after murdering two civilians, the *Life* magazine war hero is walking the barren Sicilian hills with his bodyguards. The American national story of ethnic consent has been arrested and reversed in Puzo's deft diachronic play with destinies.

The Godfather's Silences

In the past several decades, America has become introduced to the concept of *omerta* or silence through immersion in Mafia narratives. *Omerta* is a characteristic of Southern Italian culture and a cornerstone of powerful male authority in negotiation where euphemism is as close to revelation as a speaker gets and a host of aphorisms countenance public silence.[10] Often Don Corleone's power is most terrifyingly demonstrated by his reticence, by his refusal to comment or by forcing his partner in dialogue to bow to the inevitable rightness of his aims. Silence can be performed as it makes other speakers change their responses and subsequent actions. *Omerta* is most strongly demonstrated by the transgression against it. For example, when an overeager Sonny lets Solozzo know he's interested in potential drug business, the Don tells him to "never let anyone outside the family know what you're thinking" (75). Sonny's eagerness sends the message that he, the family heir, can be approached by other families and leads directly to the Don's shooting, which catalyzes the family crisis.

This centuries-old Italian code of *omerta* governing what can or cannot be said according to situation is a male constant that leads to an extraordinary if isolated power. It has lines to several literary and cultural definitions of silence in our time. For example, silence can be an ethnic sign, a narrative strategy, or a modernist signature of the exhaustion and debasement of language. Don Corleone repeatedly reserves comment or silences his opponents in implied threat. Popular fiction in general operates on a principle of silence, a monologue of unbroken, configurational, plot-oriented action without the interstices of reflection and ironic commentary. Popular fiction is silent on questions that go beyond its boundaries and is generally content to reproduce a fictional form of common sense (Bromley in Ashley 154), though the subjects of the fiction are generally the subjects that the culture is deeply interested in (desire, money, morality, power, family). The popular dialogues about these subjects often appear the very antithesis of silence, indeed become a cacophony of voices. The mock-formality in which *The Godfather* unfolds is an anomaly and tends to further mask the philosophical and moral chaos of the novel. *The Godfather* unites both the ethnic silence of the Italian American and the narrative silence of the popular form. The Italian ethnic speech acts through the characters' internal discipline, which is wary of cultural dissent and repercussion, while the popular narrative unfolds through a welter of censoring breaks: need to reach the widest audience, sensationalism, conventional wisdom on serious moral questions, authorial failure to render those questions in depth.

Silence is also a certified elite literature trope expressing an author's thoughts on both personal and historical despair. In Melville's *Pierre* (1852), his hero, caught in a spiraling parody of popular romance's grotesque familial distortions, says of virtue, "If on that point the gods are dumb, shall a pygmy speak?" (321). Hemingway's classic dictum in *The Sun Also Rises* (1926) is Jake Barnes's "You'll lose it if you talk about it," a holding in of one's painfully constructed self against trauma and breakdown. In *A Farewell to Arms* (1929), Hemingway's further commentary on the historical justification of silence is that after World War I "there were many words that you could not stand to hear and finally only the names of places had dignity"; one should only name the sites of battles, "the names of the regiments and the dates" for "abstract words such as glory, honor, courage, or hallow were obscene" (185). The charnel house of the Holocaust has led some contemporary writers to posit silence as perhaps the only acceptable response to the aboriginal catastrophe about which God appears to be silent. Narrative minimalists from Samuel Beckett through Don DeLillo reinforce language's terminal points in a philosophical commitment to Wittgenstein whom DeLillo lauds in *End Zone* as championing silence about what cannot be said: "Two parts to that man's work. What is written. What is not written. The man himself seemed to favor the second part" (233).

What links the Italian American ethnic silence to the silence of modernism in modernity is the need for control and authority, a deeply masculine need exhibited best through a male dominant narration, which, of course, suffuses *The Godfather*. Thus silence is observed and performed by Puzo's Sicilian-Americans in *The Godfather* but is not credited there by elite literary criticism, which wants to privilege silence only when it is metacommentary on language and history, not when it is an ethnically based custom of language and gesture. The mimetic representation of silence in hundreds of pages in Puzo novels carries not so much interest for critics as that expressed in one Beckett title: *The Unnamable*. DeLillo, Italian American fiction's "outed" major novelist after *Underworld* (1997), responded in a 1982 interviewer to the question "Why do reference books give only your date of birth and the publication dates of your books?" He answered, "Silence, exile, cunning and so on. It's my nature to keep quiet about most things" (Interview 20). Not only did DeLillo get away with naturalizing his silence, but he pitched the literati the famous Joycean phrase from *A Portrait of the Artist as a Young Man* where Stephen Dedalus states he will fly by his own nets of religion, family, and country in what becomes recognized as high modernist evasive action. Until quite recently, interviewers would query DeLillo on Wittgenstein, not on his ethnic-linguistic heritage. He had passed into the assimilated canonical discourse of postmodernism, a more legitimate family business. In light of the study of a best-selling author such as Puzo, what's key in DeLillo's response is that he signifies *omerta* in cross-ethnic and elite literary language, but he also appropriates *cunning*, after *destiny*, the most revealing and pervasive word in Puzo's fiction that takes us close to the locus and conception of his power as a writer. Puzo never gets artistic credit for the creation of *his* silences and cunning, which are read as only the ethnic framing of a best-selling author. Popular fiction study never makes the text's language the subject of investigation because it does not render that language as complex or allusive. Popular fiction never dictates to its critics its own agendas, merely its empirical constructs, which critics then turn on with alacrity as under-imagined, over-determined, and ideologically obtuse.

Yet the popular, elite, and ethnic categories of silence share traces in many ways. Puzo attempted to be a Hemingway with his tough guy World War II veterans in *The Dark Arena*. Hemingway's minimalist style became a fundamental narrative voice in popular genres such as the

Western and detective story, and Puzo's Corleones are thus familiar to readers from these other generic contexts. The largest popular frame for silence in the contemporary reading climate is that of "male silence" in general, an inability or refusal to "get in touch with feelings," a refusal to share emotions with others, specifically women. Silence is reinforced as male and negative. Small wonder that it can also be powerfully and conservatively reinvented simply as male power and thus be part of traditional literature's arsenal against "feeling" and emotion, which are relegated in another corner of the popular to female sentimentalism and always pejorative.

Upon his return from Sicily, Michael and Kay have an extended dialogue after sex in which Puzo dramatizes *omerta* from several viewpoints. Michael has been secreted in Sicily after his killing of McCluskey and Sollozzo. During his time there he married Apollonia and watched her die in a revenge assassination. Kay chides him that he could have written her, that she "would have practiced the New England *omerta*. Yankees are pretty closemouthed too, you know" (360). Puzo hybridizes the ethnic sign as he always does with Kay, an Adams from New England. Yet Michael will lie repeatedly to her; the surface talk that he constructs always maintains a barrier to real intimacy. When Kay tells him, "I never believed you killed those two men. . . . I never believed it in my heart," Michael answers, "It doesn't matter whether I did or not" (361). Each character speaks from a different genre. Kay in sentimental romance won't believe her man capable of such an act; Michael in the strictly segmented world controlled by *omerta* believes that women live in separate spheres, that his status as a murderer is not relevant to their life together. When Kay presses her question, she then argues herself out of it through romance language, that what she really cannot accept was that Mike didn't call her when he got back home. When Mike's cigarette ashes fall on her bare back, she attempts lame humor from his world, "stop torturing me, I won't talk," but Michael is not amused. He tells her that when he saw her tonight, he was glad: "[I]s that what you mean by love?" (360–61). Suddenly Michael is a Hemingway existentialist in the vein of "what's good is what I feel good after."

This bedroom banter is tepid by any dramatic standard, popular or elite, but the clash between the eager heroine and her stony hero continues as she tests his resolve to keep silent, and he replies in phrases such as "I can't tell you about anything that happened"; "I won't be telling you anything about my business"; "[Y]ou won't be my partner in life, as I think they say . . . that can't be." Kay lamely guesses that she's married a monster. They make small jokes about his blasted face and drippy nose. He gives her the All-American speech about joining the general American family in the future. He tells her that, like his mother and father, if she stays with him and makes him her first loyalty for forty years, "after you do that maybe I'll tell you a few things you really don't want to

hear" (364). Michael concludes with a speech he calls a "final explanation" that makes the Don into something like an ethnic Ayn Rand figure:
"He doesn't accept the rules of the society we live in because those rules
would have condemned him to a life not suitable to a man like himself,
a man of extraordinary force and character" (365). When Kay calls him
on the ethics of that remark, asking what if everyone felt the same way,
Michael pulls back, grins, and says, "I'm just telling you what my father
believes" (365).[11] In their long exchange, Kay speaks for love, openness,
trust, and American pluralism. Michael tacks between complete silence,
half-truths, general explanations, and family justification. In no case is
the dialogue internally persuasive, and, as a producer of authoritative
discourse, Michael is a second-hand agent for his father. On the lovers'
bed, *omerta* meets romance, and as Michael finally says, "This is really
getting us no place. But maybe I'm just one of those old-fashioned conservatives they grow up in your hometown. I take care of myself, individual. Governments don't do much for their people. . . . All I can say is
that I have to help my father. I have to be on his side" (366).

The Sicilian American returned from his Old World hideout justi-
fies his life and that of his father. Although America is warily held at bay
through bribes and influence, Michael expresses a hard American fact
that individualism is the American religion and a rueful but hard Sicilian
fact that governments are useless. He seals his case with the universal
justification that his father needs him, that family trumps any national or
ethnic sign.[12] Though Puzo's sentiments are conventional, their scope is
very large. Michael and Kay are speaking about nothing less than American private and public trust, within the home and within the society.
That Michael is wrong and Kay ultimately submissive does not undermine the relevance of their dialogue. That Puzo, an author rightly scorned
for his often vulgar and mythical attempts to write about sex and women,
could have the patience to inscribe such a dialogue even simplistically
tells us that some portion of his more androgynous view remains from
The Fortunate Pilgrim.

Genco Revisited

Armed with the elements of *bella figura* and *omerta*, the reader can
return to Genco's entreaties to Don Corleone in a broader frame that
allows an enhanced appreciation for what the two old confederates are
signifying in their dramatic interview. It's easy to read past the opening
section of Genco's deathbed scene. A young "exasperated" Dr. Kennedy
leaves Genco's room, "serious-faced and with the air of one born to
command, that is to say, the air of one who has been immensely rich all
his life" (45).[13] To him, the crowd of Corleones and Abbandandos waiting
outside the dying man's door are undifferentiated, even Don Corleone,

"the short heavy man in an awkwardly fitted tuxedo" who informs the
doctor that "we will take up the burden. . . . We will close his eyes. We
will bury him and weep at his funeral and afterwards we will watch over
his wife and daughters." At this moment, Genco's wife weeps bitterly,
but the Don has accomplished his role in public performance. He has
told her the truth in proper mourning language and established his responsibility. All Dr. Kennedy can do is shrug: "it was impossible to explain to these peasants. At the same time he recognized the crude justice
in the man's remarks. His role was over." Puzo crosses the ethnic performance with the Anglo scrutiny. To the doctor, the Don is an older man
with a melodramatic set of flourishes. He doesn't understand the underlying gravitas of the Don's role nor its production in *bella figura*, yet even
he notes the "peasant's" "crude justice" in the face of death. Then he
turns and walks away, "his white coat flapping" (46), medicine's signature uniform as is the Don's wedding day tuxedo. The modern world of
medical science and efficiency, often referenced by Puzo in *The Fortunate
Pilgrim* as well as *The Godfather*, has for a brief moment looked back at the
ethnic Corleones and has collided with deathbed ritual, the ethnic type-
scene here prefaced by the antiseptic gaze of Dr. Kennedy.

Once Dr. Kennedy cedes the body of Genco over to the families, the
Don is in his element. When Genco asks to be saved in the several urgent
entreaties previously discussed, the Don's final recourse to calling it
"blasphemy" may also be seen as Genco's unwillingness to go through
the script of *bella figura*, which inherently will conceal the murderers' true
relation to each other. To tell Genco to "resign" himself is to admonish
him not only to prepare himself for death but to get back in the ethnic
social script. The slippage described in the scene between the natural and
the historical, between authoritative and internally persuasive language,
may also be seen as the slippage between *bella figura* and *brutta figura*, a
transgression of an ethnically specific performance act. Genco who wishes
to historicize becomes an aesthetically ugly (*brutta figura*) dying body. To
"speak death" is literally to break confidence with performative codes,
with all that is known to be meaning. To say, as I did in chapter 3 that
after the Don's interview with Genco, Puzo closes down the affirmation
of Don Corleone as a murderer is to say, in effect, that the rules of *bella
figura*, briefly transgressed, have been restored as the novel's operative
rhetorical mode. Because both participants in this stylization must agree
to its enacting, *The Godfather*'s narrative logic makes it extraordinarily
difficult for a character to obtain any more self-knowledge than that
yielded by the speech act itself. *Bella figura* will not signify to a literary
criticism searching for self-scrutiny or a privileged individual consciousness, the hallmarks of elite fiction. Characters must maintain their roles
as, for example, in slave narrative or in women's narrative in which the
protagonist mimes the dominant discourse to appease the master or man
while retaining some residue of personal control.[14]

The reader of popular fiction most often takes the melodramatic presentation of a scene such as that at Genco's deathbed as "true" and "powerful," that Puzo's concluding "as if the Don could truly snatch the life of Genco Abbandando back from that most foul and criminal traitor to man" (48) is demonstrably the case. Deathbeds famously yield "deep" thoughts, and we obviously stand in awe of death's power. Yet Puzo's benediction in authorial voice could be seen as a weaker signal broadcasting *bella figura* without an antagonist, popular wisdom in extremis. Puzo commented in *The Godfather Papers* that most readers and critics missed the "casual irony" in his novel, that he really was "on the side of the good guys," and that his work was more moral than had been suspected (70). "Casual irony" does not appear as a rhetorical category from Aristotle through Wayne Booth, as far as I know. It's difficult in the midst of the disorder in which ideas are presented in *The Godfather* to believe that misread "casual irony" is anything more than *bella figura* not being recognized by the critical and general readers. *Bella figura* is verbal indirection of a specific sort, and Puzo perhaps intuits that readers miss it because they don't read for euphemisms in performance by dint of academic training or lack of ethnic background or both. A cornerstone of *bella figura* is dual participation. Speakers must be in cahoots, or the speaker and listener must interpret the presentation in a certain situation. The feigned ignorance on a surface level that irony presupposes is always replaced by a shared knowledge of irony's trope on another level. "Casual" well describes the studied outcome of a *bella figura*; a "*sprezzatura*" or studied carelessness may be the result (Nardini 24), a situation in which the Don and Genco, Sonny, or Michael want to show little interest or strain, to make performance look accidental or random with no agenda when, in fact, it is the very theatre for the conducting of family as business, business as family. To divine the level of indirection in a conventional modernist text would be to ascertain the tenor of its irony. However, when ethnic criticism is the critical tool, *bella figura* and *omerta*, tools of historical and social survival in centuries past, have to be privileged as well. They coexist in New World settings with the plain speaking and open speech of imagined American individualists. At this point in critical debate, elite literary silences have cultural capital, whereas the silences in ethnic performance do not. The American ethnic novel is most often read in a predominantly nonethnic specific speech community where a general misreading of its inflected performance is the norm.

The Fortunate Pilgrim: Elite Ethnic Fiction

The Godfather in which Puzo said he wrote "below his gifts" was published only five years after *The Fortunate Pilgrim*, his well-received ethnic novel that resolutely stayed within the ethnic ensemble to chronicle the family of Lucia Santa Angeluzzi-Corbo on the Lower East Side of New York City. *The Fortunate Pilgrim* is by acclimation a fine achievement; Boelhower thinks Puzo's work meritorious enough to place it in a hypothetical curriculum for a course on novels of ethnic pragmatics along with *Huckleberry Finn, Light in August, My Antonia, Invisible Man*, and Henry Roth's *Call It Sleep* (36). Such a listing would finally achieve Puzo's dream of inclusion in a canon with American classic writers. What makes *The Fortunate Pilgrim* a critic's choice over the omnipresent and world famous *The Godfather*? One answer might be found in an estimate of Puzo's handling of a scene that has real reference to the Genco–Don Corleone interview in *The Godfather*.

Lucia Santa's husband, Frank Corbo, is in the throes of a spiritual and emotional breakdown that is sapping his will to live. He becomes involved with Colucci, an Italian Protestant evangelical whom he met at work. Lucia Santa isn't scandalized because Colucci isn't Catholic; indeed, she has very little use for religion. When Colucci comes to her home with three other men, they ring themselves around Frank's bed like "disciples," and Frank accuses them of falsity: "You told me there was never any need for doctors, that God decides, man believes. Now you are false. You are Judas" (*The Fortunate Pilgrim* 104). Colucci's reaction is the extreme opposite of the Don's in Genco's deathbed scene:

> Mr. Colucci was stunned. He sat down on the bed and took Frank Corbo's hand in his. He said, "My brother, listen to me, I believe. But when I see your wife and children to be left so, my faith wavers. Even mine. I cannot make my faith your destruction. You are ill. You have these headaches. You suffer. Dear brother, you do not believe. You say God has called you and you say you are dead. You blaspheme. Live now. Suffer a little longer. God will have mercy on you at Armageddon. Rise now and come to my home for supper. Then we will go to chapel and pray together for your deliverance. (104–05)

Colucci charges his supplicant to live, not resign himself to death, to have faith and seek a doctor's care. The blasphemy is that Frank speaks death, and Colucci can't believe it. Puzo has him exhibit the self-knowledge to reference the cariacature of the parable of Christ and the true believer. Colucci assures Lucia Santa that Frank will be home at nine that night and that she should have the doctor there. Colucci will come and offer prayers with his friends, and Frank's "soul will be saved" (105). The scene so far is completely in the hands of the male who wishes to practice an alien ritual akin to but not identical to *bella figura*, an evangelical raising of spirits. But Lucia Santa is having none of it, and Puzo gives her a stinging subjective appraisal of male religious rhetoric beyond Colucci's consciousness:

Lucia Santa became coldly, implacably angry at his touch. Who was this man with his single child, a stranger to her grief and suffering, to presume to comfort her? Callow, criminal in his meddlesome religiosity—he was the cause of her husband's illness. He and his friends had disordered her husband's mind with their foolishness, their obscene and obsequious familiarity with God. And beyond that she had a feeling of disgust for Mr. Colucci. . . . She hated him. It was she who would feel the anguish, the rage of the sufferer who must bow to fate; as for Mr. Colucci, his would be the easy tears of compassion. (105)

Here Puzo imagines the woman's critique of such male ritual and confident vanity in a perspective wholly missing from *The Godfather*. Her understanding of the scene is deep and angry, a monologue in a character zone far beyond Puzo's tamer "As if the Don could truly snatch back . . ." Colucci's attempt to transact a ritual leading to a cure is not what Lucia Santa would think of as *bella figura*. She believes his rhetoric an "obscene and obsequious familiarity with God," a succinct statement of what men do as far as she's concerned and an excellent place to initiate a moral criticism of *The Godfather*. This indictment is Puzo's own pre-*Godfather* leveling of its sonorous piety in the face of all the death-dealing. Lucia Santa is never silenced by the male narrative and gives her own criticism of Colucci "and all men who sought something beyond life, some grandeur." She knows her agonies will remain when Colucci and perhaps her husband himself are gone. Then Colucci's tears would be "the easy tears of compassion." It's as if Puzo has let Genco's wife speak for herself to provide moral knowledge of the emptiness of the male melodrama around a deathbed. Such a place of sex, childbirth, conception, and childbirth is simply not the men's place. The "easy tears of compassion" are not Lucia Santa's tears or those of women in general. She weeps more specifically through "the rage of the sufferer who must bow to fate." Lucia Santa previously expressed "that secret contempt for male heroism that many women feel but never dare express" (80), that men never risk their bodies day after day "as all women do in the act of love" as their "bodies open up into a great bloody cavern year after year" (81). Puzo demonstrates he is fully capable of writing more complex scenes from the woman's view. Unlike the Genco deathbed scene he would write five years later, this scene in *The Fortunate Pilgrim* contains a rich dialogism between male and female viewpoints that does not depend on Mafia dynamics of the Corleones versus the United States of America for its effects. To keep *The Godfather* on sensational point, Puzo omitted much of the richness of family dynamics, of women's domestic role and maternal power—strong elements of *The Fortunate Pilgrim*.

Puzo may also have been freed to write of his Italian American subjects so sensationally in *The Godfather* because Puzo, a Neapolitan, was writing about Sicilians. If Naples is coded as the colorful south of Italy to most northern Italians, then Sicily is Naples' own violent lawless southland. Puzo's one Sicilian episode in *The Fortunate Pilgrim* is quite simplistic if not derogatory in its rendering and shows just what happens when a Sicilian comes slumming around in this more highfalutin' ethnic novel. Lucia Santa's eldest son, Larry Angeluzzi, is sleeping with a matronly woman of his mother's generation, while her husband is busy making and selling bootleg wine. When the husband is briefly jailed, Mrs. Le Cinglata is badgered by suitors. One is a "dark Sicilian," who holds her skirt in the "innocent lechery" of a "childish man." He mocks Larry as a rival ("[D]o you serve children here?") and tosses everyone "a look of excruciating slyness" as he asks in "deferential broken English," "Itsa your son? Youra nepha-ew?" When the Signora tells him to stop his insults and find somewhere else to drink, the Sicilian threatens to tell her husband about Larry, sticking out his chest "like a singer at the opera." The Signora instructs Larry to throw him down the stairs, whereupon the Sicilian "roars" in broken English, "You little shitta American cockasickle. *You* throw *me* down the stairs? I eat you up whole anda whole." Larry easily knocks him to the kitchen floor and realizes "the man could not use his hands and had not meant him real harm. He had come like a hugging bear to chastise a child, grotesque, human without being cruel" (43–44).

Nothing in this scene prepares the reader for the omnipotence of Sicilians in *The Godfather*, in which they not only dominate other Italian Americans but have invisible control over much in the larger American society. Puzo doesn't even give his character a name here: he is Sicilian, a type, dark, crude, sensual, comically menacing, the only character out of the scores in *The Fortunate Pilgrim* whose speech is rendered in broken English. Such a comically negative portrayal of a Sicilian suggests something other than writing "below" his gifts, as Puzo described the writing of *The Godfather*; it suggests that he is writing "below" his class and region and is not invested in portraying the humanity or complexity of the Sicilian in *The Fortunate Pilgrim*. Similarly, to stand outside the Corleones as Sicilian is to be able to manipulate them in ways that might not have been available to him in the more autobiographical *Fortunate Pilgrim*. However, in a darker elite fiction stab at understanding Puzo as author, we might allow for the improbability, after assimilating Puzo's Sicilian fool in *The Fortunate Pilgrim*, that *The Godfather* is a radical novel of manners since melodrama itself is always dangerously close to tipping over into burlesque in its broad gestures. Suffice to say, Puzo's cameo Sicilian in *The Fortunate Pilgrim* remains caught in *brutta figura*; he makes all the wrong moves in the Neapolitan Italian immigrant world.

Besides banishing Sicilians to comic relief and placing women in control of major scenes, Puzo's work in *The Fortunate Pilgrim* is distinguished from *The Godfather* in the way that it forces many confrontations between Italian Americans who have multiple roles in its culture. All the Italian characters in the novel interact with Lucia Santa's family, and they are a more varied group economically, socially, and culturally than the Italians the reader meets through the tightly controlled Corleone family, which is surrounded mainly by supplicants and victims. Lucia Santa's experience is restricted to events that impinge on her children's lives and fortunes; she sallies forth heroically on several occasions to protect her family's honor and survival. I want to look at several contact scenes to demonstrate Puzo's commitment in *The Fortunate Pilgrim* to a wider world of ethnic forms and emendations than he allows himself to depict in *The Godfather*, how the logic of the blockbuster melodrama would have ended in mayhem while analogous scenes in *The Fortunate Pilgrim* end in the negotiations of Lucia Santa, the mother and woman who wields a similar yet different *bella figura* than Don Corleone.

For the preface to a 1997 edition of *The Fortunate Pilgrim*, Puzo made the significant admission that the figure of Don Corleone was really modeled after his mother: "whenever the Godfather opened his mouth, in my mind I heard the voice of my mother. I heard her wisdom, her ruthlessness, and her unconquerable love for her family and for life itself. . . . without Lucia Santa, I could not have written *The Godfather*" because the Don's "humanity came from her" (xii). This statement sent readers scurrying back to the text in some chagrin for having missed such a possibility. In a changed reading climate for multiethnic and gendered fiction at century's end, could the great Don, most famous of ethnic American male heroes, ultimately be feminine in sensibility and traditional wielding of his family's might? Lucia Santa might join Steinbeck's Ma Joad in *The Grapes of Wrath*, Arnow's Gertie Nevels in *The Dollmaker,* Morrison's Sethe in *Beloved*, Erdrich's Marie Kashpaw in *Love Medicine*, and Tan's Joy Luck Clubbers—but Don Corleone? The contemporary fictional hero most segregated from true dialogue with women, the most powerful patriarchal figure in American popular fiction history? A few speculations are in order.

The most cynical reaction would be that reissuing *The Fortunate Pilgrim* with its conflation of Lucia Santa and Vito Corleone was Puzo's attempt to join the *lingua franca* of current fictional dialogue with a classic ethnic American novel at a propitious time coinciding with the publication of *The Last Don* (1996). However, I tend to take Puzo at his word about the link between Lucia Santa and Vito Corleone for several reasons. First of all, what's obvious from Puzo's own family history (a father disappearing when he was very young, a dead stepfather) is his search for both a father in his fiction who would be a guiding force in his life and his fictional creation of sons who would have to live up to the father's example and courage. Michael Corleone in becoming his father's son becomes his father, and a male familial order is established. Lucia Santa and her son battle in wounding ways throughout *Pilgrim*, with none of the resolution that occurs in *The Godfather.* It's a stand-off between mother and son. Gino Corbo buries his father and then leaves his family for good when he leaves his mother's influence. Ultimately, the only guiding "father" in Puzo's life was his mother, and it is her rhythms of speech and negotiation that he recreates in his Sicilian American Godfather.

Furthermore, if we entertain the possibility that Puzo was "going down" in subject matter to write about Sicilians at all, as evidenced in the one reductive Sicilian scene in *Pilgrim,* Puzo needed to draw on the authority and moral courage of the Neapolitan Lucia Santa to imbue Don Corleone with his great dignity. *The Godfather* might then be seen as hybridized *within* its ethnic materials, male and female centers of authority, and Sicilian and Neapolitan "class" statements. Also, if Lucia Santa becomes Don Corleone in Puzo's mind, such a metamorphosis would help account for the minimal role Mama Corleone plays in the novel. Like the boorish Sicilian in *Pilgrim,* Mama Corleone is never given a name and is described in her few scenes in *The Godfather,* in "grim, Italian old crone fashion" from "a more primitive culture" (393, 268). With her "wrinkled, leathery, olive-skinned face" and "heavy Italian accent," she informs Kay when Michael is in hiding, "You forget about Mikey, he no the man for you anymore" (236–37). The irony is extreme, not casual. Puzo writes about his mother as his mother, making her the heroine of *The Fortunate Pilgrim,* only to have critics applaud and the public ignore him. Puzo writes about his mother as the Godfather only to have critics ignore him and the public make him rich and famous. The infusion of maternal power and vitality into the silent, strong patriarch who always guides his family, who "reasons" with his enemies, who is "very strait-laced" in sex is yet another cross-gendered sleight-of-hand in the American popular culture whereby the role of a strong woman character is recast into that of a "domestic" and "multiple" male character. All is negotiated through heterosexual family roles within melodrama's rigid and sensational plot lines. *The Godfather* needs no true female characters since Puzo's mother, alias Lucia Santa recycled into Don Corleone, is in firm control of the family's destiny.

Therefore it's instructive to read from several scenes in *The Fortunate Pilgrim* to see where Lucia Santa is and is not Vito Corleone in training, to find where Puzo without the constraint of funneling all power and knowledge through the great Don was able to allow more play in his ethnic semiosis and more realistic confrontations across Italianita and with the American culture. Although Lucia Santa is the unquestioned matriarch in a family with first an absent, then an unbalanced husband, her forays into Italian America on behalf of her family's well-being show her in a more complex negotiation of her power and its limits, constrained as an illiterate immigrant woman in an urban American setting that perplexes and bewilders her. She first angrily ventures out into the foreign land of New Jersey by ferry and streetcar to reclaim her infant son, Vincent, who had been tentatively boarded with an Italian family while she regained her strength after the death of her first husband. Their house "had a pointed roof, like nothing she had ever seen in Italy, as if it were a plaything, not to be used for people fullgrown. It was white and clean, with blue shutters and a closed-in porch." She finds baby Vincent in "the prettiest room [he] would ever have" with a "blue crib, a white stuffed horse" where he "lay in his own piss." Lucia Santa "stared around the pretty room with the dumb anger of an animal" and "then what a drama was played" (36–37).

Into the American one-family home comes the immigrant mother, furious with righteousness. Filomena, the middle-class wife and Vincent's caretaker, sloughs off Lucia Santa's accusations of maltreatment and hints that the boarding arrangement was to have been permanent. After all, she argues, look at the baby's new clothes and pretty room. He would be happy, go to the university, "become a lawyer, a doctor, even a profes- sor. . . . What was she? She had no money. She would eat dirt with her bread her whole life long" (38). The ethnic frame here contains both the poor and the advantaged women, both still Italian Americans, with Filomena closer to assimilation. With her view of Vincent's future, Filomena espouses Don Corleone's view to Michael in the first *Godfather* film that he hadn't wanted him in the family business, that his goal had been for Michael to become Senator Corleone, Governor Corleone. Michael's reply is "We'll get there, Pop. We'll get there." In *The Fortunate Pilgrim*, oppor- tunities come through similar Americanization but not at the threat of violence. Becoming "legitimate" is leaving the ghetto and New York City, coming to the pretty American room with toys. The choice for the ethnic mother is to leave her baby son in suburban Italian America or take him back to the tenements. Lucia Santa rears back and spits in Filomena's face, then flees from the house with her child in her arms. Such is the proper female counterpart action in melodrama to the male's decision to do any- thing to provide for his children. The woman's role is maternal, to enclose the child in her arms; the male's role is usually couched in economic terms, "to feed my kids." The most intimate male personal justification is to take vengeance on a physical humiliation or unmanning, as when Michael's injuries to cheek and jaw finally provoke him into aligning himself with his family against their enemies. With the woman, it's often more primal action to keep her children at all, the starkest narratives provided by slave mothers from Stowe's Eliza through Morrison's life and death choices for Sethe. For example, Lucia Santa's defining rhetoric as matriarch in domes- tic ethnic narrative is "Don't fear. I'm your mother. No one can harm my children. Not while I live" (40).

Her resolve is tested again and again. Counterpoint to her scene of rescuing baby Vincent from the wilds of New Jersey is her rescuing her teenage son from an older married woman. Determined to bring seventeen-year-old Larry home to sleep in his own room, she goes to the Le Cinglata apartment where he has been sleeping with Signora Le Cinglata, whom Lucia Santa grew up with in Italy before they both emigrated. Their confrontation over Larry affords Puzo the opportunity to show a women's dialogized ethnic scene in which the leverage they each seek in argument comprises another example of *bella figura*, which ultimately collapses. The Le Cinglatas, husband and wife, begin in the most flowing language. The husband, a knowing cuckold, praises Larry for helping guard the bootlegging business when he's away from home. Lucia Santa tentatively breaks in to ask if Larry hadn't slept there some night. The wife chides Lucia Santa that her "son is a grown man," and "we are not in Italy," prompting Lucia Santa, "met with rudeness," to voice her true feelings":

> She said coldly, politely, "Ah. Signora, you don't know what trouble children make. How could you, you who are so fortunate not to have any? Ah, the worries of a mother, a cross pray to Christ you will never have to bear. But let me tell you this, my dear Le Cinglata, America or no America, Africa, or even England, it does not signify." (68)

Lucia Santa in one sentence manages to score Le Cinglata for her barrenness, laud her own maternal suffering, and take her stand behind a universal code: her son will sleep at home; regardless of ethnic origin, that's the way things should be. They now meet verbally in bitter insult, Le Cinglata reminding Lucia Santa that no one in Italy with the name of Angeluzzi or Corbo was nobility, that her husband, "the closest friend and fellow worker of your son's true father [Angeluzzi], almost a godfather, *he* is not to be a friend to Lorenzo?" Lucia Santa feels "trapped" and curses the other woman's "slyness" in speech. How has she been parried by Le Cinglata? Clearly because the other woman has hidden behind male patrimony and rank and has cleverly shifted the insult from herself to her husband. The women begin to joust over men's names and reputations, as they must with the husband in the room. The speech rules are dictated by audience and setting as much as by speakers. When Le Cinglata plays her best card: "Now tell me. Does the boy's own mother believe the worst of him?" Lucia Santa *"with the husband looking down her throat* [emphasis mine] said hurriedly, 'No, no. But people talk. Your husband is a sensible man, thank God.' " But just then, Larry Angeluzzi enters familiarly with a suitcase and "the tableau that this made explained everything to the mother" (even as Kay knew all she needed to know when she sees through the parlor door that Clemenza defers to Michael at the end of *The Godfather*). Lucia Santa still is able to maintain her indirection and asks Larry if her cooking does not please him anymore. Larry tells her to stop kidding; the husband takes his cue from

Larry, the other male, and speaks to her ever more familiarly. Now "truly shocked for one of the few times in her life," she orders Larry to get all his things "and come back to your own roof. I don't leave here until you come" (70).

Puzo shows how supple Lucia Santa must be in tacking through the field of argument. Besieged by a husband and wife and her own son, she indirectly accuses the older man of being cuckolded by her own blood and yet keeps track of her primary goal—to bring that son back to his own home. The signora taunts Larry that he's a baby, Lucia Santa hits her son in the face, and Larry pushes her against the kitchen table. She hisses, thank God his father is dead because he should "not see his son beating his own mother for the sake of strangers"; Larry feels "guilty, conscience-stricken, to see tears of humiliation in his mother's eyes" (71). The greatest sin and crime here is the loss of control, of crumbling as a family to outsiders. Lucia Santa in the strong woman's role is, however, subject to many curbs on her authority: a woman, a woman alone, a woman alone against an intransigent husband and a promiscuous wife, a woman whose son is beyond her physical control, an immigrant woman alone in a strange land. Puzo's writer's task here is as intricate as Lucia Santa's. He must portray in much more subtle and shifting mimetic rendering what in *The Godfather* he might bring abruptly and sensationally or ominously to closure through the threat of major violence. However, Lucia Santa runs out of weapons, rhetorical or otherwise, against Larry and the Le Cinglatas, so much so that she sins against *omerta* by threatening to go to the police if he isn't in her home that evening: "[S]elling wine and whiskey is one thing but here in America they protect children. As you said, Signora, we are not in Italy" (71).

Lucia Santa invokes Americana, the necessary threat albeit in heresy of a mother without a godfather to mediate the problem. She hybridizes the scene into one of interpenetration with American authorities beyond the Le Cinglata apartment, and her ploy works. That night a Black Hand "lawyer" appears to say, in effect, how did we all let things go so far? The hidden agenda is, of course, that the bootlegging operation needs continued protection from the police: could Larry have one more night out to save his manhood, and then he'll come home? Lucia Santa was "pleased and flattered and recognized the truth. She nodded assent" (72–73). I've stayed with this complex domestic negotiation to point out Puzo's care in registering the nuances of immigrant family crisis. The heroine of *The Fortunate Pilgrim* in her need to speak through alternate power and submission moved Puzo to depict each and every role in the sort of heteroglossia that Bakhtin makes a cornerstone of fictional exchange and that ethnicity and gender roles both enrich and qualify. Lucia Santa must speak through a woman's muted heteroglossia, must appropriate what is most often a very male seminal concept in Bakhtin.[15]

Lucia Santa and her daughter, Octavia, have a much more varied
and dynamic relationship than that of Vito and Michael Corleone in *The
Godfather*. Octavia is her mother's confederate against the male society
but just as often her fierce critic and antagonist as she fights for her own
emancipation as a second-generation immigrant in America. When Octavia
returns to her mother after six months in the hospital recovering from a
serious pleurisy, she encounters La Fortezza, a hapless young Italian
social worker who has been helping the family get money in her absence
while taking a little kickback on the side. Lucia Santa is resigned to this
traditional way of doing business, but Octavia flares when La Fortezza
begins to patronize her. He observes no forms of respect, no reserve but
"abandoning his Italian manner, said in a friendly American voice, briskly,
casually, 'I've heard a lot about you, Octavia. Your mother and I have
had some good long talks. We're old friends' " (178). This alien speech
overture makes Octavia furious that he'd take her for some easy working
girl, and she scrutinizes him further as a sorry hybrid of Italianita and
Americana without "that slim American debonair charm" who became
"more and more animated, loquacious and charming as his two dark
circled owl eyes would permit" (178). He continues to devalue her sensibility without ever inquiring as to its depth and tells her she should
read Zola to learn about her station in life. Finally he invites her to go to
the theater using cut-rate tickets he gets from the city, urging her to
accept because "it will be a new experience" for her (179).

Octavia is incredulous. She'd been to the theater, all the girls in the
dressmaking shops got tickets, too, and she'd read all about the "generous witless maidens who exposed themselves to shame" in popular novels
for the pleasure of young men tempting them with a good time. She
thinks that "this stupid starving guinea college kid thought he could
screw her" (180). She drops the forced ritual of a sham ethnic courtship
overture and spits out, " 'You can go shit in your hat, you lousy bastard,"
a preface to:

> You take eight dollars a month from my poor mother, who has
> four little kids to feed and a sick daughter. You bleed a family
> with all our trouble and you have the nerve to ask me out? . . .
> You're old-fashioned, all right. Only a real guinea bastard from
> Italy with that respectful Signora horseshit would pull some-
> thing like that. But I finished high school. I read Zola, and I
> have gone to the theater, so find some greenhorn girl off the
> boat you can impress and try to screw her. (180)

Octavia speaks politically, correctly assessing what La Fortezza sees
as her gendered and class role. Unlike Kay or Connie in *The Godfather*,
she has no need to play the game of euphemisms in *bella figura*. She has
no power to conserve, no agenda to strengthen, and is under no male or

family protectorate, nor must she bow to one. Openly expressing contempt for his Old World male-dominant assumptions, she point-for-point discredits La Fortezza's ethnic act ("only a real guinea bastard from Italy") while establishing markers to counter him. The first is education; she has finished high school in America. Second, she has read literary naturalism (Zola) and gone to plays. Thus La Fortezza must revert to finding a "greenhorn girl off the boat" because Octavia is already an American girl backed by the cultural capital to prove it. To further sever Octavia from the Italian maternal immigrant imaginary, Puzo has her marry a Jewish poet who writes in both Yiddish and English, and she bears no children. Puzo pointedly does not deliver her into some generalized American future; as Lucia Santa thinks, "my most intelligent child, picked for a husband the only Jew who does not know how to make money."

Puzo's work with cross-cultural and gendered ethnicities in *The Fortunate Pilgrim* is always complex and realistic in continual negotiation and surprise. In contrast, Puzo in *The Godfather* consistently polarizes a deadly and unrelenting Sicilian family presence against a general American family that Michael and the Don reference when it pleases them but that has no real life in the novel except in the highly stylized chapters on victims (Woltz, McCluskey) or in the fealty owed to the family by the outsiders it absorbs (Kay, Tom Hagen, Jules Segal). *The Godfather*'s absolutes further the world of melodrama. Characters in *The Fortunate Pilgrim* touch and are touched by more currents of cultural interpenetration and influence since they are never in positions of power to conserve or take over. The motions of the novel are more democratic among male and female characters who are more or less equals in want, hopes, dreams, and cultural conditioning. However, within Italianita, they occupy an array of positions and responses dictated by a number of external indicators of education, class, and economics with the resultant play in their sensibilities. In *The Godfather*, Michael hustles Kay with images about what their children and they themselves will become: "I want them to grow up to be All-American kids, real All-American, the whole works" and "you and I will be part of some country club crowd, the good simple life of well-to-do Americans" (363). This flat national script is lifeless and reductive, not interesting as language or sociology and without drama, referencing image bites that do not even make sense, as in "simple" country clubbers. Puzo made Lucia Santa a more vivid critic of the Italian past and a more articulate visionary of what America could mean:

> America was not Italy. In America you could escape your destiny. Sons grew tall and worked in an office with collars and ties, away from the wind and earth. Daughters learned to read and write, and wore shoes and silk stockings, instead of slaughtering the bloody pig and carrying wood on their backs to save the strength of valuable donkeys. (267)

Lucia Santa's American sons will be more like Alger boys, climbing the ranks of management rather than covert murderers in the name of reason. Daughters granted literacy will be freed from centuries of ties to a bloody earth where animals have more value than women. The vividness of her metaphors are what contribute to making *The Fortunate Pilgrim* a true ethnic novel, rooted in the unmourned-for earth and uprooted to the transplanted concrete tenements of New York City. In comparison, *The Godfather* is artificial, not interested in growing lives as much as holding on to rigid advantage, closing in and closing down. At root, Lucia Santa's intimation of woman's physical reality, her body "open[ing] up into a great bloody cavern year after year" (81) is the violence and terrible beauty of new life in a new land, which Puzo knew intimately in her novel and conveniently forgot in the epic of the great Don who is acquainted only with death by male *fiat* and violence.

Dr. Barbato and Dr. Segal

The social worker La Fortezza smugly addresses Octavia from what he believes to be strengths. He speaks "college Italian," owes his father money for law school, and has read about the poor in books. Whenever he comes to visit, Lucia Santa fixes him an American ham and cheese sandwich on white bread for he has a weak stomach and "turn[s] up his nose at honest Italian salami and tingling sharp provolone, the crusty gum-cutting Italian bread" (166–67). La Fortezza represents one foot on the ladder of American assimilation; he's become too American to be Italian but has little acquired American capital, only just enough to draw Octavia's scorn as some sort of alien creature who belongs in neither world; he's an easy target for both Octavia and Puzo.

A more complex figure between two worlds in *The Fortunate Pilgrim* is Dr. Silvio Barbato, who "was young but he had no illusions about the Hippocratic oath. . . . [He] was too intelligent in his own right to be sentimental about these southern Italians who lived like rats along the western wall of the city. But still he was young enough to think of suffering as unnatural. Pity had not been squeezed out of him" (106). Rather than simply displaying his newfound cultural capital, Barbato broods about the plight of the immigrant Italians because "he always wished that the people who gave him money were a little better dressed, that they had better furniture" (108). Although "his escape was complete" (107), his medical treatment of both Octavia and Lucia Santa finds him conceptualizing them in ways with strict reference to Bourdieu's designations of class-bound distinction through differing aesthetic perception. "Dr. Barbato was simply a man who could not stand the sight and smell of poverty" (161), and his guilt about that fact frustrates him enormously as it isolates him from the class from which he came. Unlike the simplistic La

Fortezza, who makes moves on Octavia, Dr. Barbato aestheticizes Lucia Santa and her daughters as a stay against both his sentiment and his desire, the driving forces of a more popular narrative than Puzo writes here. As Lucia Santa bathes the feverish brow of her young daughter, Barbato first casts them in a religious painting with "the reposing mother tending the child" and the dim yellow electric bulb "casting a beatific glow" on the walls. Rather than moving swiftly to treatment, he "tried to isolate the resemblance" and "realized from his reading that it was simply a peasant upbringing, the child's complete reliance on its mother. These were the people that famous painters had used" (170). Also, Lucia Santa's "swelling buttocks" "like her daughter's" were those "of the sensual Italian nudes hung in Florence, great, rounded . . . but they aroused no desire in him. None of these women could" (171–72). Barbato finds art a way to deflect both his sympathy and his desire. To move the family into the realm of classic paintings absolves him on many fronts while stamping his sympathy with a more abstract cast, its relation in art casting out all rage and frustration. Dr. Barbato is making a classic use of cultural capital to erect barriers against his own ethnic confusion and guilt.

Dr. Barbato makes two more philosophical-aesthetic moves that distance him precisely in the manner of elite fiction into an abstract or symbolic relation to his medical practice. When he leaves the Corbo house, he "ponder[s] the world and humanity. He [feels] something resembling awe" (172). An allied strategy to aestheticizing is universalizing, and Puzo has Dr. Barbato follow this tack to the point of sounding almost as if Puzo has cribbed from another American doctor, William Carlos Williams, in a classic poem such as "To Elsie":[16] "[Dr. Barbato] felt angry, challenged, that this had been permitted to happen in his sight, as if his face had been slapped, as if he were being dared to interfere in some cosmological bullying" (173). Such liberal *tristesse* converted to ironic shaking of fists at the universe is, on a more sustained ontological plane, the stuff of tragedy. Puzo rehabilitates the poor doctor just in time. Having cycled through Renaissance painting and intimations of the negative sublime within a page-and-a half, "his blood now turned hot" and "for the next two months Dr. Barbato, out of pure rage, practiced the art of healing" (173). After art galvanizes him into action, he tends the Corbo family without stabs at final questions or tasteful excursions into art to manage his conflicts. These varied responses by the young Italian American doctor are very well done by Puzo and show a range of understanding of the representation and consciousness of the sensitive ethnic subject-as-outsider beyond any insight Puzo gave to any character in *The Godfather*. If Vito or Michael Corleone had stopped to ironically ponder their roles through art or philosophy, their souls might have been saved, but more likely their lives would have been lost. The logic of their text does not admit self-scrutiny, nor does popular fiction.

To get a second opinion on doctors in Puzo, consider once more Dr. Jules Segal, one of *The Godfather*'s triad of Jewish American minor characters, along with villains Jack Woltz and Moe Greene. Puzo divests Dr. Segal of his ethnicity, never having him interact with Jewish American patients or with his family. He's another wronged crusader recruited from unjust infamy by the Corleones. Once "one of the youngest and most brilliant surgeons in the East," he claims he has "gone bad" performing abortions and facing subsequent investigations. He is cut from the first *Godfather* film, but in the novel, his major claim to fame is as the sculptor of Lucy Mancini's newly snug vagina and Johnny Fontane's newly scraped throat and vocal cords. He is, then the medical man who can "arrange" and "fix" like Amerigo Bonasera with corpses. When Lucy can barely talk about her perceived deformity, practicing gynecological *omerta*, Jules does not take refuge in art or philosophy but says, "You dope, you incredible dope. . . . Are you really that innocent" (312). He preaches, "Now listen to me, if you had a decent modern raising with a family culture that was part of the twentieth century, your problem would have been solved years ago" (311). Naturally such sensitive handling of the problem dictates that Lucy fall deeply in love with Jules, and the reader moves step-by-step through her shame, operation, the jokes about it, and the rehabilitation into great sex. Little wonder that Coppola in 1972 performed surgery to remove Lucy and Jules from his film.

Jules Segal confidently and self-righteously tenders medical advice to everyone, berating Nino Valenti's death wish, challenging Johnny Fontane to "be a man," so he can examine his throat. He bewilders Johnny who "knew why Jules irritated him. The doctor's voice was always cool, the words never stressed no matter how dire, the voice always low and controlled. If he gave a warning the warning was in the words alone, the voice itself was neutral, as if uncaring" (372). The medical rhetoric is a specific speech that Johnny simply cannot fathom; there's no *bella figura* that he can identify. Without gesture or performance, Johnny, steeped in such language in personal and professional life, cannot believe in Jules's statements. Puzo encapsulates the miscommunication between the two perfectly when Jules snaps, "I warned you," and Johnny shoots back, "You didn't warn me right" (372). This exchange is a microcosm of *The Godfather*'s language play, one that has ominous result. When a Corleone message is misinterpreted or not received "right," consequences are stark. *The Fortunate Pilgrim* just as often breaks into its language transactions with the American script as a powerful external determinant. Ethnic fiction is fundamentally about misreading, the tragicomic lot we fall heir to from differing language and cultural backgrounds, and reified in a set of gestural and behavioral characteristics. Ethnic fiction tells how to "warn [us] right" and sharpens our apprehension of how much we often miss collectively when a reader discounts group and national speech dynamics and culture. Like Dr. Barbato, it's often too much altogether for us, and we want to get all our quarrels with the world into one image, one speech, one character. Yet *The Fortunate Pilgrim* by staying in one tenement amongst a dozen raging, living souls portrays a wider humanity and range of literary argument under Lucia Santa's regime than *The Godfather* lurching from New York to Hollywood to Sicily to Las Vegas and back, while straining under the monolithic power of one man and one law without self-reflection.

Gino and Michael Want Out: The Critics Come Home

For Puzo, Gino Corbo's battle with his mother is the autobiographical center of *The Fortunate Pilgrim*. Gino is the restless family explorer, the son most interested in the great city beyond the Italian ghetto. Puzo does not craft Gino as the sensitive artist-in-training; he is no easily wounded, reflecting moral center of consciousness; rather he has Puzo's wary fear of "going under" at a young age to family pressure and responsibility. As has been previously discussed, Michael Corleone has a complicated ethnic passage in the extended *Godfather* narrative. He escapes into World War II America, rescues the family in crisis, flees to the Old World in Sicily, and finally becomes his father by the end of the novel. *Godfather II* and *Godfather III* show both the power and the pressures that threaten to break Michael and the family apart as Puzo and Coppola's epic becomes darker and more moralistic. What remains in this chapter on reading the ethnic Puzo is to chart Gino and Michael's attempts at "breaking away" and how they relate to Puzo's own continued attempt to both be the chronicler of his ethnic identity and to strain against it.

Such chronicling and "straining against" became in the 1990s the extraordinary fact of a generation of prominent American literary critics and theorists becoming more overtly interested in aligning their writing with their Italian American roots. Such an interest is providing a new literature of memoirs and novels according to a process that Boelhower calls "imaginative circling" ("Adjusting Sites" 58). The list of critic theorists who have commented on their Italianita or made it the subject of their writing comprises a quite extraordinary roster in the 1990s, a veritable who's who of modern and postmodern criticism: Sandra Gilbert, Josephine Gattuso Hendin, Linda Hutcheon, Cathy N. Davidson, Marianna DeMarco Torgovnick, Robert Viscusi, and Frank Lentricchia.[17] They reflect on what this dual status has meant for their writing life (Gilbert, Hutcheon, Davidson). They write realist memoirs (Torgovnick) or allusive and experimental fiction (Lentricchia, Viscusi). These writers all combine an extraordinary self-knowledge of what it means to write from a professional, knowing position within Bourdieu's *habitus*, with an equally sensitive vantage point of memory from within the spatial coordinates of

Boelhower's *habitare*, what he most recently calls "the art of dwelling" (64).[18] They combine deep critical knowledge and formal training with the lived experience of Italian American family ties to explore in a synthesis of the ethnic realism and ethnic semiosis from the inside. Already semioticians in their own careers, they now study themselves in relation to self.

This latest generation of Italian American writer-critics practices a sophisticated midcareer version of what Garadaphe calls "breaking and entering" (1995), the desire of the Italian American writer to enter literary conversations and culture and through their ethnic ensemble, to "come back in" rather than "want out" as Puzo repeatedly did. They possess a deep knowledge of modernism and postmodernism, a commitment to criticism and theory that is now not sufficient for them, and a desire for formal experiment and the use of tropes. Finally they have the potential to understand both ethnic purity and cross-cultural hybridity and to move between them in their writing; that space is the writing itself within both a cultural and a literary dialogue. This most recent literary emigration arriving back at an autobiographical self suggests a coherence and integration that Puzo could never muster in his writing, since he hardly respected his own literary or ancestral origins enough. At age seventy-six, on publication of *The Last Don*, he told an interviewer that the "public loves for me to do the Italian stuff" (Fleming 2) so what can [he] do? Puzo fought against being a pilgrim, fortunate or otherwise. He never wanted to be an emissary from or to Italianita. Yet in a curious way, much of the autobiographical-fictional energy now extant in Italian American writing was provoked into existence by Puzo's notoriety, by the force-field surrounding *The Godfather*—what it provided in pride, consternation, disgust, envy, or recognition.[19]

While the imaginative work of these Italian American writer-critics and its potential is beyond the scope of this chapter, it's instructive to hypothesize what Puzo's achievement and writing ethic might have meant in light of this expansion and dialogue. Puzo splits himself into Gino and his brother Vincent at the outset of *The Fortunate Pilgrim*. In chapter 1, ten-year-old Gino runs through the nighttime tenement city, exuberantly zigzagging from one street to another in a playful chase by other boys; he screams "burn the city, burn the city" in "hysterical triumph"; Then at his own front stoop, "he aimed himself at his mother's enormous menacing figure . . . and swerved away through the door and up the stairs." Lucia Santa intent on striking him lets him pass in a mixture of "fierce pride and tenderness at her child's wild joy" (21). His brother Vincent—sadder, quieter, already "melancholy by nature" at thirteen— watches the street scene from the window, "brood[ing] to the softened whispery sound of the summer night. . . . He was self-exiled" (19). Vincent has a putative aesthetic consciousness, in line with modernism's artistic rebellion for the ethnic hero in a *bildungsroman* or *kunstleroman*, but he transmits weakly without an artist's drive; he's destined to be a victim. Gino, however, takes evasive action in America.

Puzo bestows on Vincent the honor of portraying in fiction his own happiest days of childhood, his summers from ages nine to fifteen as a Fresh Air Fund kid. He and other "slum children were boarded on private families in places like New Hampshire for two weeks" ("Choosing a Dream" 21). In the essay, Puzo describes a veritable encyclopedia of antiethnic Americana: cows, pastures, clear brooks, hay wagons, Bible classes, flower gardens, swings, see-saws, sizzling frankfurters, roasted corn, unlocked houses, no quarrels, no raised voices (21–22). Vincent adds to the picture in Puzo's fiction with an Edenic report to his family: "raspberries grew on bushes wherever you went. You just ate everything when you felt like it. . . . Everybody had a car because there were no subways or trolley car. . . . Then Vincent showed them his pajamas. He was the first one in the family to own a pair" (*The Fortunate Pilgrim* 83). Puzo has immigrant mother Lucia Santa gaze back at this wondrous America: "There were good people in the world, then, that made strange children happy. What kind of people were these? How safe they must be that they could squander love and money on a boy they had never seen and might never see again. Vaguely she sensed that outside her world was another as different as another planet" (83–84).[20]

Lucia Santa's view that anywhere outside her world might as well be another planet leads to Puzo's own interplanetary retelling of the ethnic narrative for the film of *Superman* (1978),[21] called a "meta-narrative of immigration" where the hero's power lies in a "secret identity hidden . . . under a disabling Anglo conformity" (Ferraro "Blood in the Marketplace" 283). In the ice crystal scene at the North Pole, young Clark Kent is surely brought into knowledge of his destiny; he has no way out of it because assimilation is not an option. Marlon Brando, who plays both Vito Corleone and Superman's father Jor-El, presents a postmodern image cluster for Puzo in wish-fulfillment; wherever he turns, there's a father. Certainly the broad outlines of the comic book hero's origins and maturation were most congenial to fatherless, ethnically conflicted Puzo—the all-powerful father on another planet (Jor-El on Krypton), a literally disintegrating "Old World," sends his son adrift in the universe toward an Earth that miraculously morphs into the Kent farm, a perfect reincarnation of Puzo and Vincent Corbo's Fresh Air Fund summers in New Hampshire.[22]

In his essay recalling his fresh-air summers, Puzo describes these New England forays without any irony as simply the happiest part of his childhood. They provided him a snapshot of a secure rural America, surely the one Michael Corleone so off-handedly suggests is worth joining in *The Godfather*. It's Kay Adams country, and Puzo preserves it in the trace of American antiquity and virtue she brings to the Corleone family. Even so, Puzo is unsure how to use the referent beyond an inert America that lies beyond his characters' reach, as it always does for his Sicilians in *The Godfather*. As always, the contact zones of a truly dialogized ethnic and American clash are beyond him. Puzo mistrusts the opportunity as

author for such tension, what writers such as Viscusi and Lentricchia
inherit from Fante and Mangione. Except for his summer American interlude, Vincent comes to the reader as always stunned and yoked to the
immigrant's work world of responsibility and exhaustion, the same dead-
ening image that Puzo intimated in "Choosing a Dream." Vincent cannot
imaginatively "circle" in Boelhower's phrase ("Adjusting Sites" 64) for
Puzo will not allow him to become a literary ambassador, as Gardaphe
writes of Mangione's "sense of adapting to two different worlds" ("Breaking and Entering" 10). To build that circuit, the conflict between "Who
Am I" and "Where is Here" (Boelhower 66), would have meant remaining the vital artist, and after creating cameos such as Dr. Barbato in *The
Fortunate Pilgrim*, Puzo was never interested, beyond the structurally
suggestive fact that Corleone (a "here") became an "I" (Vito and his
son Michael).

Gino watches Vincent's submission and resists being placed in the
family's economy. He journeys all the way to Central Park where "his
childish dreams did not include thoughts of money. He dreamed of brav-
ery on a battlefield, of greatness on a baseball diamond. He dreamed of
his own uniqueness" (127). "Uniqueness" is part of the complex American birthright of equality for all. Uniqueness is the elite literature signature for the privileged sensibility or character of a major fictional
protagonist. A unique character does not disappear into a melting pot or
a degrading urban poverty. Most important, a unique character does not
remain easily in the ethnic family and work for its survival. Lucia Santa
battles Gino for control of his own life, sensing in this son her true renegade. When the increasingly hapless Vincent dies in a trainyard accident, much of Lucia Santa's frustration over losing two husbands and
now a son is focused on Gino: "You never went to see your father in his
coffin. And while your brother was alive, you never helped him" (254).
She banishes him from Vincent's funeral, even though Octavia tells her
she's being crazy. Gino slinks in anyway, plays the role of an usher,
speaks to all the older women. Larry comes up to him and says, "me and
Octavia are gonna help you carry the load," and Gino thinks, "all the
years had been spun away to bring him finally to what had always been
waiting for him. He would go to work, sleep, there would be no shield
between himself and his mother. He would be drawn into the family and
its destiny. He could never run away again. . . . It was almost good news"
(260). Tentatively, Gino "grows up" and thinks about getting a job. More
firmly, he has been claimed by the ethnic family. He can stop the "unique"
struggling now and relax into what had always been there. Such is
Michael's "destiny" in *The Godfather* as well. By extension, to be drawn
into the family describes Puzo's decision to finally write both *The Fortunate Pilgrim* and *The Godfather*, to accept the ethnic subject, to quell his
terrors about feeling outside his family on the one hand and feeling
pulled under by them on the other. Such a surrender into the life and

control of ethnic and family environment was both Puzo's great relief and his worst fear. To truly engage that fear or probe that relief was beyond him.

At his core, Gino knows he still remains separate from family and everyone else. As he spends the night by Vincent's coffin in the darkened funeral parlor, he lies awake letting his mind "tell what it truly felt, that [his mother's] grief was excessive, that she made a ceremony of death" (264). Ironically his reaction to his mother is the reverse of what Lucia Santa had truly felt about Colucci, the evangelist, that his "obscene" ease in the face of life and death had been unconscionable, like that of all men. Thus Puzo brings men and women to their largest impasse in *The Fortunate Pilgrim*. Gino's final thought in a dream is to "chain himself in the known, lightless world he had been born in" (265), the ethnic womb claiming him "to be a man." However, history suddenly claims Gino for the American narrative, offering him a chance to break away. On the first Sunday of December 1941, Larry's son is receiving First Communion, Lucia Santa is making her special ravioli, and the entire family gathers along with Lucia Santa's neighbors and old friends. The setting is the most familiar ethnic type scene of them all—a traditional meal, where food preparation and consumption are meticulously described. Gino is now working the midnight-to-eight shift handling billing for the railroad and has reacted to this job with "pure hatred, physical" (271). The radio is tuned to the New York Giants football game when suddenly Gino's head is bent very close, and then he is watching his mother intently: "There was a smile on his face. It was a smile that was in some way cruel." Octavia asks Gino what is happening, and "Gino turned his back to hide his face. 'The Japs just attacked the United States,' he said. He turned up the radio and drowned out all the voices in the room" (274). In this sentence, Puzo signifies how the national narrative has shockingly taken precedence, how all the Italian American striving and individual adjustment or maladjustment is a secondary story to be swallowed whole.

"Pearl Harbor" as plot-turning determinant is certainly an all-American cliché by the time Puzo invokes it in 1964 after its use in a score of films and novels. However, as theorists of the Great Depression contend that only the World War II economy truly brought America into its postwar prosperity, it's perhaps worth noting that the war hastened and produced the first true melting pot in American history, melted into the returning soldiers and their young families demanding opportunities for an industrious conformity. Furthermore, if as the New Historicists suggest, we start with the historical event and work back to the literary narrative, we can find a cluster of energy around "Pearl Harbor Sunday" that includes the ethnic celebration within a more generalized American tradition very prevalent in 1941, that of "Sunday dinner," the leisurely early-to-midafternoon heavy meal on the Christian day of rest. In a secularized country made up of so many vestiges of specifically marked ethnic and national traditions, this meal, centered on family, is as "sacred" as we get; that the "non-Christian" Japanese would bomb Pearl Harbor on Sunday morning and that mainland America would hear about it with their families at table makes Roosevelt's "day that shall live in infamy" even more heinous. Novelists and screenwriters have repeatedly returned to December 7, 1941, and they do so knowing, even subconsciously, that the contract between America as a country isolated from the world and its ethnic sons from all over the world still isolated within her was destined to change irrevocably and change the social and civic life of the nation through the global struggle that followed.

Gino's triumphant teenage escape in *The Fortunate Pilgrim* is deepened into endless consequence by the conclusion of *Godfather II*. Puzo doesn't follow Gino into World War II in *The Fortunate Pilgrim* any more than we see Michael Corleone as a soldier. Puzo waits and brings Michael back from the war as a hero, only to be plunged into the family's war in 1946. Puzo and Coppola returned to "December 7, 1941" as social text in *Godfather II*'s terrific coda that allows for a possible thematic rewriting of Michael's career in that film and by extension in his life. *Godfather II* plunges Michael into the struggle to hold the Corleone empire together in the 1950s; the relation between the film's historical sweep and its major scenes is too complex to go into here. Michael must deal with family drift and traitors, Kay's increasing independence and moral rebellion, treacherous associates, corrupt politicians, Senate committees, expanding markets, and the Cuban Revolution. He becomes both more melancholy and more paranoid in his wielding of power. Late in the film, he talks to his mother about how strong "Pop" (the Don) was and asks if by being strong, you could lose your family. She replies that "you can never lose your family," the ironic truth of which is never more devastating than when Michael orders the death of his brother Fredo for conspiring with Johnny Ola and Hyman Roth against the Corleones. To have an identity as a Corleone is what follows you into death and moves you to murder.[23]

Michael is alone in the glass-walled main room of his Lake Tahoe mansion when he hears the crack of the gunshot that signals Fredo was shot in the motor boat by Al Neri. Coppola then crafts one more major flashback scene, this time not to young Vito Corleone in Sicily or New York City but to young Michael at the Corleone dinner table on December 7, 1941, or four years before the present time opening of the novel.[24] The segue begins with Sonny (James Caan) fading into focus to announce (as if to the viewer who believes the movie is over), "Hey everybody, pay attention." He introduces Carlo Rizzi for the first time to Connie, Fredo, Michael, and Tom Hagen. Sonny says "that droopy thing over there is my brother, Michael, we call him Joe College." Michael is isolated "over there," sitting alone on the right side of the long table with Sonny at the head and everyone else on the left. He dresses differently, wearing an open-collar white shirt and checked sport coat, while the other male Corleones are in coat and tie. It is the Don's birthday, and the family is waiting to surprise him when he comes home from a Christmas shopping errand. After Tessio arrives with a huge rum cake, Sonny turns the talk to the "nerve of them Japs," those "slanty-eyed bastards" dropping bombs "on Pop's birthday," as he unerringly reduces probable world war to Corleone life. Tessio observes that thirty thousand men have enlisted already. When Sonny answers that they "risk their life for strangers," Michael replies, "[T]hat's Pop talking." Then he announces that he himself enlisted in the Marines. Sonny has to be restrained from pummeling him. Sonny says Michael will break his father's heart on his birthday; Fredo shakes his hand; Tom stares hard at him and says his father had talked about his future, that he has high hopes for Michael. Michael flares slightly to Hagen: "[Y]ou talked to *my* father about *my* future." Tom and Sonny run out of arguments and anger; there's a bustle in the hall announcing the Don has arrived home, and everyone goes out to meet him except Michael, who remains seated in the now-deserted room, listening to the calls of "[S]urprise!" and the singing of "[F]or he's a jolly good fellow." This deft scene resurrects Fredo, Sonny, Carlo, and the Don; suddenly Michael has a family again. However, the table is curiously void of women, children, Italian food; even the cake is store-bought. The scene has the dreamlike quality of a pared-down abstraction with no quotidian markers of either an immigrant generation or of an Italian American life. Every ethnic fictional meal is potentially a Last Supper, but Michael has summoned no ghosts/guests for such redemption, merely to show how alone he really is and always has been.[25]

The family voices drown out Michael's "American" announcement. By the end of *Godfather II*, Fredo's murder triggers Michael's memory of the day he announced he was *out*, that he had made his escape, the day he thought he could "lose" his family by joining America's struggle. Instead, he lost his family through his return to family, his leadership, violent rule, and alienation of each and every one of them. Coppola has one more even briefer flashback, this time to an earlier scene in the film in which a younger Vito Corleone holds a tiny Michael up to a train window to help him wave good-bye as the train pulls out of Corleone, Sicily, after Vito's triumphant return to take vengeance on the aged Don who had slaughtered his family. For a few silent seconds, Coppola frames a "wave good-bye, Michael" scene that has many resonances for the adult Michael as he sits brooding.[26] The very young son whose hand is being waved by a father is similar to baby Michael's hand being held up by a wondrous Vito Corleone on the tenement front stoop after he comes home from the day's work of killing Fanucci. A small cog caught in a predetermined plot. Being counted in before he could ask to be counted out. Becoming a murderer himself who returned to Sicily on the run. Leaving Sicily to return to America and try to become his father. Coppola asks the viewer to believe that this is Michael's earliest memory, one that entwines father, Corleone, Sicily, and leave-taking in ways that he will struggle with his whole life before being returned to the Sicilian earth at the conclusion of *Godfather III.*

Conclusion

Puzo richly explored Italianita in *The Fortunate Pilgrim* and sensationalized and simplified what he could carry into *The Godfather* before the coda to *Godfather II.* All the time, he was, as his commentary has shown, a reluctant son, husband, and Italian American. Breaking away, being sucked back in, going under, going bad, and trying to become legitimate are constant pressures in his work, both overt on the page and felt in the allegiances and abdications of his characters to family and to work. In "Choosing a Dream," Puzo described the millions of new American soldiers in World War II "making their innocent getaway from baffled loved ones" (26), as in leaving the scene of a crime, one which they will never be accused of by family who will never understand the need. *The Fortunate Pilgrim* is Puzo's one perfectly pitched ethnic novel about his first escape. Puzo mapped the ethnic terrain in rudimentary fashion in *The Godfather,* with monsters in the American blank spaces and initially brought this Italian American subject to countless millions. *The Godfather* is the American melodrama that greatly complicates all potential escapes and shows Puzo fully understood in Michael Corleone's odyssey toward identity across continents and worlds, both ethnic and naturalized, that you can never lose your family.

chapter five

Barthes and Puzo:
The Authority of the Signifier

If I focus on a full signifier, in which I clearly distinguish the meaning and the form, and consequently the distortion which the one imposes on the other, I undo the signification of the myth, and I receive the latter as an imposture. . . . This type of focusing is that of the mythologist: he deciphers the myth, he understands a distortion.

—Barthes, *Mythologies*

Even in matters which are, as it were, just within our reach, what would become of the world, if the practice of all moral duties and the foundations of society, rested upon having their reasons made clear and demonstrative to every individual?

—Edmund Burke, "A Vindication of Natural Society" in Francis Canavan, *The Pluralist Game*

To describe how power and authority are negotiated through Italianita in *The Godfather* is not to sanction the text's immorality and violence just because it is more colorful or dramatic when analyzed through ethnic markers. To relax into that satisfaction would ultimately be an insult to the richness of Italian American culture or any ethnic culture and its universe of forms. Ethnic semiosis does not exist as a concept to efface other questions about a novel's forms and messages. This chapter traces the interaction of structural and ideological questions about *The Godfather*'s semantics, about the immediate and long-range consequences of the novel's signification in character zones and their relation to and articulation of pluralism's premises.

Fiction best-seller lists are replete with novels that expound on every sort of public and private virtue and vice. No subject is taboo; indeed, the function of popular fiction is to talk about everything, albeit in deflecting and manageable ways. Best sellers constantly broadcast messages about sexuality, morality, politics, crime, and punishment, about all the hegemonic

systems of society's control. All fiction certainly communicates these messages through characters and their paradigmatic conflicts. However, in
popular fiction these messages often appear largely out of even the author's
initial control. Little effective causality is demonstrated in the actions and
reflections of the characters. Surely all fictional characters are instrumentalized by authorial agendas to become materialists or monists or ironic
avatars of self-scrutiny. However, even within one subgenre, between
popular melodrama's heroes such as Vito and Michael Corleone and an
elite melodrama character caught in a sensational plot such as Conrad's
bemused and idealistic Axel Heyst in *Victory* (1915), there's a great range
of characterization. Critical questions about such characterization always
center on which characters are chosen to reach the reader with what messages and what are the readerly consequences? In a study of *The Godfather*,
the question thus becomes how Puzo presumes to disclose his most vexing
moral issues.

   In popular fiction, this disclosure may be addressed through an analysis of the fictional voice's investiture as it contributes to the effect of the
narrative's authority. What does it mean to discourse on morality through
murderers? On lawlessness through criminals? In a Macbeth or a
Raskolnikov, the answer is "absolutely everything," as characters become
fully realized psychological, ideological, and aesthetic creations who challenge and satisfy an enormous audience over time through the moral and
emotional power of their representation. Furthermore, beginning with tragic
heroes in antiquity and biblical sinners in Christian parable, fictional and
dramatic narratives have always preferred "barbarous" knowledge to
any other kind. In the contemporary era, we are used to learning about
good and evil from putative villains who have become more interesting
to us than traditional heroes and have become heroes in what Philip
Fisher calls "the Romance of Consciousness" (98). Millions read best sellers
for instruction and edification, in line with the novel's traditional duties,
as well as for all definitions of pleasure. At the same time, however,
modern and contemporary readers accede largely without protest to
identify with fictional outlaws of all persuasions, who, unquestionably,
one hundred years ago would have been cast in popular fiction's outer
darkness of pulp and sensation tales. Elite fiction criticism's take on these
issues is to warn about the impossibility of achieving instruction or edification at all, least of all in popular narrative, and to seek comfort at the
abyss where the pleasure is in knowing the vast impossibilities of knowing anything without attendant irony and further self-consciousness.

   Popular fiction is more direct in its approach and disclosure. The
rhetoric of popular fiction may be grasped by attempting an analysis of
its signification that contributes mightily to the rhetoric's overall effect
on the reader. An analysis of the signification process exposes the interplay of rhetorical powers by which certain realities in the fiction are
revealed, as well as the text's ground of social fact. I want to apply the

dynamics of signification in key scenes involving Jack Woltz in *The God-father* by reference to Barthes' *Mythologies* and then speculate how an extension of the climate of Woltz's world determines much of the novel's representation of girls and women. Puzo's text alternately raises a body of issues about the Corleones and then masks or recontains them by deflecting the reader's attention from the Corleones toward other societal agents. *The Godfather* can be seen in a familiar pattern whereby best sellers often probe a wound on the surface of society, then numb the pain, and appear to make all contradictions cease. Puzo's pattern of selective outrage and moralizing when convenient helps build a readerly consensus about the heroism of the Corleones by making them "familiar" and by making their enemies in the novel "other" or strange. The creation of this pattern is negotiated through identities, first those of the Corleones and their enemies, then extending to the pluralist identities of *Godfather* readers and viewers. What this pattern of signification will show is that no attitude or action can be negative if exemplified long enough by the compelling Corleones; similarly, no outcry against their dominance, no matter how demonstrably or objectively true, can survive in *The Godfather* if articulated through the discredited or the powerless.

The Godfather is a particularly relevant text for Barthesian study. Puzo's novel anatomizes the American social and legal structure across a wide range of family and business practices and situations. The Corleone's are a tightly knit group that settles its own scores and prospers to great wealth. They care about the preservation of family and keep a sober if secretive upper-middle-class profile in their compound-fortress in the wilds of Long Island. On one level of wish-fulfillment, the Corleones as Our Gang appear to be the prototype of togetherness in our collapsing family structure, as close as the kitchen table, as powerful as the corporation; in the end, the family that murders together stays together, provisionally after Michael Corleone's "cleanup" at the end of *Godfather I*, while in *Godfather II*, Michael's crimes increase to fratricide; at the end of *Godfather III*, his tragic melodrama culminates with his daughter's death on the steps of the opera house in Palermo, Sicily.

The Corleones' indirect flouting of every form of constituted American authority and societal norm puts the reader in the position of rooting for the "good" murderers, the Corleones—because we come to know and care about them—against the "bad" murderers, their enemies of whom we know nothing except compromising flashes of impersonal brutality and decadence.[1] The Corleones operate more efficiently, swiftly, and in accordance with their sense of justice than do all the legal and police authority. Thus Puzo manages a potential crisis of reader identification by priming them to agree with Don Corleone's assessment: the system has grievously failed its citizen-adherents; often no recourse exists; we do not know where to turn in such circumstances. Never mind that the Corleones could be perceived as the breakdown of the system itself. The

logic of *The Godfather*'s signification suggests that the Corleones represent the only alternative to a system of justice that has failed.

The resultant signification of Don Corleone as heroic, omnipotent,
and well-nigh eternal is Puzo's achievement, one that can be approached
and provisionally deconstructed so that other issues may be exposed.
Not the least of these issues is the uneasy response of reader-viewers to
the Corleone reign of terror—*what if everyone acted that way?*—the response of those quintessential readers of *Godfather* power, Jack Woltz and
Kay Adams Corleone. *What if everyone* is the true nightmare disorder at
the heart of individualism. To describe how Puzo effects the management of this powerful sentiment within a pluralist society that tentatively
but largely agrees on normative conduct, I want to adapt Barthes' *Mythologies* to provide critical tools for popular fiction study. *Mythologies*
collects his essays written for newspapers and magazines in the mid-
1950s when Barthes was "trying to reflect regularly on some myths of
French daily life" (Barthes 11). His overview to the 1970 edition explained
the "double theoretical framework" of his text: "on the one hand, an
ideological critique bearing on the language of so-called mass culture; on
the other, a first attempt to analyze semiologically the mechanics of this
language" (9). Barthes examined a wide variety of "collective representations" as "sign systems" from wrestling to margerine to plastic, from
the "writer on holiday" to "the face of Garbo" to "the brain of Einstein."
He concluded with a long conceptual essay, "Myth Today," which constitutes an analytical tool most applicable to *The Godfather*. Barthes's largest aim was to "account *in detail* [emphasis Barthes] for the mystification
which transforms petit-bourgeois culture into a universal nature" (9).
Barthes considered this transformation the central facet of "ideological
abuse" in the ways in which the historical, the concrete, the political
were converted into essences that had reference to the natural, the eternal, the unchanging, "the way things are." Everywhere he perceived the
confusion of "history" and "nature" and the meretricious treatment of
the two in cultural discourse. Our postmodern awareness of the politics
of historicizing and naturalizing began in large measure due to Barthes'
landmark semiologics in *Mythologies*, which continued through *Writing
Degree Zero* (1968) and *S/Z* (1970).

Barthes distrusts the easy equation of a physical state for an emotional or moral one. His primary example is from Joseph Mankiewicz's
film of Shakespeare's *Julius Caesar* (1953) in which sweat glistening on the
actors is equated with "moral feeling" and "Roman-ness" (26). Puzo's
symbolizing all the way through *The Godfather* gives vivid evidence of
such equation. Michael Corleone's face is shattered from a blow by a corrupt New York City police captain. Again and again Puzo uses Michael's
fractured appearance to suggest his "double nature." One side of his face
looks cruel, hulking and swollen, "giving him the appearance of depravity
when viewed from that side" (Puzo 327). The other side is a classic profile

(presumably of Romanness). Just so is Michael presented to the reader, first as American war hero and then as hero of the Five Families War of 1946, which leads to his becoming the Don. Puzo establishes this inscription of Michael's duality and calls it "natural" on the level of the novel's action: a divided face is signifier of a signified divided nature between good and evil. Rather than construct an aesthetic that might allow for a featureless bland murderer or sainted physical monster, Puzo wants the easily identifiable hybrid character visually marked as good/evil in the broad melodrama. Puzo works in the same vein with Sonny Corleone, who has a "gross Cupid's face" (15, 27, 70, 245) and earns a reputation as a violent family soldier and prodigious lover. The size of sexual organs is a Puzo constant from Sonny's "enormous blood-gorged pole of muscle" (28) to Lucy Mancini's large vagina. Sonny makes women swoon in anticipatory fear, while Lucy lives in innocent self-disgust of her "ugliness." Puzo's overt signifiers are emblematic of a staple of popular fiction in which the nature of a character is presumed from physical facts that shade toward the mythic in size or potency. No one would deny that a disfigured face or genital abnormality would call up some version of "anatomy is destiny" thematizing. What Barthes would label "reprehensible and deceitful" (Barthes 28) is Puzo's explaining in the guise of "the way things are" some tacit thematic object.

In addition to his basic physical coding, Puzo strives for metaphysical configurations that expose the limits of his conceptualization and underscore the potential manipulation of his signification. A statement variously expressed by both Kay Adams and Jack Woltz in *The Godfather* is that if the Corleones are able to operate with impunity, "there couldn't be any kind of world if people acted that way" (Woltz) or "what if everyone acted that way?" (Kay).[2] This statement may be called a signified expressing a tentative democratic American consensus about the consequences of individual lawlessness. It may also trigger more than the trace of a resentful conviction in the reader that everyone *is* acting that way and that then "I'd be a damn fool to act in any other way." "What if" might be posed subliminally as a question that an individual reader might indeed ask ("what about it, eh? what sort of anarchic power would that be?"). Genuine curiosity about possible answers to this question proliferate in an American society in ever-more fluid discussion over the construction of legitimation and authority within an identity-driven pluralism.[3] By locating several articulations of the "what if" sentiment in the novel in *The Godfather* and then appraising the sites of utterance, their narrative authority, and their cluster of messages, we can find how Puzo credits and discredits character utterances on the "what if everyone" issue and what historical and political questions are provoked by his renderings? It is clear that "what if everyone" has both an individual and moral collective register and is a complex question in any society's dialogue about order and disorder. The constant exposure of such basic conflicts of the social organism is the business of best sellers as they deflect and defuse narratives that raise the largest of issues only to dispose of them in premature conclusions and affirmation.[4]

"What Kind of Man . . . What Sort of World?"

Barthes begins "Myth Today" by stating that "myth is not defined by the object of its message, but by the way in which it utters its message . . ." (109). He places most of the act of critical interpretation on divining the authority of the signifier. Language is adopted by a certain predisposing subject, and the content, especially in a novel, is yoked to a character or to a narrative voice in charge of the utterance. Barthes sees "mythical speech" as "made of a material which has *already* been worked on so as to make it suitable for communication"; the mythical speech "presuppose[s] a signifying consciousness" (110), the message situated in narrative so as to take on a logic of its own.[5] Barthes's leap from a linguistic to a mythical structure is both organic and ingenious. He flatly states that myth is a second-order semiological system but one that is catalyzed by the linguistic sign: "that which is a sign (namely the associative total of a concept and an image) in the first system, becomes a mere signifier in the second" (114). Thus, Barthes sees (115),

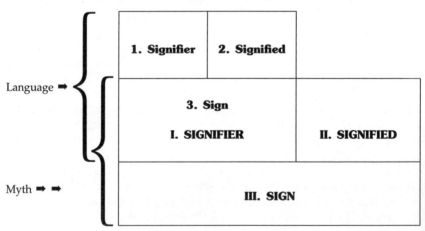

How might this second-order system be adapted to the analysis of fiction,[6] in this case, Puzo's *The Godfather*? Perhaps the novel's scene most vividly remembered from the first *Godfather* film does not feature one of the myriad human victims but that of the stallion Khartoum's severed head lying in a pool of blood at the foot of Hollywood producer Jack Woltz's bed. Woltz has refused Tom Hagen's "suggestion" to cast Johnny Fontane in a major motion picture and suffers the inevitable consequences of the Don's displeasure. In this sensational and visceral scene, Woltz's first thoughts when he stops screaming concern the cash value of the horse. He equates power with money in economic discourse: "[W]hat kind of man could destroy an animal worth six hundred thousand dollars?" (69) Then he extends his musings to a maxim saying that "the ruthlessness, the sheer disregard for any values, implied a man who considered himself completely his own law, even his own God" (69). Puzo lets Woltz get right at it. Even this early in the novel, Woltz shows he's been an attentive if not particularly enlightened reader of the text's violence by concluding, "There couldn't be any kind of world if people acted that way. It was insane. It meant that you couldn't do what you wanted with your own money, with the companies you owned, the power you had to give orders. It was ten times worse than Communism. It had to be smashed. It must never be allowed" (69).

Puzo is clear enough on the specific viewpoint of Woltz who asks that this "it," this Corleone anarchy out of feudalism visited upon him, be checked by some limits, an order that should prevail over freedom and license. An apostle of American capitalism and its licenses, he cannot see past power and money in the implications of his statement. Puzo crucially allows Woltz, Don Corleone's capitalist double from the larger society, to review the Godfather's power, aims, and consequences from a dominant Cold War paradigm ("ten times worse than communism") that demands retaliation. Popular fiction does not often allow for such checkpoints and reflective anger on systems because the narrative must continue to hurtle forward in sensation and melodrama. Yet Woltz's analysis is exactly where the reader-critic should stop, according to Barthes, for as Bakhtin reminds us, the activity of a character in a novel is always ideologically demarcated (*The Dialogic Imagination* 335). Woltz as a site of crisis both exposes and drives exploitation underground in his private dissent. Woltz says rules are rules, procedures in America that allow him to operate as capitalist predator. If we apply Barthes' diagram like a grid over the dynamics of Woltz's reasoning, we have the following:

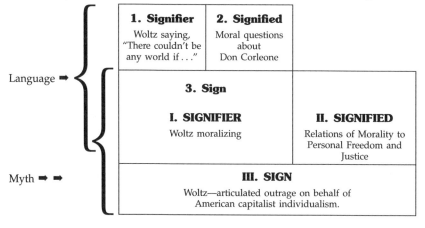

The key point in my adaptation of Barthes's diagram is the shift when the Woltz-articulated sentiments change from being the linguistic sign and become the mythical signifier at the outset of the second-order semiological operation. The mythical signified is where the reader-critic begins to imply his or her own content, what Barthes categorizes as a confusing welter of opinions, goals, values, and relations that are actually our own emotional castes, mind sets, and personal experiences and contribute to whatever "taste" judgments we make of any artistic creation.[7] These are dictated through our gender, temperament, education, social class, and political philosphy (Barthes 119). Although now we'd add race, ethnicity, age, and sexual preference, Barthes's inclusive list holds up remarkably well more than four decades later to describe reality perspectively formed by readers and the processes by which we affiliate. These associations work to make up what Barthes calls the "concept" in the mythical signified, what I would call both our yearnings and identifications toward "the good life" (Barthes mentions richness, kindness, and wholeness (121)) that influence our interpretation; our response is shaped here with regard to the most inclusive subject we can then frame and ask: what does "Woltz-articulated outrage on behalf of American capitalist individualism" *mean*? Barthes is correct to see the signified/concept open to the "whole of history" (120), which must include our own personal histories as we negotiate our priorities in a pluralist society. Furthermore, we encode our signifieds in collective formations through liberal procedural values that will enhance the possibility of their achievement.[8]

Barthes sees the signified/concept as rich while the signifier/form is "a repository of rarefied meaning" (120), making its choice by the author all the more crucial. Barthes finds an abundance of forms but few concepts, which are more universal. Also, forms may be characters, voices, or statements. Concepts may include beauty versus ugliness, truth versus lies, and goodness versus evil as we strive to give shape to our own subjectivizing reactions and touchstones that yield our views of freedom and value. In Woltz's utterance of the concept "there couldn't be any kind of world if everyone acted that way," is his own subjective history. By "Woltzing" around with it, Puzo has made what looks like an inevitable yoking of character and outrage. The mythical signification is then exactly "Woltz-articulated outrage" as it interacts with relations of morality and systems of value such as civic and financial order and becomes allied with patriotic sentiment: "it [Corleone rapacity] was ten times worse than communism" (69). Such a new signification is heavily ideological because Woltz, as we shall see, represents discredited and discounted checks and balances in the American system. To undo "Woltz-articulated outrage" is to begin to gauge the inevitable distortion of any signifier; but to answer "what sort of world?" we must first ask, what sort of man/signifier is Woltz who moralizes? on our way to asking what sort of writer is Puzo who has a Woltz moralize?

One last Barthesian set of distinctions is very useful in seeing how Puzo has positioned Woltz's in *The Godfather*'s symbology. Barthes focuses on three different types of reading, which must be differentiated to grasp what he calls the "duplicity" of the signifier. These focuses are the Empty, Full, and Mythical Signifiers. They could be labeled the signifiers of the author (Empty), critic (Full) and reader (Mythical). In Woltz's case, the author, Puzo, wishes to signify the omnipotence of Don Corleone. "Woltz moralizing" is an example of that omnipotence; he is a symbol for it after his devastating horse lesson from the great Don as to who has the real power. The critic's task with the full signifier is to distinguish once again between the form and the meaning, to expose the full form of the signification. The critic may see "Woltz moralizing" as the alibi of Corleone omnipotence, the distorted imprimatur sanctioning the correct decision made by Don Corleone to take action against him. The mythical signifier is the reader's form as he or she receives a union of meaning and form. "Woltz moralizing" reflects the very presence of Corleone power; his devastation as an assimilationist Hollywood loudmouth is the object-lesson. The reader hurtles on to the next example of family power, having acknowledged, yes, Don Corleone is omnipotent, and Woltz got what he deserved. No distortion or localizing element impedes the reader. Whereas the Empty and Full Signifiers are static in the sense of arrest, the Empty is (in Barthes's terms) "cynical" and the Full "demystifying." The focusing through the Mythical Signifier by the reader is "dynamic, it consumes the myth according to the very ends built into its structure" (Barthes 128). "Woltz moralizing" appears to "naturally" call up indignation and then Puzo "naturally" disposes of him.

However, a Barthesian analysis would only begin there. Because Woltz has been severely discredited in advance, his signification as the locus of societal outrage is cancelled by prior significations. Hence, Puzo lets readers know they need not worry about what has been done to this victim and, by implication, to any Corleone victim. If Woltz is to be at the center of a major statement on American values, Puzo has insured that reader response to him will be negative because Woltz, potential ethnic double as power magnate to the Don, is nonetheless the antithesis of Don Corleone in every detail that could matter to the reader. At age ten Woltz had "hustled empty beer kegs and pushcarts" on the East Side in New York, and at age twenty "he helped his father sweat garment workers"; yet he has remained neither in New York nor in a family business. A movie pioneer in Hollywood, he transformed himself socially by taking speech lessons and learning dress and manners from an English valet and butler. He marries an actress, collects master paintings, serves on Presidential committees; "his daughter married an English lord, his son an Italian princess" (55–56). This cacophony of signs portrays an assimilated American tycoon with tantalizing, undeveloped ethnic accents ("his son [married] an Italian princess) who has fragmented his strengths to take up a position in the larger American society where he can threaten to call up his "friend" J. Edgar Hoover if Tom Hagen puts pressure on him. "Woltz moralizing" is a corporate America loudly protesting that its protection from such criminals as the Corleones is its due for playing the American game as opposed to the ethnic identity game of the Corleones. Woltz is totally isolated in his huge mansion; his is not the Corleone compound on Long Island with spaghetti in every pot and "family" members in every bungalow. To Tom Hagen, Woltz's office is full of "shrewdies," not trusted subordinates personally indentured to him.

However, it is not enough for Puzo to run Woltz through this collective register of negatives. He must also discredit him intimately through his sexuality. The Don is "notoriously straitlaced in matters of sex" (73), and this fact is the moral control that Puzo invokes when it pleases him. Woltz, on the other hand, has "real love in his voice" when he croons to his horse, Khartoum. That Khartoum's blood fouls Woltz's bed hints that Woltz's simulated bestiality is realized in the animal's murder. In case the reader doesn't get it, Puzo has Hagen see a child star stumble from Woltz's mansion, "her exquisitely cut mouth seemed to have smeared into a thick pink mass. . . . her long legs tottered like a crippled foal" (63).[9] Woltz— horse lover, child seducer, friend of Hoover, American success story—is a thoroughly discredited figure *before* he utters his cry for checks and balances in a pluralist America. Yet he knows none himself and has committed three major sins in *The Godfather*: he has denied his ethnic origins, become "Americanized," and been sexually deviant. The three signifieds merge into an indictment that makes Woltz's outrage a sham contrivance to the critical reader and strongly undermines the potentially idealized message of "there couldn't be any kind of world if."

Puzo insures Woltz's downfall when he remains impervious to Tom Hagen's attempt at dialogue as discussed in chapter 4: "the guy was taking his words at their sentimental face value. He was not getting the message" (63). Woltz here is a bad reader of the Godfather, but readers as myth consumers of *The Godfather* perform a different activity as readers of "Woltz moralizing" as a mythical signifier. His words are not taken at their face value, and *he* is the message. Given a choice, there is little doubt that the reader will identify not with Woltz as victim or as a moral questioner of this text but with another victory by Don Corleone, whose power appears universal. Woltz's power is merely political and temporal, compromised and specific. Here Puzo performs a contemptuous politicizing in the service of eternalizing. Woltz significantly parses out most of his reactions in an interior monologue and "laughs wildly" (70) at his own conclusions. He has no real dialogized existence and is totally isolated by Puzo except through manipulation in authorial statement.

As Barthes points out, "myth transforms history into nature." In Barthes's terms, Don Corleone's power is "frozen into something natural; it is not read as a motive, but as a reason" (129). The myth consumer may

renounce Woltz's pain and protest since it is inimical to his prior signification as assimilationist, American, and deviant. Thus "Woltz moralizing" is canceled through his negative historicization and "naturally" calls
up the concept of Corleone omnipotence. Here the mythologist may intervene to challenge the author's cover-up. At this juncture, an ethical
reading suggests itself, one that carries the weight of the collective society's
liberal consensus. To open the signified/concept to the "whole of history" (Barthes 120) is to posit something like the following: the Mafia is
a natural, eternal force dislocates it as an historical and political entity
that has been created in time and could be addressed as a culture-specific
evil. To privilege Woltz as outraged victim belies the real victims of
Corleone power in the novel who are never seen, the whole marginalized
and buried culture of deprivation, weakness, and desire (gambling, prostitution, addiction, extortion) upon which the Corleone empire is built.
We only see the beleaguered family responding to specific evils and
provocations by their murderous peers in Puzo's drive to keep the novel
on course as melodrama of family life and death.[10]

Puzo, at his most distressingly cosmic, reasons that Don Corleone
helped people "not perhaps out of cunning or planning but because of his
variety of interests or because of the nature of the universe, the interlinking
of good and evil, natural of itself" (392). The contingent, fabricated historical quality of Corleone terror, the murder and the pillage, is laundered into
a natural force against which Woltz is worse; Kay is a woman; and police,
courts, and politicians are subject to mortal error because they are "made
up" in civil society, not natural. Puzo has stacked the narative against them
or willfully left them uncreated. He has turned reality inside out, turned
a horse-loving child seducer into a moralizer. Woltz as signifier cannot
survive the prior pressure toward his discrediting. Puzo here has turned
the narrative against fiction itself. He has chosen, in Bakhtin's terms, a
single-voiced myth over dialogization. Woltz's signification stands in sharp
contrast to the positive restating by the Don and Michael that "there couldn't
be any kind of world if." As opposed to Woltz's protest, the Don dies in
the "shade of his . . . patio," whispering, "Life is so beautiful" (409), and
Michael dissembles oxymoronically to Kay about "the good simple life of
well-to-do Americans" (363). Such falsely affirming moments calm and
reassure the *Godfather* reader that its first family knows what's really important. Woltz, however, goes unheard and decidedly punished. So much
for Puzo destroying through negative agency a massive signified about the
balances of a pluralist society.

Naturalizing the Signifier

Naturalizing the signifier counters specific politicizing and creates
inevitable tensions in any fiction. In "Myth Today," Barthes is frustrated

to the point where he asks, "Is there no meaning which can resist this capture with which form threatens it?" (131). This question dominates the conclusion of *Mythologies*, where Barthes contends we are "condemned to speak excessively about reality" (159), to either "ideologize" or "poetize." He could not in *Mythologies* posit a reconciliation between these strategies, and the succeeding decades have proved him correct in the contentious evolution of contemporary critical theories. Woltz was ideologized by Puzo in order to *be* poetized as villain. His specific associations with the American system and with a deviant sexuality are created only to cancel him as a spokesman for victimization by the Don. Here is the problem for all fictional narrative where meaning must come through a signifier, either a character zone or a narrative voice identified through its accents with the author. The inevitable situatedness of fictional messages marks the contingency of all novelistic statement. The content of the message uttered by Woltz takes on the greatest of its implications through Woltz as form. The mythical signifier "Woltz moralizing" has specific marked properties. To ideologize them on the critic's part is to reinvent content that the text may suppress or leave unexpressed. In this vein in *The Godfather,* Don Corleone's real victims may be invoked in their absence. The question of the Don's relation to the organized Catholic church, a key suppressed text in the novel, could then be discussed as Puzo's necessary evasive action to protect the omnipotence of his protagonist.[11]

On the other hand, to "poetize" is to search for inalienable meanings on levels beyond the narrative. This search is everywhere inimical to the artifact being examined in popular culture study. Such strategies propose value judgments about "common humanity" and "individual freedom," to name two of the most popular signifieds in the lexicon of practical literary criticism that flow from a pluralist society's deepest beliefs and goals. For a number of reasons, such signifieds now carry the burden of being labeled elitist in their "naturalized" form. Popular fiction critics are moved to restore the ideological component to texts even as elite fiction critics are moved to poetize what they deem to be complex texts about social and cultural issues, often to the exclusion of such issues. To break into Puzo's attempts at universalizing in a melodramatic novel such as *The Godfather* is to attempt to restore the historical and narrative contradictions that gave rise to its sonorous, concealing surface in the first place. It is to become Humean in the extreme, to locate sites of feeling such as Woltz's lament and block Puzo's rhetoric with sentimental response of equal feeling that the author has gotten it wrong, that "Woltz moralizing" cuts bad corners indeed.

Fiction has a naturalness of the very text that is combed for universals. What is made to look natural in *The Godfather* is, in the Woltz example, a prior coding of the signifier. This coding is inescapable if utterances are to be in the province of characters but need not be so blatantly at cross-purposes with the morality of the signified as in Woltz's speech. The more coherence between the signifier and the signified, whether achieved symbolically, rhetorically, or ironically, the greater the achievement of the author is said to be. What constitutes this coherence fuels the widest possible range of debate among critical methods and individual critics.[12] How this coherence might relate to an ethics of fiction as well as a poetics is an even larger question.

In *S/Z* (1974), Barthes is more congenial toward the naturalizing process, seeing it as an inevitable component of the production of meaning rather than an inherently reductive feature. Barthes finally asks if any sentence, whatever meaning it releases, doesn't appear to be telling us something simple, literal, and primitive, something *true*" (*S/Z* 9). In *S/Z*, "denotation" replaces "naturalizing" as "the old deity, watchful, cunning, theatrical, *foreordained* to *represent* the collective innocence of language" (9). Here Barthes's linguistic configuration shades remarkably close to a description of Don Corleone himself, shaping any specific message into an articulation of his power; he is a deity, in producing gestural performance in *bella figura* and full of "cunning," Puzo's favorite noun of praise for any character. If Puzo has inscribed a mythical center of power beyond which no other fictional dialogue may flourish in his novel, the corollary must be that his critics also naturalize as soon as they isolate his language for analysis. To snip out any text segment as in the Woltz examples under discussion here or the Genco–Don Corleone dialogue analyzed at length in chapter 3, is to arrest the narrative at a second-order level, that of multiple levels of critical scrutiny. As soon as we perform any critical act, we have substituted a further naturalization and have created a deformed text of examples in our own narrative.[13]

Barthes' largest point is, of course, that as soon as we *utter*, we naturalize. Barthes finally matures the "natural" into something like the inescapable base of the narrative: "paradoxically, language, the integral system of meaning, is employed to de-systematize the secondary meanings, to naturalize their production and to authenticate the story" (*S/Z* 23). "Connotation" is the wealth that Barthes invests in *S/Z* in terms of semes to be identified and combined. The connotations are quick, extrinsic acknowledgements and citations rather than the close-reading, second-order politicizing of *Mythologies*. In what he calls the "classic" or "readerly" text, Barthes concludes that the author moves from signified to signifier (what do I want to say, whom shall I find to say it). The author is "god" of the signifier, the critic is "priest," deciphering the full signifier and working back toward content (174). A signifier becomes a rich collection of semes. Thus Woltz could be called a "point of convergence" for power, authority, decadence, [il]legitimacy, and order: "the proper name enables the person to exist outside the semes whose sum nonetheless constitutes it entirely" (191). Their proper names throughout the American elite and popular canon could be Hester, Uncle Tom, Huck, Gatsby, Scarlett, or

Sethe, names that mythically take on a set of characteristics and convergences that allow the characters to float as ambassadors with critical portfolio toward other characters, texts, and eras, seeking answering words and embodying powerful significations.

Jack Woltz's Stable: Khartoum and the Girls

Woltz himself is a site for much bad-faith moralizing about American capitalism, its power, rights, and privileges. Radiating out from Woltz's Hollywood empire as a model of that capitalism is also a set of significations that involve the marketing and abuse of women, Hollywood's major capital asset, as it controls the sexual dream world of American culture. Much of the absolute male power of the Corleones is segmented sharply off and away from female eyes and influence. However, the Hollywood world of Jack Woltz, the anti–Don Corleone, is founded almost solely on the business of trading in women. This implication and inability to separate male and female spheres dooms Woltz's influence in the novel as surely as his refusal of the Don's offer on behalf of Johnny Fontane. For women in *The Godfather* become essences, colors, animals, ripe or rotting fruit, virginal New Englanders, shrews, spoiled "guinea" daughters, old crones, Hollywood bitch wives who are "out fucking." Barthes writes that "what is sickening in myth is the resort to a false nature . . . as in these objects which decorate their usefulness with a natural appearance. The will to weigh the signification with the full guarantee of nature causes a kind of nausea: myth is too rich, and what is in excess is precisely its motivation" (126). We need to examine, as best we can, Puzo's "motivation" in signifying the *Godfather* women.

Women in *The Godfather* are characteristically both too rich and too instrumental to the male plot to really live on their own. The way they function as mythical signifiers is, first, to deny them agency and then to build sensationally on physical attributes or economic functions. None of this is exactly news in popular fiction. However, Woltz Productions is at the heart of this narrative and re-creates something like Woltz's desiring imagination. The most imposing sexual animal in *The Godfather* is Woltz's stallion, Khartoum, whom Woltz croons to like a lover, admiring his "great brown eyes" which "glinted like golden apples, the black skin over the taut body was silk." Woltz proudly tells Hagen, "Look at that cock on him. I should have such a cock" (60). Thus while the Don has his mythically endowed son Sonny as lieutenant and heir, Woltz has a male horse that dies savagely and its head placed in his bed, the same bloody bed, it is presumed, where Woltz violated the twelve-year-old girl starlet, the "crippled foal" with her "mouth smeared into a pink mass," "whose sea-blue eyes were filmed over" whom Hagen watches stumble to the car outside Woltz's mansion. The Don "murmurs *'infamita'*" (66) when told of Woltz's action. Sonny is hung like Khartoum and slaughtered like him as well; his cock is alive in Lucy Mancini's hand, where "it pulsated in her hand like an animal" (28). Lucy herself has a sexual "deformity" to be rectified: a large vagina caused by a weakening of the pelvic floor. This cluster of sexual organ sizings in horses, men, women, and girls is clearly confusing. Is Woltz homosexual in orientation? Is Sonny no more than an animal? Is Lucy a vagina in soft core fantasy? Does the young girl starlet only exist to be raped by Woltz? Is Khartoum another innocent victim?

Girls and women are used across a direct, visceral, and reductive field of signification in *The Godfather*. The description thickens rather than the plot. A scene from the novel not used by Coppola concerns a Woltz side enterprise, the euphemistically named "Hollywood Movie Star Lonely Hearts Club" (182), a Friday evening affair hosted by Woltz's press agent at which aging star actresses who had "been desensitized physically" and could "no longer 'fall in love'" or assume the role of "hunted women" could prey on younger lovers in Woltz-approved one-night stands. Rather than "raced" (given movie roles) like Khartoum, these women are put out to stud, servicing and being serviced by younger male actors, presumably for practice and their upward (no pun) mobility in the ranks. The scene is hardly one of a brothel or an orgy. The house and grounds comprise a movie set, which features patio lighting "artfully arranged to flatter feminine faces and skin." The seductions take place in a well-appointed screening room where each aging star has her own couch and younger lover in dark "semi-privacy." The fiction decrees that a movie be up on the screen as each young stud is serviced in the dark (a working definition of Hollywood film intent) by the female star who might until recently have been the on-screen fantasy. This funny and nasty little conceit shows Puzo in a rare comic moment of control; it's our neighborhood Italian fella, Nino Valenti, now on the loose with Johnny in Hollywood, who is taken through his paces by one Deanna Dunn, who makes "a voracious plummet on his sexual organ without even a courteous and friendly word of preparation" (185). When Deanna comes up for air, and Nino is working on a fresh drink and cigarette, he cracks, "This looks like a pretty good movie." When she admires him for being "big as a house," he shrugs her off, saying, "That's the way it always is. You should see it when I get excited" (186).

Here Puzo has moved into a jaunty rendition of Nathanael West's Hollywood in a relaxed mode that Hollywood often signifies for him. He is almost off-duty in the satiric sketch about Nino in movie sex heaven. Hollywood is out beyond the straitlaced Corleones in sensibility and sexual preference. Johnny and Nino are at play in the sexual fantasy world that Hollywood demonstrably is producing all the time and that popular narrative almost establishes as the predominant reality. This more contemporary text dangles in *The Godfather* in 1969 where it's Jack Woltz's viciousness that is the main line of the novel's sexual development, not this satirical sideshow, and Puzo revisits this sexual Hollywood in both *Fools Die* and *The Last Don*. However, in *The Godfather*, the critical advice is to follow the line out from Woltz, who not only signifies degenerate sexuality himself (bestiality, child rape) but who controls American production of sexuality on film. For Puzo to really say something about this fact beyond its mere representation is well beyond his conceptual agenda for Woltz as Hollywood double for the Don.

The Godfather's "positive" or "innocent" portrayals of women include Johnny Fontane's daughters and the Girls of Sicily, including Michael's great love, Apollonia. However, the jumble of symbolism and putative links to Khartoum make an incoherent cluster of statements about women and their victimization. The reader is forced to conclude that for Puzo, sexuality and its representation are charged, but not intelligible, visceral without viewpoint, and heedless as to which feminine body is on display for what sensational or sentimental reason. Without a viewpoint, ironic or otherwise, the women in *The Godfather* are the strongest examples of reading for the mythical signifier, for "consum[ing] the myth according to the very ends built into its structure" for using women up as readerly capital in the way they are used by the men in the narratives themselves. Their ornamentation, which is made to look natural or in essence female, is a stew of innocence revered and defiled, of explosive sex between organs, not people, and of the victimization such moments inevitably yield. None of this struggle and pain appears to have concerned Puzo very much; as Nino said at the "Lonely Hearts Club," it "look[ed] like a pretty good movie."

Two young girls putatively outside the Woltz stable of sexual energy are Johnny Fontane's daughters who are kept in virginal simplicity by their mother for Johnny's occasional notice and favor. Yet Puzo can't seem to keep sexual signification out of his scene. On one of Johnny's infrequent visits home (one of Puzo's great bourgeois fantasies, of "dropping in occasionally" and finding dinner on the table, the kids dressed and shining, and the wife all attentive), his "two small daughters" wheel a breakfast cart to his bed in the middle of the afternoon: "They were so beautiful it broke his heart. Their faces were shining and clear, their eyes alive with curiosity and the eager desire to run to him. They wore their hair braided old-fashioned in long pigtails and they wore old-fashioned frocks and white patent leather shoes." These signifiers of tradition and innocence stashed somewhere in the middle of Woltz's Hollywood, perhaps called up by central casting for an antiquated family picture, are kept by Johnny's ex-wife in perfect genteel order, recalling Sicilian girls dressed for a holiday. Yet the scene changes when "they came running to him. He pressed his face between their two fragrant cheeks and scraped them with his beard so that they shrieked" (165). In another author, this fuzzy friction of a famous lover-father in bed between two young girls' "cheeks" who "were too old now for pillow fights or to be tossed around" could be very suggestive at the least or grimly revealing. Puzo, who signifies for the plot, not for psychological depth or grim irony, sees Johnny Fontane as the "romantic, old-fashioned guinea" reveling in his daughters' "freshness." Johnny's daughters are the nonsexual counterpart to the virgins he takes for sex. For Johnny without his voice (read masculinity), "the last two years had been hell on his ego, and he used this simple way to restore it, sleeping with a fresh young girl for one night . . . and then brushing her off" (158). In this way Puzo shows us a rather sad man, incapable of differentiating between dewy starlets and his own daughters and nostalgic for the original cleanliness of it all—clean phrasing in singing, clean young bodies. Johnny "smooth[es] their mussed hair" and thinks of the "Hollywood punks" who will soon be after them (166), failing, of course, to place himself in that category.

It doesn't occur to Puzo that Johnny has some defect in his relation to women, only that he's shy, victimized, and nostalgic, which is Puzo's signature dreamy vein where male musing on the feminine is concerned. Armed with psychology, elite critical reading patterns, and a moral skepticism, the reader can conclude that Woltz and Johnny Fontane are *equal* in depravity, the one in gusto as a villain, the other in soft denial, but that would not be Puzo's message. In each case, that of Woltz's twelve-year-old starlet with the torn mouth and Johnny's giggling daughters of the same age in daddy's bed, the reader is not asked to connect the dots but rather to acknowledge in popular fictional plot logic that the raped girl starlet makes Woltz bad and pigtailed daughters in bed make Johnny good. What's evident in both scenes is that Puzo contrives to get the older man into bed with young girls. We read that Woltz is "a raging wolf ravaging helpless flocks of young starlets"; we know Johnny is in thrall to young women. Yet Puzo won't give the material any internal dialogism; there's no arresting of the mythical signifier ("Woltz raping," "Johnny as loving father") to consider the consequences of an older man's love of young girls nor what is Hollywood's role in addressing and fostering such desire in the culture. The most that can be said for Puzo is his desire for a weak or casual irony in the two presentations. He's more interested in his grand comedy: the Brothel of Overaged Stars. Any concern about sexual violation and exploitation vanishes in the reader's smile at Nino's wisecracks, in the reader's applause as Woltz gets his just equine desserts.

At this point, the reader of this chapter might wonder if she is now to endure an attack of umbrage about the animal rights violations in Khartoum's portrayal. There is, to be sure, a level beyond which a critic's hammering at an author's depiction of character and characters obscures the actual authorial purpose in such quick and extrinsic character portrayal. Yet no woman in *The Godfather* is given more than a violent, external, or mythical brushstroke. Kay is a New England Adams, Apollonia a fawn, Mama Corleone a wrinkled old crone, Connie Corleone a shrew in training, Lucy Mancini a vagina. Such perfunctory characterization is, however, in line with melodrama's need to shuffle the emotional intensities around rather than provide release, mastery, or insight, to elicit the desired emotional response from the audience. Popular fiction does not give the reader a reason for, or point toward, a structure where a thoughtful pause to consider Woltz raping the twelve year old will give any more insight to Johnny Fontane breakfasting in bed with his daughters. Consuming the myth dictates that the reader experience Woltz as depraved and Johnny as innocent or, as Barthes says "live the myth as a story at once true and unreal" (128).

When Michael is exiled to Sicily and meets the "thunderbolt" that is Apollonia, Puzo again essentializes her portrayal, this time to signify a mythic female Sicilianness. The images could be taken from a child's myth picture book, a lush commercial travel guide, or a garish foreign cinematic copy of Hollywood "epic"-ness dubbed into English. This young Sicilian goddess is glimpsed in the fields with her friends: "[T]hey were still in their teens but with the full womanliness sun-drenched flesh ripened into so quickly. Three or four of them started chasing one girl [Apollonia], chasing her toward the grove. The girl being chased held a bunch of huge purple grapes in her left hand. . . . She had a crown of ringleted hair as purple black as the grapes and her body seemed to be bursting out of its skin" (333). Apollonia is "delicious ripe fruit" (345) even as the overaged stars in Hollywood had been "wax fruit" (184). What's more disturbing is Apollonia's strong resemblance to Woltz's stallion, Khartoum. The horse had "great brown eyes glint[ing] like golden apples" and the "black skin over the taut body was silk" (60). Apollonia with the aforementioned purple black hair has "honey-colored skin" and "huge brown eyes"; her signature is "silk": Puzo uses the word in numbing succession in the same page ("silky naked skin," "silken electricity," "her flesh and hair taut silk" [344]). Like Johnny's daughters, she has "a wonderfully fresh smell" (345). However, like Khartoum, she is destroyed as Michael's wife and property, a beautiful sensuous animal blown to bits in revenge against the Corleones. Did Puzo understand Apollonia's close resemblance to Khartoum, and if so, what did he make of it and what should the reader do with the doubling? The most potent and similarly described desirable objects in the novel are the male horse of the rapist villain and the Sicilian dream girl of the novel's hero. Once more, a potential for some radical conception of desire and retribution exists, but Puzo doesn't link the scenes in any way.

In similar fashion, Puzo doesn't connect other potential doubling scenes. Lucy Mancini, whom Puzo actually likes, is described at the Corleone wedding as "this young girl, fully aware . . . at a garden table in her pink formal gown, a tiara of flowers in her glossy black hair" (16). Innocent Lucy is only pages away from Sonny's "enormous blood-gorged pole of muscle" (28) and a sister to Woltz's violated girl with her "exquisitely cut," "raspberry-red mouth" turned into a "pink mass" (55, 63). However, any notion of equating Sonny's "rape" for Lucy's "pleasure" with Woltz's abuse of the girl is not in Puzo's semantic row; the two scenes pass on the visceral power of Sonny and the decadence of Woltz. What's most probable is that Puzo had a limited repertoire of violent and desiring rhetoric and images, that violence and sex were bound for him in a way that he did not or would not investigate, that his own art was not to decode or deconstruct his desiring imagination but to simply repeat it over and over in the novel's urgent moments.

Such a hypothesis might be proven by one other improbable link in this signifying chain—the description of the death of the human weapons system known as Luca Brasi, the Corleone's most feared executioner, the unreconstructed Sicilian brute whom Sollozzo and Tattaglia lure to his death to smooth the way for their attack on Don Corleone. Luca's wrists are pinned, and a "thin silken chord" is wound round his neck; his face "became purple," his "eyes were bulging out of his head" (111), reminiscent of the "mottled, dead hemorrhaged blood" in Khartoum's dead eyes (68) or the "sea blue eyes filmed over" (63) in Woltz's girl. Luca is worse than Woltz for he has murdered both his infant child and its mother. This New York anecdote told by an old woman fills the space between Michael and Apollonia's wedding and her assassination. "Silken" and "purple," Luca in death resembles Apollonia as well as Khartoum, and the link between them is extraordinary bodily value, either sexual or violent, the currency of the book's economy. Luca, Apollonia, and Khartoum become physical markers of the stakes involved. These are the weavings of the literary critic because Puzo only knows one way to write about violence and sex together, forcing him to fall back on the same rhetoric so that the descriptions merge but do not clarify.[14]

One more silk reference intrigues and is related to Connie Corleone, prized only daughter of the Godfather, a "not quite pretty girl, thin and nervous" (19) on her wedding day while the bridegroom's Carlo Rizzi's, "eyes kept flickering toward the huge silk purse the bride wore on her right shoulder" (20). Connie's money, not her body, is silk, but by possessing the purse (more valuable than Lucy's vagina), Carlo goes for the money. Does Puzo want to equate Connie's silk purse with the bodily silk of Khartoum and Apollonia? No evidence supports the pattern; rather a taxed vocabulary and repetitive image seem more to the point. One can only guess how many "silk purses" have been made out of novelists' "sows' ears" over the decades by intrepid critics whose business is making meaning and pattern, but the logic of melodrama says *onward* rather than "reflect on this set of correspondences for awhile." However, Puzo's missed chances or connections can only be mourned by critical readers. Woltz's "protege" whom Johnny "ruined," the starlet who precipitates the whole crisis with Johnny Fontane, is not even named. What if the child Luca Brasi murdered along with its mother, "a young pretty girl who looked Irish"

(347) had been allowed to live and had grown up to be Tom Hagen? Hagen's Italian wife is a "college graduate, " "rare at that time" (52), but she merits only a line or two before disappearing. What would be her ethnic and educated take on the novel's carnage? Could she be a potential Octavia from *The Fortunate Pilgrim* or an ally or rival for female articulation along with Kay? Finally, Jack Woltz's son "married an Italian princess" (56), but to what end? Why even provide the titillation for the reader if that particular gun is not going to go off in the novel? This ethnic marking of "Irish" and "Italian" women appears heedless and without follow-up. The throwaway Irish girl, female Italian college grad and Mafia wife, and Italian princess are potentially more interesting female characters than Kay, Lucy, and Apollonia, but they are barely introduced. When expectations on simple character marking and consequence are frustrated, the critic can say with reasonable certainty that interlocking patterns of ethnicity and ironic doubling are beyond the author's capability or interest, as, in this case is any careful representation of any female character in the most totally male world in the history of the American blockbuster best seller.[15]

The God of Immanence

So Jack Woltz has a horse instead of Don Corleone's three sons, a twelve-year-old girl instead of a wife. Instead of honoring his ethnic father, he jokes to Hagen that perhaps one of his grandmothers was raped by a cossack (60). However, it's not the sex that shocks Hagen but the fact that sex consumes Woltz's time and affects his business judgment. "In Hagen's world, the Corleones' world, the physical beauty, the sexual power of women carried not the slightest weight in worldly matters" (62), thus establishing a residual moralism that frees the reader to root for the Corleones, damn Woltz, and enjoy the Hollywood sex follies, all at the same time. Woltz pedals the old, seduces the young, and loves his horse. The Don, freed from all desire, may reason while Woltz explodes (ejaculates). Men who "go off," Sonny Corleone included, are finally the dangerous men. Michael gets "colder" during all crises, starting with "that strange delicious chill filling his body" (150) just before he murders Solozzo.

All these significations are easily obtainable from *The Godfather* as Puzo repeats their import again and again. In melodrama, good and evil, hot and cold, love and hate are drawn as maps on the faces of the lead characters, so there can be no mistake of their place in the *agon* that loudly proclaims their travails. Barthes's "The World of Wrestling" in *Mythologies* evinces a great nostalgia and fondness for this signifying world. Professional wrestling is exactly what it appears to be with no obfuscation of its process in the morality plays of broadly drawn heroes and villains. Barthes unpacks wrestling thusly: "This emptying out of interiority to the benefit of its exterior signs, this exhaustion of content by the form, is the very principal of triumphant classical art" (18). For Barthes, wrestling "always accomplishes completely" (24); "there is no symbol, no allusion, everything is presented exhaustively" (25). This admirable aesthetic for Barthes is as close an approximation to a simulated state of nature as he can find in popular representation. Wrestling is a creation almost coextensive with its truth; it is what it is, the audience is not tricked or taken advantage of.

What this might mean for fictional representation is expressed most movingly by Bourdieu, surely one of Barthes's godsons, who at the end of a long essay on Flaubert's *Sentimental Education* states that he admires most Flaubert's "refusal to give the reader the deceptive satisfactions offered by the false philistine humanisms of the sellers of illusion" (*Field of Cultural Production* 210–11) and that Flaubert is to be found, "like Spinoza's god," "immanent and co-extensive with his creation," that here is Flaubert's point of view (211). Here is an attempt to find the morality of an aesthetic that binds realism and literary impressionism. Also, Bourdieu is looking for the same principles of austerity and great laboring artistic humility to apply to a canonical work such as Flaubert's that Barthes is trying to find for the "authentic" public spectacle. For both critics, their tristesse is before the artifical complexity of all critical discourse that yearns for the equivalence of truth in its dialogue with the rhetoric of the artifact that it examines, even as they hold the artifact itself before the bar of immanence and coextensive social and moral truth. The desire of the critic for collapse into some sort of equivalence with the work is to not lose the value of the work in the critical dissection, re-creating the anxiety of a critic such as Jameson for something demonstrably *true*. Thus Puzo's watershed statements of nervous management and interrogation—"as if the Don could truly snatch back"; "there couldn't be any kind of world" are, set against this fierce critical ethic, false universals and bad-faith questions, "keys with which to open nature" as Barthes wearily writes about wrestling, searching for the "form of a Justice which is at last intelligible" (25). Barthes can't keep his wry exasperation out of this last line. To be "intelligible" about the universe through Don Corleone's sonorous management of his world is Puzo's message to his readers. Yet any large novel is a more sprawling and open-ended messy canvas that produces slippage through the interrelations of dozens of people who walk out of the novelist's control into history, ethnicity, gender, and nation.

Mythologies finally provides tools for an inventory of *The Godfather*'s necessary set of dialogic relationships. Barthes' method is clearly a place to start in an examination of popular signification. The author's dominion over the signifier constitutes an imperial command of the signified.[16] Bakhtin has stated any novel's potential power best by saying that the truly novelistic denies a single unitary language (like that of Don Corleone) "as the sole verbal and semantic center of the ideological world" (Bakhtin

364). The hypothesis here has been that in popular fiction, the mythical signifier is often where history is denied by an authorial sleight-of-hand that refuses to decenter language into true dialogue. Puzo exposes our universal yearnings and fears for the characters and ourselves through forms (Woltz, the Don, Kay, Khartoum) that then must be politically reinvested to retrieve the outrage beneath the obfuscations. Who *should* say what Woltz says in *The Godfather* on behalf of an American consensus moralism? Wouldn't that be in another novel with a different agenda? What *should* Apollonia say, if anything? Should *The Godfather's* real victims speak, and who are they? The middle class? The poor? The readers? To restore the muddle that popular texts prematurely move to clarify about the individual and the family, law and justice, freedom and authority, men and women may appear a negative step toward a reinstitution of an elitist critical pessimism but is necessary to counter the affirmation of the patriarchal and capitalist power represented in *The Godfather* and wrest a set of conflicting values and commentary as to what constitutes the "good life" in Puzo's America.

The criticism of popular fiction must continually gauge the containment strategies practiced within the authority of the signifier, whether it's a Yankee seaman telling the reader to "Call me Ishmael" or a devastated young black woman addressing her letters to "Dear God." As Gerard Genette comments, all literature should maintain "as long as possible that opening, that *uncertainty of signs* which allows one to breathe" (Genette 141). Barthes adds in the same spirit: "if there is a 'health' of language, it is the arbitrariness of the sign which is its grounding" (*Mythologies* 128). This almost ebullient belief in language's pure potential is an affirmative gesture that may buttress our sensibilities and give hope to our ethical and sentimental imaginings that studying popular fiction might yield the moral dialogue we seek within our differences. Hume wrote that it is "natural for us to seek a standard of taste; a rule by which the various sentiments of men may be reconciled; at least a decision afforded, confirming one sentiment and condemning another" ("Of the Standard of Taste" 309). Barthes always knew that such a critical agenda was both necessary and exceedingly difficult, especially in less-than-innocent popular forms. Writing is always worked on and traversed, "the signifier of the literary myth . . . a form which is already filled with meaning and which receives from the concept of literature a new signification" (*Mythologies* 134). To understand *The Godfather's* seductive power is to police the signifiers and keep acknowledging the dialectical flow between naturalizing and historicizing, even when Puzo refuses to maintain such a dialogue—especially because he refuses to do so.[17]

Part III

Positioning *The Godfather* in American Narrative Study

chapter six

The Godfather and Melodrama: Authorizing the Corleones as American Heroes

Let me say that we must always look to our own interests. We are men who have refused to be puppets dancing on a string pulled by the men on high. We have been fortunate here in this country.

—Don Corleone, *The Godfather*

Tom. Don't let anyone kid you. It's all personal, every bit of business. Every piece of shit every man has to eat every day of his life is personal. They call it business. OK. But it's personal as hell. You know where I learned that from? The Don. My old man. The Godfather.

—Michael Corleone to Tom Hagen, *The Godfather*

I believe that it can accurately be said that the entire history of the novel as a popular form is critically tied to its sentimental texture and to its melodramatic scheme of action. The two are nearly inseparable.

—Philip Fisher, *Hard Facts*

To read sympathetically becomes synonomous with reading like an American.

—Elizabeth Barnes, *States of Sympathy*

Chapters 3 through 5 were centered on ways to read *The Godfather* critically according to tenets extant in contemporary theory. By reading key scenes and characters through dialogics, the ethnic ensemble, and the politics of signification, I attempted to show how Puzo worked through issues in his fiction, not always toward greater clarification and deepening meaning but rather by performing the conflicts in his own nature as an Italian American son, an aspiring elite author, and a writer in the marketplace. I stressed how Puzo's treatment of writers, women, the family, male power, and authority were managed and contained in his sensibility and portrayed in his fiction.

A case could be made that *The Godfather*'s climate of reception in 1969 was in part dictated by that historical moment (patriarchy under severe stress because of the Vietnam War, collapsing American families, and generational conflict, a craving for law and order beyond compromised American institutions), but such hypotheses do not account for the *kind* of alternative Don Corleone and his family provide. The largest fiction that *The Godfather* allows its readers to inhabit is that of enormous and unqualified American security and success: the fantasy of a self-reliant, upward mobility within a total identity in family. The full power of the Corleone family and its victories is affirmed through the most compelling melodrama. John Cawelti has called melodrama "one of the basic archetypes of moral fantasy" in which "poetic justice" is its essential shape, and the movement is from disorder and chaos toward a "benevolent moral order" (262).[1] Melodrama is not a genre in and of itself, but it can cut across all the popular genres and, in fact, is the driving engine of most of them.

The Godfather is a text that always tries to have it all ways. The ultimate end of this inclusive family fantasy is suggested by Michael's speech to Kay just before he orders the murders of the heads of the Five Families: "[He'd] like to make [his] children as secure as possible before they join that general destiny" of America (365). Vito Corleone's death in Michael's arms comes right after he whispers to his son, "[L]ife is so beautiful" (409), and one must conclude it certainly is if the force of his life and victories has implemented the Corleone empire. The historical legacy of Sicilian oppression that the immigrant carries to the New World is that society is oppressive and hierarchical. The mythic formulation of the American melodrama is that man must strive for individual self-expression. These two major strands—the historical and the mythic—feed into one another as dispensation for their dual identity: the Corleones may go outside of society because of both their prior history and America's a-historical call for individual freedom. The "freedom from" servitude in Sicily is matched by the "freedom to" pursue an American individualism through extraordinary claims of character, exceptionalism, and the sheer force of the personal.

The Godfather decrees that, in America, one can achieve anything through force without denying origins or becoming legally or morally culpable. An immigrant can retain ethnic identity and yet succeed in America beyond belief in an open society without becoming "open" him- or herself. Indeed, Ferraro comments that within this Mafia clan occurs a merging of social and business functions into kin-centered enterprise and that the cost of employing blood in the marketplace is finding the company at home (183, 193). The corollary is that *The Godfather* makes murder "famil-iar" as well. Such is the powerful new contract that *The*

Godfather writes with America, denying any obligation to its national narrative as well as to its civic contracts.

If *The Godfather* is this melodramatic social text that is always evolving the family's power and authority, what sort of cultural and historical tracks is the novel laying down? What work is it performing in the American consciousness? Puzo writes the melodrama as man overcoming historical circumstance and class disadvantage. Destiny becomes optimistic evolution. How does Puzo achieve the sonorous flow of this master narrative? Philip Fisher in *Hard Facts* depicts the power of American historical and sentimental novels and their cultural acts of forging a prehistory for national self-definition. Fisher's prime nineteenth-century examples are Cooper's Leatherstocking Novels and Stowe's *Uncle Tom's Cabin*, which succeeded brilliantly in ordering massive American psychic and historical materials that were then consigned to the commonplace and forgotten as literary achievements. I suggest that in *The Godfather*, Puzo wrote both a historical and a sentimental novel. The grounds of Corleone power, the bloody massacres and their forgetting, are akin to Cooper's chronicles of Indian warfare and Anglo settlement prior to the staking of the land. Puzo adopts the popular historical novel form with his chronicle of the establishment of the family business. Furthermore, he places the drama of this establishment within the family itself, the locus of sentimental fiction, in which, through the complicity of a readerly amnesia, full normality is extended to the Corleone fathers and sons as they receive our sympathy in their battles against their enemies. As purveyors of a fated violence, Corleone men act swiftly and decisively, while the Corleone women consistently are denied any dignity in a domestic space that is always the site of male domination and sexual hypocrisy. The helplessness of Vito Corleone [Andolini], first as the Sicilian peasant boy and then as the immigrant father, is transformed by the benign dispensation to "go bad" in search of American power and authority. An empire is inaugurated by killing a man. A sentimental domestic fiction, putatively the locus of real female authority and multiplicity, is subsumed in a male takeover.

Melodrama is the preferred mode of the newly arrived, the already excluded, the ambitious, the outsider, and the socially conscious. However, "melodrama" has taken on another strong meaning in current literary-critical discussion. Nina Baym's landmark essay, "Melodramas of Beset Manhood: How Theories of American Fiction Exclude Women Authors," (1982) has defined for this generation of critics the sense that the very act of male self-creation is a dramatic ur-narrative running through the conceptualizations of post–World War II American critics who unconsciously extrapolate from the American hero's crisis apart from society and make it into the author's crisis: "[T]he mythic encounter of hero and possibility is a projection of the artist's situation" (76). This melodrama has already been projected in chapter 4 as the most congenial form for Puzo's situation and trajectory as an author. Puzo can, through the creation of Michael Corleone, reconcile himself to Italian American culture by becoming the good son to the father he never had. By Michael "going bad" in renouncing American heroism and education, he regains his Sicilian status. By "going bad" in literature, Puzo renounces the quest for elite literary status and writes *The Godfather*. Such is Puzo's American author melodrama, one in which the indignation of the Corleone characters channels the indignation of the veteran novelist with little to show for his twenty years of toil. Melodrama often operates through a great resentment, usually on the part of characters who feel hugely wronged, whether unlucky in love or in some injustice done to them by another person, a culture, a universe. Puzo's skill is in applying melodrama to the business subject, making the male role into one that is deeply personal, even as the plotting against perceived enemies is coldly, patiently carried out.

The Godfather and American Fiction in 1900: Force Philosophy, Capitalist Heroes, and Escape

The Godfather articulates American psychological certainties and capitalist victories long since won and criticized by modern critics during the twentieth century. *The Godfather* can be placed in dialogue with a now-extinct line of American naturalistic-realistic novels that took Darwinian-Spencerian force philosophy as a guiding principle, its heroes struggling in a hostile world that is always moving according to principles of individualism, intense debate about the value of humanitarianism, and dislike of any control, be it that of the government, the "system," or any form of social regulation or obligation. The flowering of American literary naturalism at the turn of the twentieth century featured male novelists such as Norris and London, creating forceful heroes who tried to drive through all social contradictions to stand alone in authority and achievement. Ronald Martin states that "the universe of force became part of the intellectual superstructure of American capitalism" (94). That capitalism was best transposed and expressed through the melodrama of individual strivers who countenanced no checks against their ambition or vision, who practiced an unbridled power until or unless authors defeated them, through fated weaknesses, over-reaching or simple determinism, what Puzo grandly calls in *The Godfather*, "the nature of the universe" (392).

Late-nineteenth-century inheritors of Herbert Spencer's evolutionary optimism such as John Fiske had assured Americans that "the nature of their society—the industrialization, the competition, the unremitting change and growth"—was not only inevitable but "it was right, that these were God's ways" (Martin 60). Spencer's deploying a series of vast metaphors from physical science over the entire array of social sciences in his synthetic philosophy preached a cheerful determinism that coincided perfectly with the American temper to justify any conceivable competition, monopoly, or social inequality. Fiske asserted that American captains of industry were truly heroic high points of human evolution (Martin 74–75). Spencer conceived of "a lawful cosmos evolving inexorably toward Something Better" (Lears 21). Such yearning fit seamlessly into the romance of American capitalism. Individualism of every variety could thus find underwriting through Spencerian doctrine; William James called Spencer "the philosopher whom those who have no other philosopher can appreciate" (Martin 86), and certainly the middle-class eagerly embraced a vision of personal success that stipulated anyone could proclaim him- or herself exceptional and thus validate any action. Michael Corleone is a Spencerian (on the way to becoming an Ayn Rand hero) when he says, "My father is a businessman trying to provide for his wife and children. . . . He doesn't accept the rules of the society we live in because those rules would have condemned him to a life not suitable to a man like himself, a man of extraordinary force and character" (365). Nothing that society offers will be as meaningful or valid as what the individual establishes as existing within himself. A powerful self-installation leads to an exceptionalism that is All American on the one hand and most familiar in popular melodrama on the other.

In one sense, *The Godfather* can be posited as a throwback text, an archaism that endorses a cosmic force philosophy more akin to that found in novels of the early 1900s such as Norris's The *Octopus* (1901), London's *The Call of the Wild* (1903), *The Sea Wolf* (1904), and *Martin Eden* (1908), and Dreiser's *Sister Carrie* (1900) and the Cowperwood novels, *The Financier* (1912) and *The Titan* (1914). Norris's Magnus Derrick and Buck Annixter struggle for heroic self-definition against Norris's vast symbols of wheat and railroad in the most extreme genre clashes of sentimentalism, naturalism, and melodrama. London's Buck, Wolf Larsen, and Martin Eden rage in extreme paradigms of heroic individualism but end in isolation or in madness, depression, and death. Dreiser knows both the quiet, relentless fall of a Hurstwood in *Sister Carrie* and the calm, steady rapacity of Frank Cowperwood. Such extreme tests of the universal order or disorder are often best expressed in fiction through a broad melodrama. *The Godfather* can be posited as a later inheritor of this American literary tradition of predestined force and melodramatic presentation as exemplified within the specific forms of the immigrant saga and popular novel. Puzo sought to catch that force in his odyssey through famelessness as a writer in the 1950s and 1960s. Such force was often the compelling riddle that Dreiser and London had plumbed in their fiction and commentary. Doctorow in *Ragtime* posits a Dreiser, "suffering terribly from the bad reviews and negligible sales of his his first book, *Sister Carrie*," turning and turning his chair in a furnished room in Brooklyn, "seeking the proper alignment" (23). Doctorow's characters in *Ragtime* all look to find ways to tap into the main line of modern American energy, to situate themselves within its momentum (see chapter 7). Puzo's midcentury quandaries and American dreaming about fiction and success have antecedents in the struggles of his fictional ancestors Dreiser and London, two authors who constantly sought an "alignment" within generic conventions, philosphical issues, and their own thinking through of careers and force.

Dreiser and Puzo show uncanny similarity in the rhetoric they used to look back on their early writing days and desires from the vantage point of great success. Both idealistic and pessimistic, they evince a studied confusion within the certainty that America promises much to the writer who can find its force fields.[2] Dreiser cast himself in the 1890s as a young writer who believed, in his first flush of post-Darwinian scientific knowledge, that "Man was a mechanism, undevised and uncreated, and a badly and carelessly driven one at that" (Matthiessen 41). In his own bleak family life in Terre Haute, Indiana, Dreiser had watched his sisters drift away to larger cities and fall into urban iniquities. He could rail against magazine fiction of the 1890s, saying, "Love was almost invariably rewarded . . . dreams came true . . . with such an air of assurance, omniscience and condescension, that I was quite put out by my own lacks and defeats. . . . I had no such tales to tell, and, however much I tried, I could not think of any" (*A Book about Myself* 490–91). Such views predate the Puzo who flatly stated after *The Godfather* made him famous that in his youth he "never heard an Italian singing," he knew no "lovable Italians," and he wondered "where the hell the moviemakers and storywriters got all their ideas from" ("Choosing a Dream" 13).

Such compensatory demystification from Dreiser and Puzo suggests they were compelled to it by a sense that sentiment and melodrama as stays against inexorable force were finally what they must bear witness against. Yet along with their debunking of their own beginnings and felt subjects comes an extraordinary belief in American Dreaming expressed through sentiment and melodrama. Dreiser writes that "having two hundred and forty dollars saved, I decided to leave this dismal scene and seek the charm of the great city beyond, hoping that there I might succeed at something, be eased and rested by some important work of some kind" (Matthiessen 42). The force of the magnetic pull mixes the language of Horatio Alger (to the city with "two hundred and forty dollars"), literary naturalism ("dismal scene"), and romance ("the charm of the great city beyond") and continues with vague self-made hopes ("succeed at something") laced by what can only be called "evangelical" verbs ("eased and rested"), and concludes by the haziest of capitalist desire ("some important work of some kind"). That "important work" might require unstinting effort and driving ambition or that "unimportant work" of a kind exemplified by sweat shop, assembly line, or day labor would give the lie to "rested" and "eased" is not an option. Dreiser effaces the pain and suffering of such work in the melodrama of "Coming to the City" in *Sister Carrie*. Such an extraordinary mixed rhetoric of accents, impulses, and yearnings calls up Dreiserian multiple energies through vague and shifting language that nonetheless powerfully defines "American Dreaming."

Puzo is a less articulate inheritor in his own musing a half-century later when he writes that as a child, "I myself had a hundred dreams from which to choose. For I was already sure that I would make my escape, that I was one of the chosen. I would be rich, famous, happy. I would master my destiny" ("Choosing a Dream") for "I believed in art. . . . It gave me a comfort I found in no other place" ("The Making of *The Godfather*"). For Puzo, leaving the family to go to war in 1941 is the equivalent of Dreiser's leaving Terre Haute for Chicago and St. Louis. Puzo evinces Dreiser's earnestness, his refusal to judge or moralize, his view of anarchy in family relations, as if a hole had been blown in his affective life. Puzo and Dreiser also share a coarseness and a sentimental commodity hunger about success. Both writers have a lumbering style and little humor. Puzo's "great city beyond" is Las Vegas, rather than Dreiser's Chicago or St. Louis, where all American wraps are off. After the failures of heroine-driven Sister C*arrie* and *Jennie Gerhardt*, Dreiser licked his wounds, as did Puzo, by magazine and pulp writing in the city, until finally becoming a success with his novels of the tycoon Frank Cowperwood. Likewise, Puzo had to turn to his male "tycoon" hero Vito Corleone after *The Dark Arena* and *The Fortunate Pilgrim* did little to establish him. In the trajectory of their careers and their constructed narrative of their early years, both Puzo and Dreiser catch a terrible and inexorable under-rhythm of American desire and force to effect their escapes into and through fiction and thus achieve success.

In *The Financier*, Dreiser's Frank Cowperwood is the key expression of force philosophy in action within the business realm. He has instrumentalized destiny and sharpened his mind and will into cold dead tools to reach his ends. A financial speculator, he has no product or yield in the commodity world beyond money itself. The Civil War, a momentary annoyance in his drive to wealth, he deems not profitable. He gazes on social structures such as family and calibrates what they mean to his need. Worrying about what happens to "superior people," he thinks, "force was the answer—great mental and physical force" because the "little guardians of law and morality" spoke only in great platitudes and hypocrisy. Recognizing this is the organization of the world, Cowperwood decides "the thing for him to do was to get rich and hold his own, to build up a seeming of virtue and dignity which would pass muster for the genuine thing. Force would do that" (121). Such lines preview Michael Corleone's appraisal of what the Corleone family needs to simulate before it can join that American "general destiny," though Dreiser's Cowperwood is always more candid about his goals. He parses out that good and evil are "toys of clerics by which they made money" (205); therefore, he need not fear any opposing force since no transcendant reality reveals itself to him. Cowperwood then falls back on pessimistic evolutionary theory to suppose that "life was a dark, insoluble mystery, but whatever it was, strength and weakness were its two constituents" (241). In 1920 after Cowperwood had established Dreiser as a successful novelist, his general description of "the American Financier" includes phrases such as "his aggressive organizing mind . . . finds itself blazing to get some new thing done . . . [and] is inspired with some great enthusiasm for something." Dreiser is describing the business man as artist (Smith 74). In 1922 he assumes the same rhetoric to describe his own literary dreaming in the 1890s as the business props can then fall away. For Dreiser, tycoons, financiers, shopgirls, novelists, and midwestern boys on their way up all possessed a seamless narrative, one and indivisible. This indiscriminate tonal deafness imbues Puzo's essays and fiction as well.

While Dreiser sought "important work," and Puzo was certain he would be one of the "chosen," no one chose Jack London, nor was he the vague dreamer of Dreiser's fiction. After a tempestuous childhood and young manhood, London began in his early twenties to write like some late Victorian engine, working sixteen to eighteen-hour days. Papering his walls with rejection slips, he would not be denied. He signed his first book contract at age twenty-three in 1899 and became the first milionaire novelist in American history (Lynn 77). London sought extreme locales for much of his fiction, the harsh sites of a natural world (the Yukon, the high seas) or the lower urban depths or majestic California. In contrast, Dreiser and Puzo are indoor novelists for the most part and do not seek the extremity of natural setting. The one London novel most analogous to trajectories in Puzo's career was *Martin Eden* (1909). The protagonist by dint of will forces his way to a successful writing career in which he leaps over barriers of class and education only to find his triumph hollow, bereft of any true capital he can carry forward into an integrated life of creation and achievement. *Martin Eden* is an unadulterated Bourdieuian text of a young adventurous tough who becomes a writer and vainly attempts to bridge all the gaps in his background of taste, environment, and pleasures. Martin painstakingly corrects his own diction in front of Ruth Morse, the upper-middle-class girl he worships. He is Pygmalion-on-the-way-to-Gatsby, working in self-fashioning, telling Ruth, "I want to breathe air like you get in this house—air that is filled with books and pictures, and beautiful things, where people talk in low voices an' are clean." He pragmatically concludes, "Now, how am I goin' to get it? Where do I take hold an' begin? (97).

Martin wants to regulate his own individualism and possess his own capital. His intellectual property is himself but finally he turns on himself, and his labor. In his early exuberance at his growing powers, he finds Spencer's *First Principles* and believes that "here was the man Spencer, organizing all knowledge for him, reducing everything to unity, elaborating ultimate realities" (149). Martin takes his Spencer as an intellectual act of faith, while more mundane realities trip him up. He charts his writing plans, believing he can alternate between hack work and masterpieces (like Merlyn in *Fools Die*), grinding out enough of the former to buy time to write the latter. London faithfully shows Martin laboring over long and short pieces of fiction and philosphical essays. No other American novel has ever had hundreds of pages of plot devoted to the mechanics and economics of Grub Street and the quarterlies, or to the calculated labor of the writing desk. Martin becomes facile enough to frame a dozen marketable short stories in half an hour and "fill [them] in at his convenience" (301). He knows the newspaper "storiette" formula, which stipulates a piece should "never end unhappily . . . never contain beauty of language, subtlety of thought . . . real delicacy of sentiment" but must contain plenty of pure and noble sentiment (300). When Ruth tries to tell him the truth about his failure as she sees it, he protests he has greater talent than published writers; her answer is the awful utilitarian truth of the middle class, the bottom line nightmare that Martin has repressed in his writerly heroism: "But they sell theirs and you don't. . . . I don't think you were made to write" (326). After he slowly begins to place his manuscripts, the acceptance rate becomes a torrent. He suddenly is welcome everywhere, even by Ruth's father and wealthy business acquaintances. Yet the long struggle to make it on his own idealistic terms has empited him of writerly ambition or more stories to tell. All his success comes for "work performed," the anvillike phrase that keeps hammering in his head. He rejects his success as completely as he had defied what looked like his destined failure. Ruth is seen finally as a chimera of safe opinions, someone from a deader and safe bourgeois world that he does not even wish to join. When he sells his last manuscript, he sees himself as "the fad of the hour." The engine that was Martin Eden shuts down, and he takes his own life.

In *Martin Eden*, London depicted the intellectual and emotional journey that Puzo would actually take through his decades-long attempts to become an honored novelist, the success that *The Godfather* brought, and the sourness that became him after its amazing public reception. Taken together, Dreiser's hope for "important work of some kind" and London's aggressive and constant assault on the literary marketplace chart two exemplary careers of American writers who unswervingly worshipped both force and the idea of literary success and knew in their bones the endless rejection before that success and the facts of fame thereafter. Frank Cowperwood and Martin Eden are their heroes— Cowperwood the artistic capitalist, Martin Eden the capitalist artist. In Vito Corleone, Puzo would create his Cowperwood with one very different attribute. Instead of family as merely another appurtenance, Puzo makes family survival the center of all Vito Corleone's predations. Puzo also lived the life of Martin Eden pre-*Godfather*, with many of the same pure protestations about the efficacy and glories of art and then the great disillusion at its failure to transform him. Dreiser and London preceded Puzo by a half-century, but all three writers' extreme attraction to and repulsion from art and success were in themselves melodramatic in nature, projected through the fiction of the essential writer's anxiety about the author as both energy source and pure American product.

Such capitalist heroes were largely forgotten after World War I, when modern American fiction began to cast the businessman as Babbit rather than as a Spencerian giant. Mencken's appelation of the "booboisie" discouraged any serious fictional treatment of the heroic capitalist, and the Depression made such a figure an anachronism or part of the problem of a wounded American society. Fitzgerald had Gatsby, Dick Diver, and Monroe Stahr, Promethean heroes deeply involved in the new economies of bootlegging, psychiatry, and cinema, while Faulkner had Thomas Sutpen, a relentless backwoods tycoon. However, these capitalist heroes in modernist classics were never presented without being embedded in issues of romance and race, patriarchal power and longing. By the end of the 1950s, elite American fiction posited young heroes with no sense of vocation or aptitude in a capitalist society, characters abstaining from the customary ways of making due along the whole spectrum of relative privilege to deprivation: Percy's stockbroker and closet existentialist Binx Bolling in *The Moviegoer*; testy librarian Neil Klugman storming the Patimkin gates for his Jewish American golden girl in Roth's *Goodbye, Columbus*; Updike's ex-basketball star Rabbit Angstrom demonstrating a potato peeler in the window of a dingy department store in a Pennsylvania factory town in *Rabbit, Run*. The personal crisis of the young male character was defined against the absurdity of the work role he was expected to inhabit and the success he was to emulate. No Vito Corleone to emulate and no Michael Corleone to become him.

By 1969, in the year of *The Godfather*'s publication, the American novel could not include a true capitalist hero without intense melodramatic presentation in popular fiction or through ironic deflation in elite fiction. Even middle-brow fiction had begun to abandon the figure after World War II, except for the more popular work of John O'Hara and James Gould Cozzens and the truly fanciful metamorphoses of John Cheever. The avatars of businessmen heroes ran the gamut from Ayn Rand's philosophically based capitalist supermen such as Howard Roark in *The Fountainhead* (1943) and John Galt in *Atlas Shrugged* (1957) to Harold Robbins' sensationalized and loose fictionalization of young Howard Hughes in *The Carpetbaggers* (1961). Rand's visionaries found themselves in the wrong timid and spineless society, while Robbins's hero sought to eradicate the nightmare power of his father by becoming him. Without such intellectual or pathological justification, American businessmen in fiction were most often depicted as middle-class bores, frustrated fathers, and husbands full of ennui as depicted in Sloan Wilson's *The Man in the Grey Flannel Suit* (1955), a key realist text of post-war disaffection with corporate life.[3] Such a novel affirms what *The Godfather* will underscore a decade later in sensational fashion: that family and home are primarily important. Wilson's hero Tom Rath is suffering in the culture of David Reisman's "lonely crowd" and is a node in an economy controlled by large corporations.

The Godfather shifts the focus of corporate power back to a text of private clans which operate in the smallest possible effective unit for protection. Puzo converts all strategic family business decisions into strongly emotional justifications and transforms all structural details of business decisions back into the naked, personal, and instinctual. The novel never shows a Corleone in a true business meeting as the term might be known, nor does a Corleone ever have money change hands or handle money. All talk about market capitalization, raw materials, labor, the infrastructure of collection at the street level, the mechanics of buying off and into the courts and political system—such is all left to the reader's imagination. We are as far in *The Godfather* from real insight into Corleone business and its complex workings as we are from understanding Gatsby's world as bootlegger or in knowing how Heathcliff made his money in Liverpool and returned to Wuthering Heights in the clothes of a gentleman. The material underwriting of the business plot is always a given, a suppressed and phantom history, so that we can keep on point in a family melodrama about life and death justifications and action of men who are, in the ruse of the text, "natural" forces.

Kinship functions as bureaucracy; Corleones never fear unemployment, never feel anxiety, rootlessness, or insecurity (the collective anomie of modernity), and they always knows the chain of command and the task at hand. In a society increasingly centering on processing information or making endless images or replication of available goods or services, the Corleone economy creates no jobs and sends nothing into circulation but rather feeds off the larger economy's sin and error, its predilection for gambling, its desire for sexual pleasure, and its need for ready cash. Human, all too human, and hearkening back to a residual American Protestant ethic of self-reliance and individual striving that the Corleones tweak in the reader's consciousness. Finally, the Corleones satisfy the immense nostalgia for values, stability, and tradition, placing such yearning in an uncomplicated capitalist and benign Freudian imaginary, even if the world thus posited belongs more to the era of Theodore Roosevelt or in such jocularly nostalgic patriarchal popular successes as the play *Life with Father* (1935) or *Cheaper by the Dozen* (1948), where efficiently expert Frank Gilbreth lovingly bulldozes his wife and twelve children with modern methods. Such authority in the home begins in the office. The Corleone father and son are the darker immigrant twins of such American patriarchal icons and staple fare, off the boat, into the ghetto, standing behind their predations with unconquerable family. Within the triple hybridity of immigrant saga, sensational crime narrative, and business novel, an increasingly uncontrollable American social existence is dramatized on the deeply satisfying level of family. The ethnic status of the Corleones enriches their drama and exoticises their struggle as "others" who are nonetheless just American folks, ruled by a powerful and loving father, who's just taking care of business.

Melodrama as Fictional Business

American best sellers in the twentieth century ignored much of the century's philosophical, aesthetic, and epistemological debate and treated both the observably social world and its varied explanations as entities to be comprehended by broad strokes of a realist melodrama. *The Godfather* is particularly well adapted to a consideration of melodramatic effect. The novel and films produce a wide range of feelings in readers and audiences, from pity to fear, from sentimental identification to moral indignation. The Corleones' externalized sense of justice and order moves swiftly to right any wrong done to the family and those it protects. The novel's various climactic points are always enacted through sex (Woltz's girl, Johnny's girls, Lucy's angst) or violence (the shootings of the Don, the deaths of Fanucci, Sonny, Khartoum, Luca Brasi, Sollozzo and McCluskey, Appolonia); in the novel's quieter moments, business is transacted through the interplay of broad gesture and euphemism (the wedding day supplicants, Sigonora Colombo's landlord, the Dons' "convention"). Barzini makes the point that Italians don't countenance life reduced to unadorned truth and that acting out a character's role is an essential part of that character's life (90). This broadly conceived and heightened sense of presentation, mediated crucially by *bella figura*'s ordering of gesture, is everywhere inimical to classic definitions of the quotidian nature of realism. Yet Barzini also points to the fact that such an active dramatic mode is one developed "by a pessimistic, realistic, resigned, and frightened people" (75). Melodrama then may be what staves off the inevitabilities of fate that a naturalistic strain of realism represents, reenacting deep Italian historical structures in an excitement of surfaces and bodies engaged in significance.

Peter Brooks in a most intelligent study of melodrama writes, "One might be tempted to consider melodrama as a constant of the imagination and a constant among literary modes; it could be one typological pole, detectable at all epochs" (14). Thus melodrama is not a genre or subgenre. Clear-eyed and somewhat dubious, Brooks calls it "a reductive literalistic version [of any] mode" and "a temptation" because it offers a complete set of attitudes, gestures, and phrases "coherently conceived toward dramatization of essential spiritual conflict" (20). Social melodramatists, among whom Brooks considers Balzac, James, Dickens, Gogol, Dostoevsky, and Proust, engage man's social existence and its "moral drama" in which characters represent and undergo extremes (22, 36). Brooks sees melodrama as remarkably egalitarian in which "the democracy of ethical relationships passes through the sentimentalization of morality, the identification of ethics with basic familial psychic patternings" (44). Certainly any *Godfather* reader or viewer has felt the intense affiliation for the band of murderers we come to know as the only "moral" group in the novel. The text's signification assures that Don Corleone's ethics are superior, no matter what the situation. The reader is encouraged to forget misgivings about Corleone actions because sympathies are so strongly elicited for and on behalf of children, a place in America, a better life. Melodrama's open seduction of the reader/viewer with its action and resolution occurs over and over again within narratives where otherwise stark or humdrum realities would make life not worth living or not interesting enough to think on. Melodrama qualifies naturalism and animates realism by cutting determinism and vivifing the quotidian. It may be employed sparingly by an author to great effect (Dimmesdale dying on the scaffold in *The Scarlet Letter*) or become a long cry against injustice and the implied call for its refutation (the Victorian preference brought into popular classic form by Dickens in a novel such as *Bleak House*).

Melodrama does not lack for definitions and applications. Richard Chase calls it "tragedy in a vacuum" and the suitable form for "writers who do not have a firm sense of living in a culture" (41), while Brooks labels it a "democratic art" (43). Brooks also cites Eric Bentley who invokes Freud when he calls melodrama the "naturalism of the dream life" and, in Victorian times, "the poor man's catharsis" (198). Ronald Martin calls Frank Norris a "melodramatist of realism" (150). Finally, Fisher believes that "the entire history of the novel as a popular form is critically tied to its sentimental texture and to its melodramatic scheme of action" (92). What makes the form so specifically American for application to Puzo is precisely his insecurity about a foothold in American culture, specifically literary culture, but also his status as a second-generation immigrant and his determination to have the Corleones partake of America's promise while preserving a fantastic distance from any of its institutions. Puzo also sees the Corleones as deeply wronged and demanding justice after living in a prior tragic servitude in Sicily, one that, when transferred to the promised land of the American twentieth century, does indeed occur in a vacuum, where Puzo can construct spectacular victories against all foes, a melodramatic pattern endlessly satisfying to readers and viewers.

Chase provides a catalogue of melodrama's variants to which can be attached *Godfather* examples: "strict conventionalism" ("the Don was notoriously straitlaced in matters of sex"); "cruel victimization" (why should the Don's family suffer?); "violent indeterminacy of events" (murders bringing almost every plot line to conclusion). Chase believes melodrama "demands abstract and conventionalized characters" (characters of "Destiny"); "clash of ideas and forces" (the Don as a natural force) (37–41). Chase is combing melodrama to help articulate what would come to be known as the American Romance Paradigm, the critical attempt of the American 1950s and 1960s to establish a literary canon for the American 1850s. The intensely symbolic American authors Chase and others were establishing as America's great writers (Poe, Melville, Hawthorne, Thoreau) partook of melodrama for their greatest extreme effects but "transcended" (the verb form of the privileged noun defining a writerly generation) melodrama to enhance comedy and tragedy. For Chase (and for his mentor Lionel Trilling), melodrama itself could produce only a "vast body of inferior fiction," which basically invoked "sensation and sentiment"; such melodramatic novelists "do not have a firm sense of a social arena" (41). This last opinion could surely be contested because the most melodramatic and powerful text of Chase's 1850s is *Uncle Tom's Cabin*, a key American document in the social arena as well as a defining best seller. Finally, for Chase, culture and society are quite different and sundered. Ideology and psychology make a culture, whereas society must be engaged by the novelist in a muddy business of representative men, actual conflict, and class structures. Chase wants melodrama to help man prevail, but he has to be the right sort of man, a Promethean figure, an ironist who is somehow universally significant rather than culturally specific. Melodrama must be enlisted as a form which would culminate in the mature art of a Henry James and texture a heroine such as Isabel Archer. In short, Chase would recognize Puzo's machinery but not his novels. "Universally significant" to Mrs. Stowe would signify "Christian" and "millennial." For Puzo, it might be "the nature of good and evil," a phrase that could be espoused as easily by Chase or his mentor Lionel Trilling. Puzo doesn't reinvest melodrama in "the best that has been thought and said" because he simply doesn't work at that level. The problem with most of melodrama's critics and benefactors is that they all know it when they see it, but whether they endorse it depends upon the complexity of the vehicle in which it appears. Brooks and Chase both find James a melodramatist to great effect; neither would give Puzo a second look.

   Popular fiction more easily affirms or juggles what elite fiction affirms after a hard-won moral struggle. What popular melodrama finally concludes in a form of piety, with religious and bourgeois overtones, elite literature finds at the abyss in barbarous knowledge. There are, as Barthes reminds us, only so many universal signifieds (goodness, kindness, wholeness, humaneness, and so on [*Mythologies* 121]), and they are shared by popular and elite narratives. Thus melodrama is and could be an essential part of any novelist's repertoire. Puzo is especially called to the potential of the form. To write of an immigrant's passage in American culture, the novelist is immediately confronted with cultural uncertainty, a heritage suddenly under erasure, emotional leave-taking and arrival, potential sudden reversals in fortunes and wondrous new experience, no everyday reality to depict in known patterns, often great suffering and want, stories of escape and reconciliation, and mourning for those left behind. The immigrant as hero, the immigrant family as unit, float in a tentative relation to the new country, both not there and not yet. Nowhere is this dynamic more keenly felt than in the economic sphere since so much depended upon the man getting work to feed, clothe, and shelter his family, whether on Puzo's Lower West Side of New York or on the American Great Plains.

The deeply personal always threatens to come to the surface in *The Godfather*. Michael begins *The Godfather* as an ironic commentator on the Corleone wedding day festivities; he is doubly marked an "American" by his war heroism in the marines and his Ivy League college-boy status. However, outside the French Hospital, he is branded by McCluskey's fist as just another "punk," a Five Family War casualty; following the assault, he swiftly joins the melodrama as a full family business partner. When the family war council is planning the execution of Sollozzo and McCluskey, the ever-cautious Tom Hagen warns Michael that he shouldn't let his broken jaw influence his judgment, since "it was business, not personal" (146). What Tom signifies is that McCluskey is a hireling, following orders from the other side. Hagen then sees Michael metamorphose: "he saw Michael's face freeze into a mask that resembled uncannily the Don's."

> Tom, don't let anybody kid you. It's all personal, every bit of business. Every piece of shit every man has to eat every day of his life is personal. They call it business. OK. But it's personal as hell. You know where I learned that from? The Don. My old man. The Godfather. If a bolt of lightning hit a friend of his the old man would take it personal. He took my going into the Marines personal. That's what makes him great. The Great Don. He takes everything personal. Like God. He knows every feather that falls from the tail of a sparrow or however the hell it goes. Right? And you know something? Accidents don't happen to people who take accidents as a personal insult. So I came late. OK, but I'm coming all the way. (146)

A terrific Puzo speech. In such an outburst, his vivid rendering of the strands of family and business is unparalleled in its jumble of personal resentments and practical applications. With Michael's emotional outcry that business is personal every day, the male melodrama of a victimized outrage is in place. Man's life itself when checked or bound is always personal. The ugly "every piece of shit" maxim totalizes the theatrical and universal nature of Michael's metaphoric rendering of the male plight. An inescapable slavery dogs man's destiny. An unseen force dictates man's lot, cast as an endless and repetitive coercion that is deterministic, involuntary, and unacceptable. An unacknowledged "they" might say it's "business," but Michael knows otherwise. The father changes into the God who is watching over his creation to the miunutest detail. In the middle of the speech, the dialogized accent becomes biblical, even in impatient secular citation ("however the hell it goes") to deflect anything in Michael's vendetta from the personal or the material. Then comes a perfectly pitched euphemism in *bella figura* about "accidents" that once again deflects the cause and effect of a "business" decision or competition. Michael is "coming," the arch-angel of family and business deliverance. Within the son's powerful justification for avenging his own honor and aiding the stricken father is an old, old story. The specific American scaffolding is kicked away, and Michael may be launched on his familial destiny, which is to confront the evildoers who would strike his family down. Michael cuts through all contradictions when he stops justifying himself to Kay: "All I can say, I have to help my father" (366). Such blood allegiances in melodrama override any other possible connotations and considerations.

Real-world business considerations in *The Godfather* also come through a more no-nonsense business tycoon, the already much-maligned Jack Woltz. Not burdened with biblical and ethnic responsibilties for family and destinies, Woltz delivers a harsh market critique of the Corleones' power; it gets swallowed up in the melodrama but has dialogized markers that belong to a real-time American world of monopoly capitalism. Puzo's discrediting of Woltz was thoroughly established before he protested that "there couldn't be any kind of world if [people were allowed to behead prize race horses]." But what it "meant" to Woltz is of import: "It meant you couldn't do what you wanted with your own money, with the companies you owned, the power you had to give orders. It was ten times worse than communism. It had to be smashed. It must never be allowed" (69). Far from melodramatic universals, Woltz's rhetoric sees the "obscure importer of Italian olive oil" as a national . threat, one to capitalism itself, to corporate power, and, ideologically, perhaps the heralding of an internal Cold War enemy more implacable than the Soviets, lawlessness within the structure of individual freedoms.

Woltz may be right: the Corleones as an inner rot may be much more injurious to the American way, but Puzo won't follow this line of reasoning for long. The structure of business in league with government is at stake, "despite all his contacts with the President of the United States, despite all his claims of friendship with the Director of the FBI" (69). All Woltz can mutter after being sedated is "six hundred thousand dollars"—the price of Khartoum. This *Godfather* villain has a balance sheet in mind as he parses out the injury done to him and the structures he represents. His questions are more material and rational than Michael's prebattle cries that "business is personal" and that the degradation of the common man is his daily lot. Yet the logic of the social melodrama demands the blood of Khartoum, Sollozzo, and McCluskey, not the tunneling down into capitalist realities. Woltz may draw his conclusions on behalf of unfettered capitalism as businessman and cold warrior, but the readers and viewers are encouraged to vote the straight Corleone ticket every time. Although Woltz may have Hoover for a friend, the Don is cited as the best friend any Italian American citizen could ever have. Historians and psychologists can grapple with the question of how this "invisible" mob government so fascinates the American public that it can't get enough of it in popular melodrama while international communism was a shadow government causing a half-century of American national paranoia. A quick guess is that backwater Sicily had no trappings of "evil empire" and as no external nuclear and economic threat, was perceived as no internal threat where the melodramatic structure could turn the subject into an endless reader's market and where the Corleone business practices look disturbingly familiar.

The Constitutional Convention of "Our Gang"

The richly dialogized and accented scene of the Dons' "Constitutional Convention" in *The Godfather* (287–93) shows how business mutates into nothing less than American statecraft itself, with full reference to history and politics. The Dons often rail against the American government that opposes them, but they have become their own nation state beyond the boundaries of business and accrue to themselves the highest powers of male authority: those of "founding Fathers" with a self-contained world as American as 1776 or 1787.

Melodrama is a powerful form in *The Godfather* that tilts the novel of business not only into an underside of family wars and personal scores to settle but onto a hyperbolic plane of mutated structures. Such is always the ability of popular fiction to place the narrative of sentiment and sensation "set against the backdrop of [war, business, politics]" that empties out these collective subjects to feed the personal.[4] Another way that *The Godfather* as a novel of business can be deflected toward more familiar American image for the reader/viewer is to cast Don Corleone in the role of an American statesman, nothing less than a "father of his country," a political figure who rises in time of crisis to manage affairs in the interests of all the people. Not the least of *The Godfather*'s powerful American fantasies is precisely that of the Mafia as not so much a criminally marauding business sucking the life out of the real economy but rather as a "state" with its own rights, treaties, and problems. In fact,

Vito Corleone consolidates his power and authority in the 1930s as the depression threatens to break America apart. Even as "honest men begged for work in vain" "from contemptuous officialdom," "the men of Don Corleone walked the streets with their heads held high, their pockets stuffed with silver and paper money" (215). The Don's New Deal works very well on the domestic front, "far better than his enemies ran the greater world which continually obstructed his path." He became advisor to block groups of voters for candidates in state legislatures, city offices, and Congress. "He consolidated this power with a far-seeing statesmanlike intelligence," sending boys to college who would become lawyers, district attorneys, and judges, planning the future of "his empire with all the foresight of a great national leader" in "the great war of 1933" (216, 217). Without ever crossing the line into any interaction with this larger America, Puzo invests Vito Corleone with more ability than Franklin Delano Roosevelt (also in a great domestic "war" in 1933); the Don is also a "foreign" policy specialist who manages "to bring peace to all the warring factions in New York City and then in the nation," culminating in Puzo's grandiose claim that the Don's problems were those of "other great rulers and lawgivers in history" (222). When "peace and harmony reign" in New York City by 1937 after selective Corleone mayhem, the Don notes with dismay the coming of Hitler and the fall of Spain; by 1939, the Don becomes the "underworld apostle of peace." Characterized as "more successful than any Pope," he hammers out a working agreement amongst the most powerful underworld organizations in the country. Puzo brazenly calls it a "Constitution" which "respected fully the internal authority of each member in his state or city" (224). From rampant fear and murder, we pass dizzyingly to papal authority and founding government documents without ever considering what the consent of the governed might mean. The final allegorical detail is sprung in the neat reverse parallel universe: "And so when World War II broke out in 1939, when the United States joined the conflict in 1941, the world of Don Vito Corleone was at peace, in order, fully prepared to reap the golden harvest on equal terms with all the other industries of a booming America." The Corleone family then has a hand in all the black market food stamps, gasoline stamps, and travel priorities" (224). The ironic shadow world that the Don manages calls for equal parts CEO, executioner, law giver, visionary, and freebooter, one who marches diagonally across history in his own interests. He's beyond both patriotism and personal appeal. The world stage has his play always running in a corner of the set, always finely tuned in its improvisations and revisions to the drama on that main stage.[5]

It's at the Dons' "Constitutional Convention" that Vito Corleone makes his most far reaching pronouncements about business and government from within the melodramatic form. Puzo sets the scene with considerable care in a clandestine summit meeting in a commercial bank director's conference room. The Dons sit gravely and calmly under a portrait of founding father Alexander Hamilton, the conservative financial genius of the early American republic (280). The mob rulers are depicted as heroic individualists who have "refused to accept the rule of organized society, men who refused the dominion of other men." They "guarded their free will with wiles and murder. Their wills could be subverted only by death. Or the utmost reasonableness" (287). Surely free will has never been defended with more persuasive weapons. "Free will" to Puzo is the Dons' license to threaten mayhem against any enemy; no "reasonableness" in the novel is divorced from murder's implied threat. Puzo's "casual irony," the complacent author's implied commentary, is a kind of *bella figura* of the moral life, as "reasonableness" and "free will" become markers in a fallen world of signification.

The portrait of Hamilton brooding over the scene legitimates the gathering of mobsters as serious and concerned high capitalists hoping to carve out a pact that will enable their "nation" to prosper. Puzo's choice of Hamilton is either lucky or inspired. In the Revolutionary War period, he "made his bones" on every level of American life. Born out of wedlock in 1755 on the Caribbean island of Nevis, he was orphaned, then sent to America by a benefactor to be educated. He was an officer on Washington's staff by 1777 and as a colonel persuaded Washington to let him lead an assault on a British position at Yorktown in 1781, the same year he wrote his first treatise on public finance. Hamilton was the financial architect of the new nation during its first decades and led the American Treasury Department (established 1789). He exhibited sound and conservative principles as he sought ways for the young nation to improve and manage the flow of revenue. Hamilton believed that a small class of old families, including merchant-shipowners and financiers along the East Coast, should be permanently installed as government's staunch allies. Samuel Eliot Morison stated that Hamilton wished to "give the people who controlled America's wealth a distinct interest in its permanence" (Morison 323). Such a profile well describes Don Corleone's "historic" maxim at the Dons' congress that "we will manage our world for ourselves because it is our world, *cosa nostra*" (293). The prevailing historical view is of Hamilton as a visionary who brought financial order out of chaos, concentrating power in the few, believing in a governing elite. He had little use for the competing American vision of Jeffersonian democracy, which he feared as the ultimate anarchy in the making. The irony is that the Corleones and their mob compatriots are the beneficiaries of the extension of democracy in the vast waves of European emigration that punctuate the beginning of the American twentieth century. Vito Corleone stands at the financial pinnacle of the mob empire in *The Godfather* espousing Hamilton's fiscally sound policies but living under Jefferson's egalitatrian dispensation. One suspects it was not lost on Puzo that Hamilton of all the Founding Fathers stood most outside the country's radical republican rhetoric as its most "managerial" figure or that he died in a melodramatic duel with Vice President Aaron Burr in 1804. When Michael tells Kay that maybe he's just "one of those real old-fashioned conservatives they grow up in your hometown" (366), he may be gesturing toward the New England Adams connection, but his father more surely resembles the prudent New York urban financier Hamilton in Puzo's fanciful American mythography, an anti-republican immigrant banker for the mob and its exclusive interests. Thus does Puzo inscribe American crime, business, and history in a rhetorical mix of accents. Vito Corleone would be the immigrant Hamilton would most fear, but he would admire his financial and organizational acumen.

The speeches made by the Dons show the accumulated wisdom of the cautious old men who have survived their reigns of murder and mayhem to now stand at the pinnacle of a business network too important to be left unregulated. Rather than the young firebrands of the American 1770s, these men are true conservators and mappers of territory. Once more, it's difficult to gauge what Puzo means by the repetition in this scene of several of the novel's most pointed signifieds about the nature of mob predation. For example, Don Corleone utters the by-now familiar lines from Woltz and Kay, "What would the world come to if people kept carrying grudges against all reason?" (287). More to the point, what is this *novel* coming to if Puzo has the Don and Woltz mouthing the same sentiments? Is the statement then given more weight? Is Woltz redeemed in some way? Has the Don become just another querulous capitalist, an old, cranky mob father who's lost a son? Puzo does not seem to realize or care that his hero and villain hold similar political views, or if he does care, he's not enough of an author-in-charge to make the pattern meaningful. Don Barzini, the Corleones' arch foe and the architect of their misfortune, repeats another Woltz line when he says "we're not communists after all" (288); he is finally shot to death in Michael's orchestrated assasinations as he "stood over a bed on which lay a young girl. . . . Rocco pumped four bullets into his belly" (430) in a replica of Woltz's Hollywood attack on the starlet. The "Don of Detroit" adds the familiar litany, "We just can't let people do as they please"; he's "tender-hearted" like Sonny but also tells the assembled mobsters that they shouldn't worry about selling drugs to "the dark people, the colored" because they're "animals" (290). Is Puzo using some comparative rhetoric here, saying that these views from mob "elder statesmen" are very mainstream American, from the prejudices to the law-and-order conservatism? At some level, he's doing just that, but I think it's rather his inability to create more than a few signifieds. Characters in *The Godfather* repeat key phrases and views not in an intricate doubling or a pointed comparative satire of American institutions but because Puzo has nothing more to say on the matter beyond Woltz's intimations early in the novel. Don Corleone conducts business on a specific scale of concern. He ironically joins Woltz in condemning rogue elements and violent intiatives. However much Jack Woltz is the anti–Don Corleone in personal life and decadent practice, they both argue quite convincingly for a conservative freemarket capitalism and the monopolist right to do whatever they deem necessary. That's Puzo's oft-repeated fictional conclusion on the matter, and he sticks to it.

It's the rendering of the Don as a statesman in a quite self-conscious historical frame that gives Puzo the opportunity to legitimate Vito Corleone's vision and Americanness. The aura of the Dons' Convention is rich with accents of nation-building at the table under Hamilton's portrait. In a speech that Puzo self-consciously historicizes as "famous" prior to its delivery by a "far-seeing statesman," Don Corleone begins, "What manner of men are we then, if we do not have our reason?" (292). "Reason" in *The Godfather* very pointedly calls up the Enlightenment tenets that drove the framers of the Constitution such as Hamilton and the Virginians to hammer out the documents and agreements that solidified the American nation. Don Corleone continues:

> Let me say that we must always look to our interests. We are all men who have refused to be puppets dancing on a string pulled by the men on high. We have been fortunate here in this country. Already most of our children have found a better life. Some of you have sons who are professors, scientists, musicians, and you are fortunate. Perhaps your grandchildren will become the new *pezzonovanti*. . . . But we have to progress with the times. The time is past for guns and killings and massacres. We have to be as cunning as the business people, there's more money in it and it's better for our children and grandchildren.
>
> As for our own deeds, we are not responsible to the .90 calibers, the *pezzonovantis* who take it upon themselves to decide what we shall do with our lives, who declare wars they wish us to fight in to protect what they own. . . . We will manage our world for ourselves because it is our world, *cosa nostra*. (292–93)

Of course, this is a dream of the freest agency, which also demonizes a "they" as the unnamed "men on high" who are the true enemies of unbridled mob commerce and control. The speech pulls at very traditional American patriotic and life world comforts. The time for guns and killing is over, and civilization nominally reigns, as in 1787 with the British vanquished and laws to be shaped for the new country. Children have prospered and have become artists and professionals. But progress also means learning to steal within the law, to be as "cunning" as the "business people," the post–Civil War architects of the national future. The echoes and accents here stretch back to the American colonies taking umbrage with "men on high" in Britain and forward into the modern postindustrial America. Weaving through the sentiments are family members: sons, children, grandchildren. To yoke "manage" to "our world" is to join both a cosmos and a bureaucratic regulating of it. "Our World" equals America itself: Don Corleone holds this to be self-evident as well as the Dons' privileged place. Such an enormous subjectivizing of an individual's proprietary rights has reference to Gillian Brown's view of the American logic of "possessive individualism" in which she traces DeTocqueville's projection in the liberal democratic state evolving out of Locke and Hobbes that "every man has property in himself and, thus, the right to manage himself, his labor, and his property as he wishes." Brown calls this "a market society's construction of Self" and one foregrounded by the American Declaration and Constitution in which government would protect rights of self-determination (2). The Dons take advantage of their freedom to be rapacious within it while they cast the government and regulation in America as their enemies, the successors to land-holding Sicilian oppressors. The great leap is from control of self and property, incarnated in family, to the whole world both personalized and miniaturized under their control, a powerful and pervasive, if not particularly moral or idealistic version of the American Dream.

The Godfather claims the authority to address very powerful historical constructions of American democracy and privilege. Melodrama shifts the questions of "managing" (a bourgeois term with echoes of Alger)) into divining the forces of good and evil. Melodrama itself always leads to an exceptionalism in which all economic, social, and cultural battles are personalized into the drama of the present where the intensity of the familiar/familial is everything. Indeed, the Don's speech suddenly shifts from the vision of "Our World" to his own family. He's willing to make a lasting peace, he says, but only if he can guarantee Michael's return from Sicily as a free man. He states that he will take it personally if Michael is struck by lightning, if he should catch a "mortal fever," if his plane or ship should go down (294). Yet he concludes again, "are we not better men than those *pezzonovanti* who have killed countless millions of men in our lifetimes" (294)? When Don Corleone sits down, the other Dons applaud him and rise to kiss his cheek. He has equated all world strife with public men (the absent figures would include not only the known monsters Hitler and Stalin but also, presumably, Roosevelt and Churchill among others). What's terrifying but compelling is the "statesmanlike" rhetoric that dissociates everyone in the room from any war that America might undertake. Any collective goal of American society, or any freely chosen or thoughtfully embraced allegiance to the new country is never even a possibility. "The men on high" is the catch-all signifier for American power, as is "our world," and there will be no interpenetration. The Dons then become at their convention the rulers of their postwar world in America, an entity they know as almost a parallel universe.

What Puzo never cares to accomplish are the dialogic possibilities of such a transformative encounter between America and the mob, how the immigrant sons might be caught up in American idealism or openness and modify rhetoric or praxis in unexpected ways. Instead, the promise of freedom in the nation is to let the Dons operate with impunity in the shadows, which, of course may be *the very dispensation to business itself in America*. Such would indeed be a hard saying. The Dons reign between the poles of communism and anarchy, between state control and total lawlessness. They are conservators, good American business men, prudent and far-seeing.

Puzo's verbal and conceptual repertoire at such moments is scant and contradictory. He certainly does not want to stress the hypocrisy of the Dons. Within three pages, *pezznovanti* is uttered in three contexts: as what or who their granchildren might become, as the arbiters of where and whom and how these men are governed in America, and as murderers of millions in the 1930s and 1940s. Puzo goes back to such a word because it's an all-purpose equivalent of *big shot*. He's seldom concerned with verbal precision, nor is the repetititon supposed to cohere in an irony that would disentangle the concepts of the role of government in relation to the governed or constituted authority set against those who would flout it. Recall Puzo invoking the pope and the Constitution in the same paragraph in which Don Corleone was a Johnny Appleseed of conciliation traveling the United States in the 1930s (224). Puzo portrays the Don and his associates as broadly as possible, providing them with signifiers that quickly and extrinsically convey both moral power and political legitimacy, regardless of context. The mob's Constitutional Convention can become whatever the reader wants it to be—a boardroom meeting, a town hall assembly, a primer on political policy, a father's plea for his son. By starting at the high end of inflated signification, melodrama always has a surfeit of sensational capital on hand to portray these "businessmen" in any moral context necessary.

Destiny as Authorizing Melodrama

Destiny appears as supple and profligate a term as can be found in *The Godfather*, and Puzo invokes it in both general and specific terms. There's a "general destiny" in America to join or refrain from (365); Michael's "curious destiny" is to replace his father (411). Vito Corleone is ready "to start on his destiny" when he decides to kill Fanucci (203). Sonny's destiny is to become a murderer, even though as a boy he was truly tenderhearted (266); his destiny was decided when he saw his father kill Fanucci, causing the Don to observe, "Every man has one destiny" (222). Whether the will of absent gods or the fated result of a human action, destiny in *The Godfather* is always played in an emotional and powerful register, the force that trumps cause and effect with great consequences. Destiny is irrevocable, a course of events in which the actors walk through large motions in an imposed inevitability. In popular fiction, destiny is conveniently decreed by authorial fiat, often out of context and specifying neither a good or evil course, merely one "destined." Destiny can never be character-based or rooted in character development. Most often, the "destined" character conceives his course as a natural fulfillment of some fated wrong or good. Self-annointed, the destined character forgets immediately that his destiny has been made out of history's manipulations and circumstance. Realism's web of connections spun in any life-world is elided through destiny's plot victories. A-historical though it appears, destiny emerges out of history's randomness itself, a capstone opinion as to why what happened *has* happened or *will* happen.

On the one hand, Vito Corleone—illiterate, oppressed, terrorized—emerges from a Sicily where his ancestors had been peasants for a thousand years. He escapes that predetermined course but not without being deeply marked by a mistrust of all governments, authority, and social bonds. In truth, he is perhaps "destined" to mistrust America and its forms and promises. On the other hand, to be an immigrant is to follow a fated narrative already in place—the flight from one country to another, the loss of tradition however oppressive, including family, language, customs, food, culture, and environment. The immigrant is trading one history for a blank slate in another that is yet conditioned by the immigrant's presence in a land predisposed to consign him to "immigrant" status and by the past that he carries forward into a new destiny. To place the dynamic in Corleone terms and family, the immigrant passes from a pawn with an absolute lack of freedom and individuality in Sicily into a pawn within the capacious idealism of an America that in its rhetoric is dedicated to erasing precisely the fated circumstance of the immigrant's experience up to the moment of arriving in America itelf. Once in America, the immigrant's new history may begin. However, Puzo conceives of the Corleones conceiving *themselves* still in patterns of destiny; their personalities and experience prepares them however incongruously for the pure possibility of America, destiny's New World child.

If destiny forgets that it has been made, so does America itself. Fisher cites the power of the American "Manifest Destiny," the wedding of "self-evident" status to American dominion over the continental landscape in the nineteenth century, and the fiction and history written out of this impulse.[6] As he says gnostically, once destiny is manifest, the writing of history can begin, as well as that of historical fiction (25), and he cites examples from Parkman, Longfellow, and Cooper on clearing of the land of Native Americans that marks a period when history is inaugurated by a series of massacres. Once violence and appropriation are safely consigned to prehistory by history and fiction, the nation can build.

The Corleone empire may begin with the killing of Fanucci, a neighborhood figure of no great import, but through this act, Vito Corleone establishes himself as a man of reason, not as a murderer, but as a force backed by the threat of a massacre, a latent primitivism that will surely destroy those who do not sustain the fiction with him of civilized dialogue and compromise. Thus murder is not destiny but inaugurates destiny and is a malevolent god or first cause. Perhaps the most stunning acting by Al Pacino in *Godfather I* is in the few seconds before Michael kills Solozzo and McCluskey in the Italian restaurant. Whole worlds appear to pass before his eyes as he lives through what has led up to this act and what may flow from it. His unfocused stare is abstracted yet terribly dramatic as, adrenaline pumping, destiny is about to be made manifest. His gun shots rip open bodies, he drops the gun on the floor, the Nino Roti score hits bottomless tragic notes, and Michael stumbles out to a waiting getaway car. The college boy/war hero disappears forever in an instant. Michael has joined the family business in vintage melodramatic fashion. Puzo did not stop to make much of this scene in the novel, but Coppola knew how to frame and underscore destiny's moment. He understood the defining act as Michael begins his real life and all else falls away.

In mob narrative, murders are public declarations of vocation and authority, as surely as a diploma hung on a wall or office space rented out and a name placed upon a door. Furthermore, murder is "self-evident,"

Michael Corleone (Al Pacino) begins his destiny (*Godfather I*).
Courtesy Museum of Modern Art/Film Still Archive.

destiny made "manifest," a revealing-as-present. American exceptionalism becomes the individual's violent exceptionalism. For a Sicilian peasant used to thinking in terms of negative destiny, to be lifted into the American manifest destiny is to retain absolutist belief in its power but to wholly shift its registers. In terms of a historical pre-condition to destined explanation and status, the Corleones come singularly equipped on several counts. Barzini refers to the Italian believing himself to be a "unique specimen of humanity," a "distinct personality deserving special consideration," believing himself for "intricate and improbable reasons" to be one of God's favorite sons (79). As Michael tells Kay, his father rises above rules not meant for men like him, men of "extraordinary force and character" (365). A democratic exceptionalism—you are predestined because you think you are—may be endorsed by the gods or by self-election. Barzini points out that such Italian compulsions to make everyone feel as if he were privileged is often compensatory behavior for a deeper, bleak outlook on life and fate (75).

Coincident to the Italian *destino* is the popular fictional drive to portray American capitalist heroes as personally driven characters who override constraints to succeed because of some innate vision and talents. Their "world" is too small or cramped to contain them, and they must seize what amounts to their destiny. As Elizabeth Long remarks, "like Calvinists predestined for salvation they are earmarked for success" (72). Such is the prescription for writers and capitalist heroes from Dreiser's Cowperwood and London's Buck in *Call* to the heroes of Rand and Robbins. This prescription is disguised in the displaced religious code heroes of General Lew Wallace's *Ben Hur* (1880) through those of Lloyd C. Douglas (*Magnificent Obsession* [1929], *The Robe* [1942]) and the popes and towering artists of Irving Stone.[7] Rivals to *The Godfather* for most influential popular novel of the twentieth century also feature improbable capitalist heroes: the calm, natural gentleman cowboy-executive-in-training in Owen Wister's *The Virginian* (1901) and Mitchell's Scarlett O'Hara in *Gone with the Wind*, a born (destined?) businesswoman, if unlucky in love and marriage.

In writing of the individual's right to regulate himself in a market society, Brown talks of this society's "construction of self, a self aligned with market relations such as exchange value, inalienability, circulation, and competition" (2). The Corleones, like any Americans, reinterpret these relations for themselves. In Puzo's hands, these relations comprise what might be called a capitalist poetics, complete with epiphanies of the peculiar market in which the Corleones function (the need to inaugurate through murder, the ultimate weeding out of the competition, and privatizing through family monopoly). Lawrence Stone cites two key characteristics of the modern family as an intensified affective bonding of the nuclear core at the expense of neighbors and kin as well as a "strong sense of individual autonomy and the right to personal freedom in the pursuit of happiness" (Barnes 91). *The Godfather* binds everyone we care about into the family and casts out all others. *The Godfather* then casts all images of self-aggrandizement and personal choice under the bar of destiny, from the fated state of being a poor, devastated Sicilian boy to the fate of becoming a Don. Family and Destiny replace community/ country and personal responsibility. All march to several deep chords (Italian, Popular, Melodramatic, American) that blend into one narrative theme that becomes *manifest*. What happened had to happen and did. "Self-evident" takes on the appearance of the most mythic and justifiable tautology.

Furthermore, "what happened" is underscored as not only inevitable but just and proper. Fisher states that "making familiar or making ordinary is the radical 'work' done by popular forms" in historical and sentimental novels (19). He submits that popular forms do cultural work through recognition and repetition in creating a reality that returns over and over again to central facts, which become "ordinary" (7). In *The Godfather*, the litany is in the interplay of family, reason, and violence done in the name of family after all reason fails. Again and again these rhythms are played out to where the unimaginable (the murders) becomes the commonplace solution. Fisher knows that historical and sentimental forms depend more on images than on analysis. They work through sensation defined through the sort of melodramatic tableaux that work hardest to seduce the reader into affiliation. They are unforgettable rather than multileveled and intelligent: the visceral impact of Khartoum's head in Woltz's bed, Michael's broken jaw, Sonny dead at the toll booth, Apollonia exploded in the car are important lessons to align the reader with the Corleone family. They far outweigh the Don's words or Puzo's authorial commentary. These historical and sentimental forms "often seem, when quoted in moments of self-analysis, stupid, obtuse, commonplace" (20). Puzo's attempts to explain his narrative, to gloss his momentum and outcomes lead to the already-discussed banal and defective causal chains on "destiny," "reason," and "death as a foul traitor."

The hard fact at the core of *The Godfather* is that murder is the family business. On the way to the Dons' convention came the murders of Fanucci, Sollozzo, and McCluskey, as well as countless others in a cycle back to Corleone, Sicily, and "destined" oppression that started Vito Andolini on his own course to America. Murder *is* the core of the family business, but the historical frame of "Founding" is most deeply, historically American, while the "Family" frame is the most sympathetic of all American collective signs. The immigrant, in effect, must always murder self as well, perform an act of forgetting that is most self-evident as well as inevitable. The immigrant saga has a rigid phenomenological and narrative form with the loss of so much of the core culture and that which constitutes personality and shapes character. "Coming to America" is indeed a "general destiny" as well as a determinism that can only be written about through a vale of tears, in a melodrama that is extreme, rather than mimetic, since the immigrant possesses no social, linguistic, or cultural baseline to be "re-presented." In this morally fluid melodramatic universe, Saving the Family becomes synonomous with Murdering Our Enemies. The setting of the novel itself resembles that of a frontier tale: the Corleone compound or fortress, Don Corleone and Sonny ambushed, Tom Hagen abducted and held in capitivity, Michael escaping into exile and returning, border skirmishes and deaths mounting on each side, emissaries and captured warriors. Genres are truly able to mix and match through melodrama.

Fisher's most suggestive phrase speaks to how images in popular forms "invaded and then ordered massive, unsorted psychic materials" (20). *Hard Facts* centers on the "colonization" of the "national mind" of characters and images such as Cooper's Indians and frontiersmen, Stowe's Topsy and Uncle Tom, and Dreiser's Carrie to provide powerful and enduring pictures of the frontier, the slave plantation, and the American city of 1900 (20–21). Fisher's verbs of choice are *invade* and *order*, the rhythm of colonizing in its effective life-world power. *The Godfather* performs these rhythms again and again in an interpenetration of immigrant, family, business, and national materials. The *real* melting pot in *The Godfather* contains Puzo's amalgam of crime, business, and family in sentiment and sensation, melodrama's twin muses. The Corleone family functions as a corporate entity with its eye on profits, expansion, and rivals, but just as surely that corporation begins to pressure the Corleones into contorted roles as Sonny tries to live up to being a Don, Michael is recalled from America to work for the family, and Vito Corleone is critically wounded. Just as surely the Old World sense of a negative destiny under the heel of a feudal oppression is reordered into a positive American destiny of individual exceptionalism and the radical freedom to become. The Corleones inexorably drive to authority in a country that believes in its collective destiny: to "make manifest" beyond all reasonable doubt and to do so within violence that is "just business." No wonder Puzo's mob narrative has become a compelling version of our national story.

The Corleone Logic of the Sentimental: Women's Roles Usurped

Saving the Corleone family becomes a greater narrative pleasure for the popular reader than grasping the management of the Corleone world. The blanket genius of *The Godfather* is that Puzo weds the imperatives of the historical novel in nation building and eliminating rival claims—in "authorizing" or "inaugurating"—to the imperatives of the sentimental novel in establishing bonds of a social disposition, to create in the reader a caring about the Corleones and their prevailing as individuals. The bonding with the family is intense and precisely locates their suffering within the family unit. The death of Sonny, the shooting of Don Corleone, Michael's return to the family, the abuse of Connie and the sacrifice of her husband to Michael's revenge, Kay's conversion to grave knowledge of Michael's role and nature—these outcomes view the family's story in the harsh and fated violence of historical fiction (what did happen, what had to happen) through the more emotional lens of sentimental fiction (who was victimized, who grieved) to the ultimate melodramatic climax (we have been wronged; vengeance is ours!).

Barnes has written that "to read sympathetically becomes synonomous with reading like an American" and that "sociopolitical issues are cast as family dramas" in American life and letters from the eighteenth century onward (2). Surely the enduring American rhetorical insistence on "the people," derived by essayists and philosophers building on John Locke's *Essay concerning Human Understanding*" (1690) with its repeated references to an epistemology of sensation, goes far toward establishing that personal affiliations nurtured through the senses could be as important a part of a person's moral compass as reason itself and could not be divorced from it. Hume and Adam Smith attempt to make sentiment a fundament of moral judgment, in effect, tuning Locke's view of sensations to a social and evaluative key, preparing the way for the American political rhetoricians such as Jefferson and Tom Paine.

We have seen above how Don Corleone speaks to the other Dons as a statesman embodying a fiscally conservative ethic amongst immigrant partriarchs in a democratically sanctioned lawlessness within a very recognizable business framework. What has not yet been stressed is how personal and familial an aura this speech has and how intertwined it is with family. What Barnes calls "the domestication of paternal authority" in America (9–10), the move of such relations from "coercive to consensual," is what the Corleones model again and again in popular fiction. Michael's passage in the novel is to surrender himself to the father, to become the father with the father's blessings, to do for him at personal cost. *The Godfather* posits this oddly anti-Freudian passage as seamless and natural; Michael's early affiliation with America is easily overturned. The Old World virtues maintained become the rather conflictless merging with the Father, to become him and do his work. Barnes's writing centers on early American fiction and is most concerned with the construction and supression of the feminine subject within the patriarchal family tale, the way in which sympathy circulates in an incestuous dynamic. In Puzo's transformation, Michael does not kill the father but assumes his role, which is also that of nurturing force.

The Godfather suggests a total usurpation of women's roles by the central male characters in a sentimental take-over. Mama Corleone has no first name. Kay is not only stripped of her individuality but is recycled into the most Catholic of the novel's women. Lucy Mancini is a restructured sex organ in Puzo's endless sophomoric Rabelaisian conceit. Connie is a sad pawn in the family's business, a character finally resurrected from victimization along with Kay by Puzo and Coppola in *Godfather III,* when, presumably, it was finally audience-prudent to install some measure of female agency to the narrative.

To rail against the marginalization of women in *The Godfather* accomplishes little because massive male domination has been felt from the outset of the narrative's reception by readers and filmgoers. What is key, though, is to account for the work's popularity with women readers and viewers as well, since the decades-long American fascination with the Corleones has hardly been masculine alone. Clearly the novel and films make the wider audience identify with the family itself against its enemies; readers are converted from configuring the Corleones as "other" (foreign, criminal, violent, sexist) to "same" (parents, children, victims, reasonable men). Such conversions are initially resisted by the ironic and/ or ideological critic who sees them as co-opting readerly energies, who may want to intervene on behalf of the novel's silenced family of women characters or on behalf of the faceless victims not even created by Puzo, anyone the family holds in terror to its ends. Fisher tries to account for the seduction of the reader in a text such as *The Godfather* by stating that the psychology of the oppressor, when rendered from the inside or when it's all the perspective the reader is allowed, is always a humanizing narration. Fisher calls it the "Romance of Consciousness" and opposes it to the Sentimental Novel in focusing on heroic villains rather than sentimental victims (91–99). What he doesn't acknowledge is the way in which sentimental narration sanctions the victim to *become* the oppressor in a newly inscribed romance of consciousness. Such a conversion is the *Great Consciousness Shift* in popular fiction: the moment in which the victim of some horrible wrong, so atrocious, so utterly and destructively unfair, one perpetrated by an oppressive gender, race, class, society, culture, government, impersonal or personal enemy, is instantly given an enormous fund of righteous moral capital to expend on revenge for the remainder of the novel. This vengeance can be carried out slowly, according to an unfolding master plan, or in one moment of violence. Contemporary social melodrama favors a psychologically traumatized character who will stop at nothing to carry out this counterplot against the one who has damaged him or her.[8]

Not all such revivified victims are rehabilitated. They may remain the torturers of the innocent, the malignant others plaguing benign heroes and heroines. However, when they perform their acts in the name of family, the potential to win the hearts of the audiences is immense. The Corleones are constant companions to their reader-viewers; we are never out of their point of view. We are in to them like the suppliants on Connie's wedding day. Nothing happens in Puzo's text that is not directly related to their survival, their power, their sense of well-being or danger. To a great degree, we are in the parlor world of Mrs. Stowe or in the interiors of Margaret Mitchell, but the oppression and war talk is quite different. The evils of slavery or Yankees have been replaced as debate topics by the dialogues of men at work, plotting, The oppressed have been given full sanction to become the oppressors, and Auden is validated: those to whom evil is done do evil in return. This basic moral balance is the most blatant of melodramatic truisms as well as a flat-line justice that an audience of feeling can applaud. The true morality play that all vengeance narratives enact is, of course, that the victim must "become like them" to achieve desired ends. Having achieved these ends, the ruins are all around. Such consciousness pervades war novels and films most strongly as the survivors look for a sign of the virtues and precepts that sent them into battle in the first place for a "way of life" that most often is coded strongly through the protection of women, children, and family.[9]

To test out Puzo's 1996 confession that Don Corleone possessed a remembered maternal voice within a patriarchal control over the family's lives and fortunes, what scenes in the novel provide the best evidence? In the transactions with Amerigo Bonasera, Don Corleone is brought into his most intimate relations to life and death. The Don and the undertaker interact because of the bodies of their children at risk in life and death; the services they require are personal and intimate. The novel opens with Amerigo Bonasera ("America Good Evening") begging the Don on his daughter's wedding day to take the lives of the two WASP teenagers who brutally assaulted her. As is discussed in detail in chapter 4, the Don takes the occasion to instruct Bonasera in how to approach him with all due respect in a personal relationship. Finally, Bonasera bows his head in fealty, and the Don concludes that Bonasera will have justice. Then he utters the famous, "Some day, and that day may never come, I will call upon you to do me a service in return. Until that day, consider this justice a gift from my wife, your daughter's godmother" (33). This transference of the Don's favor appears as a courtesy but more strongly suggests the aura of the feminine and maternal. The melodramatic language of this opening section has Bonasera weeping bitter tears, the Don being "gentle, patient" (32) as he labors to make this parental petitioner see his true role in America. The Don should be all things to him: bank, court, emotional support. Finally, the Don assigns the "gift" as one from mother to mother, woman to woman. Bonasera, an emotional man who identifies with America itself, acts as agent for his abused daughter and his grieving wife, while the Don acts for his own wife. As Puzo says about his mother, "the Don's courage and loyalty came from her; his humanity came from her" (*The Fortunate Pilgrim* xii). Scenes such as the Bonasera exchange show how Puzo either consciously or unconsciously framed Don Corleone within this usurped maternal imaginary.

In the opening wedding day scenes with Bonasera, the Don instructs the undertaker as to correct life conduct. Bonasera, who wishes to become American too quickly, to shake hands in a "good evening," perhaps, also is too eager to call for the death of the two guilty teenagers because death is his business. Yet death is also Vito Corleone's business day by day in measured decisions. The Don holds death as last resort, although his "reason" is nothing without that implied threat and fear. For Bonasera, death is something normal and easy. His job is to brush life back into death for funerals, in effect, becoming the maternal force giving life to death. Late in the same evening, when Genco asks the Don to save him, saying that the flesh is falling off his bones, the Don replies that he "has no such powers" (47); the novel's logic suggests that it's Bonasera who performs his craft for the last moments before the body is put in the earth. The embalmer is an artist but menial in comparison to the man who can grant wishes and fulfill destinies.

Bonasera's "good evening" finally comes when Sonny Corleone is gunned down at the toll booth. Hagen calls a nervous Bonasera to tell him that the Don will be arriving in an hour, that it's time for him to repay his Don. The scene takes place in the back "work" room of Bonasera's funeral parlor, where the business of death is transacted. This parlor is the commercialized trace of the domestic lying-in at home in the nineteenth-century parlor, the American middle-class room for weddings and funerals. And here Puzo gives us a funeral evening to match the opening wedding day. When Sonny's wrecked body is trundled in to Bonasera's work room, the Don appears behind the stretcher: "his hair seemed thin over his massive skull. He looked older, more shrunken than when Bonasera had seen him at the wedding." In effect, the Don has now become Gencolike, "older, more shunken" (259); he now needs an "old friend," even as Genco had begged the Don to help him stave off death. In the earlier scene, the Don had taken evasive action. He had refused the rhetorical and politicized suggestions of the dying man that they were old confederates in death. In that earlier scene, the Don had ushered all of Genco's women out of the room and had become the sole nurse and mourner. Here again, over the body of a dead male child, it's the two men who keep vigil as women. The Don asks Bonasera to use all his powers "as you love me" for "I do not wish his mother to see him as he is" (259). The earlier "gift" to Bonasera had been to his *wife*; now the Don asks for a gift for his *own* wife, Sonny's mother. Extraordinary that the business of caring for the dead should devolve upon the two men. Women are not present at such times, nor are they needed; the intimacies are between the death bringer and the death-in-life artist. The Don's remark refers to the grotesque body but also should remind the reader,"see *him* [Sonny] *as he is——murdered son and murderer, born of a murderous father.*" To sublimate that truth, all possible sentimental framing is employed to make the Don humble, pathetic, maternal.

The mourning over the ruin of Sonny, his first born, brings the Don into a compassionate relation for one of the few times in the novel. He is bereft of all authority with no one to kill, no one to reason with, no orders to give. He is a supplicant himself on another family occasion, moving from wedding day to a day of family death. Such a scene is as morally fraudulent and yet emotionally powerful as any scene in *The Godfather*. It provides no consolation or recovery and offers what Fisher calls "training in pure feeling and response" that "[lie] at the heart of sentimental politics" (123). It's most difficult for the reader to remember the Don's culpability in death when he stands in pain at the undertaker's worktable, taking the full brunt of the grieving. Such a scene could be act 2 in any melodrama on any stage, the moment just before the victim cries out to the heavens for redress or strength.

Puzo concluded his preface to *The Fortunate Pilgrim* with a melodramatic lament about his own mother: "Behold how she was wronged" (xiii). In the male adaptation, the Don's final phrase to Bonasera weds the historical novel plot to a sentimental identification in a moral blindness that refuses to acknowledge his complicity: "See how *they* [italics mine] have massacred my son" (259). The true terrors of the novel are never the Don's. Can Sonny's dead body be suitably "fixed" like Michael's face, Johnny's voice, Jules's medical practice, Lucy's vagina? Such physical "fixing" is emblematic of everything "arranged" on a societal level in *The Godfather*. What should be noted is how this scene punctuates the male and paternal colonization of grief in the novel, the exclusion of women from even this relation to their children, and the eerie male business over children's bodies in the name of the absent mother.

When Connie Corleone accosts Michael as the murderer of her husband, Carlo Rizzi, the transactions amongst dead bodies in the Corleone home reaches its conclusion. Michael has ordered Carlo's death and has engineered the assassinations of the heads of the Five Families; Sonny's "massacre" is avenged. However, Connie bursts into the male space of the Corleone "living room," shrieking, "you lousy bastard, you killed my husband. You waited until our father died. . . . You blamed him about Sonny, you always did, everybody did. But you never thought about me. You never gave a damn about me" (436). Connie has it right; Michael doesn't think about her, to be a Corleone daughter is to be disposable. The novel has come full circle at conclusion. Connie, who was married in the novel's first pages, when her father dispensed favors in her name on her wedding day, is now a widow and charges into the house to accuse her brother of killing her husband. The violence has wound its way in incestuous fashion throughout the family plot. Connie speaks politically, joining Genco, Woltz, and Kay as truth-bringers about Corleone real-world relations and crimes. Yet Michael can dismiss her as hysterical, can for one last time answer Kay's searching eyes with his final denial that he is not a murderer. Nonetheless, Kay quickly realizes

the truth when he receives Clemenza and other family soldiers and bodyguards and is called "Don Michael" for the first time.

Puzo frames her realization in a *bella figura* scene where the family
capos give him fealty. In Coppola's framing, Kay is looking into the living
room from a hallway and sees the men massed there in formal recognition. Someone moves to close the door, barring the living space from her
in the film's final frame, a door-closing that is repeated in *Godfather II*
when Michael slowly, coldly closes the glass back door on her desperate,
plaintive face, cutting her off from her children after her stealth visit to
the family compound in Lake Tahoe. In the novel, Kay sees Michael as
a Roman emperor, his body language proclaiming a "cold, proud power."
Convinced that Connie is telling the truth, "she went back into the kitchen
and wept" (437). Excluded from the living room by her knowledge of the
truth and by the men's dominion there, she can only join Connie in
complete irrelevancy.[10] From funeral parlor to Corleone parlor, the women
do not stand a chance while the deadly men are humanized even more
by their grieving for the dead and honoring their Don. They are always
"at home."

There are few significations that Don Corleone does not ultimately
embody in the American experience within the melodramatic form, wholly
usurping in male authority all the various family roles of sympathy and
parental concern, yet acting swiftly and surely in the most sensational of
male arenas, as a businessman, a statesman, an immigrant success story,
a God, a father. He operates in a modern America in which the legacy of
Calvinism and predestination was expanded and historicized by Manifest Destiny. A country that descends from Puritan patriarchs through
national messianic errands is surely a country with a readership that can
believe in a Don Corleone, can see in him the particular election from an
American exceptionalism, one reaching back to Founding Fathers in the
historical paradigm, to a "wartime" leader of men, to an immigrant
patriarch in the ethnic paradigm, to the self-made man in the success
story, to a father with sons, to a figure who can bring life or death but
who can also "manage" "our World." A powerful affirming correspondence amongst these traditional male roles accounts in full measure for
The Godfather's sustained popularity. The male strain of melodrama finally effaces capitalist predation and alters it into cosmic force, just as its
sentimental strain in *The Godfather* changes murdering men into grieving
maternal substitutes performing the necessary rituals over their broken
children. The historical and sentimental novel forms that cross in *The
Godfather* authorize power and validate sympathies toward the most
powerful and popular family in American fictional history. The myopic
outcome within melodrama's always excessive signification is the full
extension of that sympathy to the Corleones as oppressed family men on
the one hand and justified murderers on the other.

The Godfather's unoriginal and repeatable large motions within melodrama account for *The Godfather's* power, its ordinariness in seconding the Spencerian optimistic power philosophy that has become the twentieth-century business religion in America beyond any particular epistemological or historical challenge to its authority. Corleones are born into their American history by killing men. *The Godfather's* popular genius is to turn such violent individual destiny into Manifest Destiny, a familiar American conversion. Self-evident American truisms about business and family within affective forms sanction the violence that allows men the full take-over of sympathy from women as subjects and objects without denying the powerful readerly identification. Despite all reasoned misgivings, Puzo's audience can feel "at home," "like," and "same" with the Corleones. We may have better angels in our nature, but *The Godfather* does not summon them, nor do we feel their presence in the text.

chapter seven

The Corleones as "Our Gang": *The Godfather* Interrogated by Doctorow's *Ragtime*

Father had always felt secretly that as a family they were touched by an extra light. He felt it going now. He felt stupid and plodding, available simply to have done to him what circumstances would do.

—Doctorow, *Ragtime*

[Jack London was] the kind of writer who went to a place and wrote his dreams into it, the kind of writer who found an idea and spun his psyche around it. He was a workaday literary genius hack.

—Doctorow, *Jack London, Hemingway, and the Constitution*

The completed struggle for survival and legitimacy in any historical novel must take on the character of destiny in the reader's consciousness and in the historical present. One way to contextualize and contest Puzo's picture of the Corleone hegemony in *The Godfather* is by way of contrast with another historical novel, E. L. Doctorow's *Ragtime* (1975), which is as self-reflexive and multidimensional in its portrayal of American immigration and evolving power and authority as *The Godfather* is monolithic. What happens when *The Godfather* or by extension any bestselling novel is placed into dialogue with its elite fictional twin? What can be learned by examining the novel against *Ragtime*, asking what Puzo was doing and what he was eliding or refusing to comment upon? The goal is not to use *Ragtime* as a club with which to beat *The Godfather* in a canonical versus popular mimetic stakes game but to articulate the full range of issues that both novels confront about American immigration, assimilation, and the family. A larger goal is to discuss how paradigmatic popular and elite fictions presume to disclose about the representations of these subjects. Taken together, *Ragtime* and *The Godfather* are the most powerful late-twentieth-century statements about an

earlier European immigration, an American epic subject that has heretofore not created the fictional or critical climate for excitement that the
tropes of Indian removal, slavery, women's roles and rights, and the
frontier and its mythos have fostered in the last few decades. Puzo and
Doctorow both write when the melting pot had long been accepted as a
controlling American myth, but actually both novels appeared when deep
divisions within America contested such a myth: differences between
black and white, parent and child, young and old, civilian and military,
men and women, establishment and counterculture.

The *Godfather* and *Ragtime* relentlessly cover the same terrain from
different viewpoints and fictional objectives. *The Godfather* exemplifies
the motions of popular fiction, while *Ragtime* shows how popular fictions
are created and how they work. Puzo creates an ur-father for the twentieth century. Doctorow dismantles and reconstitutes the very notion of
a patriarchy. Puzo drives the hard fact of "killing a man" as inaugurating
and incorporating a line; Doctorow's new hard fact is "creating an image" as the father, the immigrant, is made up of broken initiatives and
American reconditioning of the figure. Puzo offers the truly strong man
as immigrant protagonist creating his own history. Doctorow makes
history itself his protagonist, the goal of characters being to point
themselves along its lines of force; the immigrant becomes metaphorical
and universal.

Both novels imply historical forgetting, but only Doctorow makes it
the moral subject of his own acknowledgment. The whole structure of *The*
Godfather is about erasure of acts in favor of their forgetting. Puzo's family
truly becomes "Our Gang," the prototypical mob family in American fiction. Doctorow's Our Gang image concludes his book in the immigrant
socialist-turned-movie producer's Beverly Hills intimation of the Little Ras-
cals, a willed melting pot group of kids for popular consumption that
belies the violence of *Ragtime*'s story and the victims strewn over its pages.
Ragtime's deep ironic image of Our Gang ends the individualized suffering
tale of immigration as we know it.

Puzo renders a historically capped figure, the heroic capitalist, and
fantasizes him as unremitting patriarchal hero. He sketches lightly in a
popular form of the realist-naturalist novel. Doctorow appropriates that
precise form for an ironic rendering backed by a liberal commitment to
history's victims and threads his narrative through a postmodern depiction of the birth of the replicated image culture. Puzo's novel drives
through modern America without giving notice that a popular culture
exists, although becoming a great artifact and product of that culture. *The*
Godfather gives no sign that whole eras of history are turning over with
consequences; the only history that matters for Puzo is the history of the
Corleone family. *The Godfather* retains the status of immigrant and stubbornly keeps on point as one family's triumph over its enemies. Such
heroic individualism exists as further grist for Doctorow to scrutinize as

another exhausted category. In *Ragtime*, he clears the land of immigrants and describes the process by which the melting pot is installed in popular culture through mediation and forgetting. The dialogue between a popular classic and its elite subversion reveals to us how each fiction discloses its messages through narratives that are alternately opaque and concealing about aims and practices.

Popular Fiction and Elite Fiction: A Contest?

At the outset, it's important to understand why a dialogue between *The Godfather* and *Ragtime* is useful. Energy flows through such an exercise when a critic attempts to describe one text by reference to another, to find out what a text means through what it suppresses, in effect, to define a novel by what it is not. Too often, elite novels are discussed by taking their assumed complexity as far as the critic can go in one direction or another, either ideologically, structurally, or semantically. We follow writers there to label their work as exceptional, singular or unrepeatable, and we inscribe them in a "great tradition" of other such singular, texts. With popular novels or best sellers, we use more prosaic categories to deem them important. We may write that they "touch a nerve" or express a "conventional wisdom" or a "false consciousness," that they "manage a conflict" or perfectly exemplify a subgenre. Conversely, although all popular fiction categories are always available for elite fiction to provide ironic and self-reflexive commentary, it is assumed that popular fiction steadfastly refuses to interrogate its own premises. A critic might say that Doctorow would understand Puzo's novel very well as a late-twentieth-century example of sensation and sentiment, an adventure tale of great violence in which nonetheless the central family characters gather great sympathy from the readers. Popular fiction logic expects the reader to affiliate with the Corleones, wants their cult to carry the reader along through whatever they do. *Ragtime* puts the father and businessman under scrutiny and deconstruction and hypothesizes that hero in a constellation of other recognizable early-twentieth-century figures, all competing for imaginative space and self-definition in a novel where no one can truly be identified as the protagonist. *Ragtime* would suggest that Vito and Michael Corleone are not omnipotent or directing their destinies but are subject to an array of forces and desires that endlessly loop them back into a collective that would make them part of an ensemble of Americans caught in a particular time of history.

Ragtime, of course, does not know the Corleones, but its dynamics can explain them in different fictional rhetoric that can supply the missing social and historical context, which so abstracts this suspicious Sicilian family and its activities. *The Godfather* hardly recognizes the historical force fields of the early twentieth century and suggests little of what its characters may be up against as immigrants in New York City. *Ragtime* moves in the New York of Jacob Riis's outrage at the harsh life of immigrants in slums filled with poverty and disease; Puzo is not interested. The early years of Vito Andolini in Corleone, Sicily; the assassination of his father, the hiding of the boy and his being shipped to America; the arrival in New York city—all these subjects are covered in less than a page in *The Godfather* (194). The murder of Vito Andolini's mother, the arrival at Ellis Island, the name mistakenly changed to "Corleone" by an immigration officer—all is added in Coppola-Puzo's screen version that begins *Godfather II*. All the young life of Vito Corleone is centered on learning about power and consolidating a neightborhood role. *The Godfather* is plot-driven by its hero's rock-solid need to establish himself. Yet it's not an immigrant novel and partakes of little social realism or even naturalistic, deterministic commentary. Its tale is how Vito Corleone inexorably becomes a Don. *Ragtime* expresses its outrage about immigrant struggle and child abuse in a controlled tone that never wavers or lets the reader be comfortable. The voice is that of harsh irony undercutting every self-aggrandizing or Promethean plan of its characters. Vito Corleone will succeed because it is his destiny to do so. *Ragtime*'s male strivers, from Father to Tateh and Coalhouse Walker will find themselves in places they do not choose to go, in roles foreign to them.

The cost of Puzo's singlevoicedness in writing the Don's success is a linearity that never swerves and that we can identify as a popular literature structural principle. Doctorow's commitment to a constant thwarting of the yearning and intention of his characters provides a circuit of "dissatisfaction" that calls sharply to attention the chronotopes of space/time coincidence on which all fiction thrives but does not usually flaunt. Through statements such as "at that exact moment" and "as it happened," Doctorow always seeks to keep the reader moving on many levels or "tracks." Puzo never allows contemplation of a Corleone action or decision to become the narrative center of *The Godfather*. The Corleones must, like sharks, keep moving through the plot or die. Doctorow writes through and of the melodramatic form from the vantage point of postmodern parody, irony, and understatement. Nonetheless, he compresses imagery to categorically state his anger. When he describes the immigrants at Ellis Island being herded and bullied by officials, he can write that "such power was dazzling. The immigrants were reminded of home" (15). Without going into any detail with a prior history or an individualizing of anyone involved, Doctorow references an ideology, a historical comparison, an ironic construction, a rueful glimpse of powerlessness. The image is absolutely full at the same time it's abstract and generalized. The image succeeds in being the trace of melodrama, of potentially hundreds of pages that could describe both the country of origin and the New World replication of oppression and want; the reader clearly recognizes that the author has positioned himself as caring but cool.

Neither the popular fiction melodrama of the Corleone family history in America nor the ironic treatment of the immigrant experience in *Ragtime* provides anything like what multiethnic criticism has identified as the ethnic novel or fictionalized ethnic autobiography. Puzo simplifies and passes over the facts of the immigrant experience to get to crime and power, family style. Having provided readers with a full fictional field of Italian immigrant life in New York City in *The Fortunate Pilgrim*, he apparently saw no reason to favor readers with such detail in *The Godfather*, which is built on different fictional premises. Doctorow ultimately presents "immigration" in a chain of references that stretches from the particular to the universal, from intense imagery of slum conditions to metaphors that control the novel. *The Godfather* may sound rich and multiform because of its large cast and adventures in many locales, but it's really one long tale of male power and secretiveness with no consistent authorial voice beyond the family commenting or controlling the issues raised. We cannot imagine any other contexts than what we see for the Corleones or their enemies. We cannot see them exploring new lives, acquiring new skills, or showing a curiosity about a world outside the family. They exemplify the fallacy of total control in their essential woodenness. Interested in nothing but the family, they are uninteresting themselves beyond their instrumental frame. While *Ragtime* sounds the same on every page in a declarative monotone, its verbal resources, wit, and grasp of American and media history are prodigious. Its characters are all restless, "dissatisfied," imaginatively licensed to metamorphose into other Americans, to pursue other selves. Immigration in *Ragtime* becomes not a fixed one-time action (Sicily to America in *The Godfather*) but a constant human changing that extends from fathers through all the characters in *Ragtime*.

Fathers and Immigrants:
Power, Escape, Dissatisfaction

Fathers in both *The Godfather* and *Ragtime* are the true centers of power, but they function in very different ways, emblematic of the different intents of popular and elite fiction. Puzo writes of the unbroken succession of authority that passes from Vito to Michael Corleone, a succession that occurs without visible oedipal trauma and with victory for the family over all its enemies. Doctorow systematically shatters the authority that his unnamed "Father" possesses on the first page of *Ragtime*. Every major plot initiative runs through Father and his family, bringing the news of a much more heterogeneous America, one comprised of social unrest, immigrant longing, racial prejudice, and the changing roles of women. In *Ragtime*, Father is more and more bewildered as a failing representative of American exceptionalism. With Father's world changing all about him, Doctorow writes, "Father had always felt secretly that as a family they were touched by an extra light. He felt it going now. He felt stupid and plodding, available simply to have done to him what circumstances would do" (189). No longer at the center of his own errand or America's, Father's rhetoric is very close to that of a helpless immigrant. Destiny has fled Father personally; he is now done to by events, and he cannot evolve quickly enough.

In *Ragtime*, Father takes the hits; in *The Godfather*, Vito Corleone *orders* the hits. Puzo does not question the "extra light"; Vito Corleone is exceptional in his survival, restraint, and vision, secured through a personal force he consolidates. Father in *Ragtime* builds his "house on a hill" in New Rochelle, New York, in 1902,; Vito Andolini arrives at Ellis Island in 1901 (film version) and accepts the change of his name to "Corleone," the name of his town in Sicily: "[I]t was one of the few gestures of sentiment he was ever to make" (194).[1] He succeeds in re-creating himself as a Sicilian within America, taking the Old World town into himself along with its suspicions and feuds. He remains static and unchanged in America. Doctorow, however, writes of Father that he was, even in death, "the immigrant, as in every moment of his life, arriving eternally on the shore of his Self" (269), a maxim Doctorow extends to an organic vision of human life in a later essay when he writes, "Everyone all the time is in the act of composition, our experience is an ongoing narrative within each of us" and "[P]eople find the meaning of their lives in sequence" (*Essays* 114–15). Characteristic of Doctorow and elite fiction is the major trope making that elevates a plot line and a character trait to both a metaphysical and a metanarrative principle. "Immigration" in *Ragtime* is always metamorphosing into escape, growth, and the most simple and awful temporality. Such internal intellectual energy within a concept derived from metaphor is what drives elite fiction's production and the critical attempt to realize its multiple meanings. In a novel such as *The Godfather*, immigration is not suggestive in its meanings but reductive. The concept is retained but with all its potential richness (immigration as family melodrama, customs, language, food, mores, religion, vocation) placed in skeletal forms. In a sense Puzo borrows against this ethnic richness but provides only the silhouette of it, the snapshot, precisely what *Ragtime* is in the process of analyzing. Elite fiction raises a trope to a metaphor. Popular fiction reduces a trope to its semantic outlines and then trades on the aura of its richness, its authentic life. What fast food does to "taste," what Disney does to nature and animals, what television does to "middle-class experience," Puzo does to ethnicity and the immigrant in *The Godfather*.

The status of immigrant puts the father under great stress. Patriarchs thrive most under stable systems of long duration when tradition, order, and custom rule work and days. Also, the logic of immigration itself is toward transformation; the death of the immigrant is the assimilation into the new land. Immigrants must die away in the American narrative. They are a species whose "destiny" is to adapt or die, but, as Doctorow knows, that adaptation to or absorption by the new land is never a fixed state, an endless composing and recomposing of self and one not limited to people from foreign shores but to all of humanity. The immigrant of 1900 is a prisoner of sorts within the city of different language, customs, and culture, confined to economic servitude and a victim of prejudice. For Doctorow, such states prompt outrage rendered in irony and paradox: children as "happy elves" worked to exhaustion by factory bosses, immigrants who waited for their lives to change after Jacob Riis took their pictures (15, 34). For Puzo, the immigrant plight and its powerlessness replicates the Old World oppression and is the justification for "going bad," for not accepting oppression and not waiting for change. Furthermore, in *The Godfather*, immigrant fathers and their sons stand together against their enemies in common enterprise in a straightforward and most uncomplicated binding, rewriting Freud and Darwin in their solidarity without angst, resentment, or decline. Corleone family business does not go deeply into neurosis or evolution.

The immigrant in twentieth-century America is the modern metamorphosed vanishing American, falling away in a symbolic genocide that is destined to occur in the very temporality of the plot within which the immigrant is inscribed. In organic terms, the immigrant is always doomed to disappear and to be lost to history, either in poverty or disease or in an American rebirth. With that rebirth, the new American's history truly begins, always at the cost of a prior self. *Ragtime's* central figures all go through this American process, even Father and his family, for Doctorow finds no one exempt from change at any time. In contrast, *The Godfather* posits a total denial of the need to change, as if it were a choice renounced. Puzo's Sicilian immigrants enact that American immigrant fantasy, one buried deep within the experience of millions of Americans arriving here in the early twentieth century. Within the Corleone compound and organization, the immigrant is never in an estranged role. The Corleones resist adaptation and never admit to dissatisfaction. Their hard fact of purchase in American society is "killing a man," which authenticates their "reason," but which does not partake of any American structure of law, business, government, or culture. They do not sow or reap; they do not make or replicate. They desire to be no one other than themselves. In many ways, the Corleones are as terrifying and inexorable as Faulkner's Snopes clan in their intervention in American capitalism, the urban plague to match the rural one, omnipotent and unchallenged.

Doctorow knows that immigration, while a human constant and thus a "universal" currency, has its stranger analogues. Father signs on for Peary's expedition to the North Pole, where Peary ultimately cannot say exactly where they are because the ice shifts endlessly. A watery planet defeats his stern will and measure; he must simply declare himself "there." There is no place to plant the American flag, for the world is too vast and inhospitable. Evelyn Nesbit ministers to Tateh's Little Girl and ultimately desires to affiliate with the immigrants in their poverty: "she was insane with the desire to become one of them . . . for a few hours each day she lived as a woman in the Jewish slums" (43), before Thaw's chauffeur comes to pick her up and drive her back to the mansion. Evelyn casts herself in a movie role before Tateh even helps invent the medium. She is "having an experience" as a living sentimental character in relation to an external object on which she lavishes her feelings, yet it is only a shift of her desiring imagination from herself, from sensation to sympathy. In succeeding decades, future Evelyn Nesbits might "take a role" in a such a sentimentally serious "breakthrough film" to enhance a career. Doctorow frames the scene showing Evelyn "so desperately in love that she could no longer see properly" but rather seeing "everything through a film of salt tears" (43). Her tear-filled eye becomes the camera, a living medium of emotional representation. This metafictional critique of sentimentalism, while representing the scene through it, is Doctorow's double reference and postmodernism's great ploy: to allow us to know as we read the manipulation of the very responses that make up our reading. Doctorow takes the risk of the elite author that the reader will not lose primary allegiance to the character while sharing an insight both at the character's expense and the reader's own naive emotion. Such an emotional balancing act is everywhere in postmodern reader response, and no author describes its workings better than Doctorow. Evelyn is an aimless "immigrant," wandering with her body through women's roles and costume changes as mistress, sex object, and nurturer. Finally bored with both the slums that are closed to her and with Younger Brother's neurotic attentions, she wants back in her most comfortable popular genre: "she wanted someone who would treat her badly and whom she could treat badly' (74).

Such a multileveled investigation of Evelyn's meanings as popular heroine within genre is beyond Puzo's goals and reach. He wants to use Kay Adams Corleone as a moral touchstone and also as a site of America ultimately absorbed into the family. An Adams daughter from New England finally gets the truth about her murderous husband, at which point, she goes back into the kitchen and weeps. In what amounts to *The Godfather*'s epilogue, Puzo gives Kay the novel's last perceptions. Having converted to Catholicism after internalizing the enormity of Michael's sins, she attends daily mass and takes communion Puzo shows her emptying "her mind of all thought of herself, of her children, of all anger, of all rebellion, of all questions. Then with a profound and deeply-willed desire to be heard, as she had every day since the murder of Carlo Rizzi, she said the necessary prayers for the soul of Michael Corleone" (446) Puzo never writes in self-reflexive commentary about the very forms within which he works, but often he wants the reader to make comparisons with other scenes and large motions in the novel. Here, what Puzo has called "casual irony" operates for any and all readers. Kay has been Michael's most insistent interrogator from the large American society about "what if everyone . . ." She is his wife whom he has not trusted. She has learned from becoming a Corleone how to put herself in the hands of a higher authority. Yet she does so to save Michael, not be dominated by him. Kay's supplications are in line with the favors asked of the Don on his daughter's wedding day. Now he is gone, and she needs to appeal to a different God.

Another author might weave a feminist argument through "profound and deeply willed desire . . . to be heard" as indicting the silencing of women or an ironic religious comment about a final reinstallation of God as the true arbiter of human wishes, but Puzo is not that author. There's no pattern for such a reading to take shape in the language or images. More than likely, Kay's abjection and conversion are in line with an unasked question: how powerful is Michael, son of Don Vito? So powerful that his wife must become Catholic, must pray like his Sicilian mother for his redemption. Just so does Kay go back into the kitchen to weep, because that's what women do, at least Puzo's women. That kitchen is a real kitchen, not a symbolic space. It's a woman's place because that's where Corleone women can be found, and the parlor is occupied with mobsters—nothing more.

Evelyn Nesbit's attempt to become a woman of the slums exists in her sympathy, which Doctorow wants to deconstruct. Her "arriving" on the "shores" of a new self is provisional and mediated by popular responses. The reader is always held back from primary identification with Evelyn. When she first makes her way to Little Girl, who is tied by a rope to Tateh so she won't be abducted, "she knelt down, her eyes dewy, and looked into the face of the dry-eyed girl. Hey pumpkin she said" (38). Evelyn's "Hey pumpkin" is incongruous, colloquial, nonethnic, and naive; it is sympathy at its most bland as Doctorow turns the scene from pathos to bathos while not losing it for the reader. Evelyn is banal and familiar; the "dry-eyed girl" is not moved by her own plight nor by Evelyn's attention. In her final scene in *The Godfather*, Kay Adams Corleone is the object lesson. Her role is to express Corleone power, not to call attention to her contingent status through gender or genre. Evelyn, no less an innocent character caught up in response to suffering, is the text herself for Doctorow—her maternal concern in her acting through a salty camera eye. Doctorow concludes, "[H]er voice became husky because her throat was bathed in the irrepressible and continuous crying which her happiness caused her" (43), linking the two indispensable facets of sentiment (crying and its happiness) but also grimly recalling Evelyn's salty throat when Thaw demands her to perform fellatio on him in the Tombs; she is tied to him by need of money no less than Little Girl is roped to Tateh. The last image of Evelyn's tears tells the truth that when

Evelyn cries for Little Girl, she cries for herself, which, as a true narcissist in brief remission, is fitting for her as a melodramatic heroine.

When Emma Goldman writes to Evelyn that she's using her as an example in ideological critique, "Evelyn didn't know what to do with such remarks" (71). She is a mystified popular reader, not knowing what she exemplifies. As a character fueling the culture's dreams of sexuality, she has no dreams not made by that culture nor any vantage point from which to see herself not claimed by her self. Puzo in *The Godfather* never introduces any character from whom a critique may be offered, excepting Jack Woltz and Kay Adams, the one silenced by violence, and the other, by marriage vows. There's no privileged information not vouchsafed to the Corleones themselves or parsed out by them. Their world view is the novel's limit and the reader must live coextensive with them. Self-reflection would destroy the purity of their heroism and release the monolithic control they have. It would simply be weakness. When Doctorow speaks of Grandfather's fascination with Ovid and transformation, he writes that "forms of life were volatile and that everything in the world could as easily be something else" (97). *Ragtime* unfolds within this fluidity, as does America. Bakhtin's concept of 'heteroglossia', the primal sea of language acitvity that washes over all discourse, no matter how worked up or styilized, is ideologically very democratic in its ethos, touching all parts of discourse and all speakers. Puzo by restricting his novel's information and scrutiny refuses to let his characters join in this life. Popular fiction always censors such multiform richness.

Arriving at "Our Gang"

Much has already been said in chapters 3 and 6 about Puzo's use of destiny to describe Don Corleone's passage through *The Godfather*. The family passes under the sign of fate that is Puzo's ticket for them to ride out any crisis that threatens their authority. Bakhtin well depicts this narrative world as that of the epic (see also chapter 8), one that he calls the "world of fathers and founder of families," a world in which the hero is absolutely equal to himself and has already become everything he could become. Epic characters for Bakhtin are bounded, preformed, and individualized by various destinies (*The Dialogic Imagination* 13, 34). He notes that an epic past is preserved and revealed only in the form of a national tradition, which is given as sacred and sacrosanct (16). In *The Godfather*, the national tradition is merged with the family as sacred and political entity to form Cosa Nostra. "Our World" is defined by the boundaries of the Corleone family, and all actions taken and decisions made are within that world. The family becomes the nation, and "Our World" becomes "ourselves." Such equating serves the popular fiction plot well when readers want and expect strong actions and emotions on behalf of clear goals by consistent characters. In effect, everything in popular fiction is punctuated, every syllable expressed, and all relations ultimately stand in the light.

Elite fiction is wary of the epic's opaqueness and wants to break into its monolithic narrative and sonorous surface. In *Ragtime*, Doctorow clearly wishes to speak of what is momentous in the American experience. He has a passionate feel for the epic sweep of our history, but in an oxymoronic gesture, he strips the patriarchs of their authority and the American exceptionalism of its clarity and assurance. Instead he exposes the brawling and contesting set of forces behind the American epic/errand, in which no character or set of ideals can ever be co-extensive with the nation or with self. Fisher has commented that the struggle of any historical novel takes on the appearance of destiny in the reader's own time (115) because the reader is inevitably living in a world that must accept certain outcomes. What Doctorow does is work forward toward the fact of Hollywood's rewriting of the immigrant struggle into the Our Gang vision of neighborhood kids, an image that stands for suppression of history's hard facts in the lives of the characters who have contributed to Tateh's vision on the lawn in Beverly Hills. To amend Fisher on Cooper's conclusions to the Leatherstocking novels, in *Ragtime*, "on the way to [the lawn in Beverly Hills], "there was a massacre . . . there was a massacre . . . there was a massacre" (Fisher 73).

Moreover, Doctorow drives the reader of *Ragtime* back from the reader's present in America to the birth of the replication and image culture that created the Our Gang image in the first place. Destiny is contested by such invention and innovation, which is not epic but insurgent, even if on behalf of a material ethos. The novel's double historical frame moves forward from 1900 to roughly 1920 in the novel's pages, while its conclusion in Hollywood puts the half-century between 1920 and the novel's publishing (1975) in firm perspective. Both the form of the American historical novel and its function in the present are served and satisfied by Doctorow's narrative. When Father begins to lose the "extra light" that had touched the family, it's American Exceptionalism waning in its surety. Doctorow places the light in aesthetic terms when he writes of Winslow Homer's painting: when "a certain light was still available along the eastern seaboard. Homer painted that light" (4). The "eastern seaboard" references American vision from the Puritans through the Founders to the Transcendentalists, finally come to reside in the flickering light of the early movie projector on the "western seaboard" as the families in *Ragtime* pass through its transforming lens into "Our Story" of who we are as a modern nation.

Ragtime's last image of the novel's children about to be converted into Our Gang cuts away the individualized suffering of immigration and of family struggle as we know it. Tateh is a survivor and a booster, as well as a tycoon. He has performed the makeover of social motion, death, and desperation into powerful popular art, and he has not been cynical. Recall Michael Corleone's bland view of becoming legitimate and joining "some country club crowd, the good simple life of well-to-do Americans" (363), what Puzo also describes as "that general destiny" (365). Tateh's view is Michael's, which is in actuality an Our Gang of country club adults. Neither Tateh or Michael is reflective or counts the cost. Doctorow, however, drives the Our Gang image to devastating implications, whereas Puzo simply references the stolid, monlithic "good" American life as out there for the Corleones to join when they're ready. What Puzo takes for granted, the American world that Cosa Nostra cites when convenient, becomes the controlling image for Doctorow's conclusion about how popular narrative is produced. The stunned reader asks of *Ragtime*, is *that* what Coalhouse's struggle and martyrdom were for? Sara's lingering death after being assaulted by the vice presidential bodyguards? Father's mystification and death on the *Lusitania*? Tateh's wife banished by him after her defilement on the cutting room floor? In *Ragtime*, the reader has seen every step to the lawn in Beverly Hills and weighs the sanitized outcome. The melodrama is expunged in favor of children "getting into trouble and getting out again" (270). In *The Godfather's* final pages, the reader may also pray with Kay and over Michael's massacre in the name of his father and the Family. However, the terrible Corleone power holds sway over her silent entreaties, and the melodrama is complete with no lessons beyond the family plot.

However the two novels arrive at the last image of Our Gang in their disparate meanings, each posits a history without tears, Puzo by showing us the family we've come to know and love as triumphant, Doctorow, by Tateh's sentimental rewriting and collapsing of families' struggles. If we believe Michael to be a hypocrite or a liar about "the country club" or the general American destiny, we must as readers provide the image with a concept, a richness of association that Puzo never provides. What *The Godfather* lacks is any tension generated by the language outside the plot itself, any referential or dislocating trope that would take the Corleones into a hybridized relation set against a power equal to their own or at least contestatory to it. *The Godfather* ends with the consolidation of Michael's power. He has become his father, order is restored, and the family is impregnable. We are where we were at the beginning of the novel, even with all the deaths tallied. In *Ragtime*, the reader experiences a great shock in Our Gang as it becomes a mythical signifier in a tremendous rush of insight; the reader feels what the entire novel has been "meaning toward." No such sublimity is possible in Puzo's text, where each moment is equivalent to itself and no other. In *Ragtime*, the families have been dissolved and reconstituted, and the stories of that pain and striving are rewritten by the "father" who has first reconsituted himself. The Our Gang story will be popular because it will be free of the violence of the prehistory that conditioned it. We are not back at the beginning of *Ragtime* but at the beginning of our own modern era of media culture in cinema's new way of telling that culture its truth—what will become the catch-phrase of Disney-fication. The actual surviving family in *Ragtime* is made up of children, a widow, and a widower, yet it includes an orphan of color, a little boy and a little girl whose parents have been lost to history. The widow and widower are an ex-socialite and an ex-socialist; the murder, madness, racism, rage, and despair are gone. What remains is a sentimental view of childhood that remembers a past that never existed for these children but will exist in a media future, where we all get along.

Ragtime works to describe how Our Gang came to be, an image that only crystallizes on the last page and allows the reader to speculate about the power of a popular image, what Puzo never does through such notable protagonists as Vito and Michael Corleone, who are solely heroes in a tale of vanquishing enemies. Tateh is more problematic for readers, the inscrutable survivor of Doctorow's converging plot-lines, the grim and oppressed socialist immigrant who becomes optimistic American image maker. He becomes the historian America wants to "read" through his comedies, which began as silhouettes and outlines that suggested emotion. Any freedom that he now possesses in Hollywood to produce his visions comes after the jettisoning of his ideals, his wife, his name, and his past. Yet Doctorow doesn't judge him. Tateh has found a way to tap into the main line of American energy. He has given the culture what it wants; he reads his audience. He has become a benign Jack Woltz in a tale free of a Vito Corleone to plague him with comparisons of remaining "authentic."

Linda Hutcheon writes of the "inscribing into history" in the 1960s of previously silenced groups in literature, who are defined by the differences of "race, gender, sexual preferences, ethnicity, native status, and class." From the 1970s through the '90s, such "ex-centric" groups have been rapidly and completely inscribed into andro/phallo/hetero/Euro/ethno centrisms (61). In effect, *Ragtime* writes the prehistory of this recent social motion and literary absorption of the margin into the new hybridized center but completely within the novel's early-twentieth-century frame, making the point that any historical novel is about both its created era and the time of its own creation. *Ragtime*'s three major families are dispersed and reconstructed into multiples of new social demographics. The revolutionaries, artists, and women are silenced by the new culture industry of which Tateh is a godfather. America knows which stories it wants to hear, and it chooses Our Gang on Tateh's lawn and Our Gang in the Mafia. America truly does not care if the Corleones assimilate or not as long as they thrill us in their family violence, and America does not care who or what disappeared into the melting pot as long as Tateh's kids are cute. What fades away in postmodern historicism for Hutcheon is any sure ground upon which to base representation and narration (89).

Thus we come to Our Gang, which finally denies in *Ragtime* what the third page of the novel had so rudely announced: "Apparently there *were* Negroes. There *were* immigrants" (5).

Popular and Elite Fiction: Aims and Practices

The Godfather denies multiple subjects all the time in its representation, but Puzo never makes the reader aware he *knows* that. The elite novel consistently calls attention to the problems involved in its own making and reception. To find these problems in a popular novel is often to deal with the issues that are not foregrounded and then do much of the work in framing them. In essence, Puzo is free to write of a turn-of-the-century immigrant hero without ever taking the reader down into the ghettoes of the Lower East and West Sides of New York City to show poverty, disease, and despair because someone like the fictional Tateh had shown how to create the narrative melodrama that outlined and silhouetted characters without cause and effect, without the myriad ironies and historical reversals making up the large social march called "immigration." How fresh and unassimilated Tateh appears, a character like no one and nobody, yet largely unknown to us, even at novel's end. What, finally, would his story be, if narrated by himself? For such honesty, a reader might turn to the classic fictionalized autobiography of the immigrant era, *The Rise of David Levinsky* (1917) by Abraham Cahan, or to Doctorow's *Billy Bathgate* (1989).[2] Both *The Godfather* and *Ragtime* are past such mimetic reflection for different reasons. Puzo certainly doesn't risk his Corleone family being dragged down into power relations in an equal and mystifying field of desire Doctorow can't let his characters live individually beyond his orchestrated ensemble, so committed is he to history's power and the contortions of desire and dissatisfaction. Puzo won't create a dialogized world, while Doctorow won't let his characters alone. Neither author trusts the power of realism to bring issues fully into focus. Puzo fears losing his authority. Doctorow, too, would lose authority if he were to naively acknowledge the power of the "everything said" that he admires in Dreiser. He would lose the intensely worked up narration of *Ragtime*, as complete a center of control as is Corleone parlay of reason and fear as mounted by Puzo. What Puzo imposes in the popular novel as the dominance of characters in *his* gang to control the plot, Doctorow in the elite novel imposes on the narrative voice and the interrelation of the American ensemble that finally allows the reader to see that the whole sweep of *Ragtime* before its final page. Here is the true tale of our diversity and metamorphosis, one that also belies Tateh's last reductive image.

Ragtime's truest "gang" is found on the skater's pond at the foot of the Paine Avenue hill within the criss-crossed skaters' tracks where Little

Boy, Doctorow's historical consciousness, sees the mystery and power of history and fiction welling up from a popular visual image of community and civility, one that glosses and displaces the other incomplete "tracks" images throughout *Ragtime.* Such is the novelist's grid of multiple perspectives and personalities that always contains more fluid and more suggestive plot lines than the rigid positing of destiny. This rewriting and morphing of the deeply American symbol of the railroad, an epic monster in Norris's *Octopus,* within the classic Currier and Ives village print domesticates its power and brings it back toward family and collective. On the metanarrative level, the skater's pond "map" is *Ragtime's* rhetorical template of erasures and coincidences in all the characters' lives, which cuts away at their individualism and free will in vintage elite fictional fashion. Elite fiction often predicates its power on its multileveled meanings and deep structures, but at the core of its narrative complexity is often the simplest and most inclusive of images (the skaters' tracks) and the most daring commitment to potential human freedom and diversity, while often showing its impossibility on the level of the fiction itself. Popular fiction, which usually purports to be "populist" at its core, deals with issues of its lead characters' oppression and drive toward authority and/or freedom, but it is finally elitist in its refusal to ever grant its characters pure possibility or openendedness. The fiction for the common reader is author-itarian, and Don Corleone is the perfect exemplar.

Popular fiction fears the power of the quotidian with which realism would challenge melodrama. Elite fiction must complicate the quotidian to prove that the individual's mind and sensibility are the most privileged centers of truth that outstrip anything the material world can render. Doctorow remains committed to both the hard fact of the material culture's obstinate presence and the mandarin view of individual autonomy and subjectivity that chronicles but never masters it. How he reconciles his social outrage at American inequalities in an elegant and highly aestheticized narration dictates his creative tension in novel after novel. Puzo has no consistent inventive style, no master trope or organizing principle beyond telling the story. Rather, he draws on the power of traditional "moments" (weddings, funerals, beginnings, and endings) as reference. A good example of reader association that Puzo probably hoped the reader would grasp is the fact that *The Godfather* begins and ends in the Corleone compound on Long Island, juxtaposing the marriage of Connie and Carlo Rizzi with Connie's final accusation that Michael has killed Carlo, that he would never have done it if their father had been alive. The interlocking scenes of marriage, wedding day favors, the death of the husband, the sister coming not to ask for a favor but to label her brother a killer, Kay then asking Michael if it's true, Michael "using all the mutual trust they had built up in their marriage" (437) to lie to her— all the correspondences fit and round off the family plot. Yet they call attention to nothing outside the plot itself. They make the serial unfolding of Corleone power symmetrical and satisfy a low-level readerly need for "similarity," whereas *Ragtime*'s beginning and ending take the idea of a house and a family into ironic reversals as well as recomposition. Father's "house on a hill," part of the earliest imagery of American compacts from John Winthrop onward and suggestive in the domesticated emblem of the prosperous American state, is transported to Beverly Hills, with the reconstituted family on the lawn in California, the image in the mind of Tateh, the producer. He will "make" this child-dominated family group into an image that America wants to believe about itself, having adventures "in their own neighborhood" (270), a place that is now everywhere and nowhere through the power of film and that effaces the deaths that allowed them to arrive there. Tateh as film producer would immediately understand the narrative drive of *The Godfather*.

Ragtime asks the reader to consider the consequences and erasures of popular narrative manipulation, whereas *The Godfather*'s resonances happen only on the plane of the novel itself. *The Godfather* more simply records Michael manipulating Kay and then has Tom Hagen justify Michael's action for her. *Ragtime* consistently moves to a metacritical examination of the processes by which the American popular culture authorizes itself in forgetting American history. *The Godfather* records the inexorable Corleone victories with only Kay's dedicated prayers, an essentially futile gesture, as comment. Puzo looks to neither the popular culture, the larger American history, nor the agonies and promises of immigration. So much is cut away that, in effect, the Corleones are the real silhouettes, instrumentalized into action on behalf of the family, as machinelike as anything a material *Ragtime* culture could conjure up in the age of Ford. No public life is evident in *The Godfather*, whereas *Ragtime* is a Bakhtinian carnivalized text. *Ragtime*'s power is in its intellectual and ideological energy, exhibited by restless evolving characters such as Houdini and deployed through brilliant deadpan language conceits. Puzo reserves the novel's power for the Corleone victory in the plot, whereas characters in *Ragtime* do not "win."

Doctorow in a 1985 essay, "The Belief of Writers," lays out his fictional ethic:

> The young writer who picks up tonally, philosophically on the Hemingway romance, is in danger of misperceiving the predominant condition of things, which is that the future of any of us is not individual. As independent entrepeneurs of ourselves with no control over our destiny, we may be failing the task. How will we be able to stay true to the changing nature of our lives if we hold to a myth that is being nullified by history? If our response to what is going on today were appropriate, it would probably produce books ... with less polish

and self-consciousness, but about the way power works in our society, who has it, and how it is making history. (117)

Within Doctorow's dismissal of the individual at the center of fiction in our time is a fundamental renunciation of popular's fiction imperative to rely on the aggrandizing power of a Corleone or a Corleone family. "Destiny" is always beyond the control of our "changing selves" and is "nullified by history." Doctorow wants to show how power works, and that includes narrative power. Within that charge, he must work from the "myth" of individual power itself. He must show the fruitless quests of, for example, J. P. Morgan to transcend himself at the top of a gross materialist pyramid of money and power to seek more irrational secrets of his spiritual nature, to watch Houdini, the immigrant genius, replicate that metaphysical escape on the level of the physical, night after night for American audiences, as he uses up his body and its resources in seeking the riddle of death. Younger Brother sublimates his gusts of romantic passion into the radical who knows how to blow things up. Coalhouse Walker grieves and then demands his redress from America, which slaughters him in his excess of pride and then violence. Mother and Tateh learn to evolve in the new century as versatile new woman and American image maker. America itself is reinvented as the Franklin Novelty Company, the name of Tateh's first employer in—where else?—Ben's Philadelphia. Doctorow might, indeed, call for someone like a more morally aware Puzo, who could produce books "with less polish and self-consciousness," but, unfortunately, having passed that part of Doctorow's test, the Corleones exemplify power in society but fail to make any point about how it is distributed or whom it harms or what its relation to a larger American history might be; they remain mythic and do not believe in history.

Doctorow has a great admiration for the inventions of the male titans of American fiction in 1900, such as Dreiser and London, exemplars of "less polish and self-consciousness." Dreiser in *Ragtime* is the "morose novelist" seeking "the proper alignment" in his rented room in Brooklyn by doggedly moving his chair in a complete circle, hoping to break into the main lines of the culture's force and energy. Of Dreiser's *Sister Carrie,* Doctorow writes that the feelings of the major characters "brilliantly exceed . . . the magnitude of their minds or the originality of their problems" ("Theodore Dreiser: Book One" 31), a fine description of Carrie, Drouet, and Hurstwood, as well as *Ragtime*'s major players, and finally a key source of all sentimental and melodramatic fictional power. Who will care about, for example, Michael or Vito Corleone's logic or consistency of argument as long as they may identify with the universality of their family problems? Doctorow also writes with affection about London as a writer "who went to a place and wrote his dreams into it, the kind of writer who found an Idea and spun his psyche around it. He was a workaday genius literary hack . . ." (13) No better description of a best-seller writer, one who brings forth a mythos through the intensity of his capture of material, can be found. Puzo himself may be strangely ennobled by such ascription. The saga of the Corleones is an emigration without true poverty or pathos, a rise to power without friction with the larger culture by a male family without affect but with great coherence and solidarity. The Corleones are a sombre clan, which embodies Puzo's "spun" psyche, his need for a powerful father, his early flight from ethnicity, his justification of going bad as an author, his ultimate transposition of ethnicity into conservative family virtue, his selling of violence and murder in the name of sentiment and reason. Not only did Puzo write his dreams into the Corleones, but he wrote the Corleones into American dreams, where they embody those dreams.

In writing of London's *Call of the Wild*, Doctorow is fascinated by the great dog Buck, his affiliation with mankind until his master is killed, and then his decision to run with the wolf pack, all ties cut with humankind. Here is the *primal* going bad saga, the going outside not only the law but also civilization and humankind as Buck had known them. Doctorow sees very clearly that such is London's parable of prehistory, the reversion to an earlier being not caught in civilization's narrative about itself. Buck may be a dog, and Vito Corleone a Don, but the parallels are clear. Doctorow writes that *Call* speaks to "what is momentous," and that the novel asks not what is Buck's survival but "what is his philosophical destiny?" Such is the question all the characters mutely ask by implication in their actions in *Ragtime*; such is the question that Puzo hammers at in the repeated mentions of destiny in *The Godfather*. Buck takes revenge after John Thornton's death and moves off with the pack. Michael is lost to the larger America when he rejoins the family to stand by his father in what Doctorow, writing about *Call*, labels "the dream life of our atavistic selves" (17), in which London wrote a "mordant parable," "a parody of sentimental education wherein the hero is de-civilized" (18). Such is Michael Corleone's reversion as well, but it's into the family itself, the substitute for the nation he has joined and then renounced. Michael in effect is now "where life triumphant belongs to the most fit" (Doctorow 18). The Corleone ascendancy minus the claustrophobic allegiances that the family fosters in the reader is one more desensitizing challenge to our moral natures. As Doctorow concludes about London's *Call*, "This is not a sweet idea for a book, it is rather the kind of concept to justify tyrannies and the need of repressive social institutions to keep people from tearing themselves to bits. But London's Nietzschean superdog has our admiration if the truth be told" (18).

Within the curve of this thought, Doctorow exactly catches the largest of contradictory frames in which *The Godfather* lives in our dreams. Doctorow suggests a bit of Woltz's reaction to the Corleones in his uneasiness about *Call*, in his fear that there couldn't be a world if we all were to be like Buck; but within that fear, a larger sentiment carries his emotional sway over to Buck as one who can cut it, who breaks through all hesitancies and restraints to act as the dominant male. That's finally what audiences want most from *The Godfather*, not the moral riders to its constitution (Corleones indivisible with dominance over all, all checks and balances held by them, all three branches of government—and executioneer). Doctorow knows that *Call* "never forgets its sources as a magazine frontier romance" (19) any more than Puzo ever forgets *The Godfather* is a melodrama of broad action and simple passions. Doctorow concludes that it's "Jack London's hack genius that makes us cheer for his Buck and want to lope with him in happy, savage honor back to the wild, running and howling with the pack" (19).[3]

No better description can be found to explain what *The Godfather* does to us as readers who occasionally want nothing more than to go off-duty as guardians of our own moral nature and, in this most democratic and egalitarian of all systems, cut through all responsibility except the primal one, to know where our natures are and to act on them, though beyond such simplification is the fallen world of society, history, and other people. The Corleones are "Our Pack," too, beyond our world and even theirs in the implication of their freedom, which quite simply knows no competition that can't be defeated. *Godfather* readers and viewers voluntarily surrender to join Puzo's gang and its atavistic competence.

chapter eight

The American Inadvertent Epic:
The Godfather Copied

The epic gives form to a totality of life that is rounded from within; the novel seeks, by giving form, to uncover and construct the concealed totality of life.

—Georg Lukacs, *The Theory of the Novel*

Most popular literature tends to be weak on the cognitive and formal levels so that we cannot pretend to ourselves that we relish it because it makes us wiser, subtler, or more delicately responsive to beauty.

—Leslie Fiedler, *What Was Literature*

He is Al DeNiro and I am Bobby Pacino. Then I'm Al and he's Bobby. Recently, visits from Marlon Keitel. Roles assumed daily. We move as rapidly as we can from imitation to parody to the grotesque, the monster versions, contortions, screaming the lines in the exhilarating ridiculosity of our everyday lives. Throw away the movies. Do each other, go directly to the gargoyle faces emitting gargoyle voices.

—Frank Lentricchia, *Johnny Critelli*

Writing novels is a dead end, like being a blacksmith. It's all movies and TV now.

—Puzo, *The Last Don*

If there is reason to contrast a best-selling novel such as *The Godfather* with an elite text such as *Ragtime*, then surely the novel should be displayed against other best sellers of comparable scope as well. Is there a transhistorical, genre-busting popular category that might contain Puzo's novel? Leslie Fiedler, long the bad boy of American literary critical paradigm making and popular-elite fiction relations, suggested in *The Inadvertent Epic* (1979) that "works which long endure win our assent not rationally and logically, like history, philosophy, or science, but viscerally, passionately, like rituals in primitive societies or dreams in our own. They tend, that is to say, to reinforce our wildest paranoid delusions along with our most utopian hopes . . ." (84).[1] Fiedler as a psychoanalytic critic of American mythography was most interested in novels "rooted in demonic dreams of race, sex and violence which have long haunted us Americans" (17) across our history, such as *Uncle Tom's Cabin*, *Gone with the Wind*, and Alex Haley's *Roots*, with excursions into Thomas Dixon's *The Clansman* and D. W. Griffith's adaptation in *The Birth of a Nation*. Fiedler sees readers at these sites licensing themselves "to be driven out of control," to "return to psychic states which [they] have theoretically abandoned in the name of humanity and reason" (84). The "humanity and reason" thus overturned could comprise, for example, the larger collective body of moral questioning about *The Godfather*'s view of men and their responsibilities to society and to common law beyond the fierce family position. Such works, then, says Fiedler, do not have to pass the test of being able to "instruct and delight" but rather move through us in "dreams awake" (85). He thus agrees with Doctorow's assessment about such compelling narratives, that they draw on our atavistic reader's affiliation.

Fiedler broadly outlined his theories about a master American mythos as early as *Love and Death in the American Novel* (1960) and then spent the next two decades shifting his theses from elite to popular fiction, where the libidinous energies he identified could be more overtly exemplified. *The Inadvertent Epic* also charted the deep American structures of miscegenation and symbolic color lines in the familial tale in slavery and reconstruction periods as a subject of enduring emotional power and significance. At present, any move in American literature study toward critiquing best sellers or identifying incest and miscegenation as controlling American tropes owes much to Fiedler in *Love and Death* and *The Inadvertent Epic*, as well as to a renewed historicism evident in the study of slave narratives and all manner of identity narrative. *The Godfather* epic reworks the incest and miscegenation in more coded terms on the level of the isolated immigrant family and its mighty fear of assimilation. The novel and subsequent *Godfather* films bind the family members within a network of personal relations while positing assimilation in America as unacceptable.

The Godfather stands for a great, heroic dream of immigration and family, the epic modern subject so notably missing from our twentieth-century popular classics and sense of ourselves as Americans. Furthermore, if Fiedler is right, we would want such an epic to elide all the difficulties and contradictions of identity and its submersion and affirm the bond of an original, patriarchal culture within the fluidity of the self-made American life. It is the peculiar genius of *The Godfather* that the novel suggests Americans can have it all, their rooted identity and their mobility. The core immigrant family attains unimaginable power and indirect influence along with the wealth that only coming to America can provide. This miracle and dream can be negotiated in a world in which men and women stay in their assigned roles, where family authority is revered and American success is paramount. *The Godfather* unites two epic strands of American twentieth-century experience. First, it contains the Corleones within the great migration of Italian Americans from 1890 through 1920, the pinnacle of southern European emigration to the United States and the high point of the powerfully symbolic Ellis Island entry into this country as represented by Vito Corleone. Then *The Godfather* extends its story into the World War II generation represented by Michael Corleone, who is sensationally emblematic in his fashion of the millions of Americans who settled down as husbands and wives, fathers and mothers to join that "general destiny," as Puzo rather benignly but contemptuously called it, to become in the 1950s the most obsessively family-ed generation in American life since the 1850s. On a macro level, how does *The Godfather* disrupt and rearrange the American love of family and self-reliance and wrap its dream around them? How does the bourgeois epic of immigration become, by inference, the business fable of success that the culture needed? How do its domestic and power arrangements both mirror and challenge American post–World War II family and business life?

Puzo and Coppola chart the melancholy murderer Michael becomes (*Godfather II*) and the death of both Michael and his daughter (*Godfather III*), while the epic itself becomes more compromised by exposure to actual American life and society as it fell into fiction. However, as shown in chapters 3 and 5, Puzo misses countless chances to dialogize his characters and their roles. Outside *The Godfather* per se, Puzo returns to his epic's roots in *The Sicilian* (1984) and copies himself in *The Last Don* (1996) and *Omerta* (2000). *The Sicilian*, however, misses tremendous opportunities to bind Michael and his Sicilian roots, while *The Last Don* is encrusted in rather inert Mafia material and an obsessive return to what are Puzo's true loves after 1969, tales of Hollywood and Las Vegas. This chapter will speculate as to how Puzo's epic *itself* is assimilated beyond his own productions, in this case into texts that are both copies and experiments in other media. *The Godfather* is a commodity in the image culture and is dispersed into manageable fictions in the realm of cinema and television. Like any constructed artifice that becomes monumental in postmodernity, *The Godfather*'s cultural affect is finally preserved in the virtual copies of itself, in versions of the Family in language, style, and icons. The latest progeny in *The Godfather*'s family is the extraordinary HBO television series *The Sopranos* (1999–2001), which in its first three seasons has adapted mob narrative to the small screen by wedding a series of turn-of-the-millennium American concerns to a more female-centered melodrama while retaining the male power world under stress and potential collapse (see chapter 9).

In an America that has for one hundred fifty years believed in a manifest destiny to justify our expansion, rectitude, and national energies, *The Godfather* has been an epic vehicle to portray the national errand as a business and family triumph. America is a country that has always spoken excessively about family. In our version of a national epic, as a colony of England, we broke away from the abusive "parent" country, only to reinscribe ourselves through "Founding Fathers" in a most patriarchal origin myth that nonetheless most often featured the visual iconography of a defiled virginal Anglo or Native American girl at the time of the American Revolution.[2] We then recuperated the female victim as a fair, young country and created in the nineteenth century the most domestic, sentimental, family-oriented literature imaginable, only to subsume it and the family in the late-nineteenth-century industrial civilization and accumulation of capital, thus catalyzing a realist-naturalist fiction in flight from the family, which became pejoratively "genteel" and bourgeois in the modernist excoriation. The American immigrant family in the early twentieth century enters this varied and deeply coded national family affair with its own signification and rites of passage that ultimately contributed to another obsessively domestic period in American life, the post–World War II 1940s and '50s, which culminated in the revolt against family, patriarchy, and business at the time of *The Godfather*'s publication in 1969. It is the particular destiny of *The Godfather* to enrich this centuries-old American semiosis and historical benchmarking with its facts and fantasies and to suggest ongoing narrative models for adaptation.[3]

Epic and the Fall into Popular Fiction

When we think of powerful epics in Western literature, the list of works contains familiar classics (*The Odyssey, The Iliad, The Aeneid, The Song of Roland, Beowulf, The Divine Comedy*), as well as a few late, more prose- or poetry-oriented modern and contemporary masterpieces: Joyce's *Ulysses* and Derek Walcott's *Omeros*, to name two. Epics tell of great heroic deeds that also are nation-building and that inaugurate a sense of a people and culture. The style is elevated, and action itself requires noble and brave deeds that may touch on the superhuman and feature descents into the underworld or involve angry or benevolent gods. Epics "keep general reflection at a distance" through a "naiveté" (Adorno 18); self-consciousness would only compromise the hero and drag him down into more recognizable realist dimensions. Action in the epic fills out to be coextensive with the known world as depicted. In the long secularization of Western literature and descent into more realistic narrative that culminates in the novel itself, the epic has undergone a slow dismantling into fragments, but many of its constituent features remain and can be identified in modern criticism of the novel. Georg Lukacs has been perhaps the most suggestive critic of what features of the epic are mutated to cohere in any modern view of the novel. As Lukacs puts it, "the epic gives form to a totality of life that is rounded from within; the novel seeks, by giving form, to uncover and construct the concealed totality of life" (60). Within a text such as *The Godfather*, immediate tensions can be determined between its residual epic material and its pressure to disclose in the novel form. In the case of the mob, Cosa Nostra (Our Thing, synonomous with Our World) becomes an entire society as the Five Families know it, extended in influence, determining its boundaries, including all family members within it, allowing no excess or variation. Here is the imagined "totality... rounded from within" that can account for all life and conduct with no voice or competing reality permitted. To "uncover" this rigid world, the novel exists to scrutinize and contextualize in varied ways through its full-field description of social reality, to counter the epic proscription against such description.

How does Lukacs then bridge the epic into the novel? He sees the survival of the epic in the personalized tradition of the "epic individual," the hero of the novel, driven to an "autonomous life of interiority" when an "unbridgeable chasm" has been created between world and consciousness (66), despite bonds "linking an individual destiny to a totality" "whose fate is crystallised in his own" (67). The modern hero in the novel thus is tied to history, the scrolling epic of his culture; he both determines his relation to that history and is determined by it. Lukacs concludes that the novel is the art form of "virile maturity" in contrast to the epic's "normative childlikeness" (71), in which case we might cite Achilles as a world champion sulker before the walls of Troy unless all his conditions are met, or to Tony Soprano, who, in his aptly child-centered Freudian therapy often becomes a wailing unhappy little boy who can only splutter, "But you said I was the victim of poor parenting!" The "need for reflexion" is Lukacs's touchstone for the "deepest melancholy of every great and genuine novel" (92), but as this study has shown, *The Godfather*, and by extension other mob narrative, has resolutely refused to consider its own moral positions and premises, in part because of the epic's refusal to even consider moral blindness, the province of tragedy at the high end of dramatic and literary production and melodrama at the low end.

Bakhtin in *The Dialogic Imagination* is interested in the epic as a sounding board and contrast to the novelistic. As opposed to Lukacs who sees a more organic evolution out of the epic to the novel, Bakhtin calls for a novelistic hero who would combine positive and negative features, low as well as lofty, and the ridiculous as well as the serious (10). This is Bakhtin's familiar carnivalized mode. Especially in the postmodern rendering of what *The Godfather* or *The Sopranos* means to us, "carnivalizing" could mean a mixture of forms and functions, even a nostalgia for the sombre or "epic" telling. Part of postmodern carnivalizing is to know that you are immersed in the carnivalesque, within speech genres that are already extant, as when characters in a dozen or more Hollywood movies made in the 1990s cite lines from *The Godfather* or when Silvio Dante, Tony Soprano's trusted and dour *capo*, is asked repeatedly by the Soprano "family" to reprise dialogue from *The Godfather* to the great amusement of the men caught precisely in "the life." Bakhtin uses characteristics of the epic to show exactly what the novel should criticize. He includes "stilted heroizing," "narrow and unlifelike poeticalness," and the "pre-packaged and unchanging nature of their heroes" (10). Much of the reader's tension in *The Godfather* occurs when the reader must grapple with the Don's formal speeches and gestures, Old World cunning and deliberateness, and inflexible, far-seeing sameness. Puzo never permits any cracks in this edifice, creating in a wooden style that crafts the Don much closer to an epic hero than a novelistic one but also makes him all the more powerful and impervious to novelistic constraints.

Bakhtin sees the novel operating in a "zone of maximal contact with the present" (11), and in that clash with the epic's centering on the past comes the true oxymoronic quality of mob narrative, that it enshrines for the sons (Michael Corleone, Tony Soprano) a prior world that has already been closed in by epic developments and precepts, the world of the fathers that has handed down all the rules and codes, the world that was formed by prior historical clashes and outcomes. In effect, the epic is "descent culture" par excellence as Sollors might define it, through the "blood" or pure line without any contract or "consent" that is inherently assimilationist. *The Godfather* in epic terms is archaic in its clannishness; its arguments about force; its fierce determinism and formal world view; its inability to countenance any relativity, uncertainty, or irony; as well as its refusal to scrutinize itself about any of these possibilities. The grand scale epic traces surviving into *The Godfather* as text enable it to hold its power, literally within the tale and figuratively with the audience, against all enemies—other "families," moral critics, elite readers, censors of its Italian American "defamation"—who would qualify or counter its strong effect.

Popular fiction itself could be called a fiction of epic inflation, which contains no commoners, rather mythical figures battling their enemies. The fiction often becomes of necessity monologic and centered on an outsized individual who is "the most powerful," "the richest," "the most satanic," "the most beautiful," and so on. The survival of prodigious heroes and heroines and the battles of villains and victims are the fundaments of popular narrative, and to scale down these figures into dialogizing is to play against epic sizing. Fiedler well describes how our love of such narratives is our guilty secret as popular readers. He states that we can't pretend that such works make us better, wiser, or more moral or responsive to beauty but rather put us more in touch with the "perilous aspects of our own psyches, otherwise confessed only in nightmares" (*What Was Literature* 49–50). Such were the responses generated in the "inadvertent epic." The incestuous and miscegenated themes that Fiedler sees imprinted throughout our national imaginary can certainly be traced through the immigrant's tale. To keep everything within the family, within the kinship lines of descent, is to posit a pure strain of lineage, enhanced by the family's network of personal and intimate services. The horror and fear are the prescribed assimilation or amalgamation with strangers, Americans, what *The Godfather* often calls "shrewdies" or "sharpies" or alien American beings such as Kay Adams's WASP family where her mother serves "boiled chicken" (235) and the parents hardly seem to know who their daughter is. To become American is to mingle and to belie not only epic but ethnic purity, to break into the narrative line with inflected accents from outside the descent culture. Is it possible that what American reader/viewers sense is that *The Godfather* censors this volatile American incestuous and miscegenated material in favor of a purity such as ethnic descent and nonassimilation that makes Puzo's text a newly nativist document of some mandarin antimixing? If the readers forget or sublimate the Corleones as Italian, they can wallow in a dream of "same" and "like" with no "others" outside the family. The epic cast into modern America in *The Godfather* then would become an unbroken Sicilian line of inferences, historical conclusions, and "nation-building" within one family: the Corleones are not only Our Gang but comprise Our World as readers, a world they have made that looks and feels like America. Here is identity raised to pathology.

To describe epic's fall into fiction is to engage in some complex generic tracing. Jameson is fascinated by the survival of precapitalist literary forms such as the epic within realistic and modern fiction and cites Ernst Bloch's reading of the fairy tale with its magical wish fulfillments as a "systematic deconstruction and undermining of the hegemonic aristocratic form of the epic with its somber ideology of heroism and baleful destiny" (*The Political Unconscious* 86). The genius of *The Godfather* is to encapsulate both frames, the fairy tale and the epic, within the novel so that reader's yearnings for family happiness and security are crossed with the large and mannered inevitabilities and sadnesses of the epic in which a culture hero might undertake certain actions to secure his world. Jameson's adjective of choice to describe the epic's view of destiny is *baleful,* denoting an active evil, full of pain and suffering. Jameson also uses *baleful* to describe other dualities that he wishes to hold continually in suspension when he writes of the "demonstrably baleful features of capitalism along with its extraordinary liberating dynamism" ("Postmodernism" 86) and his conception of the heroic saga unfolding under a "baleful spell," "furnishing the symbol of domination by a past which is their only future" (*Marxism and Form* 130). Such conceptions aptly describe the tragedy of the Corleones as well as their desperate compact: they live in a present in which the old loyalties and resentments in their Sicilian pasts are the only structures in which they can conceive of an American future. Jameson sees Bloch making a distinction between the peasant and aristocratic character of the raw materials of the fairy tale and heroic saga; but surely the role of *The Godfather* is to unite the formal opposites in confusion in the popular text, to fuse "those most naive and emblematic visions of the heart's desire which are the table groaning beneath ample bread and Wurstchen, the warm fire, the children back home happy at last" and "the sentence of doom" hanging "over all the heroic gestures of its characters" (130). Such yearnings are embodied in the fathers and sons who must go bad in order to sustain the vision of abundance, the urgency to maintain the melodrama of family against all enemies, Sicilian and American.

Baleful, indeed, a domestic tragedy masked as triumph, a horrifying contortion of human aims and desires "in the name of the father," an appropriation of every patriarchal role imaginable from God himself through the secular stern and wise father to a powerful American businessman who provides for his children. By collapsing capitalism, destiny, and epic under the sign of "baleful," Jameson historicizes destiny itself, exposing its ahistorical rhetoric as masking a deep background historicization of oppression and want in the feudal system that nonetheless is only exacerabated and re-stressed under capitalism. What links the feudal, precapitalist state and capitalism proper in the Marxist interpretation is the outline of the theory that matches the diagnosis or application. That is to say, destiny privileges an inevitability of a prior signification, while Marxism privileges the primacy of the signification to come.

Jameson consistently tries to distance himself from any prematurely "ethical" statement that might charge him with moral criticism; nonetheless, he tries to find a properly dialectical vantage point that acknowledges pervasive false consciousness as well as the need for a naive Utopianizing in a reconceived ethical vision. The immigrant saga is always Utopian in exchanging the present selves, the very lives of the first generation, for a vision of the future family of children and grandchildren. Immigrant narrative is always Utopian, cutting off the past in favor of a dimly signified but highly idealized future. Such a denial of the past is also a denial of epic imagining in the surety of a culture's depiction. In a more urgent historical frame than epic's sonorous one, the sacrifices of immigrants are not ordained by any austere central government that collapses individualism and history under a Democratic Year One. They are, in the spirit of fairy tales, in the service of a "magical narrative," that of the American Dream, not so much the streets paved with gold as the streets paved at all, or more to the point, streets one can walk on without fear, streets that belong to the people as citizens. *The Godfather* preserves what in immigrant narrative is the living memory of a dead past, which the birth country re-presents in stasis as an oppression (values, language, custom, tradition) and then converts to the unimaginable future for the

American children, a Utopia of education, security, and freedom. Only the present remains a huge gap or lack that can't be lived, a composite of a "never again" (will I bow the neck) and a "not yet" (as in Michael's comforting words to an aging Don Corleone, "We'll get there, Pop. We'll get there"). Such a "present" is inimical to the epic which wants only sureties about the narrative it confidently provides about a culture's unfolding. America turns out to be a trickier place than the epic can account for, a contradictory evolving society that nonetheless needs its dreams to function.

Fiedler never wrote a line about *The Godfather*. He would have been uninterested in its utter maleness, its lack of racial or gendered insight, its flat characters, and Puzo's complete ignoring of psychologized states. Fiedler's imagined epic is much more subconscious, the landscape of American nightmares of race, sex, violence, and family all intertwined, not so much articulate as chaotic with powerful image upon image taking the place of any reflective unfolding or artistic control and leading to a reader/viewer response system also unmanaged where "release of the repressed is what popular art makes possible" when "the burden of any system of morality finally becomes irksome" (50). This rather furtive Dionysian response on the part of the popular reader is unmediated by social class or professional training. Fiedler suggests this reading beast lies deep within us and in the national history, the demonic racial tale we have constructed and find ways to tell ourselves in compensation. Fiedler's criticism is never less than national psychic melodrama itself in the extreme terms with which he liberates popular fiction from any stays whatsoever. He desires, as he says, a canceling of aesthetics and ethics in favor of what he calls "Ecstatics," which would be constituted as eclectic, amateur, neo-Romantic, populist criticism, more concerned with myth, fable, archetype, fantasy, and wonder (139). That's certainly one way to move beyond the conundrum or moral interrogation of *The Godfather* or any popular text: shift to an irrational and subversive "outlaw" criterion of judgment, one as wild or wilder than the trangressive texts themselves. Fiedler may want to call American blockbuster books "epic," but he casts aside all the ponderous surface of those texts in favor of something far more psychic in them. His primary examples—Stowe, Mitchell, Dixon, Haley—are quite middle class and hortatory but appear to unleash epic in the guise of melodrama, the popular novel's rewriting of American origins and deep structures. Perhaps the epic survives only in the melodrama of contemporary popular fiction, where it can be humanized into tears, rage, and violent necessary deeds. *Godfather* readers/viewers just want to see the Corleones *cut* it, not have them *think* about it. Adorno writes of the epic seeming "to be a state of stupidity" in comparison to "the enlightened state of consciousness to which narrative discourse belongs," that this "stupidity" operates in a "restorationist ideology hostile to consciousness" (18) and, thus, inimical to psychology and the subsconscious. Such is the epic or melodramatic hero's task, to get on with the nation-building or heroic return and leave introspection to the poets and critics. The epic traits in Puzo's Mafia fiction do not mutate beyond that rigidity. After he wrote his long authorial lament in *Fools Die*, Puzo's remaining trio of Italian American novels, *The Sicilian*, *The Last Don*, and *Omerta* do not open into the more overtly novelistic but stay within the rigid and sonorous parameters he had established in *The Godfather*.

Writing the American Mid-Twentieth Century: *The Godfather*'s Historical Framing

In chapter 7, I considered how *Ragtime* not only writes the history of the early twentieth century but also writes on the origin of the popular media and entertainment forms that transmit that history to us. Doctorow is always extremely conscious of these frames. In contrast, Puzo appears to almost ignore *The Godfather*'s historical frame (1900–1950) except in quick extrinsic flashes of Vito Andolini arriving at Ellis Island (more developed by Coppola in *Godfather II*), some references to the Don acting more swiftly and decisively in the Great Depression years than Roosevelt, and in a few disparaging remarks about Hitler and Mussolini destroying "their world" and that of Churchhill and Roosevelt. On the whole, *The Godfather* appears to take place in somewhat of a vacuum, punctuated by the murder of Fanucci, a general mob "war" in the early 1930s and peace reigning until Sonny's murder finally signals the Five Families War of 1946, also an event that Puzo glosses over very quickly. Similarly, Michael is a World War II hero, but we never learn the details; we're given no flashback scenes to his moments of high courage, merely a quick reference to a PT boat heroism that almost certainly references John F. Kennedy. *Godfather II* does much more historical grounding and extends the family's history both west to Nevada and to Cuba where Coppola uses the backdrop of Castro's entry into Havana on New Year's Day 1959 to portray Michael confronting Fredo's treachery and that of Hyman Roth. Michael appears before Senate committees on racketeering; he is outed in a way his father never was, yet in many ways he is more secretive and alone, without the personal love and fealty his father demanded and received. He becomes a melancholy executive and finally a murderer of his own brother. Rather than falling into American history, he participates in the fall of his own family. Sonny tells him he's killing people for strangers in World War II, but Michael himself is estranged from any and all of them. Coppola creates a memorable scene of Michael in a limousine, making his way through the streets of newly revolutionary Havana. Coppola's extended frame films Michael from the front, turning his calm slow gaze to the moiling masses outside his window. The limo stops, and Michael emerges and calls to Fredo to get in the car, that it's the only way off the island. Coppola literally shoots Michael as the prince of capitalist and family darkness; only his silhouette is visible as he speaks. A terrified Fredo scuttles into the night of Havana's history rather than face the hand and judgment of his brother.

From Puzo's viewpoint, writing his own historical passage is clear. Gino in *The Fortunate Pilgrim* makes the first escape from the family into American history itself, joining the army after Pearl Harbor. Puzo served for four years, met his wife in Germany, and wrote *The Dark Arena* (1955) about the defeated postwar German landscape and the American presence there. The novel is very Hemingwayesque in the vein of *In Our Time*, beginning with a "Soldier's Home" vignette of Walter Mosca in the Bronx where he can no longer connect with his family nor the girl he loved before the war. Nothing whatsoever is made of his ethnicity. He's drawn back to the German ruins and the black market economy where he can at least find people who've gone through what he has. Finally, the frame changes to that of *A Farewell to Arms* as Mosca loses his wife, Hella, to complications after childbirth and then has the obligatory tight-lipped and rueful tough guy reflections on being bereft and alone in a ravaged world. *The Dark Arena* is derivative in mood but well-done in its characterizations and certainly goes against the grain of war novels in centering on the gray area of "occupation," scams, and further violence among emotionally displaced people on both sides. Taken together with *The Fortunate Pilgrim*'s exploration of the Italian immigrant experience, it's possible by the time of *The Godfather*, whatever Puzo says about "writing below his gifts," that he felt he'd historicized enough, that *The Dark Arena* was his World War II novel and that *The Fortunate Pilgrim* was his immigrant novel. Perhaps he saw no reason to truly ground *The Godfather* in either setting, though there is some connective tissue linking World War II to the family's world. Clemenza believes they should stop the Tattaglias "like they shoulda stopped Hitler at Munich"; Michael believes that "if the Families had been running the State Department there never would have been a World War II" (142); he tells Sonny that Solozzo will be an easy target: "I've been in combat against tougher guys . . . and under worse conditions. Where the hell are his mortars? Has he got air cover?" (143). Michael's intimation after the murder when on a freighter pulling out of New York harbor is hybrid Hemingway/Puzo: "[H]e felt an enormous sense of relief. He was out of it now. The feeling was familiar and he remembered being taken off the beach of an island his Marine division had invaded. . . . All hell would break loose but he wouldn't be there" (153).

If we can place Michael Corleone in the frame of a World War II soldier, we can also see him as a returning American war veteran. He reflects many of the postwar facets of male experience, albeit in a sensationalized and multiplied frame. Michael comes home first as marine hero, where he meets Kay and comments on his family, largely from the outside. Then he is recruited into the Family war and becomes a combatant, first protecting his father at the hospital from would-be assassins, where he has his jaw broken by McCluskey. He then commits a double murder and is sent back overseas to Sicily, reversing the patterns of both returning war veteran and of immigration itself. Hiding in the hills of his ancestral homeland, he finds love and passion with Apollonia, but she is assassinated, another "war" casualty. Michael returns home a second time, this time as a veteran of his father's and his family's war in 1950. Now his own stewardship of the family begins, and his career path is set. As with other veterans, he settles down, marries, has two children, and becomes an executive in training. Puzo links Michael to the millions of World War II veterans who "[made] their innocent getaway from baffled loved ones," survived, and came home to the "cage of family and duty and a steady job" (*Godfather Papers* 26).

The patterning and the outlines of an American male generation at war and coming home are ratcheted up to a violent degree in Michael Corleone. What sort of nerve does Puzo touch with Michael as postwar businessman and husband/father? Elizabeth Long has written that in American popular novels, "the entrepreneurial definition of success is celebrated in its most pure and fabulous form," often in historical or religious novels (64). Here is where the hero can mutate into roles both grand and tempestuous, while still showing the nerve and the vision to lead as a powerful hero where he can be both "god" and "father." Money and wealth seem to come almost incidentally, and the tedious details of its acquisition are basically beneath the fiction. Michael supplants his father with ease, making executive decisions that are carried out by men who were of his father's generation. He carries out his father's revenge plans to the letter and achieves his father's power. The dream is complete.

No stages of neurosis or narcissism mar Michael's takeover of power in *The Godfather*. He gets to run the company. Such seamless ascension without psychic conflict clashes with the more familiar elite fiction text that Richard Ohmann has identified in the American novel of 1960–75, in which the hero is precisely in flight from the customary ways of making do in American postwar society, that the needs and values of the managerial and professional class reached a crisis point of individual and isolated "illness" in thorough retreat from the American postwar world of monopoly capitalism (210). It's as if Ohmann had attempted to invent the class analysis of Bourdieu from the ground up in the American fiction that begins after the 1950s. He identifies the figure of "childhood" as what the hero holds onto "against capitalist and patriarchal social relations" (215), where the adult masquerades as a child emotionally in crisis, where "deep social contradictions" are "transformed into a dynamic of personal crisis" and the goal for the hero is some "personal equilibrium" (217). Such would be the post–World War II American male melodrama (to amend Baym): abstention, confession, rebellion, often directed against the father or the absent father, himself a stand-in for culture or country. To be "true to yourself" is an ethnically unmarked version of authenticity where one would heroically defeat conformity and allegiance.

It would be hard to overestimate how thoroughly *The Godfather* demolishes these male crises of sensibility as indulgent nonsense. Consider Michael Corleone against the generation of age-group American fictional heroes and antiheroes of his era: Seymour Glass, Tommy Wilhelm, Binx Bolling, Neil Klugman, Rabbit Angstrom, Yossarian, McMurphy. Michael Corleone is never young or neurotic or conflicted, and he does not take flight or lead quixotic rebellions against authority: he *is* authority, more like Dirty Harry or the "Man with No Name" in popular genres of male power. He does not hesitate but plans and carries out the murders of McCluskey and Solozzo; malaise is never an option. The problems are clearly delineated, almost totally in a business sense: Who is our enemy? What needs to be done? How will I do it? He inherits short- and long-term business strategies ("Your brains or your signature on that paper"; "revenge is a dish best served cold"). The swiftness with which Michael becomes an instrument of the Corleone family will is a terrific marshaling of the son as capital resource. Such an overwhelming response, always in place and never countenancing any breakdowns, is a quite compelling subliminal message filtering through *The Godfather* at the height of the Cold War.

In fact, the Corleones running Cosa Nostra presume an Our World that needs a "Their World" in contrast and opposition, and what finally could the Corleones and their opposition signify in 1969 but clearly delineated heroes and villains in "ways of life" that would fight to the death for hegemony? Certainly popular fiction often works in code with and against huge cultural and historical formations. Thus, *Uncle Tom's Cabin* was the great cry against slavery but also expressed a deep structural lauding of women's roles as well as expressing a cross-gendered, cross-racial cry against slavery and ownership of white middle-class women as daughters, wives, and mothers. *Gone with the Wind*, partly a stock Jim Crow tale of the Old and Reconstruction South, nevertheless had its buried capitalist anthem for the devastated American 1930s readership, that a nation could rise from the ashes in a strong economy and that women could find themselves free to express their multiple talents; indeed, Scarlett is a better businesswoman than a romantic heroine. Just so does *The Godfather* provide many subliminal consolations. For an America whose children are running in the streets in 1969, Puzo posits Michael Corleone running his father's business and participating in a just war at the time of Vietnam; the family buries a brother cut down in combat but takes revenge, and order is restored. Also, the Corleones are always vigilant as an effective Cold War early warning system. No massive attack from rival superpower families can succeed, and summit meetings are held to insure just that. Even when the missile system that is Luca Brasi is defused and destroyed, the family continues with new deterrents. *The Godfather* provides a strong conservative critique of a weakened America, a "tolerant" America, which is a source of amusement to the Corleones, who count on such a society for their success. Even as they embody a never-ending vigilance to protect themselves, they bore from within through America's institutions and mores, providing a reader and viewership with twin halves of an adversarial pairing; the Corleones are both "Us" and "Them."

In such a reading climate, the secondary aspects of *The Godfather*'s structure can be seen as extremely satisfying, in the blanket security they issue as a family and the threat that thrills the millions. From the depths of the late 1960s, *The Godfather* issues its edict: that the Cold War world (post World War II and post Five Families War) is under Corleone family control, and they will stay the course. Their children will not rebel against the family or the country.[4] In this family, the son inherits deep peasant watchfulness and "cunning"; he's primitive rather than ambiguous, shrewd rather than conflicted. Action rather than reflection will carry him through, and he will honor the father. Social contradictions and hestitancies belong to the therapists and their patients in the elite fiction of the 1960s, syndromes that *The Sopranos* will inherit for the mob narrative genre in 1999–2001. The historical and cultural trauma of Vietnam in the country of the young will be dramatized at the Pentagon, Grant Park, and Kent State. Meanwhile, Michael in the created *Godfather* text of the early 1950s has work to do, he has a world to be defended so "a way of life" may survive. Thus *The Godfather* was published at the height of the Vietnam era collapse of all authority, in the teeth of the battle to justify the "domino theory" in Asia and to prevent world communism. *Gone with the Wind* was a cry from the depths of the Great Depression about America rising from economic defeat and social prostration. *Uncle Tom's Cabin* was a call for a simpler humanity in 1852 during a low decade of political and legal compromises that hoped to stave off the collapse of the American Union and that posited slavery ending in America in God's own good time, a relief to politicians on all sides. Inadvertent epics do not overtly historicize a nation's master narratives but do so through deflected and mutated material in which reader and viewer satisfactions come in coded reassurances against the symbolic cultural collapse projected in the fiction that stands in for the real American historical crisis.

Popular fiction after World War II becomes increasingly amoral and fixated on glamour and consumption. However, the middle-class heroes who come home to stay in the traces of business after the war become faceless cogs in a bureaucracy that at best gives them uninteresting work to do and at worst makes them immoral for the corporation's sake. Such definitions are best articulated through the work of sociologists such as David Riesman in *The Lonely Crowd* and William H. Whyte in *The Orga-*

nization Man. The Man in the Grey Flannel Suit is a realistic cry against this faceless and drifting suburban life. What the Corleones offer in implicit contrast to this domination of the workplace by the anonymous corporate ethic is the nostalgia of the "family-owned" business, but not a corner store or small-scale enterprise, rather one as powerful in the world as a corporation but invisible and far more intimate to the reader and viewer. As a pleased Hyman Roth says in *Godfather II*, "Michael, we're bigger than U.S. Steel." A Corleone family member or associate never fears unemployment, is not personally or politically powerless, is not bored, and does not inhabit a lock-step routine. However, as in the modern corporation, whereas Whyte commented that they want your soul, not your sweat (Long 152), the Corleones demand personal rather than professional allegiance, but the thrall is somewhat the same. Daniel Bell stated that modernist culture had repudiated the central function of all religions, "the restraint of the self in the service of some transcendent moral order" (170). The Corleones purport to be quite restrained, only acting when absolutely necessary; that is their high road. The low road or compromised version of this charge is Corleones as murdering thugs in the dregs of American capitalism, in the foul wake of trafficking in the wastes of human sin and error and preying on the weak. Take your pick. Puzo "inadvertently" creates a world in melodrama's residual rendition of epic that could stand for almost any managed and resolved crisis of American national, paternal, and business authority: constantly protect "Our World," comfort the downtrodden, defend the weak, reap the profits, and stay together.

Puzo and Copying *The Godfather*

Puzo did not become a *Godfather* publishing machine. Not a prolific writer before his great success (two novels a decade apart [1955, 1964]), he published only five more novels between 1969 and his death in 1999. No genre shelf exists to hold his collected works as is the case for Stephen King (horror) and Anne Rice (vampires). Puzo did not pursue a subgenre empire of his own. There was no "Mob Fiction" shelf (although the video rental stores certainly might offer one) to compete with "Mystery" (a legion of male and female detectives in series form) or "Romance" (many different series pitched to different audiences at various levels of explictness and age group). Other rival male blockbuster writers could write a series, such as Tom Clancy's Jack Ryan books. The spy or caper thrillers of Robert Ludlum, Ken Follett, and Sidney Sheldon also appeared with a metronomic regularity.

Why was there never *The Godfather II*, the *Novel*? Certainly agents, editors, publishers, and readers would have clamored for such a text. The answer may lie in several directions. First, Coppola's two Academy

Award–winning films (1972, 1974) for which Puzo shared screen writing credits, forever stamped the features of Brando, Pacino, Duvall, Caan, Keaton, Shire, and other actors onto a generation of American moviegoers. The second film brought Michael's story a decade further along, while using much of the immigrant Sicilian material from the novel in flashback form. As with *Gone with the Wind*, the brilliance of the first two *Godfather* films cast the novel, incredible publishing success that it was, into a secondary relation to what had become a visually stunning and rhetorically vibrant tale, one that passed visually into the culture with lasting force.[5] Furthermore, Puzo had never wanted to write *The Godfather* during his two decades of chasing the dream of elite literary success. He tried very hard to escape ethnic typing in his revered art. His wry acceptance of his destiny as the author of *The Godfather* did not include going back into harness as that author. He spent a good part of the 1970s doing lucrative work in Hollywood, writing or collaborating on screenplays after the doors had been opened for him by his *Godfather* scripts with Coppola.[6] Then the 1970s closed with his writer's lament and Las Vegas portrait in *Fools Die* and the text for the revealing picture book *Inside Las Vegas*. Puzo finally did come back to the Mafia subject in three novels, *The Sicilian*, *The Last Don*, and the posthumous *Omerta*. None of them really adds insight to his work or to the mob subject or moves beyond what had been established through the *Godfather* novel and the three films with Coppola. Each successive novel suggests that Puzo knew best that he was finished with mob narrative when he wrote the Corleones into American fictional and cinematic history and that, having become legendary to its worldwide audience, the family would have been better off without Puzo as authorial godfather "pulling a few [more] strings."

What *Godfather* fan could resist the opening pages of *The Sicilian*? Michael Corleone is still in Sicily in 1950 after the assassination of his wife Apollonia with instructions to bring home to his father the legendary Sicilian bandit/Robin Hood Salvatore (Turi) Giuliano. The frustrating truth about *The Sicilian* is that Puzo made nothing of the possibilities of this plot line. Michael is almost inert, never has an interesting thought, takes very little initiative, and is not shown with any jealousy or resentment of the young Sicilian folk hero who might be his double. They do not take up arms together, nor do they debate an Old and New World Mafia or talk of their hopes and dreams. Puzo tantalizingly has Giuliano (a real historical figure) be conceived in the United States and born back in Sicily, but this potential dialogizing is not developed. Turi and Michael never meet in more than four hundred pages, in which Puzo seems to keep Michael hovering around to tease the reader, even creating a completely irrelevant book 3 of nineteen pages titled "Michael Corleone," as was book 1. The situations that develop around Sicilian figures of local intrigue are not compelling. Puzo does attempt a history of sorts that depicts the pressures Sicily was under at the close of World War II, caught among a defeated Fascist state, a Communist insurgency, Mafia presence, and the hope to create in Italy a civil and unified society. However, all the detail sinks under Puzo's dead language, in which description of language, custom, and Sicilian society seems to have been sketched in. Turi Giuliano posesses the "the inborn tactical sense of the born guerilla" (61) and an "inborn animal ferocity" (145). When he is shot and left for dead, he "willed his body to heal" (inborn medical skill?), and Puzo allows him to forego any moral agency in the blithely dotty "he felt a new freedom, that he could no longer be held accountable for anything he did from this time on" (90). Puzo signals this new state, writing that Turi and his men "were vanishing into the beginning of their myth" (70), and readers soon wish they didn't have to follow them there. Puzo's still driving home bizarre causal chains; the "irony of heaven" dictates that the son of an abbot becomes a murderer (225); the authorial narrator argues that say what you will of Sicilians–born criminals, murderers, cunningly treacherous—"no one could dispute that Sicilians loved, no, they idolized children" (183). Saddled with Giuliano as a monologic and mythic martyr from actual Sicilian history and Michael as celebrity guest who can't save him, the novel never takes on any life.

If *The Godfather* never existed, *The Last Don* might read as a lightweight but compulsive tour through connecting worlds of Las Vegas, Hollywood, and the region known as "the Mob." Puzo created another omnipotent family in the Clericuzios for *The Last Don*. They come fully formed, indeed ossified into an aged boss, his middle-aged sons who are never really characterized, and a competing third-generation pair of rivals, vicious Dante Clericuzio and the novel's hero, Cross De Lena. The mob material is ever closer to the epic and mythic. The Clericuzios live in New York and Long Island compounds that resemble Old World gardens; one expects nymphs and fauns to leap out from behind fountains. Their ethnic fantasy enclave in the Bronx is so purely Sicilian, it should be studied by tribal ethnographers. Indeed, the longer Puzo wrote about the mob in the United States, the further it receded back into something close to retired status—calcified, an executive group of bankers and power broker elders full of wisdom but little life force. Puzo's real love in *The Last Don* was the world of movies and gambling, for which he created entertaining and sensational stories of screenwriters, directors, stars, high rollers, and casino bosses. Hollywood and Vegas threatened to break out in *The Godfather* before Coppola and Puzo pared down the rambling plot into the taut New York family melodrama of the first two films. Puzo wrote *The Last Don* in his mid-70s; it's no mistake that Puzo's three male bosses (Don Clericuzio, Alfred Gronevelt in Las Vegas, and Eli Marrion in Hollywood) are all aged potentates who mentor the young and the ambitious about money and power. Marrion and Gronevelt die in the novel after sharing their wisdom, and Don Clericuzio weighs forth at heavily staged moments. The novel's funniest character is the novelist-screenwriter Ernest Vail, a more relaxed Puzo figure than the grumpy Merlyn of *Fools Die*, who puts on both the Hollywood and literary worlds, is "earnest," pathetic, chatty, and cheerfully depressed and suicidal. His appearances are always welcome.

Omerta, Puzo's last work, is more focused than *The Last Don* and begins with an interesting generic twist. The legendary retired Don Raymonde Aprile is assassinated in New York City, and his ward, Astorre Viola, the son of a great Sicilian Don who somehow knows "in this two-year old [son] I see the heart and soul of a true Mafioso" (4); Astorre spends much of *Omerta* finding out who has committed the crime. However, the mystery frame soon dissipates into a confusing cast of overaged mob guys from America and Sicily. The potentially interesting frames involve the three Aprile children—Valerius, a West Point military tactics instructor, Marcantonio, a TV executive in charge of programming for a major network, and Nicole, an outspoken lawyer who does pro bono work for foes of the death penalty (perhaps Puzo's final example of "casual irony"). She even gingerly takes on her lordly and powerful father with generic liberal table talk: "The more we [Americans] kill, the easier it gets to kill. Can't you see that?" and the improbably chatty and scolding "Daddy, you are just too ourageous as a moralist. And you certainly are no example to follow" (50–51). Tony and Meadow Soprano they ain't! There's a very tough black lady police detective, a powerful FBI agent who can't decide (much like an American middle-class audience) whether he admires or loathes the Aprile family ("they destroyed the fabric of civilization" (19); "I don't buy this Don bullshit" (266); "You have to know these people. First they get you into trouble, then they help you out" (263); and a young Irish woman who aids and abets hit men and is Astorre Viola's great love.

Such a varied cast suggests the chance for a real opening into dialogue for Puzo but at the very end of his writing life, he can't pull off a twist beyond his conventional views on mob destiny set against "the safety of organized society" (25) as he describes the nonmob world, which, more than in any other of his mob texts, the family is ready to join. The Don's children, emissaries to more approved corridors of American power (military, media, legal), largely fall away to spectators as the novel turns into a series of sensational murder scenes that already appear as separate screenplay action segments as Puzo remembers the meaning of the occasion of *Omerta*. Puzo cannot follow through in detail on the possibilities of Marcantonio Aprile's power within television America or have Valerius Aprile show himself a brilliant tactical killer like his father. For the last time, the interpenetration of mob world and "other" is not realized by Puzo. However, he does provide a very fitting end to his Mafia chronicles by having Astorre Viola and Rosie, his love, return to Sicily to live after all their New York enemies have been vanquished. They ride horses up through the hills to the town of Corleone, where Astorre gets down or one knee to propose marriage: "she threw her arms around his neck and showered him with kisses. Then they fell to the ground and rolled together in the hills" (314).[7] Home in Sicily has been reclaimed. Marcantonio and Valerius "were working together on a project based on their father's FBI files" and believe "the Don would have appreciated the idea of receiving large sums of money for dramatizing the legend of his crimes," as close to postmodern self-reflexivity as Puzo ever got. He's more than ready to conclude his mob tales because "the old Mafia was dead. The great Dons had accomplished their goals and blended gracefully into society" and "why would anyone want to bother with the rackets when it was much easier to steal millions by starting your own company and selling shares to the public?" (315). With this final pragmatic opinion about American capitalism circa 2000, Puzo closes his books, with Astorre promising Marcantonio Aprile that he'd be available as a consultant on the TV series about the Aprile family. Puzo himself died in July 1999 after the conclusion of *The Sopranos'* first season on HBO.[8]

Accounting for *The Godfather's* takeover in the last three decades in American popular narrative and culture depends on forces beyond Puzo's occasional energies and output. In *The Last Don*, Ernest Vail says it best in one of his oddly upbeat negative speeches: "Writing novels is a dead end, like being a blacksmith. It's all movies and TV now." He continues, "[W]hat can you write about passion and the beauty of women? What's the use of all that when you can see it on the movie screen in Technicolor? . . . Actors and cameras doing all the work without processing through the brain. . . . Now the one thing the screen can't do is get into the minds of their characters, it cannot duplicate the thinking process, the complexity of life" (325–26). Vail may be giving the general novelist's brief against cinema, but he also describes Puzo's own refusal to ever psychologize his mob characters and give them any inner life in his novels. Furthermore, the melodrama itself works much better on the screen than on the page, where adventure, broad gestures, and sensational action can be much more vivid. Melodrama does not reward the reader as much as the *viewer* over and over again in its strengths. Therefore, the mob family narrative's continuance predominantly in movies and television since *Godfather II* in 1974 can be accounted for in large part by the visual presentational logic of the generic form best suited for its production.

No one film or even combination of films really bridges the period from the *Godfather* hegemony (1969 novel, 1972, 1974, 1990 films) to *The Sopranos* (1999–2001). Instead, a number of writers, directors, and actors have contributed to sustaining mob narrative in one form or another, and only an outline will be sketched here. Sergio Leone, known primarily for his Italian "spaghetti Westerns" that launched Clint Eastwood's film career, directed *Once Upon a Time in America* (1984), a four-hour epic heavily symbolized and playing upon memory with most of the action taking place in the 1920s and '30s. Stylized and lyrically presented, Leone's work is the most artistically experimental of the major mob films. Along with Coppola, Martin Scorsese has been one of the most honored American directors in the period, one whose skill had been initially identified with the presentation of Little Italy in *Mean Streets* (1973) before he weighed in with *Goodfellas* (1990) and *Casino* (1995). These films provided a speed and drive that took the mob out of Coppola's dimly lit formal rooms and solemn enclaves, past the Old World formality of the Don and the brooding spirit of Michael Corleone into adrenaline-driven and vivid dynamics that resemble the rhythms of *Sonny* Corleone. Scorsese also domesticated the mob family into scenes from a marriage in the drawn-out battles between husband and wife in both films. *Goodfellas* and *Casino* pulsate with greed, desire, and sheer menace in ways that *The Godfather* trilogy never did. One never knows when scary Joe Pesci is going to go off as a human timebomb. The shrewd but manic scufflings of Ray Liotta as mob informant Henry Hill in *Goodfellas* and the violence between DeNiro and Sharon Stone in *Casino* animate the mob cinematic genre in moment-to-moment intensity and allow Scorsese to give the entire subject a more realistic feel; he described *The Godfather* as "epic poetry, like *Morte D'Arthur*," while his own mob "stuff" "is like some guy on the streetcar talking" and said that his goal in *Goodfellas* was to convince the audience "it was hanging out with these guys in a bar" (Keyser 201). The closeness of audience contact with the Paulie Cicero crime family in *Goodfellas*, however, is mitigated by Scorsese's impersonal almost documentary style filming, "as if you had a 16mm camera with these guys for 20, 25 years" and screened "what you could pick up" (Keyser 197).[9] *Goodfellas* is closest to *The Sopranos* in its anarchic middle-class energy but fails to be intimate with its characters.

In many respects, the post-Godfather film resurgence of mob narrative is also a throwback to the Hollywood gangster genre of the 1930s. The early talking pictures, especially before more restrictive production codes in 1933, dealt with ethnicity, morality, and families split apart (the proverbial bad apple of a son, his priest brother, and their sufferin' ma). The Italian American characterization was often self-evident but not stressed. Mervyn LeRoy's *Little Caesar* (1930) with Jewish American Edward G. Robinson as "Rico" and Howard Hawks's *Scarface* (1932) with Paul Muni, subtitled *"Shame of the Nation"* upon its release, were both loosely based on the life and times of Al Capone. William Wellman's *The Public Enemy* (1931) allowed James Cagney to chew the scenery for the first time; his molls were Jean Harlow and Mae "Grapefruit" Clarke.[10] Humphrey Bogart made a memorable starring debut as on-the-lam mobster Duke Mantee in Robert Sherwood's *The Petrified Forest* (1936). *Film noir* kept the crime genre alive in the 1940s and early '50s, although the films were not necessarily ethnically inflected. Academy Award–winning classics such as Elia Kazan's *On the Waterfront* (1954) and George

Roy Hill's *The Sting* (1973), kept eclectically referencing the mob within story lines, as did Billy Wilder's *Some Like It Hot* (1960) with George Raft's sublime portrayal of Spats Columbo and Nehemiah Persoff as "Little Bonaparte." The mob came to television with *The Untouchables* (1959–62) on the FBI's battle with the Capone family, and Brian DePalma made a film version of *The Untouchables* (1988) as well as a remake of *Scarface* (1983).[11]

Al Pacino has devoted a significant part of his career in reprising roles in mob-related films, though usually playing against the formal, cold Michael Corleone persona that made him a star. Pacino's film vehicles have included gangster reprises in *Donnie Brasco* (1987) (as a career mob soldier), DePalma's *Carlito's Way* (1993) (as a Puerto Rican gangster), and *Scarface*, as a cop in *Serpico* (1973) and *Sea of Love* (1989), and in an over-the-top role as the SatanFather in *The Devil's Advocate* (1997). Other films have been quirkier at working with pieces of the mob tale. John Huston's *Prizzi's Honor* (1985), adapted from the novel by Richard Condon, posits a hit woman married to a hit man and both eager for career advancement, which can only conclude by taking each other out.[12] Careers of real-life gangsters were run through Puzo's formula as well. Barry Levinson's *Bugsy* (1992), starring Warren Beatty, went into detail about the founding of Las Vegas (touched on in the Moe Greene subplot in *The Godfather*) by Bugsy Siegel, Mickey Cohen, and Meyer Lansky in the early 1940s. The Coen Brothers' *Miller's Crossing* (1990) gave the mob tale their particularly claustrophobic and horrific aura.

Various memoirs and novels are turned into made-for-TV movies or Hollywood features: *Honor Thy Father* (1973), an adaptation of the Gay Talese book about a Bonanno family son's tale; the women's laments *Mob Princess* and the comic *Married to the Mob* (1989); and the women mob boss fantasy, Jackie Collins's *Lucky/Chances* (1990). The most playfully postmodern film spinoff is *The Freshman* (1990), in which Brando plays a mob boss running the ridiculous "endangered species" Diners Club, who looks and sounds exactly like Don Corleone but isn't; he has to continually deal with "aren't you . . . ?" statements from stunned characters. Don Corleone has almost become a brand name, as has Brando's raspy voice and cheeks stuffed with cotton.[13] Thus cinema kept the mob genre alive, along with a scattering of television series such as Stephen Cannell's *WiseGuy. Analyze This* (1999) with DeNiro as a mobster in need of a shrink and Billy Crystal as his psychiatrist, while graced by old pros, had the misfortune to match whimsy against the intensity and intelligence of Tony Sopranos's psychoanalysis on *The Sopranos*. Italian Americans and all other Americans begin to "speak mob," as certain phrases and verbal styles make their way into the mainstream along with products and brand names.[14]

Undoubtedly the biggest cinematic generic influence in the 1990s on the road to *The Sopranos* was Quentin Tarentino's *Pulp Fiction* (1994), which added crucial formal elements to the mob narrative that heretofore had been ignored. First, Tarentino's two hit men, Jules and Vincent (Samuel L. Jackson and John Travolta), are terrifically verbal creations, riffing on their jobs, the universe, and fast food in France, with Jules quoting passages from Ecclesiastes to validate his wrath. They are grumbly working men in funereal garb with intensity and a rather dotty earnestness, as well as a purity of action. Yet they most often shade closer to Laurel and Hardy or a Rosencrantz and Guildenstern as they wait for for orders from their bosses. Tarentino's particularly pop sensibility is replete with references to other films and directors; his energetic Hollywood collage has a bounce that oddly humanizes his mob guys by scaling them down through comedy. They are also righteous in their instrumentality, taking vengeance on those who deserve it on orders, always subject to powers from above as soldiers in a larger mob world. Two more significant features of *Pulp Fiction* were its pulsating score of eclectic rock music and constant use of strong obscenities in dialogue, both features that *The Sopranos* adopted, further overturning *The Godfather*'s formal, mournful Nino Roti score and generally less explicit language. Travolta in his major comeback effort as Vincent Vega was a disheveled, overweight smiling killer who cleared the way for a James Gandolfini to play Tony Soprano as another large, amiable predator. Tarentino's deadly duo, however winning, still were free-standing islands of rage and snappy lines. No family was on display for them in *Pulp Fiction*, which was a series of interlocking short sketches rather than a serial. That reassociation of family and business was also left to *The Sopranos*.

Ernest Vail's writer's view in *The Last Don* that it's "all movies and TV now" (325) suggests Puzo's resignation from really believing and working in the novel form. Aging Don Clericuzio in *The Last Don* has few pleasures left in his eighties, but one night, after a particularly satisfying Italian meal, he is in such a good mood that he sits down to watch television with his daughter, Rose Marie. After four hours "filled with horror," he says to her, "Is it possible to live in a world where everyone does what he pleases? No one is punished by God or man and no one has to earn a living? . . . Where are the people who understand a piece of cheese, a glass of wine, a warm house at the end of the day is reward enough?. . . . Who are these people who yearn for some mysterious happiness? What an uproar they make of life, what tragedies they brew up out of nothing" (299–300). It speaks volumes that Puzo's most antiquated Don is reduced to a querulous TV critic and singer of traditional Italianita. The Don voices real audience concerns about "pleasure" and "happiness" and the centering on the individual's nebulous tragedies. He speaks for hard-core bourgeois values with a dash of peasant solidity for good measure, almost out of Bourdieu in his precisely naming his simple pleasures. He can't understand such an American television world, but it is the one that will inherit mob narrative and adapt it beyond the Don's and Puzo's imaginings. At the end of of his night as TV critic, Don Clericuzio does darkly intone, "Everyone is responsible for everything he does" (300), and this is Tony Soprano's paranoid truth about his social role as well as his ideal self, to be the responsible man and on television to boot.

chapter nine

The Godfather Sung by
The Sopranos

*All my life I wanted to do movies. . . . But I wound up in TV and it pro-
vided a good living. . . . But for me it was always cinema, cinema, cinema.
Now this has been so good. Where am I ever going to go where it's going to
be this good again?*

—David Chase, creator of *The Sopranos*

*Tony Soprano: We wanted to stay Italian and preserve the things that mean
something to us. Honor and family and loyalty. And some of us wanted a
piece of the action.*

*Dr. Jennifer Melfi: What do poor Italian immigrants have to do with you?
And what happens every morning you step out of bed?*

—*The Sopranos*, 2, 9

When a depressed Tony Soprano is prodded by his psychiatrist, Dr.
Jennifer Melfi, to open up about his father and describe the family dynamics at home during his childhood, he tells her, "My mother wore him
down to a nub. . . . He was a squeakin' little gerbil when he died" (*Sopranos* 1, 1). Such an admission announces we're not in *The Godfather* anymore, though the ghosts are everywhere. Tony is a midlevel mob boss,
but he's no godfather in powerful control. He is in therapy, on Prozac
and Xanax, in deep conflict about his roles, and convinced that "everything is trending downward" (1, 1). Clearly the genre rules have changed
in *The Sopranos*; *omerta* is honored in breach rather than observance. Indeed, Tony Soprano is encouraged to talk about absolutely everything
that's down deep in his identity. What is most revealing, in the revision-
ary scope of *The Sopranos*, is the presence of women with powerful determining roles. Tony's mother Livia, is a controlling monster. His wife,
Carmela, feels deeply religious misgivings about her and Tony's life and

would hold him to a higher standard of truth. Dr. Melfi is Italian American *and* a shrink. Taken together, the Soprano voices in *The Sopranos* sing
maternal, therapeutic, and moral songs that herald the fact that the series
title is no accident; the heretofore excluded and deflected female characters of the family business melodrama rise to battle for control of Tony's
life. The male melodrama still holds center stage, but the songs of the
sopranos are overtures to Tony to know himself, to change, to be a good
man. Such a goal is still a long way off at the end of the third season of
The Sopranos after thirty-eight installments, for it's the nature of serials to
hold off closure by all means possible.

The second most significant change wrought by *The Sopranos* in
the mob narrative as bequeathed by *The Godfather* and its successors is
its televised series format, which allows for and dictates a greater commitment to realism and a more intimate relation to the Soprano family,
in the tradition of America's time-honored television family dramas.
The TV format also invites comparisons of Tony Soprano to other famous television fathers. Tony Soprano may be no Vito or Michael
Corleone, but he's no Jim Anderson or Ward Cleaver or Ricky Ricardo
either. No previous American TV series has featured a murderer in a
continuing heroic role and certainly not a father and husband as murderer. A two-hour movie often attempts to push an audience toward
such heroic identification by defining the "justifying" circumstances in
outlaw psyches, a cinematic tradition most often linked to *Bonnie and
Clyde* (1967) and *The Godfather*; however, Tony and his crew are there
week after week clubbing and murdering rivals when necessary, in
between family gatherings, soccer games, college tours, trips to see
Mother and to the gardening center to get weed killer, attendance at
confirmation parties and school chorales. They just do what they do.
"Leave the gun. Take the cannoli," Peter Clemenza's famous instruction
in *Godfather I* after Paulie Gatto is shot in the head in the Meadowlands,
gave a disorienting quotidian twist to mob assassination. Clemenza's
wife had asked him to go the bakery and her "order" was of equal
importance. Such an incongruity in *The Godfather* is built into moment-
to-moment structural fact in *The Sopranos*.

Television, the most intimate of American appliances and most
routinely used in the home, is equally the most fitting place for the
Soprano family to be captured by narrative *at home*. Even as the American Western moved from *The Virginian* to *High Noon* to *Gunsmoke*, even
as the detective genre moved from Hammett and Chandler to Bogart in
The Maltese Falcon and *The Big Sleep* and then to *Dragnet, Miami Vice, Hill
Street Blues*, and *NYPD Blue*, so the mob narrative follows what seems to
be an iron law of media's copying logic: from the page to the large screen
to the small screen. The destiny of generic popular forms is finally to be
domesticated and turned back to the American public in the most comprehensive cycling through bourgeois values and their interrogation on

television. To bring mother-haunted Tony Soprano before the bar of his female psychiatrist's principles and his wife's prayers is to finally force godfathers in mob narrative into a moral inquisition in the home in the popular medium best suited to domesticate the entire subgenre in ways that Puzo could never countenance or conceive. *The Sopranos* is always already mediated by *The Godfather* and self-consciously aware of the fact as it continues the popular business of producing the family business. To score *The Godfather* as sung by *The Sopranos* on television is to establish the suppleness of the American form of mob narrative to continue to develop and acquire new significations in a different medium.

Living in *Godfather* America: *The Sopranos* and Self-Reflexivity

What most centrally links *The Godfather* to *The Sopranos* is that Tony Soprano and his family live in an America that has been completely colonized by *The Godfather* itself. Indeed one constraint on Puzo in making his later novels such as *The Last Don* and *Omerta* more contemporary is that he was the one mob narrative writer who couldn't reference *The Godfather*! The novel was the best-selling American fictional text of the 1970s. Coppola's unprecedented two Academy Awarding–winning films (1972, 1974) established visual images and language sequences for millions of viewers worldwide. Testimonials of *The Godfather*'s influence on individual lives as well as art come from quite valid sources. Sammy "The Bull" Gravano, self-confessed murderer of nineteen men for the Gambino crime family, who turned evidence against flamboyant New York crime boss John Gotti, spoke of his admiration for Puzo "knowing the life cold" and through *The Godfather* making "our life seem honorable"; "Sammy the Bull, " himself the subject of a made-for-TV movie, calls Puzo "some kind of genius" (*NYT Magazine*, January 2, 2000).[1] Michael Imperioli, the actor-screenwriter who deftly plays Christopher Moltisanti, Tony Soprano's volatile young nephew and boss-in-training, said in an interview, "[W]hen we were kids, *The Godfather* was hero worship to us and made us proud to be Italian. We had pride in these characters. We didn't feel revulsion for them" (*Fresh Air Sunday*, March 12, 2000).[2] These admissions from a convicted murderer and a key *Sopranos* player indicate the enormous influence of Puzo and Coppola's texts in defining verisimilitude, courage, and ethnic pride over several decades. Living in the wake of Puzo's imaginary, both the actual mob culture and its representational mirror were wholly captivated; the audience for *The Sopranos* was "made" by *The Godfather*, "made," too, in the sense of personal fealty, having killed for the family and been bound over to them. The Corleones "made" the audience by compromising the viewers' primary sense of outrage over their deeds. Having sympathized and affiliated with the mob family for more than thirty years, the audience long ago joined Sammy the Bull and Imperioli in assent and complicity.

The aura of *The Godfather* hangs over *The Sopranos*, not only in the way the culture treats the Sopranos as dangerous mob "celebrities" but also in the very language they use among themselves to describe themselves. Precious little humor exists in Puzo's writing; his Corleones have no figures to imitate. However, Tony's gang is full of spontaneous *Godfather* turns. Silvio Dante is always ready with his hangdog face and droopy lip to do a Michael ("just when I thought I was out, they sucked me back in"; "our true enemy has yet to reveal himself"). Tony, curiously, never joins in the riffs; sometimes he smiles, but more often he simply tolerates the by-play. It would appear he is having enough trouble trying to *become* the Godfather. Father Phil, Carmela's young priest and shy romantic admirer, is also a movie buff, who hovers around the Soprano home and asks Carm about Tony's movie tastes: "which movie does Tony like best, [*Godfather*] I or II?" and "what did Tony think of *Goodfellas*?"

Other uses of *Godfather* material are more intricate and playful. *The Sopranos* (2,4) opens with a screen shot: "*FBI Warning*" on copyright infringement about pirated or stolen tapes; we quickly see that it's Tony and the boys in the back room of their strip joint Bada Bing, trying to screen a print of *Godfather II* on a stolen DVD player, one of a shipment they're fencing. Silvio and Paulie make much of the fact that these are "the alternate takes" on a "bootleg" version. Just so is *The Sopranos* the latest alternate take or creative infringement on Puzo's formula. Furthermore, in the real-time world of the Soprano gang, FBI Warnings are everywhere. Tony's closest confederate and childhood friend, Salvatore "Pussy" Bompensiero, has turned informant for the FBI; the bureau has the mob's photos stacked up on its office wall in order of rank, like movie posters or Politburo members; agents regularly search the Soprano home. When the DVD player doesn't work, the guys alternately curse it and hit it. Tony asks, "[W]hata ya' gonna do? Call Coppola for ideas on how to fix it?" Paulie adds, "Someone should tell Paramount Pictures to get their shit together. We're gonna be stealing thousands more o' these tings." As usual, the *Godfather* rap begins, Silvio intoning, "It was you Fredo . . ." Asked "what's your favorite line?" Tony moans, "I can't have this conversation again," but when pressed, he speaks of the old Don's villa in Corleone, Sicily, how quiet it was with the crickets and the great old house; he feels there the peace he wants and needs in the present. Always impatient, Christopher lives in the present and doesn't like to trade *Godfather* trivia with his elders any more than Tony. A movie buff and aspiring actor-screenwriter, he just wants to see the film and impatiently fusses with the machine until Paulie provides the usual solution to a Soprano gang problem; he beats the DVD player with a baseball bat.[3]

The Godfather epic never takes itself as anything less than utterly seriously. It does not know itself as the object of cultural adulation with the resulting terminal stiffness of its already formal presentation only heightened in retrospective reading and viewing over the decades. However, Chase's conception of the mob narrative is thoroughly at home in the postmodern self-reflexive and image culture. *The Sopranos* tries to work within as many frames as it can, including those of *The Godfather*, keeping them all alive and keeping its audience edgy and slightly off-balance, generally in a ceaseless delight at the cultural interpenetration. In the very first episode of year one, Christopher pushes a body into the Jersey Meadowlands swamp and intones, "Lewis Brazi sleeps with the fishes," which makes Pussy, a generation older and a *Godfather* purist, wince and tell him it's "Luca Brasi." "Whatever," Christopher retorts, in true contemporary slackness. *The Godfather* has become general cultural currency. Chase can use the citation to limn the communication problem between Christopher and Pussy and create within comic frames. The "sleeps with the fishes" reference comes brutally home in the last episode of year two when Tony figures out that Pussy is a traitor to the family. In a dream sequence he confronts Pussy as one of the fish packed in ice at a beach stand at the Jersey Shore; Pussy as fish says, "[T]hese guys on either side of me, they're asleep" and reveals his treachery. By the end of the hour, Tony and the gang have shot Pussy to death at sea; the last image of *The Sopranos'* second season is of the Atlantic waves rolling in. The extended scenes with Pussy are sad, hilarious, and moving, yet begin as wonderfully referential to the source in *The Godfather*. One of postmodernism's more simple aesthetic pleasures is the audience's acknowledgment of self-conscious borrowing or quoting of material from other texts, creating the tacit assumption that familiar, exhausted, or plundered styles and subjects created in a new mix become the definition of the "new."

No single vehicle has so well captured America's decades-long affair with mob narrative as does *The Sopranos*. Chase is unrelenting in his portrayal of a culture and media industry so deeply imbued with what could be called "Godfatherness" that there is no way out to an original or summary statement of influence and effect, origin and separation. The most brilliant single *Sopranos* hour to capture the climate of America's cross-referenced and utterly implicated relation to mob narrative is the seventh show of year two in which Christopher gets to be with a film company on location, and later the film's "development" director and writer tentatively walk on the wild side with him as they strive to be "authentic," to enhance what they think of as the power of their work. The sadness and hilarity that result form a grimly comic picture of a culture so in love with sensation and violent imagery that Christopher, a truly dangerous and troubled young man, becomes a literal savant of instinctive movie-making and a source of mob lore, even while retaining his explosive core personality and exposing the craving of the industry and audience for more such stories.

Christopher's relation to film and narrative production is the most complex in *The Sopranos* and most in line with the postmodern. Christopher is enamored of movie-making and figures if he can't be "made" by and for Tony, then he can go to Hollywood to write, perhaps star in films about the mob and play himself. He sends away for "Movie Magic Screenwriter" software and is baffled when it doesn't magically do most of the writing for him. He quits an acting class after battering another student in a class exercise; his classmates and the instructor are very impressed with his fire, but Christopher finds it much too close to his real life. He then pitches his script in a garbage can, where it's retrieved by his faithful girlfriend, Adrianna. Chase's truth, of course, is that Christopher perhaps can make more money by writing a film about the mob than by joining it as a fully made member. The work would be lucrative, easier, less threatening, and who could know more? When he actually hooks up with the film company through his cousin's girlfriend Amy, a script development girl, his crisis of allegiance to Tony heightens. The film's screenwriter, played perfectly in character by Hollywood actor-writer Jon Favreau, comes sniffing around Christopher as the real thing, whereas Christopher himself wants to turn his mob reality into film and money.

When Christopher visits the movie set in Soho, he's like a star-struck kid during the shooting of the movie's climactic scene. Amy explains that the director, fresh from a triumph "at Sundance" with a "lesbian romantic screwball comedy," is now into "more mainstream" work and the film, *Female Suspects,* is about lesbian spies and girlfriends. The two lovers, played by Sandra Bernhard (Christopher gauchely points and blurts out, "I know her. *King of Comedy,* right?") and Janeane Garofalo, have just shot each other; they both lie bleeding in a garbage strewn alley, and Favreau and the woman director are looking for some pithy dialogue to cap the big climax. Christopher goes wide-eyed when he sees Bernhard hold a huge gun with a silencer; it's too close to his real life. Amy solemnly whispers to him that the silencer symbolizes the heroines' silenced voices in society. The director calmly wonders whether Bernhard should shoot Garofalo again and what she might say: "bitch" seems too tame for the occasion. They debate a bit, whereupon Christopher strides forward and points to Bernhard, saying, "Have that one call that one *"bucchiaccio."*[4] When everyone draws a blank, Christopher repeats the word. Favreau and the director say it sounds pretty good—but what does it mean? "It means 'cunt,' " he answers. No one bats an eye: sounds good to them. So be it, and Christopher has become an instant script doctor. The amoral blankness of the movie company's decisions in the empty, vulgar climax to the scene perfectly reflects its vacuous and violent movie itself. Christopher's instant expertise comes out of his own obscene and violent world from which he is an ambassador in his vitality and "authenticity." Thus does Chase satirize the movie company with his own production company that nonetheless is exploiting precisely what

Christopher knows and what Chase knows the audience knows about what Christopher knows.[5] Postmodern critique here takes on a complexity rarely achieved on television through any genre.

After the filming, Favreau and Amy go into a neighborhood joint with Christopher, eager for more "authentic" experience. They want to hang with him to enhance what they think of as the power of their work. Christopher points out that across the street where a laundromat now stands was the restaurant where Willie Moretti stuck his gun in Tommy Dorsey's mouth and bought Sinatra's contract from him for a dollar. Favreau thinks it's so cool: "[T]hat's like the inspiration for Johnny Fontane and the studio boss in *GF I*." Having immediately shifted the historical anecdote to the movie reference, because it's both his job and the culture's desire, Favreau says that he'd like to do a film on mobster Joe Gallo, to show that he really wanted to grow, to learn, and to paint (presumably like Christopher), that he was a "flawed and blinkered guy." Christopher dismisses the Gallo reference, saying that it happened when he was three years old, and besides, he says "learnedly," there'd already been a film made of it, *The Gang That Couldn't Shoot Straight*. Christopher also worries that Favreau isn't authentic enough, that he doesn't understand the life or culture; he frankly tells Favreau that his heroes in *Swingers* (1996) were modeled on "Frank and Dean," but there was a "pussy-assedness" to it, to which Favreau readily caves, becoming more obscenely colloquial to converse with a native, adding eagerly that "you can tell me the way shit goes down, the way people really talk."[6] Finally, Christopher sees a shadowed figure out the window, shudders, and tells Favreau and Amy a chilling story about her, a transsexual hooker whose customer, a mob guy, was so outraged at finding out she was a man that he poured acid all over her. At which point, without a tear or missing a beat, Amy says, "*Crying Game*." Instantly the horrifying story is converted to a movie I.D. and a response referencing another film. Throughout their conversation, Favreau and Amy convert life into film reference, whereas Christopher knows to keep them separate. Christopher warns them that the anecdote compromises the masculinity of a made man and cannot be told: "[T]his kinda thing is unacceptable where I come from," both the male sexual humiliation and the telling of it. Sure enough, Amy immediately writes a script treatment of Chris's story, and, when he goes ballistic over her pillage, her defense is, "[Y]ou said the guy met the transsexual at a swing set in the park. This guy gets his dick sucked at the Statue of Liberty." To cinch the deal, she adds, "Oliver [Stone] wants to see it."

Absolutely everything in *The Sopranos*, no matter how grotesque, violent, or intimate is instantly to be converted into genre or quick, extrinsic reference. No boundary line exists between "material" and "product" for Favreau and Amy who are just as fragmented as poor Christopher. Christopher has story conferences with Amy and then with Favreau, in which he tries to pitch his own screenplay and become bonded in the movie business. They treat him warily, always on edge about his violent potential to go off and somehow implicate them; he, however, acts like a young friendly bear, seeking advice on his work, wanting to be in *their* life. In their reactions to Christopher, Chase beautifully captures much of the audience's reaction to the Soprano mob world and by extension to all of mob narrative. Christopher overflows with "the real thing"; they want to stay tuned to the buzz he gives off, the whiff of danger, and remain safely behind the camera.[7]

Favreau approaches Christopher almost as a heroic athlete, asking haltingly, "[C]an I ask you—have you ever . . ."; Christopher toys with him, saying loudly he's not going to answer unless he asks, "[D]id I what, have I ever what?" Favreau asks if Christopher is "strapped." Christopher pulls out his gun and flips it to him, making Favreau almost queasy. As Christopher playfully cuffs him for the gun, he asks, "Whaddya think of my script?" Favreau, now really afraid of Christopher but not wanting to show it, begins to ramble, giving script advice in an impromptu story conference but all the time prudently wiping his fingerprints off Christopher's gun, implicitly reminding the audience what Christopher does for a living. Christopher is so exuberant over this Hollywood insider's advice that he exults, "Fucking brilliant!" puts the gun to Favreau's head, says "Blam, blam," and then kisses him. Favreau practically faints, so lost in Christopher's ethnic and male effusiveness that he can't script; he has lost control of his scene and is finally too close to what he both needs and fears. The audience watches fascinated, never more intimate with the potential life-threatening world of the Soprano family than when Christopher innocently plays with a vulture from the commodity culture who would capture his aura. Such a complex transaction is captured within the vehicle that is *The Sopranos* itself and would not have been possible or even meaningful without the genre and aura that *The Godfather* authorized in the 1970s.

Far from the vows of *omerta*, everyone wants to script mob narrative as product, including benighted young gangsters such as Christopher, who really does see becoming a made mobster or a screenwriter as equal career opportunities. Christopher comes trailing real danger from a world of violent men, which movie makers crave for their audiences. However, in the relationship between the mob and cinema in *The Sopranos*, it's clear that Chase sides with Christopher as more open, resourceful, and alive. He's sensual, immediate, and ambitious in ways not controlled by jargon or status, beyond his allure for Favreau and Amy as icon and "consultant." Cinema and television constantly search for vantage points and more material from which to depict a Christopher and in fact idolize and disparage him at the same time. Behind their layers of other film references, other directors, and technical jargon, they believe they do it for us—the audience for lesbian lover-murderers screaming "cunt" at each other—the same audience that chooses to watch *The Sopranos*, which not only has a viewpoint on this dynamic but *is* this dynamic. There is no way back to a clear separation of mob life or its cinematic or television presentation for the viewer or critic, nor is it possible to ignore the reified status of "mob narrative" itself as it overdetermines every relation in *The Sopranos*. As Garofalo says to Christopher when he comes back to the set, "[D]o you have more stuff like that I can use?" "Authentic" obscenity grounds the ethnic mob language that is the lingua franca of an entire subgenre. Christopher himself partially understands the game. When pointing to Bernhard and Garofalo, he objectifies them as "that one" and "that one," realizing that Sicilian for "cunt" and the possibility of more gunplay is all that the audience for this screen classic will need to know. Who cares who the actresses are or the characters they play? Anything we can use to feel more dangerous, visceral, and alive drives us to consume *The Sopranos*, which then depicts our moral nightmares with intensity and intelligence. *The Sopranos* represents its audience, the producers, actors, writers, and Soprano family members in a referential matrix that includes the legacy of decades of *Godfather* narrative and descendants

Christopher as a naif in this dreamland is both a supplicant with a screenplay and a most feared agent of doom; he finally is asked by Tony at the end of the episode to choose between "whatever the fuck is calling you out there" in a *Godfather*-besotted half-world of screenwriting dreams and their promise and where he should be with Tony: "[Y]our actions should show you want to be with me every fucking day." Christopher walks back into Tony's house on the day of Tony's son's confirmation and votes for "primary experience" with the Soprano family, his excursion into postmodern mirrors provisionally at an end. The world outside the Soprano family makes no sense to him; the world inside may be dangerous and death-haunted, but he knows the rules. It is unclear how the viewer can tell the difference between poor fragmented Christopher as murderer and peripatetic Christopher as script advisor on screen in *The Sopranos*.[8]

Chase knows that he is describing this postmodern climate from inside, from this *Sopranos* episode that is within the sensational mob narrative paradigm itself rather than above it or outside it. Indeed, while Christopher debates going back inside to join Tony, Pussy Bompensiero, who is standing up for Anthony Jr. at his confirmation, sits sobbing upstairs in the Soprano bathroom, tormented by his love for Tony, his need to save himself, and his treachery to the family. Unlike Christopher, who flirts with the movies and comes home to Tony, Pussy is giving his mob narrative to the FBI and has even agreed to wear a wire to the confirmation. As Tony gathers his family for the official confirmation portrait, he exclaims, "Where's Pussy? Where's the Godfather?" This void at the center of *The Sopranos* is always telling; no patriarch, no authoritative voice, no core reality or way in to one. Christopher has more commodity value than Pussy the informant, née godfather. What makes *The Sopranos* a dialogized delight is precisely its willingness to place itself as an artifact in the tangled intertextual web of America's love affair with what *The Godfather* has wrought, to face the mystification that is our attraction—repulsion to Christopher, Tony, Pussy, and the family and to implicate the popular arts—cinema and television—that have become dependent on it, even as the Sopranos know their commodity representation defines them as surely as any further crimes they could commit in society.

Christopher's decision to stay with Tony has its analogue in Chase's own career decision to stick with television. He admits that despite a long career in series television as writer, producer, and director, "all [my] life I wanted to do movies. . . . But I wound up in TV and it provided a good living. . . . Now this has been so good. Where am I ever going to go where it's going to be this good again?" (Carter, "He Engineered a Mob Hit" 90). In terms of his cultural capital, Chase's trajectory reverses that of Puzo. He's engaged in perfecting the popular toward an elite status in terms of aesthetics and referentiality, whereas Puzo himself slid to what he called "beneath his gifts" and couldn't really respect himself or his form. To Christopher and to Chase, "coming home" to Tony Soprano is a fortunate fall that gives much greater sanction to postmodern hybridized genres and the cutting between popular and elite. *The Godfather* in a sense fathered such generic flexibility, but Puzo no longer sired its children.

America in Therapy:
The Sopranos Sings for a Nation

In discussing the transmission of the epic through the novelistic (chapter 8), I noted Adorno and Lukacs speaking of epic as the childhood of the race, that a certain naive portrayal coheres through the unfolding of an epic tale. Lukacs shifts the focus of the surviving epic hero to the novel; he says the novel objectifies the psychology of that hero (60). Tony Soprano is an epic character being driven into a more novelistic self-reflection. He suffers true birth pangs as he enters psychotherapy in the narrative that inevitably drives him as analysand back into childhood. Fiedler also spoke of the American "inadvertent epic" as the vehicle wherein our personal and communal dreams are conflated, allowing us to express "the dark side of our ambivalence toward what any status quo demands we believe" and "to acknowledge men's hatred of women and women's contempt for men, along with the desire of parents to possess utterly or to destroy their children, and the corresponding Oedipal dreams of those children" (*What Is Literature* 41). Fiedler appears to identify the full force field of family relations all the way from popular fiction up to Greek tragedy, but he does not see this terrible truth-making in popular fiction leading to any transgressive knowledge because most popular narrative "tends to be weak on the cognitive and formal levels" (49). Tony Soprano may be depressed for all of us, but he does not often come through to any hard-won wisdom, nor do we through his story. In fact, if pressed, Tony would probably say that he is trying to become a better mob boss through therapy, to fix what is broken in order to become more *like* his idealized self in power. However, Tony is consistently reduced to a raging child who is sometimes kind or good, but most often a grown man whose power is slowly killing him in ways that he can't afford to acknowledge.

By placing a mob boss in such a vulnerable position in analysis, Chase is creating a wholly different relationship for a "Godfather" with the American audience. The problems of Tony's violence and his compromised reign at the head of the Soprano family are not only ethnically and criminally marked in the contemporary period; they are seen to be pervasive crises of maleness in America. Men circa 2000 must be rehabilitated past their abusive and wounding natures. They are encouraged to get in touch with their depression, which they mask with rage that may be covering their sorrow (to borrow from Dr. Melfi's extended explanation to Tony).[9] *The Sopranos* in serial format would portray Tony on the road to new insight through a deeper understanding and a resultant refashioning of his psyche. Tony is damaged and does damage, but *The Sopranos* hardly gives up on him; indeed, his male melodrama is still the focus of the plot in the remarkably hearty and sustained twentieth-century-long cry of the American male that job, family, and home are not nearly enough for him and that he may be perennially caught in the wrong life. This strain of American male anxiety in post–World War II America has roots in the more WASP suburban fiction of Cozzens, O'Hara, and Cheever and in many of the male melodrama films of the late 1950s, recently dubbed "male weepies."[10] That we are in a thorough revival of this familiar suburban disaffection can also be seen in the Academy Award-winning *American Beauty* (1999), though the disillusioned character played by Kevin Spacey in his free-floating and general disaffection does not touch the complexity of Tony Soprano's portrayal. The advantages of thirty-eight hours to unfold the private, public, and subconscious lives of its principals give the television series a decided advantage over its two-hour movie-formatted rival.

The Sopranos thus richly unites the contemporary culture's two strongest narrative representations of love and family: movies/television and therapy and the inevitable conflation of the two in *The Sopranos* itself.[11] If Christopher can't make it in the mob by becoming Tony's symbolic son in whom he will be well pleased, he can write about it and perhaps make his own movie. Tony wishes to cease being "Mama's Boy," to be healed in analysis, which is another fantasy form of breaking away into "freedom" and personal success. Christopher wants to break into the business family's inner circle; Tony wants to know why being there is killing him. Melodrama drives characters to internalize their social, economic, and class conflicts (Landy 14) and both Christopher and Tony strive to explain their roles through a strong narcissism and self-referentiality, the favorite middle-class conversions of choice in the ruse that everything is personal and about individual freedom in America. Such intertextuality in *The Sopranos* (Christopher wants in, Tony wants help, the movies and TV want them as product) suggests that there is no "legitimate" or "larger American society" that could be defined by a liberal pluralism, that such a touchstone hypothesized by viewers and critics is a creation of a liberal false consciousness, that nothing about the Sopranos' world is unconnected or unmediated. That is a conclusion that the wary and paranoid mob bosses and their soldiers would fully endorse on an empirical level.

Such hard facts hang heavily over Tony and Dr. Melfi, whose weekly sessions become the viewers' regular appointments with them on HBO. Tony initially begins in instinctive mistrust of the patient's role. He mumbles to Melfi on first meeting in *Sopranos* (1, 1) that everybody has to go to "shrinks, counselors, Sally Jessy," wondering for the rest of America, "where does it stop?" and points out that Gary Cooper wasn't in touch with *his* feelings; he was a "strong silent type, *that* was an American." Tony marks himself as contemporary and a class aspirant: "I had a semester and a half of college. . . . I understand Freud. I understand therapy. But in my world it doesn't go down." Tony is no stereotype of comic mistrust about psychoanalysis. Chase thoroughly depicts Tony's half-knowledge, his contemporary familiarity with analysis but also his clichéd misgivings about heroic males opening up and his firm sense of himself segmented off ("my world") where silence should still reign. He has learned as much from Vito Corleone and Gary Cooper as he has from his father, "Johnny Boy" Soprano. Melfi and Tony's sessions are fascinating for the sense of realism they impart to the analytic process and the way their insights underwrite the larger *Sopranos* narrative. They comprise the most sustained dialogue we possess to date in popular narrative on the morality of the mob and mob rhetoric in explanation for conduct across a range of individual and collective practices in American society and popular culture.

Melfi works heroically if warily with Tony, wending their way through his depression. However, after three seasons of therapy, Tony's world and world view have altered less than they have impacted on her own as psychiatrist and moral individual. Tony is a stunningly hard case, both in his revelations and in his resistance to her questions. By the end of year two, Tony has survived a botched assassination attempt, a major FBI indictment for a murder he committed, and numerous attempts to infringe on control of his business interests. Melfi, on the other hand, has developed an alcohol problem, her sessions with her own shrink are consumed by discussions about Tony, and her boyfriend has been beaten by a cop on the Soprano payroll. Because of Tony's mob problems, Melfi's own life has been placed in danger, and she is forced to run her practice for a brief period out of a motel room. She becomes increasingly involved in her responses to Tony's brutal acts and descriptions. She takes his case and progress as a great professional challenge and a matter of personal ethical and moral necessity. She is, of course, half in love with him and he with her in patient-therapist transference; their relation goes very deep, for she must represent both the mother and the wife he resists as well as his relief from the pain of both figures.

Such dramatic and sustained tension between Tony and Melfi is light years from anything Puzo cared to conjure up for the male and female Corleones. Michael's stonewalling before Kay's erratic questioning is simple wordplay in comparison to Melfi's interrogation of Tony's most cherished beliefs and defense mechanisms about himself as father, son, and crime family boss. Again and again, Melfi responds to Tony's admissions with the stock analyst's question of "[H]ow did that make you *feel*?" Her continual probing signifies the essential call-and-response rhetoric of analysis as one of melodrama with a sentimental emphasis on the emotions rather than on reason, which is seen as the line of defense against feeling that must be pushed through to a truth that is down deeper, in darkness and the past, within family trauma and early sorrow. The narrative of analysis combines powerful aspects of both elite fiction and criticism (multileveled plot and theme, complex characterization, "hidden meaning") with popular fiction (sensational revelations, sexual and violent action at root of human behavior, family "romance" in early childhood at the core of personality and character beyond historical, political, and economic referents). *The Sopranos* brilliantly exposes how analysis plays both elite and popular narrative roles.

Most of Melfi's questions drive Tony into defensive positions about his identity, where he tries to explain who and what he is. Their dialogues often speak to issues in America's love affair with mob narrative back through decades of the Corleones and their successors, who won over a vast audience. She forces Tony to ask: what did I do? what does it mean? what am I responsible for? how can I justify my life? doesn't everyone do this in some way? how did I get to be this person? These questions are the audience's questions as well and date back in mob narrative to Woltz's and Kay's quandaries in *The Godfather*. And Melfi doesn't let Tony get away with facile answers. In *Sopranos* (1, 7), when Tony gives her his seductive half-smile and says, "[M]aybe it's in the genes," Melfi counters with a more precise professional term saying that "genetic predispositions are just that," and then asks about "free will." He comes back hot and colloquial as always: "[Y]ou're born to this shit. You are what you are." Melfi then says "[W]ell, then, that is a range of choices. This is America," Tony disparagingly responds, "Right, America." Such is the barebones sparring in a much larger debate between them for the audience of mob narrative about cause and effect and moral responsibility. Melfi becomes the reader/viewer's interrogating imagination and response to Soprano predation and dominion. She's the first created character in decades to be granted the license to sit a "godfather" down and repeatedly fire away with the ethical and moral weight of society, medicine, and outraged female nurture behind her authority. The more Melfi convinces Tony that his mother is at the root of his unhappiness (which Tony reduces to "poor parenting," since he's a true son of the Freudian century and knows the language of the tribe), the more he's outraged when she questions him in his historical role as immigrant descendant, patriarch, and gangster, reminding him that he is "free" to choose a range of behavior. Ann Cvetkevich has commented that "psychoanalytic institutions and models are central to the formation of modern disciplinary power, which enables the control and production of subjectivity through claims to liberate the psyche" (32). Tony cannot live in the contradiction surrounding his "freedom": that he has both a "destiny" and the capacity to alter it if he can learn and grow and show personal courage to change. This moralism is at the heart of the *Sopranos* melodrama and beyond any goal Puzo ever had for his mob families in fiction or film.

Death is Tony's constant companion and counters his desire for growth and change. In one session with Melfi, he's concerned enough to deflect his fears onto Anthony Jr. (A. J.) who's become death-haunted from reading Camus's *The Stranger* at school and is quoting a philosopher he calls "Nitch" (Nietzsche). Melfi tries to explain to Tony that his own symptoms (fainting, shortness of breath, panic attacks) are a physiological response to emotional problems. She says that "when some people first realize that people are solely responsible for their decisions, actions, and beliefs, they can be overcome with intense dread, a dull aching anger that the only absolute is death." Tony then snaps the dialogue back to A. J.: "[T]he kid may be onto something" (*Sopranos* 2, 7). When Christopher is shot and almost killed by elements out to get at Tony, he tells Melfi disparagingly that Christopher believes he has had a near-death experience and saw himself in hell (*Sopranos* 2, 9). The pivotal dialogue continues:

Melfi: Do you think he'll go to hell?
Tony: He's not the type who deserves hell.
Melfi: Who deserves it?
Tony: The worst people. The twisted and demented psychos who kill people for pleasure, the cannibals, the degenerate bastards that molest and torture little kids and kill babies, the Hitlers, the Pol Pots, those are evil fucks that deserve to die.
Melfi: What about you?
Tony: Me? Hell? You were listening to me? We're soldiers. Soldiers don't go to hell. It's war. Soldiers, they kill other soldiers. We're

in a situation where everybody involved knows the stakes. And if you're gonna accept those stakes, you gotta do certain things. It's business. We're soldiers. We follow codes. Orders.

Melfi: Does that justify everything you do?

Tony: Excuse me. Let me tell you something. When America opened the floodgates and let all the Italians in, we weren't educated like the Americans. What'dya think they were doing it for? Because they wanted to save us all from poverty? No, they did it because they needed us. They needed us to build their cities and to dig their subways and to make them richer. The Carnegies and the Rockefellers. They needed their worker bees and there we were. But some of us didn't want to swarm around their hive and lose who we were. We wanted to stay Italian and preserve the things that mean something to us. Honor and family and loyalty. And some of us wanted a piece of the action. Now we weren't educated like the Americans. But we had the balls to take what we wanted. But those other fucks, those other—the J. P. Morgans, they were crooks and killers, too. But that was business, right? The American Way?

Melfi: What do poor Italian immigrants have to do with you? And what happens every morning you step out of bed?

Melfi asking "what happens every morning you step out of bed?" is the most direct and succinct challenge to mob narrative within the genre since Puzo began asking his audiences to justify the Corleone praxis by checking their morals at the first page or opening cinema frame. Her question also signifies an all-American response to Tony's taking refuge within an identity politics to explain his life. The dialogue carefully delineates the differing responses. First, Tony posits circles of hell like a good moral theologian and sees himself and Christopher exempt because they're in a war, an endeavor that is structured and ritualized, unlike degeneracy and appetite. He conflates capitalism and warfare ("It's business. We're soldiers") and models both immigrant identity and essential American criminality. He can't help showing his hypocrisy in a further rhetorical conflation (honor and a piece of the action). Melfi doesn't buy it. The speech sounds as if he has memorized it as a catechism from his father or other mob members or extrapolated it from *Godfather* narrative. She calls Tony on his ethnic affiliation; after all, he's third-generation Italian American. Then she asks about practice: what, indeed, *does* Tony do every day? How can he find justification in an ethnicity to commit the acts he commits? What does being Italian American in 2000 have to do with historical wrongs suffered by his people?[12]

Essentially this is a majoritarian question from the heart of a more universalized American *doxa* that says that any essentialism is not an adequate justification for socially deviant conduct. It's made all the more authentic because the question is asked by an Italian American female psychiatrist, thus conjoining her own valid ethnicity and female sentiment against violence, as well as a scientific, humanistic legitimacy as a medical professional. In blunter terms, she won't allow Tony to play the ethnic card and tells him that his life is about *him now*, every day. In American dialogues other than *The Sopranos*, Melfi's negative response could be used to block African American grievances at their historical and racial root in favor of a universal "Americanness" or to counter views on affirmative action. Melfi speaks in a backlash against identity politics as a cultural universalist, qualifying historical trauma and centering on the mythical and nonidentity-inflected monadic American who communes with conscience as sole arbiter of conduct and does not allow any multiple cause and effect, a line of argument that could date back past Hawthorne's conscience-haunted characters to real Puritan fathers. In mutated form, her critique of Tony is mainstream and comforting. Tony and his men have every reason to fear hell, but *The Sopranos* can't help both parodying and contextualizing that fear. Chase and his stable of writers maintain an archness about what is deeply troubling in American allegiances and trangressions, while not denying the trauma and perhaps helping audiences to recognize it. They do so through a relativism that contextualizes all previous absolutes in the signature that underwrites the postmodern response.

Chase won't let Tony and Melfi's confrontation end there. Tony is outraged at her questions, which treacherously strip away all his constructed defenses. Like a wounded child, he howls at her, "You pick now to act like Betsy fucking Ross!"—and this after telling him he was the victim of poor parenting! Tony is instinctively correct to hurl the "Betsy Ross" charge at Melfi, a female who criticizes his Italian American identity defense from the standpoint of an angry American patriotism. She suddenly speaks authoritatively in a mainstream American historical indictment of Tony's life after positing his mother as the probable cause of his dread. But now she kicks the crutch of the evil mother away from him, leaving him nowhere to stand as victim, certainly not in the turn-of-the-millennium's favorite jargon of excuse, "poor parenting." Still so very far from acknowledging his own guilt, he can, however, in perfect contemporary fashion, retreat into his status as "victim." Tony knows what his rights are (he watches Sally Jessy, too, after all), and they don't include being called to account for his actions. Here is a clear example of what a deft comedy of manners *The Sopranos* often is. Not once does Chase ambiguously question the seriousness of Melfi and Tony's dialogue but wryly depicts Tony perhaps more infantilized by her criticism than he was before getting hooked by the "helping" professions. Still thinking about being betrayed, he goes home to an argument with Carmela, where he projects his anger both at his mother and Melfi onto her earlier bitter suggestion to him that he get a vasectomy if he is going to continue to sleep with other women. When Tony asks her, "Isn't it a sin to undo the good work [God] has done?" he thinks he's made a telling point through her religious faith, that he shouldn't be "snipped," but Carmela comes back with, "Well, you should know. You've made a living of it." In a single morning, mob boss Tony Soprano has now been accused of being a murderer by both his shrink and his wife in the most stunning moral colloquy in the history of mob narrative, surpassing anything Connie and Kay could wound Michael with in *The Godfather*.

Angry and frustrated, Tony then badly wounds A. J. by suggesting that his "son and heir" would have been better off not born. The "sins of the mother" are visited by the son onto the grandson. Inside the nominally powerful mob boss is a very unhappy child acting "like a woman" in his hysteria and by fainting, and those in his orbit, particularly women and children, immediately pay for it. The Tony Soprano reclamation project would be to turn him into a faithful husband, a better father, and a reconciled son, but it's not easy, especially when Melfi's question about what happens when Tony steps out of bed every morning is set alongside the show's popular opening theme with its refrain, "Woke up this morning/Got yourself a gun" softly thumping through the opening credits as Tony drives home through northern New Jersey. Basically, Tony arises for work (sometimes quite late in the morning), and that work potentially always includes a gun. Other accents filter through this connection of waking and guns. If three decades after *The Godfather* we get the mob story we need, it's in an America much more hypersensitive about both identity defenses and violence than Puzo's was, while its own popular cultural production is more and more violent (the same would obviously apply to *The Sopranos* itself, constantly working though and questioning what the show itself is afflicted with and presents), the American culture's obsession with guns and their relation to violence. "Woke Up This Morning" and its less-than-subliminal vigilante message is inescapable. The song's second line states that your "father always told you, you're the chosen one," and such a role is precisely what Tony cannot inhabit any longer and why he is in crisis. Tony remains a passionate primitive and pilgrim who would like to awaken in the sadness of a fallen morning and have all things be well, but that would be giving up his gun in a dangerous world where what he and Melfi talk about "don't go down." But they *have* talked about it in therapy with the full participation of a contemporary cable television audience, which by now knows that no subject is currently blanketed in *omerta*. The analyst-analysand transaction is always in the mode of Romance of Consciousness, which in contemporary representation may allow for the sympathizing identification with anyone about anything.

Jennifer Melfi:
Psychoanalysis as Recovery Narrative

Dr. Jennifer Melfi is a forty-something Italian American psychiatrist who is the most powerful voice from the bourgeois public sphere yet created to question the rationale and moral underpinnings of mob narrative. She comes with impeccable credentials as insider and rightful inquisitor and as the mother/daughter/lover/wife typically silenced in this violent male narrative.[13] She inhabits the ethnic Italian American role used by Tony as refuge and justification, yet she represents almost total assimilation through professional credentialing and scientific-cultural capital. Her identities are multiple and intertextual. Thus while Tony in an initial bonding gesture asks Melfi, "what part of the boot [Italy] you from?" by Bourdieu's markers, they speak across a wide gulf of accrued cultural capital. Melfi is the liberal professional therapist of feeling who probes the wounded male's spirit in melodrama. As a professional "reader" of patients as texts, she asks Tony society's questions. *The Sopranos* casts Melfi seriously as a romantic heroine of power and moral authority. She appears in a long line of contemporary female interrogators and representatives of the helping professions, in fiction and cinema, Pat Conroy's Dr. Lowenstein in *The Prince of Tides;* on television from Dr. Joyce Brothers through Dr. Ruth, to Oprah, as well as the female professional authorities in books and self-help seminars (Suze Ormann, Naomi Wolff, Marianne Williamson). Melfi is thus a familiar compound character in an era of postfeminist authority. Brooks comments that "melodrama demonstrates over and over that the signs of ethical forces can be discovered and can be made legible" (Landy 64) and in Melfi's questioning, she certainly represents the professional middle-class audience caught in the thrall of Tony's violent life. She is fascinated, appalled, judgmental, and without real answers for or about him. In thirty eight hours over three seasons, Tony has broken down her belief in herself and her science. Melfi wants to demonstrate to Tony and prove through him not the existence of evil but his place in it and its roots in him, but as she tells her own therapist, "I'm in a moral never-never land with this patient," precisely the uneasy situation of the audience for *The Sopranos* as it has been for decades of *Godfather* audiences: how to balance Tony's deeds with his justifications for them, how to acknowledge his obvious heroism on behalf of those he loves and for whom he feels responsible despite the carnage he commits against others; how to root for a fledgling mob boss who is undeniably a murderer.

Melfi does not want to dislodge Tony from his place in the Soprano family. She represents in the guise of science, modernity's highest authority, an "understanding" of sin and guilt. She wants to change Tony's life by smoothing him out and making him confront awake the dreams that haunt him. In effect, analyst and patient come to their dialogues in *The Sopranos* representing epic's fall into the novel as articulated by Lukacs. Along with his identity as heroic Italian immigrant, Tony speaks for traditional norms, what he calls "codes," "rules" followed by "soldiers," but he is arrested in childhood; he is "childlike," as both Lukacs and Adorno have characterized both the epic form and hero. According to Lukacs, the epic and by extension the epic hero must take vengeance against those who trangress stable norms and strive for a "perfect theodicy" in which crime and punishment always balance out (Lukacs 61). Tony knows who the *really* bad guys are, like Hitler and Pol Pot, not him. In his traditional epic conception, Tony is vindicated in his own mind when he himself metes out justice, almost as a god[father], certainly as judge, jury, and executioner. Melfi, on the other hand, strives to acquaint Tony with "the psychology of the novel's heroes" (60), as Lukacs would say. Her discourse strips Tony of his power and makes him a seeker after his own truth, quite a reduction in rank for an epic hero and one that he sees as unmanning him, particularly when he already feels threatened just by talking about it. During their therapy sessions, they speak at cross purposes. On a more literary plane, Tony basically explains the world of epic heroism to Melfi, while she explains to him the proper psychological role of the hero in a modernist novel. The two discourses are incompatible and clash on a fault line of intent as well as genre. The epic itself "inadvertently" becomes the novelistic, and both are worked through in a family television melodrama, one of the most hybridized popular forms in postmodernism.

Beyond the obvious languages of sex-as-science and family romance that punctuate psychoanalysis, the gulf that separates Tony and Melfi in their dialogue on the morality of his role can also be seen in a class analysis of their sessions. Tony always dresses informally; for him, a golf shirt is work attire. Watching him shuffle heavily around his house in underwear and an oversized bathrobe makes us remember how formal and dignified the Corleone family appeared in the *Godfather* films. (Only Sonny Corleone with his undershirt and suspenders combination, hair-trigger temper, obscene language, and simmering sexuality could audition for the Soprano gang.) On no one's schedule but his own, Tony is a large temporarily domestic animal, padding around between feedings and kills. His negative reaction to analysis is most often a class reaction (I work for my family; I put food on the table; I do what my father did). Bourdieu writes that "there is a popular realism which inclines working people to reduce practices to the reality of their function, to do what they do, and be what they are ('That's the way I am'), without 'kidding themselves' ('That's the way it is')" (*Distinction* 200).[14] The iron-clad tautologies that Tony himself practices make him resist Melfi's attempts to extrapolate and to symbolize, to draw out lines of intent—in short to make him an elite reader of his own text. As Barthes writes of tautology,

Tony demands "the indignant 'representation' of the *rights* [italics Barthes] of reality over and above language," a refuge behind "the argument of authority" (*Mythologies* 152–53). In this regard Tony practices a great mistrust of therapy with which a popular audience can identify, especially in an era when traditional psychiatric therapy is questioned by a number of insurgent discourses, especially feminist ones, and when drugs buttress or supplant talking cures; indeed, Tony's dosage of Prozac and Xanax becomes a plot device. *The Sopranos* wants to have it all ways, to portray the contemporary reliance on mood-suppressing drugs and yet retain the romance of the analyst-analysand and allow Tony to voice the general mass mistrust of analysis. Despite Melfi's work with him, Tony continues to practice what Bourdieu calls "the practical materialism which inclines [him] to censor the expression of feelings or to direct emotion into violence or oaths" (199), a definition of maleness that succinctly describes bottom-line Soprano family conduct in business and in mob narrative.

Every Freudian analysis is an attempt at an elite literary reading, and Jennifer Melfi is Tony's critical guide, bringing him before the bar of his own history. Melfi wants to instruct Tony in how to make his life mean something other than what he thinks it means. She introduces him to allegory and symbolism and tries to push him beyond "I am what I am" and "it is is what it is." She is nothing less than the woman (mother, lover, wife, "Betsy fucking Ross") who will nurture, absolve, and enlighten him, so he may be released from the prison house of depression and dread, a fairy tale from the Freudian century with lady analyst as heroic knight. She stays the course of his therapy, fascinated, appalled, compelled to listen but reeling, as is the audience. His revelations are the stuff of her professional life, but they are extreme; his fury and impact buckle her white magic. Tony has contaminated her sense of professionalism and sharpened her sense of justice. She's finally face-to-face with what she has to tease out in more muted form with other patients, what could only be called the "problem of evil." Violence enters Melfi's personal life in *The Soprano*'s third season when she is brutally raped in a parking garage. The police botch the investigation, and Chase toys with the audience's umbrage and anticipation: when will Tony learn of the outrage and take vengeance since he believes "degenerate bastards that molest" "deserve hell"? However, Melfi refuses to inform him. Her dramatic and wordless decision underscores her principled dismay at his brutality, which she courageously will not allow to be invoked on her behalf, no matter how angry and violated she feels. She will not become part of the cycle.

The questions finally posed by Melfi's prolonged exposure to Tony Soprano are: if she is beginning to crack under the enervating strain of Tony's life and rationale and her inability to change either, what does this say about audience exposure to Tony and all the other Tonys? What are

Tony's conclusions about his life in analysis? If Melfi is able to "help" Tony through therapy, will she inevitably weaken him in his role to the point that his life will be in danger: to combat his evil, will she get him killed?[15] Finally, what is Chase's melodrama telling us about *our* identification with Tony as it orchestrates these questions? Is *The Sopranos* a serious moral investigation of mob narrative, or is that investigation only another of its strands to be pasted into postmodern collage—and how might we know the difference?

In Carm's Way: Carmela Soprano and Religion as Recovery Narrative

Just as Melfi fervently practices the twentieth-century religion of psychoanalysis, Carmela Soprano invokes the more traditional Catholic faith. Carmela is filled with dread at the life the family has chosen and hopes to make Tony, in her words, "true" to himself and to her. Taken together, Melfi and Carm practice on Tony two healing discourses of the spirit, the twentieth century's scientific talking cure and the traditional Christian religious discourse of repentance and absolution. They reinstitute both female sympathy and sentimental extension of grace to him, or at least the "normality" that Fisher prizes as sentiment's conferral on characters. Even though Tony spends no time in church except once to point out to his daughter, Meadow, that his grandfather, a stone mason, helped build it, Carmela tries to make up for his lapses and sins, since to her, her souls and those of her children hang in the balance.[16] Chase in *The Sopranos* clearly wants to restore a religious dimension to the dread expressed by a mob family member and fittingly chooses Carmela to express that dread. It's quite radical to find a genuinely religious character on a prime-time television program who is not in the clergy or who is not some sort of fantasy figure, such as characters in *Touched by an Angel*, or much more trendily expressing belief, disbelief, and interest in the "paranormal," in series from The *X-Files* to *Buffy the Vampire Slayer*. If Jennifer Melfi ethnicizes and feminizes psychiatry, Carmela Soprano retains the religious vision for a wife and mother in realism. Together these two sopranos sing to and for Tony, as they try to bring him out of his narcissistic and depressed male uniqueness and into the flow of a relational existence, postmodern culture's feminine desideratum for a reformed male.

Episode nine of *The Sopranos'* second season contains the long dialogue between Tony and Melfi about who deserves to go to hell and Tony's justification of mob life, as well as several scenes in which characters seek to learn their relation to sin and evil. *The Sopranos* hardly ever moralizes or snickers, and when it does, the narrative generally bites back. In the tradition of TV melodrama's balance, it gets out the conflicting points of view. Christopher is in intensive care after stopping several bullets and believes he's been to hell and returned to tell the tale. Hell turns out to be an Irish bar called the "Emerald Piper" where it's always St. Patrick's Day, and Christopher is playing dice with Roman soldiers and two Irish guys, and the Irish always win. Every night at midnight, Christopher's murdered father "gets whacked" again, and "it's painful," Christopher moans to Tony, as he asks for an increased morphine drip. He then tells Tony and Paulie that he has messages for them from guys they'd murdered. Paulie listens nervously and actually consults a psychic on his chances of staying out of hell and his prostitute girlfriend weighs in on predestination as well. Tony is moved to give his version of who belongs in hell to Melfi (see pages 266–67). However, he's generally exasperated by Christopher's visions. He prefers a more utilitarian approach to religion. Earlier, he had laid down the parental theological law to Anthony Jr.'s "Nitch"-inspired view that "God is dead" by telling him that "even if God is dead, you're going to kiss his ass." *The Sopranos* is never too haughty to opt for such telling one-liners. The verbal sparring at home is vintage television family banter, light years from *omerta* or any patriarchal hierarchy. *The Sopranos* also has the confidence that Christopher's trip to hell and back will be truly comic as well as very revealing for all the murdering men in their scuffling with conscience. Mixed modes rule yet again in the postmodern mob narrative.

When Carmela reaches the hospital to visit Christopher, her first reaction is to find an empty room in which to pray:

> Gentle and merciful lord Jesus. I want to speak to you now with an open heart, an honest heart. Take my sins and the sins of my family into your merciful heart. We have chosen this life in full awareness of the consequences of our sins. I ask you humbly to spare him and if it is your will to spare him, deliver him from blindness and grant him vision and through this vision may he see your love and gain the strength to carry on in service to your mercy.

Flushed with her prayers, Carmela goes to Christopher's room after the men leave to tell him of her hopes for him. Tony has given her a deeply altered version of Christopher's big journey, telling her that he had seen angels in heaven, but Christopher immediately corrects the vision. Although actress Edie Falco's deft facial expressions reveal Carmela's concern as she absorbs Christopher's story of his trip to hell, she does not swerve from her course. Without missing a beat, she corrects her vision of heaven to include his hell trip and still prays for his salvation; she's used to incorporating extremity into her prayers. Chase counters Carmela's overtures to Christopher with the facts but does not overturn either. Her sincere attempt to reach out with traditional balm and comfort becomes another competing discourse in the Soprano dialogues on good and evil. Neither her view nor Christopher's comic rendition of hell by an Italian American mob kid and murderer takes precedence as a narrative strand, forcing the popular audience to live this contradiction as she does.

Carmela is the mistress of a huge suburban house. Although she keeps refrigerator and freezer filled with baked Italian treats for when the family wanders in from school or predatory acts and skulduggery, their shiny home is void of ethnic ensemble warmth or closeness. The internal distances in the house are huge and empty, accentuated by the way Chase typically shoots the home scenes in long focus. The family is forever walking down stairways and entering doors into large brightly lit rooms dominated by a long sterile kitchen counter or a huge TV set or king-size bed. Food or conversation is doled out in raids on the fridge late at night or in midday when Tony finally wakes up. Tony and A. J. meet at the TV set or looking for food. The Sopranos are often at home together, but vast spaces separate them. To counter her loneliness, Carmela often reaches out to a young priest, but he is as much a movie buff and a childlike flirt as he is a dispenser of spiritual comfort. When Tony takes Meadow on a college tour in New England, Father Phil shows up late on a rainy night at the Soprano house for a half parish visit and half seduction. Even though Carmela is flu-ridden, she comes to the door in her bathrobe and slippers and offers him the baked ziti in the freezer in familiar ethnic ritual. He then asks about Tony and the kids, and they settle in to watch *The Remains of the Day*, a favorite film of hers. When the film reaches the unmasking of Stevens the butler as a reader of popular romances, he is literally backed against the wall, shielding himself with his novel from an advancing Miss Kenton, who wishes to break through his defenses and achieve some intimacy; his cold, bright eyes keep her away as if he is a hunted animal. The absolute lack of communication between them and Miss Kenton's agonizing unrequited love is too much for Carmela. She says, "Father, turn it off. I can't handle it. There's so much in me." Rather than be pulled into some transgressive situation at this point, she requests a confession, right there on the living room couch. They turn their backs to one another, and she begins:

> I haven't confessed in twenty years. I have forsaken what is right for what is easy, allowing what I know is evil in my house. I wanted money in my hands, I'm so ashamed. My husband, I think he has committed horrible acts. . . . It's just a matter of time before God compensates me for my sins. . . . But I still love him. I still believe he can be a good man.

Carmela in effect confesses for the audience as well and expresses the viewers' shared hopes that Tony can be redeemed. The viewpoint most strongly expressed is the sentimental one of Christian forgiveness cloaked in the more contemporary "forgive thyself" of analysis. Both discourses are articulated by the women who together hold Tony's moral balance (and that of the audience) in their hands. Jennifer Melfi provides the most trenchant questioning of Tony Soprano from behind the authority of psychiatric categories, but Carmela assumes the more traditional woman's role, familiar from *The Godfather*, of praying for souls.

However, Chase provides Carmela with the power to counter Tony's actions in other ways beyond prayer. Carmela is a tough in-fighter when she must be. When she finds out about Melfi, that Tony's seeing a *female* therapist, she tells him about her movie night with Father Phil and calls it "just therapy." She's also not a Pollyanna, not immune from the coercive life the Soprano crime family lives. When she wants to make sure that her daughter, Meadow, is accepted at Georgetown, she bakes her best pasta dish, takes it to a lady lawyer acquaintance, and never waivers in her sweet steely determination to get the message across: that a letter of recommendation would make Carmela, a Soprano after all, very happy.[17] She almost has an affair with a home contractor who is scared off by Tony's reputation. When Tony explains he's been talking his Russian girlfriend out of suicide, Carmela informs him that she's going to take a three-week trip to Rome and perhaps meet "the Holy Father," and Tony will have to drive A. J. to the dentist and find a tennis clinic for Meadow "cause if I have to do it, I may just commit suicide." She insists that Tony get a vasectomy if he continues to whore around; she won't accept the idea of contracting disease or of bastard children. At the end of episode nine, having prayed for Christopher and come almost to the end of her tolerance for Tony's lies and violence, she yet attempts to bind them together by taking him into their bed and whispering that she wants another child; they sink down together for the first time in twenty-two episodes over two seasons! The last shot cuts away to a pair of small carved angels on the nightstand by the bed with their eyes uplifted. Carm's way finally carries a day. Such a provisional happy ending is rare in *The Sopranos* but points to how many of the episodes end with Tony safe in the home, often befuddled or lonely, away from his "business."

Thus psychiatry and religion are asked to rehabilitate Tony Soprano in what is surely a male recovery narrative for our time. Tony asks Melfi if what he does and is has any meaning (an existential and individual quest), while Carmela asks him to be "true" to her and to his children (a social role in the life-world of a marriage and family).[18] Women in *The Sopranos* powerfully counter the reigning ethos of the mob family and demand that the men acknowledge their natures and try to change, what the contemporary American culture says in general to men and another example of a popular narrative speaking in code and working through a cultural syndrome in the affirmative. *The Godfather*, which always seems in need of reflection and analysis by its characters or authorial voice never doubted its own motives, values, or ability of its men to act. In contrast, *The Sopranos* brings the mob narrative to a pitch of contemporary bourgeois maturity and postmodern comedy of manners with Tony's resulting indecision and doubt. Melfi and Carmela are no mere spokeswomen and mouthpieces, either. They often reverse roles as increasingly, Melfi plumbs the nature of evil, while Carm lauds therapy; in fact, she feels initially (before learning Melfi's identity) that Tony is being very brave. She's elated that he embarks on a course to help himself.

Chase can create his episodes in the certainty that male authority is provisionally under severe erasure in 1999–2001, that any male action may be interpreted as violent, abusive, and isolated. This current popular narrative moral plot line clashes with another, more traditional one, what *The Sopranos* provides in the best tradition of mob narrative, the still operating sense of unreconstructed male action—direct, nonreflective, closed to wives and family. Men giving off that whiff of danger in their very presence. Men not reconstructed by new discourses or "authentic" to themselves but menacing and visceral.[19] The complex satisfaction for the viewer of *The Sopranos* is where the most excessive clashes occur between the overcoded male or what is left of him and the sopranos, Melfi and Carmela, who sing of balm, understanding, and the acceptance of the sorrow that underlies Tony's rage and depression. Tony mourns for what he has lost or perhaps never had, a youthful integrity of "epicness" without reflection, to be coextensive with one's physical self and desires; these desires he cloaks in ethnic identity. Psychiatry and religion would draw Tony away from this nostalgia to perfect another Utopian and reflective male self for the future; a naive American therapeutic optimism would reign there. Such a persona is incompatible with the strong father and boss of mob narrative we have come to know and accounts for the fierce oxymoronic and dramatic tension that Chase is able to sustain in *The Sopranos* and which creates a schism in Tony's psyche with no reconciliation in sight.

Livia Soprano

Tony's mother, Livia Soprano, is the most powerful figure in Tony's life. She looms over his childhood as a furious and loveless source of potential violence and manipulation. She reigns over his adulthood as a bitter older woman and widow who mightily resents both her decreased authority after the death of her husband, "Johnny Boy" Soprano, and the onslaught of old age. Tony says she "is dead" to him; her daughter, Janice, calls her "a complete narcissist"; her granddaughter, Meadow, in more contemporary jargon says that "Gramma is into negativity." Dr. Melfi suggests that in the Soprano family, "the whole idea of motherhood is up for debate" (*Sopranos* 2, 7]. Livia is also the series' hardest character to gauge. She alternately appears shrewd and dangerous and then dissolves into incipient senility; the changes often appear strategic but just as often out of her control. And yet the viewer never knows. Janice brings up the children's painful childhood, and Livia says, "You don't know the kind of man your father was. It would kill him to see me now" (*Sopranos* 2, 2). In two quick sentences, Livia (played by the late Nancy Marchand) reveals all her inscrutability. Marchand reads the first sentence ("You don't know) ominously as in "your father would have had the power to slap you down for what you say"; she follows it up with "It would kill him" read in a wail of utter self-pity and weakness. Then she pronounces a double curse on her daughter: "[S]ome day I hope you have children of your own and they treat you like this."

During analysis, Melfi encourages Tony to think back to childhood, to see if he can recall his mother literally threatening his life. He easily remembers several episodes. One has young mother Livia threatening little Tony, "You're driving me crazy. I could stick this fork in your eye."[20] Another shows Johnny Boy Soprano wanting to move the family west to Reno, so he can get a stake in gambling opportunities there, but Livia shouts him down, her children within earshot: "I'd rather smother them with a pillow than take them to Nevada." Johnny Boy's retort, "[A]lways with the drama!" signifies the fact that Livia's powerful histrionics were always in the melodramatic mode. Tony had good family coaching in melodrama, and in the final episode of *The Sopranos'* first season, viewers were treated to the extraordinary sight of Tony rushing to the hospital to confront Livia after learning that she had set him up to be "hit," only to find her being wheeled into intensive care for a possible stroke. He almost leaps onto her gurney, getting in her face, eyes wild as he demands, "[D]id you have me whacked?" Livia's eyes too get wilder, bigger, as horrified nurses and orderlies try to pull son off mother. A thin smile crosses Livia's face as she disappears through a hospital door, but it's unclear whether her smile is one of terror, triumph, or bewilderment. With Livia Soprano, Chase has both restored the power of the Italian American mother and cruelly darkened her portrait. The Italian American mother was an absent center of power in *The Godfather*, where her role was usurped by Don Corleone. Chase gestures toward Puzo's admission that he modeled the Don on his own mother when Tony ruefully acknowledges to Livia after she has stonewalled him once again, "Ma, if you'd been born after those feminists, you'd be the real gangster" (*Sopranos* 1, 7).

Indeed, what Chase has done is create in Livia all the malevolence and maternal refusal to be displaced from the center of her son's life that Lucia Santa exhibited toward Gino in *The Fortunate Pilgrim* without giving Livia any of Puzo's sympathy and veneration for that fierce love.[21] In *The Fortunate Pilgrim*, Lucia Santa asked Octavia, "Who should be [Gino's] boss if not his mother? . . . What will happen to him when he finds out what life is, how hard it is? He expects too much, he enjoys life too much" (223) and, even more tellingly, "[H]e was her enemy as his father before him . . . he treated her as a stranger, he never respected her commands. He injured her and the family name" (226). Finally, Lucia Santa cried "tears so full of gall that they could only have sprung from a well of anger, not grief" (223).

Livia Soprano turns this powerful Italian American mother's courage rancid since she has no love to temper her bitterness. It's bad enough that Livia has lost her aura of power with the death of her husband, but she can't even gain any pathetic capital in her fall from mob boss's clearly miserable wife to unloveable, unloving mother. Livia is jealous of her son and his strong wife, and she's threatened by the idea Tony's disclosing to a psychiatrist all her shortcomings as a mother. Livia takes Puzo's cry about his mother ("Behold how she was wronged!") and twists it to: Behold how I've been wronged by everyone!

Puzo concludes *The Fortunate Pilgrim* by moving Lucia Santa to a new home on Long Island, where the whole family lives in a *Raisin in the Sun* migration. In contrast, Chase has Livia Soprano ensconced in a fancy retirement home, raging in impotent fury as a senior citizen about to be warehoused toward death. Nothing any longer belongs to Livia that would allow her to work her will or feel special. Only the link with her brother-in-law, Junior, from her own generation keeps her pride and memories alive, and together they fan the fire of their mutual resentment of Tony's presumptions to be an adult and boss of the Soprano family. She feels she has lost her family—something Mama Corleone told Michael was impossible. Tony feels the terror that Santa Lucia's son, Gino, felt about his mother in *The Fortunate Pilgrim*: that he would forever have to "chain himself in the known, lightless world he had been born in" (265), a vision of womblike imprisonment in the Italian American life-world.

The attachment of an Italian son to his mother can be impossibly strong, an emotionally intense but not destructive bond (as in Greek tragedy) and most often represented through comedy. Many Italian men live well into their twenties and thirties still being cared for by mothers who never truly let them go.[22] However, this cultural characteristic becomes grotesque antinurture in a battle to the death between Tony and Livia, especially after Johnny Boy dies and Tony tentatively takes his place as head of the Soprano Family. No small gesture of Tony's is ever appreciated by Livia. When he brings her favorite cookies to the senior citizen home, she refuses to eat them, telling him "to leave some out for the lunatics." When she comes to a Soprano family barbecue, she sniffs the air and makes a face, saying, "You're cooking with mesquite. It ruins the taste." Her dinner table conversation is peppered with references to family atrocities, particularly mothers killing their babies. When A. J. visits his grandmother and says he's depressed, she replies that "the world is a jungle . . . people let you down. In the end you die in your own arms. It's all a big nothing. What makes you think you're so special?" (2, 7). *The Sopranos* gives Livia no space or sympathy. She has no protection from her accusing son and no influence over him, and that double negation drives her toward madness and violence, even as age and illness close the circle of darkness.[23]

Every psychoanalysis not only picks up on the role in which the patient casts his mother but, in effect, becomes the patient's new gestation period in which he spends a period of time learning and trying out new feelings, to be reborn into his own narrative. Thus, Tony's sessions with Melfi are not only about the mother-son relationship but are intended to replace that relationship with a stronger one. That Livia may be replaced or doubled by Melfi in the dynamics with Tony is exemplified by her becoming more and more impatient with him in their sessions, by her drinking and becoming scattered, in effect, by her repeatedly asking him the question Livia asks of the men in her family: "[W]hat makes you so special"?

In essence, Tony confesses to one woman (Melfi) the sins of another woman (his mother, Livia), while keeping the transaction essentially quiet from a third woman (his wife, Carmela). He wants the sympathy, pity, and ego support he should have received from his mother and gets it on a weekly basis from Melfi. That he also frequents his Russian girlfriend with "appointments" and that he puts Melfi on the run from his enemies, forcing her to ply her profession out of a motel, adds to the illicit quality of her role and the sense that the extension of Tony's fixation with his mother is reshaping all the roles of the women in his life as they mutate into his mother. Even his daughter, Meadow, his most clear-eyed supporter, is in thrall to Livia. In the sudden ending of the third episode in year two, Tony goes to check on his mother's empty house (his childhood home). He peeks in the window and sees Meadow. Nights before she and her teenage friends made a mess carousing there without permission, and now, bandanna on her head, Meadow is on her knees, sobbing, nauseous, almost manically scrubbing the floor clean in an obeisance and penance that her father never approaches and cannot understand; it's between grandmother and grandaughter, and Tony is excluded; he backs away in confused silence and never mentions that he saw her.

Tony's older sister, Janice, is another tormented female Soprano. She suddenly reappears in the family's life after two decades away. A recycled new ager/hippie with the commune name *Parvati Wasatch*, she's also a manipulator like her mother with a sharp eye for playing off one family member against the other in order to get a stake. When she takes up with Richie Aprile, a recently released ex-convict, the brother of Tony's former boss and a thorn in Tony's side, the viewer wonders if Janice, vital in middle age, has arrived to become a center of power equal to her mother and a real challenger to Tony. However, that speculation ends in one of The Sopranos' most arbitrary and forced plot developments. In an argument that turns violent, Richie slaps Janice's face, and she simply takes out a gun and shoots him dead. By the end of this penultimate episode in year two, Janice is hustled out of town on a bus. Tony is left to mop up after her, cleaning the blood from the same living room Meadow had compulsively scrubbed, while Christopher and Furio make Richie "disappear" by chopping up his body in a butcher shop. The irony is that Tony himself had just ordered Richie's execution, but, as usual, someone, most often a female Soprano, acts for him. True to her mother's love/hate melodrama with men, Janice wails to an exasperated Tony of Richie, "I loved him so."[24]

Janice's role points to a real problem for women in The Sopranos. None has any claim to a network of other women. Each major female character is a satellite dancing around Tony, telling him his truth. They do not come together to form a "family of sopranos." Carmela has her circle of suburban wife friends, but she has no intimates. She is essentially alone, shunned by her daughter and resented by her mother-in-law, whom she most often fights to a draw; she fears and mistrusts Melfi's presence in Tony's life. Janice is an operator, alone in Richie's volatile orbit until she snaps. Tony and Janice's sister lives near Tony but is seldom seen except to make it clear she is purposely steering clear of their mother. Meadow casts a cold eye on everyone and is willing to cut off friends if they criticize her father. In the final scene of The Sopranos' third season, however, she walks away from her father in disgust, realizing that Tony has ordered the hit on her gangster-wannabe boyfriend, Jackie Aprile, Jr. Christopher's girlfriend, Adrianna, has identified Carmela as her role model, but they seldom see each other, and she has no one her own age. Melfi acts as a *deus ex machina*, commenting on Tony's family members.

Melodrama always needs a strong enemy or antagonist, and yet in its sympathetic need for audience identification it also needs strong heroes and heroines. In The Sopranos, Livia is the villain, while Melfi and Carmela are the heroic protectors and defenders of Tony's flame. No father confers succession on Tony, and he suffers the loss of his mother with almost Rousseauistic intensity. Tony becomes a male hysteric, fainting, suffering shortness of breath, and feeling dread in a bid for love and the pathos that should have surrounded the orderly separation of the son from the maternal.[25] In searching for that maternal imaginary through Melfi and analysis, Tony also seeks it from the audience as does the melodramatic form. Viewers mother Tony and excoriate Livia, while the rest of Tony's women—wife, shrink, mistress, sister, daughter—move to fill Livia's roles. Never before has a mob boss been in a position or need to seek so much mothering from female characters and an audience. No godfather in sight to hold it all together for Tony, nor is he capable of becoming one.[26]

The Form of Television Melodrama: HBO as Home

Tony Soprano's crisis is always personal, which deflects much worry about his crimes in collective society. The farther away from his criminal conduct and social roles as an active member of society or participant in an American economy, the better the melodrama likes it. Such a reversal of audience scrutiny from the material crimes of the mob boss toward his intimate relations stamps Tony as always self-involved. However, it's instructive to look briefly at his economic status. Tony is light years away from the status of a Corleone. It's easy to see Tony as somewhat of a struggling businessman, albeit one with rolls of cash tucked in his shirt. Tony and the Soprano crime family nibble on the edges of a millennial boom economy that has "legitimately" passed them by making others instant millionaires and billionaires through a 1990's stock market boom and total emphasis on technology. In fact, Tony's "businesses" are anti-quated and piecemeal: protection, auto theft rings, hijacking truckloads of merchandise (to poke through the contents), scams selling bogus phone calling cards to lonely immigrants, attempts to establish backroom gam-bling as an "executive" card game. Tony's into a little bit of everything but has labor and management worries everywhere.[27] His new recruits are moronically eager, his most trusted associate has been turned by the FBI. He's still an underboss with no sense of Corleone grandness. Tony attends no major mob conventions to carve up the U.S. territory but instead is usually pulling up to dump sites, loading docks, and forlorn Meadowland vistas in his SUV, trying to ride herd on his impulsive young lieutenants and collect the various monies due to him out of fear. He's not letting Uncle Junior and his wing of the family "earn" as Jackie Aprile had done before his death. He suppresses incursions from other racial and ethnic groups, as well as soundings from the postmodern media and technology. Christopher wants to be a "player" in cinema and market or create "himself." Tony sets him up with a phony license in fronting a small brokerage office, where "brokerage" connotes broken bones of young traders if the Webistics stock doesn't get sold. Tony's view that "things are trending downward" and that he's "coming in at the end" (1, 1) is confirmed. The Sopranos are more of a danger to their immediate family and each other than they are a cancer on American society; they toil in an unhealthy and dangerous occupation that is fad-ing, such as coal mining. Tony's problems become more those of a midcareer executive facing obsolescence.

The Soprano family is living out Cawelti's obervation that the "es-sential social-psychological dynamic of social melodrama is one of con-tinually integrating new social circumstances to the developing middle class sense of social value" (46). The question becomes then: what narra-tives *cannot* be absorbed by the American middle class if the mob boss becomes just another tired, befuddled guy driving home to suburbia every evening? Does murder become just another "social circumstance" the audience will abide if other resemblances to themselves are strong enough? If Tony drives an SUV and commutes to work with a cell phone stuck to his ear and lives in a big suburban house and worries about his employees and a dying occupation and cheers for his daughter playing soccer, does he become one of us only? Or is he still a murdering mob boss? It is clear from the first three seasons that one thrust of *The Sopranos* is not to put Tony in prison but to rehabilitate him, help him "put it all behind him": the rage, the horrible mother, the enervating depression, his killing, his evil ways. Melodrama's Utopian hope and end point is always to elevate its hero to this virtuous state, but given *The Sopranos'* serial form and its great success, Tony's rebirth is not likely to occur any time soon.

What is so central to *The Sopranos* is what has always been at the core of melodrama: home. Home is where Tony arrives at the beginning of each episode. The show is very centered on region, and no one has captured the much-maligned New Jersey on film like *The Sopranos*. Over the opening credits, Tony emerges from the Lincoln Tunnel into Jersey, passes over the Garden State Parkway and the New Jersey Turnpike, goes by smaller row houses, weedy lots, refineries, factories, and small businesses; the roads become smaller, the houses, sleeker and farther apart. Finally the last stretch takes him down a tree-lined road, and he pulls up in his own driveway in North Caldwell, alighting from the car with a final thrice-repeated "got yourself a gun" hammering on the soundtrack. Dad is home. Tony's drive also simulates the long march (but short distance) earlier immigrants took from the now grim, older factory towns in a new migration to a suburban frontier; Philip Roth had the dynamic right decades ago in *Goodbye, Columbus* (1959) when his Neil Klugman thinks that "it would not take an eagle to carry me up those lousy one hundred and eighty feet that make summer nights so much cooler in Short Hills than they are in Newark" (10). The Soprano crime family still functions in the inner older Jersey cities; the Soprano nuclear family nestles in an upper-middle-class suburb. The series has yet to invade one turf with the other (except for a periodic FBI search warrant visit), to suggest as boldly as Puzo and Coppola did in *Godfather II* that Michael Corleone's family fortress on Lake Tahoe could be invaded by his business "life" and that his bedroom could be the site of an assassination attempt, the family place, as Michael rages at his lieutenants, "where my wife sleeps!" and then softly, in still steely tones, "where my children come and play with their toys."

To scale a putative godfather down to the small screen, Chase provides Tony with echoes of American television fathers from landmark TV programs. Tony Soprano has the discontents, strong opinions, and generally conservative leanings of an Archie Bunker in *All in the Family*, which began with a nostalgic "Those Were the Days" screeched by Edith Bunker and sung by Archie as the camera rolled through a block of modest homes on an older Queens street before pulling up in front of Archie's house, where he is indubitably "at home" in his famous battered chair. *The Simpsons'* opening features the whole family racing home from different places as Homer leaves the nuclear power plant and careens through Springfield's environs before landing plopped down in front of the TV with Marge and his brood, the credits for the program starting so fast that it seems they're watching *The Simpsons*.[28] In reversing the opening home image, the 1970s most honored and least ironic TV family melodrama, *The Waltons*, ended in a large country house, the many family members talking between the rooms, lovingly saying "goodnight" as the lights went out one by one, including those of family chronicler "John Boy" Walton.[29] The mother and father of *The Waltons* were Olivia and John, a very close fit to Livia and "Johnny Boy" Soprano in perhaps a skewed homage by Chase.[30] Without undertaking a close analysis of Tony Soprano set against these famous TV fathers, it's certain that Chase places him in a long line and wide range of very referential figures that an audience knows and appreciates—blustery, opinionated, comic, serious, conservative, liberal, interested in children, wanting to do the right things, occasionally absurd, always loved by the family. The economic function of these fathers varies. Archie's on the loading dock, Homer's in the nuclear power plant, John Walton's in his backyard lumber business, and Tony is in "Waste Management" (Chase's pun).[31]

The fact that *The Sopranos* is on HBO allows speculation about the class dynamics of the Soprano family's televised representation and also speaks to both melodrama and cable television's altering of TV viewing patterns and their analogies to movie going. Home Box Office is the most exclusive American cable television service and reaches only about one-quarter of American homes available to network broadcasts (Carter "HBO Wants to Make Sure You Notice" 97). Since it is not included in "basic" cable packages, HBO and its lauded original series are promoted and screened to a more elite audience, viwers who can pay for cable and also pay for an extra premium cable service. HBO viewers can choose from a range of programs that allow for more artistic freedom than is usually granted series television, in terms of both content and style: no checks on obscene language or presentation of sex, no commercial breaks, and the chance to run shows consecutively for, in the case of *The Sopranos*, thirteen weeks with no breaks for reruns or waiting for network "sweeps" periods. *The Sopranos* also takes on the form of the great nineteenth-century melodramas of writers such as Charles Dickens. A new chapter appears in the serial every week, with action ranging over many facets of the characters' lives without picking up the narrative thread exactly where the last chapter dropped it (every Dickens reader has the experience of going deeply into one of his characters for fifty pages at the outset of a majestic melodrama such as *Bleak House* and then not having that character reappear in the textured and cross-referenced plot until around page 400). *The Sopranos* moves confidently in the guise of such a long, unfolding Victorian novel. If you missed the flashback scene of Tony's youth with his young parents (1, 7), then you've missed a piece of his puzzle. Yet HBO, because of the popularity of the series, runs each Sopranos episode "in season" like a first-run movie, with a first presentation of a new episode on Sunday night and the repeats of the same episode in staggered hours on three or four other nights during that week. You may "go to" *The Sopranos* in your home on the evening of your choice and find it still running within a given week. Then this serial experience is repeated the following week. Finally HBO then "reruns" the entire thirteen-week cycle of shows to prepare viewers for a new cycle, becoming in effect, a second-run movie house. HBO operates as a theater chain with different show times, but its viewing is in the private control of the home, which would include taping the show for rebroadcast at the "leisure" of the viewers. Cassette and disk copies of *The Sopranos* are now available at video rental stores as well.

One prominent feature of the Soprano home is a large TV screen, where A. J. plays video games or Tony watches the History Channel on cable. Thus, we may surmise Tony gets HBO; *The Sopranos* is about the home, broadcast by Home Box Office to the home, and Tony is very much in the home as is the television set itself, an intimate part of the domestic decor of the American family dwelling, likely to be speaking at all hours, even when no one is listening, the background noise and companion to American family life. As many critics have noted, the experience of viewing films is fundamentally different from viewing television, on the level of image projection and visual response all the way up to and including the phenomenological occasion that each viewing experience suggests. Films are seen in large, darkened theaters, where the projection of an image comes frame by frame from behind the viewer toward a brightened screen in front. The audience sits scattered in anonymity, having paid for the experience of "going to" the film. The film is watched consecutively without a break. The figures on the screen are enormous in scale in comparison with the filmgoer's body. Television is far more intimate and domesticated within the home. Barthes calls television the very "opposite experience" of the cinema: "the space is familiar, organized by furniture and familiar objects, tamed. Television condemns us to the family whose household utensil it has become" (Allen 187–188). The television set, which may be lodged in the middle of many machines in a home "entertainment system," projects pictures out at the viewer, who most often is in its light instead of a cinema's darkness and may be on the move or talking, eating, cooking, having sex, walking in and out of the room, channel surfing, hitting the mute button, watching a cassette on the VCR, and so on.

Television also moves episode by episode in its regularly scheduled programs in the pattern of the everyday, which suggests family and work structures in a stable core behavior, against which almost any other behavior looks abnormal and must be defined against the normative and absorbed by it (Ellis 158). Television generally regards the world from isolated viewpoints (166), which, when added to TV production budgets that are much smaller than those of cinema on the whole, combine to make familiar repeated interior spaces the norm for series. Such stability aids what Mimi White calls television's "regulated latitude of ideological positions" (Allen, 162–63), its even-handedness in balancing viewpoints even within family disputes in an attempt not so much to disclose new problems or social formations but to work through the known in the guise of a simulated range of event and reflection. Thus *The Sopranos* can posit Tony Soprano as haunted son and murderer but also as loving father and family provider. The series may criticize Tony from Melfi's universalist professional high ground and Carmela's religious faith at the same time it retains Tony's hegemony as a male action hero without unresolvable contradiction or closure. In fact, the family itself is a crucible like television itself, where all is to be admitted and forgiven. Television in the guise of representational balancing might actually make *The Sopranos* look more revolutionary than it is simply by cracking the male monolithic mob discourse, not by a social criticism or by an insurgent feminist critique but by giving the professional woman/maternal substitute (Melfi) and the true woman/wife (Carmela) a chance to question Tony through the melodramatic form itself, that of a domestic serial with its strong links to nighttime TV soap opera such as the more business-oriented *Dallas* and *Falcon Crest,* as well as the more sentimental *thirtysomething.*[32] Lest *The Sopranos* look too domesticated, part of its evenhandedness comes from the equally strong segments of each episode in which Tony and his men act apart from the family and the women in the suburbs to do their violent business and congregate in the back room of Bada Bing to plot against their enemies. In such moments they seem women-free except for the exotic dancers wriggling in the background, until they head for home.

More recent TV workplace shows feature a mixed gendered professional family in, most often, the police station, law office, or hospital, the preferred melodramatic workplace collective family of the 1990s (*ER, Ally McBeal, LA Law, St. Elsewhere, The Practice, Law and Order*) that pretty well cancels out specific domestic space and children and suggests such segmentation to be out of date. *The Sopranos* doggedly retains a separate domestic sphere, which TV seals and penetrates at odd postmodern moments. On the TV show *The Sopranos*, Tony Soprano in his own living room watches himself be arraigned in federal court on the ten o'clock news, another television show. Carmela is utterly bereft as she identifies with the heroine of *Remains of the Day* on her television set. Tony Soprano always drives back to the home that broadcasts *The Sopranos*; presumably he can go inside and watch the show. *The Sopranos* extends the contradictions of *The Godfather* into the problems and lives of those inheritors who absorb the book and movie even as they adapt it, though no one on *The Sopranos* ever mentions Puzo or his book; it's all movie talk and culture.[33]

Finally, HBO itself is a rival gang to network television, seeking to grab its share of the audience from other TV corporate "families." Much of the early reporting about *The Sopranos* concerned its marketing and promotion, the differences between the license granted to Chase and his team set against the networks who passed on the show in development but who now have spinoffs on the air and in production.[34] HBO's goal is to make Sopranos images as widespread as possible, with tie-ins to music CDs from each episode in the series. Soprano fan "megasites" are on the Web, with instant transcripts of the show's dialogue week by week, maps of Tony's route home through northern New Jersey, the actual address and name of Bada Bing, and at the end of both seasons an on-line contest to choose the best line spoken by a *Sopranos* character.[35] Viewers were encouraged to vote on line as to what they thought would happen in the season finale. Besides *The Sopranos* regularly coming into their homes (like mail delivery and waste management), viewers can purchase Sopranos goods and images and participate in their family life as an American media phenomenon and a shopping network. It's too bad beleaguered Tony can't get a piece of the internet action on the Sopranos on *The Sopranos*.

Chase has perfected *The Sopranos* as a TV vehicle, but it wasn't always that easy for him to accept his fate. He wanted movie fame outside the medium, but now after *The Sopranos* success, he asks, "Where am I ever going to go where it's going to be this good again? (Carter "He Engineered a Mob Hit" 90).[36] Television becomes the known enclave, the cross-coded ethnic and media security beyond further exploration into other forms (cinema, cultures). Chase exhibits the classic signs of self-awareness about the cultural capital of the two media, cinema and television, but comes into a better relation to his role than did Puzo, who never accepted *The Godfather* as a substitute for his earlier aspirations in fiction nor film as a substitute for the novel. Chase's cry about what is there for him past *The Sopranos* mirrors his character Christopher's attempt to leave the family (the show?) for the movies, but he reluctantly comes back to the fold, realizing that whatever he's looking for "out there" cannot match what he knows is familiar: Tony's power, promises, and security. Chase creates within TV at a level that few other continuing drama series have ever achieved, while registering the tensions between "the life" of crime (television) posited against his own ambitions in a more elite representation (cinema). While providing the sensational action narrative that the TV audience expects of mob narrative, Chase also gives the audience what it equally expects, melodrama's making vivid all moral choice and family conflict. *His* melodrama laboring in the vineyards of TV with less cultural capital than conferred by cinema seems to be providing a happy ending for him, rather than the one depicted in Puzo's going bad saga with *The Godfather* when he wrote below his gifts. Television has become Chase's home, where he is at home with *The Sopranos*.

Jean Luc Godard famously commented, "Television can project nothing but US" (Allen 193), and so it is that Chris Albrecht, president of HBO "original programming," can say of *The Sopranos* that "these characters are all completely relatable. The only difference between Tony Soprano and me is that he's a mob boss" (*NYT* 7). With such gleeful identification, it's no stretch at all to find Tony Soprano welcomed into American homes with the values that his home espouses as the television family becomes the surrogate for the normative society that mounts the medium and controls the messages. Yet it would be a mistake to consider *The Sopranos* as merely watered down mob narrative. In fact, television sustains the dialogue with the culture that had most lionized *The Godfather* in the first place, seeing in its own power of absorption the ability to domesticate the "other" and be thrilled by the residue of freedom in violence that remains so American. *The Sopranos* also adapts, in Tony's discomfort and desire for grace, a last trace of the culture's residual Puritan insistence on individual responsibility, on the "what's wrong with me" that has driven our centuries-long idealism even as it fuels our narcissism, until we no longer can distinguish one from the other. We still revel in Tony's individual freedom to solve his knottiest business problems swiftly and without remorse. The sentimental hope to reform him to be a better husband, father, and American citizen is countered by the audience's sensational thrill about Tony's identity: stay as you are; solve your own problems; don't become like everyone else. The schizophrenic vote appears to be in: Americans no longer see much difference between Tony Soprano and themselves. In fact, he has become a "representative man," confused by business, wife, children, parents, and self; he has assimilated even in the face of his own protests as an Italian American victim. He is truly troubled by dreams he cannot fathom, but he awakes and slips the yoke of his conscience by wielding the male power that he still possesses on behalf of family. Here is America's most powerful and potentially most dangerous enduring dream.

Conclusion

The Corleones are finally welcomed at long last into middle-class homes in *The Sopranos*. Don Corleone would be astonished at such assimilation in the gaze of "strangers." In the conclusion of *The Sopranos'* second season finale, Chase provides cross-cutting scenes that reference Coppola's great scenes in the *Godfather* films where he juxtaposed religious and ceremonial family and cultural observance with murder. However, Chase scales the ending down to fit Tony's more bourgeois life of crime and his family ties. Coppola had filmed Michael in somber ritual becoming godfather to Carlo Rizzi's child, while the heads of the Five Families are being murdered (*Godfather I*). Then in *Godfather II*, Coppola contrasted the murder of Fanucci by young Vito Corleone (his first killing) with a juxtaposed Feast Day celebration on the streets of Little Italy. Finally in *Godfather III*, a crescendo of cross-references ends the film. During the opera *Cavalleria Rusticana* in Palermo, the new pope is assassinated in Rome, while the Corleone organization takes vengeance against his and their enemies; Michael's daughter, Mary, dies by an assassin's bullet. Chase's final vision in season two juxtaposes Tony's family and business. *The Sopranos* are at home celebrating daughter Meadow's graduation from high school, a suitable secular American ritual. However, earlier that day, Tony participated in the killing of Pussy, his best friend, godfather to his son, and mob informer. As the family poses for multiple pictures of an extended Soprano family, they smile, arms linked in solidarity, looking innocent enough in family snapshots. Nobody asks, as they did at Anthony's confirmation party, "Where's Pussy? Where's the Godfather?"

After each family moment, Chase cuts away to another of Tony's earning businesses: garbage trucks, adult theatres, the brokerage office, calling card scam, high stakes card game. The swift cuts beg the question: which is the real center of the Sopranos' life? The family or the businesses? What has enabled the Soprano family to gather with friends in such secure comfort? Chase cuts to a Hasidic drug dealer whom Tony shakes down and then to Dave, a sporting goods store owner and former friend of Tony, who has gambled away his son's college money in Tony's "executive game," allowing Tony to gobble up his business with no remorse. Now Dave's leaving town, having lost family, business, and respect, a father who has not been as lucky as Tony, who has survived murder attempts and federal indictments because of his menacing aura and connections. Earlier in the day Tony had walked out of Melfi's office in a cocky mood, rejecting her observations: "You're so angry with your mother. But you never say 'boo' about her trying to kill you," and even though your mother "inflicted serious childhood injuries that are still there, your father, the gangster, tough guy—did he protect you kids from this borderline mother?" Tony weeps to her in mock despair, brutally rebuffing her observation of "I pick up sorrow coming from you" with "I had a dream I fucked your brains out right on that desk; you loved it." Tony goes male primitive to counter her intuition. Melfi has rallied from her own fear of Tony to press him ever harder and the "sorrow" she senses is over Pussy's death. She, like Livia, calls him "Anthony," which is what Carmela calls A. J. Tony is last pictured contentedly puffing on a cigar in his own living room in the bosom of his family, the good life all around him, surviving another day of murder and denial with another cycle of dread and depression sure to kick in after the euphoria of triumphing over his enemies. However, the final image of *The Sopranos'* second season is of the waves at the Jersey shore rolling in, presumably over Pussy's body. The melodrama continues.[37]

The domestic melodrama would like to encompass male subjectivity and renegotiate the boundaries that might accommodate it (Torres 92), but the Soprano men don't want to explain themselves within the family space to anyone. They want the sexist divisions to remain. They want their lives and identities back before therapy and *female* subjectivity. They want, in short, to be Corleones, but their ideological position is more tenuous, and Chase and his stable of writers are shrewd enough to realize the dialogized potential of the male yearning and the outcry of the lady Sopranos. We see Tony is in charge, but he is even more desperate and ill despite outlasting his enemies and inquisitors. Pussy is dead. Carmela grows more and more distant as she weighs an affair and foreign travel. Melfi is an alcoholic and losing her vocation. Christopher is shot. Livia is remanded to the senior citizen home. Richie is killed by Janice, who flees town. Junior is slowed by old age and illness, as well as house arrest. Tony's precise fear is that everything is conspiring to push him under, literally and figuratively, a fear like that of Puzo and his Gino Corbo in *The Fortunate Pilgrim* and Merlyn in *Fools Die,* but Chase provides Tony with a relatively free pass into a fourth season with the sopranos of *The Sopranos* still on his case. Yet a large question still remains. How *did* Livia reduce Johnny Soprano from father and godfather to a "squeakin' little gerbil?" The absence of the father-godfather appears ever more glaring as a missing piece in Tony's life. Melfi calls him on this fact in their last session in year two: "[Y]our mommy tried to kill you and you give her airline tickets?" "Why didn't your father, big tough guy, protect you from her?" *Isn't that what "godfathers" do?*

Chase is much more candid than Puzo or Coppola in questioning the premises upon which his characters act and believe. Yet the *Sopranos* revisionism couldn't exist without the narrative tradition laid down by *The Godfather* for them to deconstruct. At the conclusion of *Godfather III,* Michael Corleone tries to scream in primal horror at the assassination of his daughter on the steps of the Palermo opera house, but no sound comes out; he has no more orders to give, no retribution to take, no way to eradicate his loss. He is neither a father nor a god but rather a silent scream of a tragic hero walled in pain. Coppola and Puzo cared not at all about about a female-centered form of melodrama. Opera (a traditional Italian business) and melodrama are wings of the family business, and the bass voice or *basso*—base, too, in its evil notes—is now covered in *The Sopranos* by the siren voices of the sopranos, who sing to Tony about the good and evil in his nature, about moral choice and individual responsibility. It's still all about him, but the women are coming on.

Conclusion

Mario Puzo died in July 1999 after *The Sopranos'* first season on HBO. What he felt about the series, if anything, has not been reported. Although the current of energy in the mob narrative had been out of his control for decades, having passed into the hands of other writers, screenwriters, and directors, Puzo himself never ceased to wonder at that success and provide his own stubbornly realistic view of it. In 1996 at the publication of *The Last Don*, Puzo granted a series of interviews for the first time in twenty years. He had never been interested in the rise of multiethnic literature as a study. Instead, the picture he left us with is that of a retired don of pop fiction, at peace with himself and proud of his achievements. He said that "it might have been preferable to be in the Mafia. I'm glad I'm a writer, but it's hard work. Nobody likes to work hard," and "just because a guy's a murderer, he can't have endearing traits?" (McShane 1). I miss him. I miss his amoral storytelling, his cheerful and complacent nihilism, his lack of pretense, the way he could hide as a shrewd and watchful peasant to invoke "cunning" and "destiny" at one moment and tell a delicious Hollywood or Las Vegas anecdote the next. He never dissembled, never preached, never wrapped himself as anything other than what he was.

At times in these interviews, Puzo gave what appeared to be stock answers he thought his public wanted after years of American opinion hounding him about the ethics of characters in his novels: "I don't like crime. I'm very moralistic against crime. In my work, a significant part of my writing is a commentary on America and its judicial system" (Fleming 1). One searches in vain for this crusading Puzo in his writing, except for Bonasera's lament at the opening of *The Godfather*. He observed that "in both my Mafia books I've wanted to show the parallel between the normal business world and the Mafia" (Fleming 2) and that the Corleones and Clericuzios are more "old-style Sicilian Dons: "[T]hese guys know how to use violence as a business tool" (Fleming 2), ending with "[T]he old guys were men of honor" who had "family values." By 1996, how much could Puzo recall of his original intent, and wasn't he simply doing what writers have always done: take refuge in critic and readers' versions of what they were supposed to be up to? He had long since become his success by writing about *omerta* and in doing so, he made *omerta* itself *audible*, to the point where the language of silence has been fully disclosed in language, where silence has been named.

One continuing thread in Puzo's last interviews is how proud he was of the money he had made. He cheerfully asked, "You know how many copies I sold? I got the money. Nobody said I just sold books. I got money. Statistics, they don't mean anything unless you get the money. . . . To me, money is the focus of everything you see people do (Zaleski 212). In a fundamental way, he returned to what he had stressed in *Fools Die* when Merlyn hides his bribe money for Las Vegas under his manuscripts, when Puzo sent up the *Paris Review* writers' interview format by asking them to go out and ask the real question of a Harold Robbins: how much money did he make? This firm view finally explains mob narrative to a limited degree. Is murder at last finally just a business strategy? The codes and honor at long last all do pertain to the money: that's what people get killed for in mob narrative, so that the "earnings" may continue; that's what Puzo's books are about so that sales may continue. No current American fictional narrative comes closer to speaking this hard fact about financial life in our culture.[1] For better or worse, this is where we are in consuming *Godfather* narrative, accepting it in a melodrama that endlessly goes over the intertextual bonded entities: Money/Violence/Family. Extreme violence and domestic warmth are repeatedly our most powerful visual images in mob narrative and throughout the history of American popular fiction. Before Puzo perfected violence in *The Godfather* as third term in his triad, he had Lucia Santa in *The Fortunate Pilgrim* be more lyrical and dubious about money as substitute for family. She marveled that in America, "[m]oney guarded the lives of your children. . . . Money was a new homeland" (84). The family business did indeed turn out to be murder, the first product in the line, in which various covers of olive oil and "protection" stock the front shelves. When murder becomes a practice rather than a stunning immoral interlude, we have good reason to question writers and directors and their choices, as well as an entire subgenre. Making murder familiar and ordinary is the radical work done by mob narrative, and that will always be frightening and compelling when conveyed with Puzo's storytelling power, Coppola's visual gifts, or the intelligence of Chase in *The Sopranos*.

The Godfather is launched on its fourth decade of reader and audience reception. The American audience that greeted *The Sopranos* in 1999 is very different from that which first encountered *The Godfather* in 1969. Interest in the Corleones has never flagged, and *The Sopranos* has risen to continue to shape mob narrative in one of the most acclaimed programs in television history. *The Godfather* had been written at a time of cultural revolution among the young as well as landmark moments in the Civil Rights movement. Yet it always already had a retro feel: reaffirmation of the patriarchy, uncomplicated Freudian passing of authority from father to son, the subjugation of women, the winning of a "just" war against "them." Such palatable tales within melodrama made *The Godfather* a classic conservative popular text in ways similar to Stowe's Christian millennial recontainment of slavery, which would end in God's Own Good Time, in *Uncle Tom's Cabin* or to Mitchell's apologia for the Old South and for Reconstruction's necessities in *Gone with the Wind*.

Moreover, *The Sopranos* comes to us now at the end of an era when identity politics of all kinds has shaped academic, critical, and national discussions of rights, privilege, and American passage. In 1969, the Corleones seldom called attention to their being Italian. They were aware of themselves as themselves; their solidarity and roots were understood, but Puzo in the novel never privileged that knowledge.[2] His characters were not spokespeople for ethnicity. Michael Corleone gestures toward "the good simple life of well-to-do Americans" (363) in a naive shorthand, a conflated simplicity with riches in the heyday of American postwar optimism where the goal was Main Street joining the country club, the desirable world of frozen 1950s Technicolor movies. Tony Soprano, however, is a firmly ensconced ideologue on identity. He may live in a large suburban home, but he does not worry about becoming "legitimate" or even care what that means. He has enough problems with his work as it is, and he remains adamantly Italian, even though he's more integrated into American society than the Corleones ever were. His dialogues with Dr. Melfi are a study of identity practices, often about gender issues but just as often about ethnic or class issues. He knows instinctively the identity game, how to "convert structural disenfranchisement into a means of claiming cultural and political power" (Farred 631) to rhetorically block Melfi's probes, which threaten to strip him of his tenaciously held identity, one that allows him to function as mob boss. "What do poor Italian immigrants have to do with you?" is Melfi's question from an identity critique. Kay's question to Michael ("What if everybody felt the same way?") was a universalist question from America's civic heart about license and order and was not specifically ethnic or about identity at all.

What the Corleones or Tony Soprano would be without their ethnic or mob identities is a question that postidentity politics can't answer at present. The emphasis on analysis in *The Sopranos* is also an identity search, to have Tony find himself within alternate paradigms of behavior. Freudian analysis is the perfect therapy for an identitarian century since analysands are authorized to find what selves they inhabit or want to inhabit. Such an essentially metacritical errand makes Tony an everyman for both popular and elite audiences: the ethnic son practicing self-scrutiny. Before Tony's analysis, the most a Corleone could envision was the chance to "live the fact that you are who you are can be doubled by the responsibility to be who you are" (Michaels 84): a Sicilian; my father's son; a murderer; a godfather. The Corleones had come to inhabit exactly themselves. Melfi threatens Tony's equivalence, and he has no one else to be.[3] *The Godfather* projected the creation of a powerful identitarian logic, which

The Sopranos is in part dismantling. Within the curve of these three decades (1969–2001) is the construction, flourishing, and reaction against identity politics, all carried out within essentialist and nonessentialist pluralism.

I retain my fascination for the mob narrative form and its compelling window on our national contradictions. First, consider the vehicle: poor unloved popular fiction, besieged by the right for triviality and moral slackness, by the critical center for a lack of formal complexity, and by the left for false consciousness. Only loved by millions and millions for portraying society's major concerns in sensational and sentimental fashion. Popular fiction is often a way of staying behind for the audience, in reworking narratives that never go out of fashion, no matter how literary critics might deem them tedious or simple, to reach back for families that don't seem far removed from clans, loyalties that can't be broken, affiliations of blood. Popular fiction's immediate and opaque power counters technology, evolution, maturation, assimilation, emancipation, global homogenization, complexity, doubt, secularism, and irony—for starters. Puzo appropriated ethnicity without its alternative questioning, without its individuating energy in concert with other forces in a dialogue with America. In the ethnic melodrama of business and family, he found the generic equivalent of a mythical storytelling that retained the immediate power that a more reflective and less sensational elite fiction often trades for complexity.

It can be argued that it's a mistake to ask gifted sensational writers to give us a totally balanced picture of their subject since what they do is touch nerves down deep. In 1996, Puzo himself took refuge in one of the oldest dodges that aesthetics allows, even to its rank and file: "if you're a true novelist, your first duty is to tell a story; if you want to moralize, write non-fiction, philosophy, whatever" (Zaleski 214). So I have essentially followed his advice in criticism (non-fiction), having examined why we want to moralize at times about Puzo, to ask first, who made *him* a moral free agent who could talk about murder with immunity, and then to follow out my intuitions by seeking answers in moral philosophy's debates, particularly in the Humean legacy of a criticism through and of sentiments.

Those sentiments bring me one last time to the bourgeois public sphere in a pluralist society that in its tolerance and flexibility toward all difference appears to have absorbed mob narrative and made it "like" and "same" instead of "other." The Corleones and Sopranos view their own families as worthy of absolute respect but no one else's. They reject one vital half of the American liberal pluralist tolerance of differences, the granting to other groups of essential human value and dignity, thus rejecting any notion of a common enterprise in America. In terms of the illogic of narcissistic and absolute identitarian difference, mob narrative is fundamentally obsessed with and in its isolation. In this extreme sense, the Corleones and Sopranos do not oppose the differential structures of pluralism; rather, they are the conservative expression of it. As American as apple pie.

However, within my harsh labeling of the Corleones and the Sopranos as the very expression of the American business and family life itself, I would say in conclusion that Puzo and his inheritors continue to provide a male dream of anarcho-resistance to regulation and order in a civic society in favor of more traditional and pragmatic allegiances and alliances within identity. America lives with mob narrative the same way it lives with payoffs to "benevolent associations," with unreported income, white collar crime, executive CEO salaries in the millions, union gauging, sweetheart contracts, presidential pardons, lobbying and campaign money infractions, and so on. Mob narrative becomes a more vivid and distant (hence manageable in fantasy) version of the economic facts that Americans face every day.[4]

Mob narrative also provides a psychically licensed space to hunt with the pack. Such a fierce but essentially cautious profile in mob narrative never takes that next step into a shared American optimism or idealism. The Corleones, the Sopranos, and all the other goodfellas take advantage of all American freedoms and tolerance but contribute nothing to the greater commonweal, calling all the rest of us "strangers," but oh, how we long for *their* version of community, for the decisiveness that the dream of threatened violence promises, even as we must work out our accommodations more slowly and maturely in various sublimations; myth and melodrama seems so much more thrilling than realism, when displayed back across our social contracts. The Corleones and Sopranos become potent and powerful white men, physically darker and dangerous, with personal and financial power. In the end, mob narrative must be called a deeply male dream of patriarchy and order, one that cannot account for anything like a full field of human sympathies and still only admits women and children as victims, ornaments, scolds, or justifications for all actions taken on their behalf.

A Cold War America greeted Puzo's novel in 1969, a country waging a long, tense war with an implacable ideological foe as well as fighting a highly visible war in Vietnam, a country looking for peace, détente, survival of family, and values. Over the decades as both the Vietnam War and the Cold Wars dissolved into a sustained national prosperity and technological future, the early audiences for Puzo's novel (1969) and Coppola's first two *Godfather* films (1972–74) are perhaps now at their high point of influence and power in the American media and commodity life, which accounts in part for the obsessive citations and copying of mob language and lore. Will *The Godfather*'s relevance and referentiality be passed on to new generations? A strong counternarrative in American culture is telling us we don't need aggressive patriarchal males anymore, that they are redundant and dangerous to the social organism. In social and cultural terms, as well, *The Godfather* and *The Sopranos* are ways of staying behind in strong residual formations of traditional order, even as the cracks in the edifice are everywhere. A case in point could be the difference between the older Soprano gang members who revere "Al" and "Francis" and do their *Godfather* numbers, while Christopher would rather be Vince Vaughn or Jon Favreau; he knows deep down that he'll never be Michael Corleone, anymore than will Tony Soprano, who has his own suspicions about survival. Vito (Andolini) Corleone, Michael Corleone, Tony Soprano, and Christopher Moltisanti comprise four different generations who work out their American dreams within mob narrative.

Marianna Torgovnick has called for a more responsive "I" and "We" in criticism, to take into account a more supple individual voice as well as a collective voice of responsibility and community, that we need to learn how to do these "voices" in concert and do them better (149).[5] Writing this book has taught me a great deal about this negotiation. A contemporary critique of pluralism's unexamined premises describes it as containing "a tacit supremacism [which] easily coexists with political liberalism, flexibility, inclusion, and generosity; it consists of the quiet expectation that its procedures and standards will be taken as a dispute's rules of arbitration—that its concerns count the most" (Gordon and Newfield 398). Pluralism is no privileged vantage point at long last for it includes not only those with accrued moral capital who can afford the "flexibility," "inclusion," and "generosity" in setting standards for judging *The Godfather*[6] but also a Don Corleone, who precisely simulates such lived procedures when it suits him; to patiently (flexibly) wait out an adversary, to bind (include) someone to him, to come through for his extended family (generosity), to quite simply define all the rules so that the family's concerns come first. He replicates that "tacit supremacism" all the time. In this case, we would have to conclude, as Michael in *Godfather II* tells the corrupted Senator Pat Geary, who would excoriate him, that "we're all part of the same hypocrisy, Senator." Yet such a conclusion need not only be in Michael's rueful truth shared with a villain/victim but also in the fact that the Corleones and their audience (us) are indeed more "like" than "different" in America in so many important ways that speak our yearnings and affiliations, and that fact accounts as much as any for their amazing popularity. Since American culture refuses to confer full civic status or often even a simple humanity to so many, what recourse is there except to come into the American arena arrayed in identity? This is the question that mob narrative continues to model with goodfellas who also pass as fathers and businessmen.

Analyzing how the Corleones became Our Gang in *The Godfather* has moved me to respect the view of the unassimilated and the reasons they remain so, to crack the code of myth and melodrama's understanding of the strains of living the extremities of our postindustrial capitalism and attempting to integrate our long-hallowed views of family at the center of American life. In living with Puzo, I've come to respect his long struggle against famelessness in our culture and his need to overcome it in any way possible. I regret the laziness of a great storyteller but laud his honesty. I sense even more our culture's great fascination with mob narrative and the need to express what it might mean. The writing has taught me also to understand the power of long-standing American rhythms and assumptions about family and business. The project has let me trust my reading instincts in the corners of popular texts and call the material "significant" while learning how to be morally and ethically involved in my critical errand. The question of who has the right to use violence in a society, if anyone, and how that right is sanctioned, censured, and qualified in fiction is food enough for any critic and writing project, and I hope this issue has been illuminated here.

Siting *The Godfather* in American culture is finally about how to negotiate America as a text for authors, readers, critics, immigrants, and families. It's about the things we carry as we move from one group and identity to another and back again: ideals, people, conditioning, dreams, and metaphors. Here, at last, is the American family business in popular fiction, which we read through Puzo.

Notes

Introduction

1. How Puzo and Coppola collaborated on the screenplays will be an interesting subject for both film scholars and *Godfather* critics. Puzo's papers at present have been withdrawn.

2. Tony Soprano, already a child of Hemingway-era movies, protests to his psychiatrist that Gary Cooper wasn't in touch with *his* feelings; he was a "strong silent type, *that* was an American" (*Sopranos* 1, 1). Tony references traditional male silence fostered in the Western genre as his model, but he appears as the mob boss avatar of this silence himself, as well as a historian of his own generic role.

3. I'm indebted to Gina Frangello for pointing out this important difference between *The Godfather* as *lived* and *The Godfather* as *made*.

4. Fisher pragmatically notes a large exclusion in the absorption of regions by the core culture when he comments that gender and race are what within American experience can't be altered by mobility or succession of generations.

Chapter 1. Popular Fiction: Taste, Sentiment, and the Culture of Criticism

1. Bourdieu provides dozens of examples of class-based responses to paintings in *Distinction*.

2. Kant's "Intellectual Power of Judgment" which is to lead to "moral feeling" is cordoned off from history and politics, beginning *a priori* in maxims, which craft a law for everyone through a judgment not based on any interest. However, Kant allows that the intellectual power of judgment is not based on any interest but may give rise to one. Kant's interest is in the activity of judging, which he wants to describe as procedure: "The disinterestedness of the judgements of taste is only one element of the whole characterization of these judgements" (Kemal 105). After a judgment has been made, an interest can be connected to it, says Kant (Kemal 101), but it's difficult to translate such a sequence into actual reading and interpretation of texts. Such a sequence suggests fixed opinions and programmatic assignment of effects.

3. Jane Tompkins concludes her *West of Everything* by casting the going bad frame as the Western's "retaliatory violence," that "the hero is finally provoked

and "vengeance, by the time it arrives, feels biologically necessary" (228). Writers, readers, and critics eagerly pursue such a justification in popular fiction; they do what they gotta do.

4. Jonathan Glover "is also right in believing that our hope for the future must, to a considerable extent depend on the sympathy and respect with which we respond to things happening to others" Amartya Sen, "East and West: The Reach of Reason," *New York Review of Books*, July 20, 2000, p. 34. See Glover, *Humanity: A Moral History of the Twentieth Century.*

5. John Guillory observes that "pluralism forms the basis for a critique of aesthetic discourse itself inasmuch as that discourse appears to subsume the differences between different groups into the ideological 'universality' of aesthetic value, the same universality which virtually founds aesthetics in Kant's *Critique of Judgment*" (271).

6. Booth himself is caught in the quest for the one true reading, the summary evaluation. He has no interest in the critics' hesitancies and sustained quandaries unless and until they lead to the right judgment. He also disparages the popular in relation to elite fiction and roughs up *Jaws* to show how he can assimilate and dismiss it after sampling two pages, though he elsewhere states that "to understand a book well enough to repudiate it, you have to make it part of yourself, really live with it" (202, 285). He conflates judgments (sentimental, shallow, pretentious, decadent, bourgeois) with experiencing these states in the work itself. The literary-critical naming system is not as closed as Booth suggests. He fears "collusion with the accused" (285) when reading popular texts, a contamination of the aesthetic with the moral and ethical.

7. What I am positing here through articulating Jameson's hard-won ethical negations is a more affirmative use of the massive pessimism of the Critical Theory of Horkheimer and Adorno, themselves pioneers in conceiving of popular and high culture artifacts as part of the same inadequate imaginative response, through a methodology that influences Jameson's dialectic and yet is more qualified by his residue of romanticism within the hard sayings.

8. Hume provided the best and still most encompassing categorization of our infinite variety in taste judgments: "one person is more pleased with the sublime; another with the tender; a third with raillery. One has a strong sensibility to blemishes, and is extremely studious of correctness: another has a more lively feeling of beauties, and pardons twenty absurdities and defects for one elevated or pathetic stroke" ("Of the Standard of Taste" 314).

Chapter 2. Mario Puzo: An American Writer's Career

1. Yet the rambling apologia that is *Fools Die* should remind us that success, whether achieved by a Puzo or by a Melville descending through the labyrinth of *Moby Dick* to the sentimentally grotesque and inbred *Pierre* brings its own costs in American literary life through literary creations hybrid and still-born. If the American Success Story is really the American Failure Story, as countless

American texts have shown us over the centuries, the ironic state of "late" rather than "early" literary success is a happening for which we don't have as many models.

2. If *The Godfather* were an elite text, I might go into more depth in describing Nino as the author-manqué. Rabinowitz's suggestions of what conventions we follow "before reading" are certainly relevant to the general critical view that nothing can really be learned by studying a popular novel as a *kunstlerroman* or a *roman a clef*.

3. *Godfather II* might have been the novel sequel, instead of the second Academy Award winning *Godfather* film (1974), had Puzo gone to work on that text. A collection and cataloging of Puzo's papers, including novel drafts and film scripts for the *Godfather* movies is a badly needed next step for study of *The Godfather*.

4. *Contemporary Authors New Revision Series* 42, p. 367. The wry "rich and famous" line is very much in keeping with what Puzo calls his "casual irony," that he laments reviewers did not catch in his rendering of the Corleones. Such a generic "epiphany" is much valued in best sellers, as in Scarlett O'Hara's famous "As God is my witness, I'll never go hungry again," in *Gone with the Wind*.

5. So infuriating were these pieces that James Jones kept a copy of the essay in his Paris flat so that visiting writers could jot appropriate and obscene comments in the margins next to Mailer's prose. Jones's wife, Gloria, relates another side to this group of writers: "There was a kind of closeness because these guys were very special and understood they were smarter than most people, plus they knew that as novelists they were the best around. They saw themselves as part of the same very special club, a club that you had to be real good to get into. . . . There was that sense of us against them" (Manso 275). Puzo never received bids to rush this fraternity.

6. Freed from the mob narrative and its dominated or marginalized women, Puzo's Hollywood women are more lively, interesting, and sensual characters, as the female writers, directors, and stars of *The Last Don* (1996) attest.

7. In the film adaptation of *Some Came Running*, Dave Hirsh lives, but Ginnie is shot to death, presumably for the crime of being an insufficient working-class muse for a depressed middle-class writer.

Chapter 3. Bakhtin and Puzo:
Authority as the Family Business

1. The following are Bakhtin's most familiar texts to date in English translation: *The Dialogic Imagination* (1981); *The Formal Method in Literary Scholarship* (1978); *Marxism and the Philosophy of Language* (1973); *Problems of Dostoevsky's Poetics* (1984); and *Rabelais and His World* (1984).

2. Puzo does not tell the reader that the two old confederates are speaking in Sicilian dialect, although the intimate occasion would certainly suggest it. Throughout his fiction Puzo remains careless about Italian language transaction and occasions, evincing no consistent pattern in citing the language shift. Coppola

makes much of Solozzo changing to Sicilian dialect to speak with Mike in the restaurant just before the double murder. Gardaphe believes that "Puzo's representation of Italian language throughout the books is based more often than not on aural transcriptions of Italian words and Italian American dialect" (*Italian Signs* 213).

3. Bakhtin believes that "incorporated into the novel are a multiplicity of 'language' and verbal-ideological belief systems—generic, professional, class-and-interest group . . . tendentious, everyday . . . and so forth" (*The Dialogic Imagination* 311).

4. Bakhtin writes, "In a hidden polemic . . . the other's words are treated antagonistically, and this antagonism, no less than the very topic discussed, is what determines the author's discourse" (*Problems of Dostoevsky's Poetics* 195).

5. Coppola's *Godfather I* does not capture any of the resonances or nuances of the Genco–Don Corleone interview. Perhaps Coppola felt the scene came too early in the narrative to introduce a complex, ironic viewpoint of the Don's power.

6. "Stylization stylizes another's style in the direction of that style's own particular tasks. It merely renders those tasks conventional." (*Problems of Dostoevsky's Poetics* 193).

7. In his essay on crime in America, Puzo wrote that "society, cloaked in the robes of law, masked by religion, armed with authority, sprung from the beginning of history, is itself the archcriminal of mankind" (*The Godfather Papers* 80). All the cadences from the Genco–Don Corleone passage are here in the deep distrust of the legitimacy of any man-made institutions. With society as "archcriminal" here and death as the "foul criminal" in the Genco interview, the equivalance is clear: society equals death itself for Puzo.

8. Here is an excellent example of the sloganeering of popular fiction about the moral supremacy of the truly strong man, with its uncomfortable political associations.

9. For a full discussion of destiny in its relation to melodrama and to American Manifest Destiny, see chapter 6, "Destiny as Authorizing Melodrama."

10. A classic spokesperson and high culture text for this authority would be the Lady Catherine de Bourgh in Jane Austen's *Pride and Prejudice*. In her climactic interview with Elizabeth Bennet, Lady Catherine thunders, "I will not be interrupted! Hear me in silence!" as she attempts to stop the match with her nephew Darcy. Of course, Austen has Elizabeth Bennet carry the day with internally persuasive argument, even though Lady Catherine is not persuaded.

11. Giovanni Sinicropi had an early criticism that Puzo needed "a vehicle that would have allowed him to give us a dispassionate and courageous analysis of both the Mafia and the corporation, instead of a fresco glorifying the family 'gestes.' Puzo refused to go that far." Thus, he concluded that "the Mafia, even elevated to the rank of a corporation, remains as mysterious as ever" (90).

12. See Stephen Greenblatt, *Shakespearean Negotiations: The Circulation of Social Energy in Renaissance England* (1988), especially chapter 2, "Invisible Bullets," 21–65.

13. Barthes would say that these scenes state the presence of the Don's power, where the reader "consumes the myth according to the very ends built into its structure" (*Mythologies* 128).

14. The costs to the Corleones of continual victory is a primary subject of Coppola's *Godfather II*, in part a response to negative criticism of *The Godfather* novel and *Godfather I* that the Corleones were not sufficiently "punished."

15. In *The Dark Arena*, Puzo stressed World War II as a shaping force on his stoical protagonist, Mosca. Puzo had disregarded such large historicizing by the time of *The Godfather*.

16. Wayne Booth comments that the reader may undermine the author by becoming "an intending ironist in his own right" and thus becoming "part of the significance the text may acquire" (*A Rhetoric of Irony* 39). He also states that in irony, "we read character and value, we refer to our deepest convictions. For this reason, irony is an extraordinarily good road into the whole art of interpretation" (44). Granting Booth's premises, irony is not without its own hierarchical deformations of text and message.

Chapter 4. *The Godfather* and the Ethnic Ensemble

1. William Boelhower, *Immigrant Autobiography in the United States* (1982); *Through a Glass Darkly: Ethnic Semiosis in American Literature* (1987); "Adjusting Sites" (1999). Werner Sollors, *Beyond Ethnicity: Consent and Descent in American Culture* (1986); ed., *The Invention of Ethnicity* (1989); Anthony Julian Tamburri, *A Semiotic of Ethnicity: In (Re)cognition of the Italian/American Writer* (1998).

2. Gardaphe has commented that what is called the "Southern Problem" in Italy, one even raised by Northern Italians, then became the "Italian problem" in America (5).

3. The basic outlook of people in "Southern Italy" has been described by Edward Banfield as "amoral familism" and by Robert Putnam as a "culture of distrust" (Barone 242).

4. Such a reliance on the performative aspect of language and its visual, bodily motions suggests why mob narrative has been best represented by cinema since Coppola's *Godfather I* in 1972.

5. Such as Puzo's own *The Fortunate Pilgrim* (praised by Boelhower) and the writing of John Fante, Pietro DiDonato, and Jere Mangione (see Gardaphe, chapter 2, "The Early Mythic Mode," 55–85).

6. In *Godfather I* in the same scene, Kay and Michael are coming out of a theater after viewing *The Bells of St. Mary's* (1945) starring Bing Crosby as a singing priest and Ingrid Bergman as a no-nonsense nun at a struggling Catholic school.

7. Gardaphe raised the possibility that *The Godfather* is a study in "reverse assimilation, " asking "what would happen if an Italian had the power to make America conform to his or her way of seeing/being in the world? (94). I see Michael's initial reversion to the Family's side in a slightly altered frame. To become his father's son is to *unassimilate* prior to beginning to bend American systems and society to his will.

8. Michael here shows traces of a Tom Joad in Steinbeck's *The Grapes of Wrath*. An aura of Depression-era rhetoric, Puzo's formative decade, hangs over Michael's class analysis.

9. Hagen as adopted son generally shows more knowledge of Mafia codes than anyone in the Corleone family. When the huge dead fish is returned to the Corelone compound wrapped in Luca Brasi's bulletproof vest, Tom knows "It's an old Sicilian message" (118).

10. Torgovnick's comment was that Italian Americans believe that not saying something aloud "allays the truth" and calls it "faith in euphemism" (71).

11. Michael's grin here reminds of Sonny grinning nervously after the Don drops all pretense about his role as a murderer (222). "Grinning" signifies that the jig is up and both *omerta* and *bella figura* have failed.

12. It's important to recognize the Italian American fictional tradition in which the "honest hard-working Italian immigrant family" portrayed in the fiction of Fante, DiDonato, and Mangione functions "as a community united against an alien and hostile outside world." Puzo adds to this earlier, more realistic fiction and memoir the fantasy of absolute control over the American environment (Gardaphe 86).

13. We might speculate here that Puzo is referencing *the* Kennedys as an American family of power and wealth. Certainly the trajectory of Michael Corleone's career as the son of a powerful American criminal father, his war heroism in the Pacific, his brief Ivy League sojourn, his return in 1946 to "run" for Don recalls John F. Kennedy's career (even to following in his dead brother Joe's footsteps as politician when he really wanted to be a historian or writer). Not the least of America's subconscious identifications with the Corleones may be as shadow Kennedys on a more overtly sensational side of business, "diplomacy," and leadership. Puzo's most neglected novel *The Fourth K* (1990) depicts a future Kennedy president (Francis Xavier Kennedy) who must make terrible choices after his daughter is killed by terrorists. The book turns muddled and dark rather than a moment-to-moment thriller. Kennedy becomes an embittered and dangerous fascist, and the text is strewn with questionable views of just about everyone: blacks, Arabs, Jews, and all people in power. Here is a ranting Puzo text for further study.

14. Recall Ralph Ellison's grandfather at the outset of *Invisible Man* (1952) who tells his grandson to "live with your head in the lion's mouth. I want you to overcome 'em with yeses, undermine 'em with grins, agree'em to death and destruction, let 'em swoller you till they vomit or bust wide open" (19–20). Luce Irigary in *This Sex Which Is Not One* (1985) has famously posited the strategy of woman playing with mimesis, "miming" the oppressed female role by "try[ing] to recover the place of her exploitation by discourse, without allowing herself to be simply reduced to it" (76).

15. "Heteroglossia wash[es] over a culture's awareness of itself and its language, [and] penetrate[s] to its core." *The Dialogic Imagination*, p. 368.

16. Williams' "To Elsie" (1923) is a classic, unsentimental rendering of a New Jersey hired girl from an immigrant background, so overwhelmed by life's dismal present that Williams sees her only in a grim future that mocks both nature's beauty and God's dispensation: "Somehow it seems to destroy us. . . . / No one/ to witness and adjust/no one to drive the car."

17. Sandra (Mortola) Gilbert commented, "I wanted a name that *didn't* reek of garlic and cigars, didn't ooze olive oil, had never drunk red wine. . . . I wanted—

to be perfectly frank—a name that never met a mafioso (57); Hutcheon wrote of "cryptoethnicity," having been born "Bortalotti." She also notes that Davidson, an editor of *American Literature,* prefers "Notari-Fineman-Kotoski," the sign of growing up Italian, Russian, German Jew, and Polish Catholic (247). Boelhower, the most theoretically challenging multiethnic critic of American fiction, teaches and lives in Italy.

18. Boelhower in "Adjusting Sites" calls *habitare* an *ethnos* comprised of a place, a set of characters, and a customary behavior (65).

19. Gardaphe writes, "*The Godfather* was the first novel with which I could completely identify," and "Puzo's use of Italian sensibilities made me realize that literature could be made out of my own experiences" ("Breaking and Entering" 7).

20. Such scrutiny of America from the ethnic subject survives into *The Godfather* in fragments, such as when Don Corleone wonders that his soldier son Michael "performs these miracles for strangers" in World War II, whereas Lucia Santa marvels at the *goodness* of strangers helping her family.

21. Puzo gets credit for the story of *Superman*; the screenplay is credited to Puzo, Robert Benton, David Newman, and Leslie Newman.

22. In the original *Superboy* comic strip, begun in 1942 by Jerry Siegel and Joe Shuster after their 1930s success of *Superman*, their hero is given a past as a super baby whose craft crashes into the all-American town of Smallville. The Kents in the comic strip were townspeople, older and well-dressed, with the father in a snapbrim hat and topcoat, driving a roadster when they spot the infant by the road after he crashed to earth. By the 1980s, with American cinematic images of young Clark Kent in the *Superman* film racing express trains through farmfields, the Kents in the redrawn comic strip are rattling along in a brown pick-up truck with the father wearing overalls when they find the baby; back on the farm, young Clark breaks a tractor in half. We may surmise that Puzo's Fresh Air Fund idyll in New Hampshire had much to do with moving the Kents out into rural America. (*Superman from the Thirties to the Eighties,* 12, 15, 276).

23. Michaels suggests in *Our America* that "what is most valuable is what cannot be lost," that the "thing that you cannot lose is the thing that cannot be separated from you; it is not so much yours as it is you" (97).

24. Michael is "suddenly caught by something to which he belongs without knowing it," as Boelhower cites Viscusi writing about such flashes of involuntary insight. Boelhower references Lentricchia in *Johnny Critelli* that "in 1993, at the age of fifty four, 'he had gained sudden and inexplicable access to the past' " (67). Here is Michael's first flashback in the movie, one that he's helpless to control, that comes out of nowhere. Boelhower cites Carlo Ginzburg "enlarging what appears to be insignificant" (69), and calls this an example the "Italian school of microhistory" in the mid 1970s, what is now generally labeled New Historicism.

25. Lentricchia writes from inside this dynamic series of food, people, and writing in *Johnny Critelli*: "Christ, I'm hungry. . . . *They die while you write the book, while you're writing. Eat these sentences, these are their bodies. The last supper is a supper of sentences. The only supper*" (31).

26. Rose Basile Green identified this pattern of Puzo's heroes as early as *The Dark Arena* in the psyche of Walter Mosca, who, "finding that he does not relate

any longer to his family, [he] withdraws into the state of emotional paralysis that is his personal isolation" (342). A very high modernist fate indeed.

Chapter 5. Barthes and Puzo: The Authority of the Signifier

1. Terry Eagleton provides a preliminary analysis of the reader's inevitable ideological matrix in *Criticism and Ideology*, (167).

2. Kay's statement is seconded by Grace Kelly in *High Noon* (1952) just before Gary Cooper goes out to duel Frank Miller's gang. She says, "I don't care who's right or wrong. There has to be some better way for people to live." Westerns particularly encode such a yearning as they chronicle problems of societal order in a half-built civilization on the frontier. See Tompkins, *West of Everything*, 227–28.

3. In a pluralistic view of human values, Kekes writes, "Possibilities are seen as being good or evil depending on the effects their realization has or would have on us human beings. And these effects are benefits that we may enjoy or harm we may suffer" (15).

4. The only two fictional phenomena to match *The Godfather* in both popularity and cultural staying power are *Uncle Tom's Cabin* and *Gone with the Wind*. Stowe's novel raises the horrifying spectre of slavery at the root of the Southern family but also lets all parties off the hook by stating that God will end slavery's evil in his own good time. Mitchell provides a recovery narrative for an America in the teeth of a depression in the 1930s while writing stock Southern Reconstruction history. She also provides both an emancipated businesswoman in Scarlett as well as an impossible romantic heroine: one who is frigid and who chases the wrong man for over 850 pages before her epiphany. Both novels describe women's empowerment but give it no real currency in life-world affairs.

5. Bakhtin corroborates this logic when he speaks of "the absolute hegemony of myth over language." He describes "mythlogical thinking" as a substitute for the "connections and interrelationships of reality itself." (*The Dialogic Imagination*, 369).

6. I am adapting Barthes' system of signification to fictional discourse here without a real analysis of the implications of this shift to creative language. How the fictional act mediates or changes the dynamics of this pattern is a subject in itself. For my purposes, I assume that character zones are where fiction fundamentally happens.

7. Since *Mythologies*, much more work has been done on reader response and on social discourses speaking without subjects, influenced by the work of Foucault. Differing ideological views in America on how the FBI and communism worked together in a symbolic symbiotic relationship are advanced, as well as analyses of how communism itself has "failed" as a threat. Woltz may seem a Cold War period piece as well as a bit clownish c. 2000. In fact he may resemble not Fanucci, the Don's first victim (a cool old flamboyant bird) but the

landlord who terrified, comes to see young Vito after telling him to get lost—who the hell are you?—in his splenetic lack of control and subsequent nervous contrition when he learns the truth of Vito Corleone's new neighborhood menace through murder.

8. See Kekes' discussion of such procedural values, which include "distributive justice," "human rights," "equality," and "freedom," in chapter 11, "Some Political Implications of Pluralism: The Conflict with Liberalism" 199–217.

9. Don Corleone's enemy Phillip Tattaglia, is similarly discredited as child molester. Just before he is murdered on Michael's orders, Phillip Tattaglia, seventy years old and naked as a baby, stood over a bed on which lay a young girl.... Rocco pumped four bullets into him, all in the belly" (430).

10. The only other direct cry against Don Corleone's authority comes from Kay after Michael has explained his father's "ethics." She asks him, "What if everybody felt the same way? How could society ever function, we'd be back in the times of the cavemen" (365). Kay, too, is an outsider in the Corleone world. Female and powerless in Puzo's conception, she is Michael's property, much like Woltz's horse. Kay is also part of a gesturing toward a residual Protestant ethic that Puzo only sketches out.

11. In contrast to the suppressed institutionalized church, Ferraro has pointed out that *The Godfather* is intricately "organized around the sacramental activities for which Italians are renowned..." (Ferraro " 'My Way' in 'Our America' " 512).

12. The basic primers in such studies would include Rabinowitz, *Before Reading*; Booth, *The Company We Keep*; Hutcheon, *Irony's Edge*; and Smith, *Contingencies of Value*.

13. Yet in a firm symbiosis, by finding value and key clues to Puzo's talent and temperament in Michael's ethnic and family refusal is to practice the same negation in another semantic row that Barthes' mythologist found to be the critic's melancholy task when he exposes the heart of the falsely totalizing popular narrative. The refusals are in massive distaste, a refusal that leaves the writer and reader-critic at the heart of the aesthetic-ethical debate with no clear road home.

14. In the realm of "Khartoum studies," note how in *Godfather II*, a drugged and bewildered Senator Pat Geary of Nevada finds a raped and murdered girl in a well of blood in his bed and is convinced by the Corleones that he killed her and that they are his only protection against exposure. Senator Geary had gravely insulted Michael Corleone and didn't get the message, as Woltz had not. The primal violation of young girl as animal results. She is not only Khartoum but Woltz's twelve-year-old starlet victimized again. For the origin of Khartoum's head in Woltz's bed, Puzo may be referencing the 1884 murder and beheading of General George Gordon, the British colonial hero who fell during the siege of Khartoum in the Sudan. His head was put in a handkerchief and displayed before passing tribesmen who spit and cursed at it. Gordon's death shattered the myth of British invincibility in East Africa; his powerful aura and national affiliations did not save him any more than Woltz's connections saved his horse.

15. To patiently go on symbolic reading and linking expeditions in popular fiction and repeatedly end up "no place" is not to say the trip isn't worthwhile. Such journeying may be the only way to test out the author's conceptual skill and literary intelligence. What Ferraro calls "brilliantly anti-masculinist" and "surreally gynophobic," for example, in Puzo's writing about women ("My Way" 517), I still see as childishly sexist to no consistent pattern, that real shaping by Puzo is wishful thinking. Coppola pointedly excised Lucy Mancini, the overaged starlets, and Johnny's daughters from his 1972 film. Did he do so because the material was too awful or too explosive? I suggest the former, though Ferraro's lauding of the presentation of *The Godfather*'s women is certain to launch a new critical dialogue about Puzo.

16. Consider the enormous power of Marlow in *Heart of Darkness*, telling the Intended of Kurtz, "He died saying your name." Such is the bond established between Marlow and the reader in which Marlow equates the Intended with the novel's deepest darkness. "The horror, the horror" equals herself: European sentimental idealism, incarnated in woman's idolatry and "belief" that masquerades as love and Marlow thus identifies in his misogynistic displacement.

17. It would be fair to hold elite fiction to the same "policing" standards and not rush to call them "works for the ages" without the same ideological and formal scrutiny.

Chapter 6. *The Godfather* and Melodrama: Authorizing the Corleones as American Heroes

1. While Cawelti was one of the first critics to take *The Godfather* seriously for genre study in *Adventure, Mystery, and Romance*, he ascribed it to the evolution of the crime story while he reserved what he called "best-selling social melodrama" for the likes of Irving Wallace, Jacqueline Susann, and Harold Robbins. I believe Puzo in *The Godfather* to be the most powerful melodramatist.

2. Dreiser allows the softer, dreamier Puzo to be seen as opposed to the tough guy Norman Mailer, whom Puzo both envied and disliked in his style and success (see chapter 2).

3. *The Man in the Grey Flannel Suit* (1955) actually includes a melodramatic Italian subplot as World War II veteran Tom Rath must decide to do the right thing by an Italian woman with whom he has had a wartime romance and child—and how to tell his wife in Connecticut.

4. Stephen Neale has commented that melodrama often suggests a crisis of the social order but concludes with an "in-house rearrangement" of that order rather than any radical restructuring" (Ashley 109).

5. There's a whole novel here in the absent details of a figure such as a Joseph P. Kennedy in the interlocking of crime, business, and statesmanship, the potential interactions with real world capitalists, American down and outers, provisional socialists, New Deal bureaucrats, beleaguered bankers and businessmen. That text was written by Dos Passos among others; Puzo tells but does not show. He has neither the patience nor the inclination to let such detail work slow his melodrama for long.

6. When Puzo was imagining the destined Corleones (1969), his elite literature *doppelgänger* Mailer wrote impressionistically of American WASPS themselves "emerging from human history in order to take us to the stars" (*Of a Fire on the Moon* 280). Such was Mailer's manichean conception of the space program that he did not know whether these explorers (immigrants?) exemplified the best that was in us or the devil's own blapshemous reach to the stars. Mailer's brilliant nonfiction reporting the 1960s and 1970s is decidedly melodramatic and draws heavily on notions of the individual and collective American destinies. For Mailer in a prophetic mode threaded into a national literary conversation over the the last two centuries, see Banta, *Failure and Success in America*.

7. Long suggests that success novels may be set in "pure and fabulous" form as historical novels or "novels about religion" (64).

8. Women can't "go bad" in a positive sense. The designation would only connote "whore" or "adultress" and a loss of moral nature, not a move to a higher or culturally approved state. There is no recovery for women or triumphant victory in a process of going bad; there are no female Robin Hoods.

9. In the realm of recent American war films and "what we're fighting for," note *Saving Private Ryan* (1998) for one of the more melodramatic examples, *The Thin Red Line* (1998) for one of the more austere.

10. Even the kitchen is colonized in Coppola's *Godfather I*. Clemenza stands over a pot of pasta sauce, telling "Mikey" his favorite recipe lovingly and in detail. His apron, his rotund stature, his at-home ease all suggest that he's connoted as convivially female and in his element. Why does Michael need to know such arts? Because some day he might have to cook while the men "take to the mattresses," the mob family equivalent of manning a temporary safehouse from which they go forth to do mayhem.

Chapter 7. The Corleones as "Our Gang": *The Godfather* Interrogated by Doctorow's *Ragtime*

1. Such a conversion from "Andolini " to "Corleone" signifies the end of of the Andolini family in Sicily through murder and emigration, and Vito's prehistory is closed down. Yet "Corleone" brands him ever closer to Sicily. Michael Corleone will lose a Sicilian family yet again with the death of his new wife, Apollonia. Puzo kept repeating this dynamic as the Andolini/Corleones cycle back and forth through their descent culture's tragedies and vendettas. I'm indebted to Dina Bozicas and her paper, "Never on the Outside: Mario Puzo's Sicilianization of an American Hero."

2. Doctorow joins Puzo in writing a novel about an American gangster in *Billy Bathgate*, an account of Dutch Schultz written by the "capable" and inscrutable boy Billy who tells the Schultz gang's story from an anonymous and powerful position that he has attained in American society after sequestering a large part of the gang members' fortune at the time of their brutal assassination. For Doctorow, Billy himself is a historicized Jay Gatsby, who survives and becomes an inheritor. Dutch Schultz is a demystified and horrifying Don Corleone. Billy's

comment on destiny is that "the world worked by chance but every chance had a prophetic heft to it" (29), the promise that Little Boy has intuited in *Ragtime*. In a more pragmatic moment, Billy sums up a boy's life in mob narrative: "What I was in was a thrilling state of three-dimensional danger, I was in danger of myself, and in danger of my mentor, and in danger of what he was in danger of, which was a business life of murdering danger; and out beyond all that were the cops. Four dimensions" (39). Billy in maturity has become a powerful figure in that "general American family," perhaps a tycoon or government official, but he does not reveal his identity to the reader and remains inscrutably assimilated.

3. In *Ragtime*, Doctorow shows what happens when Coalhouse Walker cuts all his ties with the larger society and does *not* move in "happy savage honor" but is cut down in miscomprehension and horrible violence, including his own. Doctorow shows how Coalhouse's story moves past its myth toward his "philosophical destiny." In another vein familiar to *The Godfather*, Coalhouse demonstrates that when Amercican society can identify a true sacrificial victim, it will swiftly act on the maxim that "there couldn't be any kind of world if people acted that way." Coalhouse gets no dispensation to go bad; he merely becomes bad.

Chapter 8. The American Inadvertent Epic: *The Godfather* Copied

1. John McWilliams has commented that as early as 1805, Robert Southey had called the epic "degraded," and in 1812, an anonymous critic said the epic "seldom succeeds, unless in a barbarous or semibarbarous age" (117). Traditionally critics have wanted to reserve "epic" "for the best, the highest, and the most comprehensive of literry artifacts" (3).

2. See Shirley Samuels, *Romances of the Republic*, for intricate analyses of this visual and verbal iconography.

3. This passage of an American symbology over two centuries is in the realistic historical vein. The American Renaissance and modernist texts work mightily to subvert this more mainstream and normative tale.

4. Darby comments that Leon Uris's *Exodus* (1958) and James Michener's *Hawaii* (1959) urge that the individual derives meaning and identity primarily from his social setting, which in turn is amalgam of historical experiences grounded in religion and geography (93). Region and place matter in popular fiction and go against the grain of Ohmann's "personal illness" narrative, which is inward and private.

5. Fiedler comments on a distinguishing feature of popular art being its ability to move from one medium to another without loss of intensity or alteration of meaning: "its independence in short of the form in which it is first rendered" (*What Was Literature* 40). It's worth noting that the film and television adaptations of *Peyton Place* were relatively undistinguished, and as a result, the novel went out of print for many years and became known as something of a 1950s period piece without a sustaining and alternate media life.

6. Some of Puzo's other screen credits include *Superman*, *Earthquake*, and *The Cotton Club* (directed by Coppola).

7. There's more than a hint that Puzo resurrected Nino Valenti for Astorre Viola's tougher job of being a doubly blessed Don's son. The FBI agent's wife tells him, "You remind me of a young Dean Martin" and "Astorre was delighted. 'Thank you,' he said. 'He's my hero. I know his entire catalogue of songs by heart' " (149).

8. Chase in *The Sopranos* pays homage to Puzo's last literary effort and perhaps to his passing. In the first show of the third season, Tony brings *Omerta* to his mother, Livia, to read. It's the last time he sees her before her death.

9. Scorsese wanted to pick up on Nicholas Pileggi in *Wise Guy* (1985), who reworked the reminiscences of Henry Hill in nonfiction.

10. Chase memorably concludes the second show of *The Sopranos'* third season with Tony watching the end of *The Public Enemy* on his VCR just after the disastrous and depressing wake for his mother held at the Soprano home. Gangster Tommy Powers (Cagney) is to arrive home from the hospital at his sainted Irish mother's front door. While she sings "I'm Forever Blowing Bubbles" to herself as she fluffs his pillows in anticipation for his homecoming, his brother opens the door to Tommy's mummified dead body that falls in the door toward the camera; rival mobsters have done him in and gift-wrapped him. Tony wipes a single tear from his eye; the contrast with his own monster of a dead mother and his still very tenuous hold on life are clear to him. Chase has commented that watching this scene from the movie as a kid was "the most frightening thing [he'd] ever seen" (*Fresh Air*, National Public Radio, March 9, 2001 interview).

11. See Lopez, for the most complete run-down of mobster films.

12. Thomas Ferraro has written on *Prizzi's Honor* as a real contender with *The Godfather* in mob narrative. See Ferraro "Blood in the Marketplace" 199–207.

13. In postmodern America, the mob is as likely to copy the fictional texts. Lentricchia writes, "I saw an elegantly dressed elderly man, utterly manicured, a shave every four hours, a haircut every five days, who would occasionally walk outside to talk to youngish guys built like bulls in flowered shirts, with envelopes in their hands who kissed him on the cheek when they left. It was a movie, post-*Godfather*. They knew they were in a movie; they were enjoying themselves in the movie" ("The Edge of Night" 30).

14. The tip of the iceberg would include Godfathers Pizza, an oldies record collection of Italian American crooners called *Mob Hits*, a short story collection entitled *Take the Cannoli* (2000), and a rock band in Boston called "Luca Brasi." Johnny Depp gives a rhetoric lesson on the multiple meanings of "fuhgedabowdit" in *Donnie Brasco*.

Chapter 9. *The Godfather* Sung by *The Sopranos*

1. Sammy "The Bull" Gravano served five years in prison, was released, and ultimately left the witness protection program. As of July 2000, he sat in a Phoenix jail on $5 million bail for supplying area clubs with the drug ecstasy.

2. In Gay Talese's *Honor Thy Father* (1971), Bill Bonanno of the Bonanno crime family already felt in the early 1970s on reading *The Godfather* that "the

Sicilians described in [the novel] were endowed with impressive amounts of courage and honor, traits that [he] was convinced were fast deteriorating in the brotherhood" (312).

3. Paulie is not always so literal. He provides a great critique of Starbucks and designer coffee houses when he despairs that Italian-born drinks such as espresso and cappuccino are now the province of yuppies and non-Italians; he's disgusted with the legitimacy and tameness of the whole affair—but manages to cop a coffee mug before he walks out.

4. My sources tell me that Christopher uses a dialect version of *bucchaccio*, which sounds more like *booc yock* and which means "filthy hole."

5. What the audience knows includes Imperioli's memorable minor role in Scorsese's *Goodfellas*, as the young gang go-fer whom Joe Pesci first shoots in the foot when annoyed and then annihilates in a memorable spasm of violence. Chase references Imperioli's career in the mob film genre when "Christopher" gets partial "revenge" by shooting a bakery guy in the foot when he doesn't move fast enough to suit him.

6. Favreau's fine work in the episode shows a willingness to extend himself and his genre-persona beyond his role in *Swingers* where he was a younger and sadder Albert Brooks. Like Michael Imperioli who plays Christopher, Favreau is a writer-actor divining the Hollywood genre game and they both play writer-actors in this episode.

7. When Christopher finally insists that "you cannot use that story [of the transsexual], do you want to see me clipped?" he adds, plaintively, "you were just gonna leave?" "I really liked you." To which Amy responds, "It's getting kind of William Inge here," putting up her barrier of a cinematic trivial pursuit tactic to defuse any possible primary feeling. Finally her corporate identity achieves verbal domination, when, without a final comeback for him, she screams, "Excuse me! I'm a vice president, you fucking asshole."

8. Gina Frangello has commented to the author, "[Christopher is] standing there with a foot in two generations, immobilized. It's fascinating, watching this young man try to act out a part of his cultural collective consciousness (the Mafia belief system) while also chasing his generation's collective consciousness (the movie star)."

9. Tony is surprised to learn that his father, too, periodically collapsed or blacked out but that Johnny Boy's boys had let it go or called it "a condition."

10. See Thomas Schatz, "The Family Melodrama," in Landy, *Imitations of Life*, 162–65.

11. Fitzgerald in *Tender Is the Night* (1935) and Nabokov in *Lolita* (1958) firmly established movie love and Freudian love to be the intertwined expressions of modern desire in their representational narrative form and showed how deeply implicated Hollywood was in the production of making sense of Freud's "family romance." Fitzgerald provided the nightmare image of "Daddy's Girl" for Rosemary Hoyt and Nicole Warren Diver, before the father, Dick Diver, who would be all things to all women. Lolita, child of the movies, will be twice abducted, once by the romantic pedophile, Humbert, and then by Clare Quilty, the director who will star her in porn flicks.

12. When Bill Bonanno is sentenced by a judge to four years in prison for credit card fraud, much of Melfi's American umbrage at Tony is evident in his remarks: "You are not the product of a ghetto. I don't see that because of the family relationships. . . . you were under any great handicap. . . . You could have gotten a job. There was no need to do what you did." (Talese 471).

13. A case might be made that Kay Adams Corleone in *Godfather II* is radically intervening in mob life and that of the Corleones by unilaterally deciding to abort her unborn son with Michael, declaring that "this Sicilian *thing* must end." However, Kay is more desperate, without authority, personal or cultural, and for her stand is denied any contact with her children by Michael. Also, how the abortion squares with Kay's conversion to Catholicism in both novel and first *Godfather* film is puzzling.

14. Michaels concludes that it's pluralism itself that causes such identities to become tautologically explicable, that in pluralism we begin by affirming "who we are," which is understood as "prior to questions of what we do" (14–15).

15. I'm indebted to Marina Lewis for this point.

16. Puzo in *The Godfather* had Mama Corleone and Kay pray only for the Don and Michael, never for themselves and their children.

17. Mimi White comments that marriage on TV is a site of disruption rather than narrative closure as it often is in movies. Allen, *Channels of Discourse*, 193.

18. Cawelti speaks of the social melodrama of 1900 where an "aggressive social heroine's" woman's role was to bring back a "morallly revitalized man" to a "truer spirituality and loving relationship," Cawelti in Landy (42). Such would be Carm's traditional way in *The Sopranos*.

19. Don DeLillo has his protagonist Nick Shay in *Underworld* (1997) say of his Italian American boyhood in the Bronx in the 1950s, that

> I long for the days of disorder. I want them back, the days when I was alive on the earth, rippling in the quick of my skin, heedless and real. I was dumb-muscled and angry and real. This is what I long for, the breach of peace, the days of disarray when I walked real streets and did things slap-bang and felt angry and ready all the time, a danger to others and a distant mystery to myself. (810)

The persona of Nick Shay's teenage lament is precisely the character and role that Tony Soprano inhabits in his own present and that *The Sopranos* would hypothetically wean him from.

20. Lentricchia in *Johnny Critelli* crafts such a passage in mutual knowledge of its play, suggesting perhaps a truer give-and-take in the Italian American family battle between mother and son: "When I was a child, my mother said, If you say bad words I'll make this sewing needle get hot on the stove and sew your tongue to your lips. I'm going to put a nail through your tongue. She was trying to stifle a smile. I was trying to stifle a giggle" (31).

21. Chase has said that Livia is based on his late mother, Norma.

22. Barzini wrote about Italian sons: "Nothing should be spared to produce them. Everything is done for them in Italy. They are the protagonists of

Italian life. Their smallest wishes are satisfied." (Tom Hundley, "Apron Strings Holding Firm in Italy," *Chicago Tribune*, May 11, 2000). Since Barzini also comments that "Jesus Christ shares, in Italy, His supreme place with His mother, on almost equal footing" (Barzini 204), the battlelines are drawn in a secularization of this most venerated Mother and Son in Italian America.

23. Livia Soprano was brilliantly played by the late Nancy Marchand who died in June 2000. Her role was already greatly diminished in the show's second season because of her illness. In the first episode of season three in March 2001, Chase technologically reembodied Marchand as Livia for an awkward last scene with Tony before Livia's death. Any further revelations of Livia's pathology and power will have to come through flashbacks to Tony's youth.

24. Tony is constantly kept off balance in such moments. Earlier after savaging him to his face, Livia comes up close to him and says softly, "I suppose you're not going to kiss me." He literally flees down the steps of her house from this oddly incestuous moment, trips, and his gun falls out. As he scrambles to put it back in his pocket. Livia titters and slowly closes her front door, having reduced Tony to a child yet again.

25. Mary Ann Doane comments that pathos can be conceived of as "a kind of textual rape" (Landy 304).

26. Interim boss Jackie Aprile died of cancer in the show's second season, while the "big" boss languishes in prison. Uncle Junior, a potential rival to Tony, never had the right stuff in his prime and remains a dangerous but largely ineffective aging irritant.

27. In contrast to *The Godfather*, Chase really depicts the everyday violent economics of the Soprano family, its infrastructure, handling of money, and brutalizing of lower-life associates. Tony is a working man. Vito and Michael Corleone were executive bankers by comparison.

28. Is it a coincidence for Chase that *The Sopranos/The Simpsons*, contemporary television's most intelligent family dramas, both begin with *S* and contain the same number of letters?

29. The Waltons's call-and-response ending is perhaps copied from James Agee's writing of the softly whispered family "goodnights" on the Gudger porch in the most moving 1930s chronicle, *Let Us Now Praise Famous Men* (1941). Economically, the Waltons were the Beverly Hillbillies in comparison to Agee's blasted tenant farmers. Agee knew a thing or two about sentiment.

30. May it be too much to suggest that Chase, a true son of New Jersey, has named Meadow Soprano for the lovely and famed "Meadowlands?"

31. Late in *The Sopranos*' second season, Tony finally goes to his office after his lawyer suggests he might want to give an occasional appearance of legitimacy to the feds who are hounding him; the office managers have to clear away boxes and boxes of stuff (they've been using Tony's digs as a storeroom) and introduce him to the office staff.

32. See Ian Eng, "*Dallas* and the Melodramatic Imagination," in Landy 473–96; Sasha Torres, "Melodrama, Masculinity, and the Family," *Camera Obscura* 19 (January 1989), 86–106.

33. Chase does plant some literary visuals with a purpose. Carmela is seen in bed reading both the Bible and Arthur Golden's *Memoirs of a Geisha*, the Bible

when she asks Tony to get a vasectomy, *Memoirs,* just before she seduces him and asks that they try for another child. Melfi in bed reads T. Coraghessan Boyle's *Riven Rock*, the tale of an utterly mad husband propped up for decades by a platoon of psychiatrists and attendants; he has a morbid fascination with and violent hatred of women, particularly his mother and wife.

34. *Falcone* was an eight-night CBS mini-series modeled on the film *Donnie Brasco* and broadcast in March and April 2000 about an FBI agent going deep inside the mob. The audience could cling to the security of a law enforcement agent in an assumed role, while never having to worry about his true colors as they reveled in the mob mayhem. The USA cable series *Cover Me* debuted in April 2000 as a lightweight mix of a *Falcone* and *The Sopranos'* family feel and flair. Both husband *and* wife are undercover agents in darkest suburbia with three kids. They move around the United States in different identities and can become Jewish or "golfers" or "San Diegoans" for an hour, getting close to their quarry in ridiculously easy fashion on the model of *Charlie's Angels*. Mom's first seen in deep "uncover" as a fledgling Bada Bing girl writhing around a pole. The "Cover Me" logo leading into commercial breaks shows five little dark blue FBI strap undershirts on a backyard clothesline. The series is narrated by a Fred Savage "Wonder Years" voice-over of one of the *Cover Me* children. *Cover Me* appears to be lite parody in the guise of naive copying. The show's creator is Shaun Cassidy, and the first episode was directed by Tony (Wally Cleaver) Dow. A *Cover Me* kid intones, "By now, we're all on the team." Ain't it the truth.

35. The competition was won in the second season by Junior Soprano, who mused immortally, "I got the FBI so far up my ass they can smell Brylcreem."

36. At this point, it's clear that when I say "Chase" in my analysis, I'm also shorthanding a term that stands for a large number of creative hands. *The Sopranos* lists eleven directors and eight writers in the first two seasons of twenty-six episodes, with many of these personnel doubling as producers. Such an ensemble team working in tandem on a tight schedule obviously bears further investigation. Do different writers work on versions of episodes? Do some writers specialize in writing for specific characters? Is there a particular thematic or verbal/visual style to certain writers or directors in the series? Or is all homogenized under David Chase's vision?

37. Chase stated that he did "a sudden u-turn" at the end of *The Sopranos'* second season, when he'd planned to end with Tony more strongly realizing that he was his own worst enemy, that he had no excuses for what he was, but that suddenly Chase "got tired of moralizing," thought "that's enough for now," and felt it more necessary to remind the audience that Tony was a mobster and a "very scary man" (*Fresh Air* interview March 9, 2001). We can see how Chase himself recreates the audience's swing back and forth in identifying with or against Tony, rooting for his rehabilitation but still both admiring and fearing him.

Conclusion

1. Fisher remarks that we haven't truly begun to explore the "long history of money and speculation in America" ("American Literary and Cultural Stud-

ies" 234). Such eras as the Civil War, Gilded Age, Populist Era, and Progressive Era remain unacknowledged in any American fictional tradition, nor do more recent twentieth-century periods get their due. Tom Wolfe provides the closest look at recent American money and its mores in popular fiction in *The Bonfire of the Vanities* and *A Man in Full*.

2. An occasional exception proves the rule, however. At the Dons' convention, Don Corleone rises to say, "[W]e will manage our world for ourselves because it is our world, *cosa nostra*. . . . Otherwise they will put the ring in our nose as they have put the ring in the nose of all the millions of Neapolitans and other Italians in this country" (293).

3. As Fredo has no one else to be when Mike reads him out of the family in *Godfather II*, telling him that since he has betrayed the family, he doesn't want to see him or know what he does, that he does not want to be present when he visits their mother. When she dies, Mike gives a chilling nod at the wake to Al Neri that it's time to put Fredo's execution in motion.

4. Other identities that *The Sopranos* comments on are the childhood abuse narrative and the repressed memory narrative. Tony Soprano in the show's third season is tracking back through a Proust-inspired catalyst of an Italian salami to memories of his father chopping off a butcher's finger for not making weekly payments linked to his mother's almost sensual desire for bloody red meat on the dinner table.

5. Torgovnick writes, "The 'I' marks experiences, life histories, emotions, and beliefs. The 'we' marks positions, group identifications and allegiances: it can galvanize people for positive goals; it does not need to be pinched" (149).

6. Gordon and Newfield comment that "pluralism itself is under more scrutiny as the racial ideology of a minority white culture." (397).

Works Cited

Adorno, Theodor W. "On Epic Naivete." [1943]. *Notes to Literature. Vol. 1.* New York: Columbia University Press, 1991. 24–29.

Allen, Robert C., ed. *Channels of Discourse: Television and Contemporary Criticism.* Chapel Hill: U of North Carolina P, 1987.

Ashley, Bob. *The Study of Popular Fiction: A Source Book.* Philadelphia: University of Pennsylvania P. 1989.

Austen, Jane. *Pride and Prejudice.* [1813]. New York: Penguin, 1985.

Bakhtin, M. M. *The Dialogic Imagination.* Ed. Michael Holquist. Trans. Caryl Emerson, Michael Holquist. Austin: U of Texas P, 1981.

———. *Problems of Dostoevsky's Poetics.* Ed. and Trans. Caryl Emerson. Minneapolis: U of Minnesota P, 1984.

Baier, Annette C. *A Progress of Sentiments: Reflections on Hume's Treatise.* Cambridge: Harvard UP, 1991.

Banta, Martha. *Failure and Success in America: A Literary Debate.* Princeton: Princeton UP, 1978.

Barnes, Elizabeth. *States of Sympathy: Seduction and Democracy in the American Novel.* New York: Columbia UP, 1997.

Barone, Michael. "Italian Americans and American Politics." *Beyond* The Godfather. Ed. A. Kenneth Ciongoli, Jay Parini. 241–46.

Barthes, Roland. *Mythologies.* [1955]. Trans. Annette Lavers. New York: Hill & Wang, 1972.

———. *S/Z.* [1970] Trans. Richard Miller. New York: Hill & Wang, 1974.

Barzini, Luigi. *The Italians.* [1964]. New York: Touchstone, 1996.

Baym, Nina. "Melodramas of Beset Manhood: How Theories of American Fiction Exlude Women Authors." [1982]. *Criticism: Major Statements.* Ed. Charles Kaplan, William Davis Anderson. New York: Bedford/St. Martin's, 2000. 586–602.

Baynes, Kenneth. *The Normative Grounds of Social Criticism.* Albany: State U of New York P, 1992.

Beckett, Samuel. *The Unnamable.* London: Calder & Boyars, 1975.

Bellow, Saul. *Dangling Man.* [1944]. New York: Meridian, 1960.

Bernstein, Richard J. "Pragmatism, Pluralism, and the Healing of Wounds." *Pragmatism: A Reader*. Ed. Louis Menand. New York: Vintage, 1997.

Boelhower. William. "Adjusting Sites: The Italian-American Cultural Renaissance." *Adjusting Sites: New Essays in Italian American Studies*. Ed. Boelhower, Rocco Pallone. Stony Brook, N.Y.: Forum Italicum, 1999: 57–71.

————. *Through a Glass Darkly: Ethnic Semiosis in American Literature*. New York: Oxford UP, 1987.

Booth, Wayne. *The Company We Keep: An Ethics of Fiction*. Berkeley: U of California P, 1988.

————. *A Rhetoric of Irony*. Chicago: U. of Chicago P., 1974.

Bourdieu, Pierre. *Distinction: A Social Critique of the Judgement of Taste*. Trans. Richard Nice. Cambridge: Harvard UP, 1984.

————. *The Field of Cultural Production: Essays on Art and Literature*. Ed. Randal Johnson. New York: Columbia UP, 1993.

Bromley, Roger. *Lost Narratives: Popular Fictions, Politics and Recent History*. London: Routledge, 1988.

————."Natural Boundaries: The Social Function of Popular Fiction." In *The Study of Popular Fiction*. Ed. Ashley. 147–55.

Brooks, Peter. *The Melodramatic Imagination: Balzac, Henry James, Melodrama, and the Mode of Excess*. New Haven: Yale UP, 1976.

Brown, Gillian. *Domestic Individualism: Imagining Self in Nineteenth Century America*. Berkeley: U of California P, 1990.

Cahan, Abraham. *The Rise of David Levinsky*. New York: Grosset & Dunlap, 1917.

Canavan, Francis. *The Pluralist Game: Pluralism, Liberalism, and the Moral Conscience*. London: Rowman & Littlefield, 1995.

Carroll, Noel E. *A Philosophy of Mass Art*. New York: Oxford UP, 1998.

Carter, Bill. "HBO Wants to Make Sure You Notice." *The New York Times* on The Sopranos. New York: ibooks, 2000: 93–98.

————. "He Engineered a Mob Hit, and Now It's Time to Pay Up. *The New York Times on* The Sopranos: 83–90.

Cassidy, John. "The Fountainhead." *The New Yorker*. April 24 and May 1, 2000: 162–75.

Cawelti, John G. *Adventure, Mystery, and Romance: Formula Stories as Art and Popular Culture*. Chicago: U of Chicago P, 1976.

Caygill, Howard. *The Art of Judgement*. New York: Blackwell, 1989.

Chase, Richard. *The American Novel and its Tradition*. Baltimore: Johns Hopkins, 1957.

Ciongoli, Kenneth, and Jay Parini ed. *Beyond* The Godfather: *Italian American Writers on the Real Italian American Experience*. Hanover N.H.: UP of New England, 1997.

Conrad, Joseph. *Victory*. [1915]. New York: Oxford UP, 1986.

Coppola. Francis Ford. *The Godfather*. 1972.

——. *The Godfather Part II*. 1974.

——. *The Godfather Part III*. 1990.

Cvetkovich, Ann. *Mixed Feelings: Feminism, Mass Culture, and Victorian Sensationalism*. New Brunswick: Rutgers UP, 1992.

Darby, William. *Necessary American Fictions: Popular Literature of the 1950s*. Bowling Green, Oh.: Bowling Green State U Popular P, 1987.

Day, Clarence. *Life with Father*. New York: Knopf, 1935.

DeLillo, Don. *End Zone*. [1972]. New York: Pocket Editions, 1973.

——. "Interview with Don DeLillo." *Contemporary Literature*. 3, 1 (Winter 1982): 19–37.

——. *Underworld*. New York: Scribner's, 1997.

Dickens, Charles. *Bleak House*. [1853]. New York: Signet Classics, 1980.

di Donato, Pietro. *Christ in Concrete*. 1939. Indianapolis: Bobbs-Merrill, 1966.

Dixon, Thomas W. *The Clansman*. 1905. New York: Gordon, 1975.

Doctorow, E. L. "The Beliefs of Writers." *Jack London*: 103–17.

——. *Billy Bathgate*. New York: Random House, 1989

——. "Jack London and His Call of the Wild." *Jack London*: 1–21.

——. *Jack London, Hemingway, and the Constitution: Selected Essays 1977–1992*. [1993]. New York: Harper Perennial, 1994.

——. *Ragtime*. [1976]. New York: Plume, 1996.

——. "Theodore Dreiser: Book One and Book Two." *Jack London*: 21–39.

Dreiser, Theodore. *A Book About Myself*. [1922]. New York: Boni & Liveright 1926.

——. *The Financier*. [1912]. New York: Meridian, 1995.

——. *Sister Carrie*. [1900]. New York: Bantam, 1982.

Douglas, Lloyd C. *The Robe*. New York: Grosset & Dunlap, 1942.

Eagleton, Terry. *Criticism and Ideology*. London: Verso, 1978.

Ellis, John. *Visible Fictions*. London: Routledge, 1982.

Fante, John. *Wait until Spring, Bandini*. New York: Stackpole Sons, 1938.

Farred, Grant. "Engame Identity? Mapping the New Left Roots of Identity Politics." *New Literary History* 31, 4 (Autumn 2000): 627–48.

Faulkner, William. *Absalom, Absalom!* New York: Random House, 1936.

Feagin, Susan L. *Reading with Feeling: The Aesthetics of Appreciation*. Ithaca: Cornell UP, 1996.

Ferraro. Thomas J. "Blood in the Marketplace: The Business of Family in the *Godfather* Narratives." *The Invention of Ethnicity*. Ed. Sollors. 176–207.

———. " 'My Way' in 'Our America': Art, Ethnicity, Profession." *American Literary History*. 12, 3 (Fall 2000): 499–522.

Fiedler, Leslie A. *The Inadvertent Epic*. New York: Simon & Schuster, 1980.

———. *Love and Death in the American Novel*. [1960]. New York: Meridian, 1962.

———. *What Was Literature*: *Class, Culture, and Mass Society*. New York: Simon & Schuster, 1980.

Fisher, Philip. "American Literary and Cultural Studies Since the Civil War." *Redrawing the Boundaries: The Transformation of English and American Studies*. Ed. Stephen Greenblatt, Giles Gunn. New York: Modern Language Association, 1992. 232–50.

———. *Hard Facts*: *Setting and Form in the American Novel*. New York: Oxford UP, 1985.

———. "Introduction: The New American Studies." *The New American Studies: Essays from* Representations. Ed. Fisher. Berkeley: U of California P, 1991. vii–xxii.

Flaubert, Gustave. *Sentimental Education*. Trans. Robert Baldick. Hammersmith, Middlesex: Penguin, 1964.

Fleming, Robert. "For Mario Puzo, a Spectacular Return to the Mafia World He Knows So Well." www.bookpage.com. May 31, 2000.

Gambino, Richard. *Blood of My Blood*: *The Dilemma of the Italian-Americans*. Garden City, N.Y.: Doubleday, 1974.

Gardaphe, Fred L. "Breaking and Entering: An Italian American's Literary Odyssey." *Forkroads: A Journal of Ethnic American Literature* 1,1 (Fall 1995): 5–14.

———. *Italian Signs, American Streets: The Evolution of Italian American Narrative*. Durham: Duke UP, 1996.

Garrett, George. *James Jones*. New York: Harcourt Brace, 1984.

Gaut, Beryl. "The Ethical Criticism of Art." Ed. Levinson, *Aesthetics and Ethics*: 182–203.

Gelmis, Joseph. "Merciful Heavens, Is This the End of Don Corleone?" *New York* 4, 34, August 23, 1971: 52–53.

Genette, Girard. *Figures of Literary Discourse*. New York: Columbia UP, 1982.

Gilbert, Sandra. "Mysteries of the Hyphen." *Beyond* The Godfather. Ed. Ciongoli, Parini. 49–61.

Gilbreth, Frank B., and Ernestine Gilbreth Carey. *Cheaper by the Dozen*. New York: T. Y. Crowell, 1948.

Giordano, Paolo A. and Anthony Julian Tamburri, eds. *Beyond the Margin: Readings in Italian Americana*. Madison, N.J.: Fairleigh Dickinson, 1998.

Glover, Jonathan. *Humanity: A Moral History of the Twentieth Century.* New Haven: Yale UP, 2000.

Gordon, Avery, and Christopher Newfield. "White Philosophy." *Identities.* Ed. Kwame Anthony Appiah, Henry Louis Gates Jr. Chicago: U of Chicago P, 1995. 380–400.

Gray, John. *Enlightenment's Wake: Politics and Culture at the Close of the Modern Age.* London: Routledge, 1995.

Green, Rose Basile. *The Italian-American Novel: A Document of the Interaction of Two Cultures.* Cranbury, N.J.: Associated University Presses, 1974.

Griffith, D. W. *Birth of a Nation.* 1915.

Guillory, John. *Cultural Capital: The Problem of Literary Canon Formation.* Chicago: U of Chicago P, 1993.

Gunn, Giles. *Thinking across the American Grain: Ideology, Intellect, and the New Pragmatism.* Chicago: U of Chicago P, 1992.

Haley, Alex. *Roots.* Garden City, N.Y.: Doubleday, 1976.

Harpham, Geoffrey Galt. *Getting It Right: Language, Literature, and Ethics.* Chicago: U of Chicago P, 1992.

Hawthorne, Nathaniel. "Young Goodman Brown." *Selected Tales and Sketches.* New York: Holt, Rinehart and Winston, 1962. 108–122.

Hemingway, Ernest. *In Our Time.* New York: Scribner's 1925.

———. *The Sun Also Rises.* New York: Scribner's, 1926.

Hume, David. *An Enquiry concerning the Principles of Morals.* [1751]. Ed. J.B. Schneewind. Indianapolis: Hackett, 1983.

———. "Of the Standard of Taste." [1757]. *Critical Theory since Plato.* Ed. Hazard Adams. Harcourt, Brace, Jovanovich, 1992. 308–315.

———. *A Treatise of Human Nature.* New York: Oxford UP, 1978.

Hutcheon, Linda. *Irony's Edge: The Theory and Politics of Irony.* London: Routledge, 1994.

Jameson, Fredric. *Marxism and Form: Twentieth Century Dialectical Theories of Literature.* Princeton: Princeton UP, 1971.

———. *The Political Unconscious: Narrative as a Socially Symbolic Act.* Ithaca: Cornell UP, 1981.

———. "Postmodernism, or the Culture Logic of Late Capitalism." *New Left Review* 146: 52–92.

———. *Postmodernism, or the Cultural Logic of Late Capitalism.* Durham, N.C.: Duke UP, 1991.

———. "Reification and Utopia in Mass Culture." *Social Text* 1, (1979): 130–48.

Jones, James. *From Here to Eternity.* New York: Scribner's, 1951.

———. *Some Came Running.* New York: Scribner's, 1957.

Joyce, James. *A Portrait of the Artist as a Young Man.* [1916]. New York: Viking, 1964.

Kant, Immanuel. *Critique of Judgment.* [1790] Trans. Werner S. Pluhar. Indianapolis: Hackett, 1987.

Kekes, John. *The Morality of Pluralism.* Princeton, N.J.: Princeton UP, 1993.

Kemal, Salim. *Kant's Aesthetic Theory: An Introduction.* New York: St. Martin's, 1992.

Keyser, Les. *Martin Scorsese.* New York: Twayne, 1992.

Krantz, Judith. *Princess Daisy.* New York: Crown, 1980.

Landy, Marcia, Ed. *Imitations of Life: A reader on Film and Television Melodrama.* Detroit: Wayne State UP, 1991.

Lears, T. J. Jackson. *No Place of Grace: AntiModernism and the Transformation of American Culture.* Chicago: U of Chicago P, 1994.

Lentricchia, Frank. "The Edge of Night." *Beyond* The Godfather. Ed. Ciongoli, Parini. 28–48.

———. *Johnny Critelli; and the Knifemen: Two novels.* New York: Scribner's, 1996.

———. *The Music of the Inferno.* Albany: State U of New York P, 1999.

Leone, Sergio. *Once upon a Time in America.* 1984.

Levinson, Jerrold, ed. *Aesthetics and Ethics: Essays at the Intersection.* Cambridge: Cambridge UP, 1998.

Liman, Doug. *Swingers.* 1996.

Locke, John. *An Essay concerning Human Understanding.* [1690]. New York: Oxford UP, 1979.

London, Jack. *The Call of the Wild.* [1903]. New York: Vintage, 1990.

———. *Martin Eden.* [1909]. New York: Penguin, 1984.

Long, Elizabeth. *The American Dream and the Popular Novel.* Boston: Routledge & Kegan Paul, 1985.

Lopez, Daniel. *Films by Genre.* Jefferson, N.C.: McFarland, 1993.

Lopreato, Joseph. *Italian Americans.* New York: Random House, 1970.

Loriggio, Francesco. "On the Difficulty of Being an Italian-American Intellectual." *Adjusting Sites.* Ed. Boelhower, Pallone. 125–51.

Lukacs, Georg. *The Theory of the Novel.* [1920]. Cambridge: MIT, 1971.

Lynn, Kenneth S. *The Dream of Success.* Boston: Little, Brown, 1955.

Mailer, Norman. *Advertisements for Myself*. New York: Signet, 1959.

———. *The Deer Park*. New York: G. P. Putnam's Sons, 1955.

———. "The Time of Her Time." In *Advertisements*. 427–51.

———. "The White Negro." In *Advertisements*. 302–22.

Mangione, Jere. Mo*unt Allegro*. [1943]. New York: Harper & Row, 1989.

Manso, Peter. *Mailer: His Life and Times*. New York: Simon and Schuster, 1985.

Martin, Ronald E. *American Literature and the Universe of Force*. Durham N.C.: Duke UP, 1981.

Matthiessen, F. O. *Theodore Dreiser*. New York: William Sloane, 1951.

McShane, Frank. "Mario Puzo Dead at 78." Associated Press release. July 2, 1999.

McWilliams, John P., Jr. *The American Epic: Transforming a Genre 1770–1860*. Cambridge: Cambridge UP, 1989.

Melville, Herman. *Pierre; or, the Ambiguities*. [1852]. New York: Hendricks House, 1962.

Michaels, Walter Benn. *Our America: Nativism, Modernism, and Pluralism*. Durham, N.C.: Duke UP, 1995.

Miller, Toby. *The Well-Tempered Self: Citizenship, Culture, and the Postmodern Subject*. Baltimore: Johns Hopkins, 1993.

Mitchell, Margaret. *Gone with the Wind*. [1936]. New York: Warner, 1993.

Morison, Samuel Eliot. *The Oxford History of the American People*. New York: Oxford UP, 1965.

Nardini, Gloria. *Che Bella Figura: The Power of Performance in an Italian Ladies' Club in Chicago*. Albany: State U of New York P, 1999.

Neale, Stephen. "Genre." In *The Study of Popular Fiction*. Ed. Ashley. 107–12.

Norris, Frank. *The Octopus*. [1901]. New York: Penguin, 1986.

Nussbaum, Martha. *Poetic Justice: The Literary Imagination and Public Life*. Boston: Beacon, 1995.

Ohmann, Richard. "The Shaping of a Canon: U.S. Fiction, 1960–1975." *Critical Inquiry* 10, 1 (September 1983): 199–223.

Palumbo-Liu, David. "Assumed Identities." *New Literary History*. 31, 4 (Fall 2000): 765–80.

Percy, Walker. *The Moviegoer*. [1961]. New York: Popular Library, 1961.

Pileggi, Nicholas. *Wise Guy: Life in a Mafia family*. New York: Simon & Schuster, 1985.

Puzo, Mario. "Choosing A Dream: Italiana in Hell's Kitchen." *The Godfather Papers*: 32–69.

———. *The Dark Arena.* [1955]. New York: Dell, 1969.

———. *Fools Die.* New York: Signet, 1978.

———. *The Fortunate Pilgrim.* [1964]. New York: Fawcett Columbine, 1997.

———. *The Godfather.* [1969]. New York: Signet, 1978.

———. *The Godfather Papers and Other Confessions.* New York: Fawcett, 1972.

———. *Inside Las Vegas.* New York: Charter, 1977.

———. *The Last Don.* [1996]. New York: Ballantine Books, 1997.

———. "The Making of *The Godfather*." *The Godfather Papers:* 32–69.

———. "Notes from an Unsuccessful Writer's Diary." *The Godfather Papers:* 233–48.

———. *Omerta.* New York: Random House, 2000.

———. *The Sicilian.* New York: Bantam, 1984.

———. "Writers, Talent, Money, Class." *The Godfather Papers:* 81–88.

Pynchon, Thomas. *The Crying of Lot 49.* [1966]. New York: Harper & Row, 1986.

Rabinowitz, Peter. *Before Reading: Narrative Conventions and the Politics of Interpretation.* Ithaca: Cornell UP, 1987.

Railton, Peter. "Aesthetic Value, Moral Value, and the Ambitions of Naturalism." Ed. Levinson, *Aesthetics and Ethics.* 59–105.

Rand, Ayn. *Atlas Shrugged.* New York: Random House, 1957.

———. *The Fountainhead.* New York: New American Library, 1943.

Riesman, David. *The Lonely Crowd.* New Haven: Yale UP, 1950.

Robbins, Harold. *The Carpetbaggers.* New York: Simon & Schuster, 1961.

Rorty, Richard. *Truth and Progress: Philosophical Papers, Volume 3.* Cambridge: Cambridge UP, 1998.

Roth, Philip. *Goodbye, Columbus.* [1959]. New York: Bantam, 1963.

Roulston, Helen. "Opera in Gangster Movies." *Journal of Popular Culture* (Summer 1998): 102–11.

Samuels, Shirley. *Romances of the Republic: Women, Family, and Violence in the Literature of the Early American Nation.* New York: Oxford, 1996.

Scorsese, Martin. *Goodfellas.* 1990.

Sen, Amartya. "East and West: The Reach of Reason." *New York Review of Books.* July 20, 2000, 34. Excerpted from Glover, *Humanity.*

Shaw, Daniel. "Hume's Moral Sentimentalism." *Hume Studies* 19, 1: 31–51.

Sinicropi, Giovanni. "The Saga of the Corleones: Puzo, Coppola, and *The Godfather* (an interpretive essay)." *italian americana* 2, 1: 79–90.

Smith, Barbara Herrnstein. *Contingencies of Value: Alternative Perspectives for Critical Theory*. Cambridge: Harvard, 1988.

Smith, Carl. *Chicago and the American Literary Imagination 1880–1920*. Chicago: U of Chicago P, 1984.

Smith, Dennis Mack. *A History of Sicily: Modern Sicily after 1713*. London: Chatto & Windus, 1968.

Sollors, Werner. *Beyond Ethnicity: Consent and Descent in American Culture*. New York: Oxford UP, 1986.

———, ed. *The Invention of Ethnicity*. New York: Oxford UP, 1989.

The Sopranos. 1999–2001.

Stowe, Harriet Beecher. *Uncle Tom's Cabin*. [1852]. New York: Penguin, 1981.

Talese, Gay. *Honor Thy Father*. New York: Fawcett Crest, 1971.

Tamburri, Anthony J. *A Semiotic of Ethnicity: In (Re)cognition of the Italian/American Writer*. Albany: State U of New York P, 1998.

Tarentino, Quentin. *Pulp Fiction*. 1994.

Tompkins, Jane. *West of Everything: The Inner Life of Westerns*. New York: Oxford UP, 1992.

Torgovnick, Marianna DeMarco. *Crossing Ocean Parkway: Readings by an American Daughter*. Chicago: U of Chicago P, 1994.

Trey, George. *Solidarity and Difference: The Politics of Enlightenment in the Aftermath of Modernity*. Albany: State U of New York P, 1998.

Updike, John. *Rabbit, Run*. New York: Knopf, 1960.

Viscusi, Robert. *Astoria*. Toronto: Guernica Editions, 1995.

———. "Divine Comedy Blues." *Beyond the Margin*. Ed. Giordano, Tamburri. 69–82.

Vittiello, Justin. "Off the Boat and up the Creek without a Paddle." *Beyond the Margin*. 23–45.

Waugh, Patricia. "Stalemates? Feminists, Postmodernists and Unfinished Issues in Modern Aesthetics." *The Politics of Pleasure: Aesthetics and Cultural Theory*. Ed. Stephen Regan. Philadelphia: Open U P. 180–201.

White, Mimi. "Ideological Analysis and Television." *Channels of Discourse*. Ed. Allen. 134–71.

Whyte, William H. *The Organization Man*. New York: Simon & Schuster, 1956.

Wilson, Sloan. *The Man in the Grey Flannel Suit*. New York: Simon & Schuster, 1955.

Wister, Owen. *The Virginian*. [1902]. New York: Viking Penguin, 1988.

Zaleski, Jeff. "Mario Puzo: The Don of Bestsellers Returns." *Contemporary Literary Criticism* 107: 212–14.

Index

Abbandando, Genco (*The Godfather*), 1, 88, 90–96, 99, 100–03, 114, 161, 205; and *bella figura*, 125–27; and *omerta*, 125–27

Adorno, Theodor, 18, 34, 237, 262, 271, 300n. 7

Aesthetics: and the aesthetically "bad," 27; and the aesthetically "good," 27; and distaste, 27; and moral agnosticism, 29; and moral judgment, 27; and Romanticism, 28; and taste culture, 31

Agee, James, 314n. 29; *Let Us Now Praise Famous Men*, 314n. 29

Albrecht, Chris, 288

Alger, Horatio, 178

All About Eve, 74

All in the Family, 283

Ally McBeal, 286

Althusser, Louis, 34

American Beauty, 263

American fiction criticism, 31; and capitalist heroes, 182

American Romance paradigm, 31, 186

Analyze This, 249

Arnow, Harriette, 131; *The Dollmaker*, 131

Auden, W.H., 203

Austen, Jane, 302n. 10; *Pride and Prejudice*, 302n. 10

Bachelard, Gaston, 110

Baier, Annette: *A Progress of Sentiments*, 20

Bakhtin, M.M., 16, 87–89, 92, 94–95, 98, 106, 109, 135, 218, 224, 233–34, 301n. 1, 302n. 3, 302n. 4, 306n. 5; and answering words, 102; and authoritative discourse, 88–89, 94, 125; and dialogics, 16, 88–90, 94–95, 98, 103, 106, 129; and epic, 233–34; and internally persuasive discourse, 88–89, 93, 125; and single-voiced myth, 159; *The Dialogic Imagination*, 88–89, 92, 94, 95, 98, 106, 169, 218, 233–34; *Problems of Dostoevsky's Poetics*, 84, 98

Baldwin, James, 71

Balzac, Honore de, 3, 185

Banta, Martha, 309n. 6; *Failure and Success in America*, 309n. 6

Barnes, Elizabeth, 173, 201; *States of Sympathy*, 173, 199, 201

Barthes, Roland, 16, 25, 48–49, 106, 149–62, 166, 168–70, 186, 271–72, 285, 302n. 13; and Bakhtinian dialogic, 106; and critical melodrama, 49; and de-politicized speech, 89–93; and distaste, 307n. 13; and Foucault, 306n. 7; and historicizing, 152–54, 170; and ideologizing, 25; and naturalizing, 152–54; and poetizing, 25; and politicized speech, 89–93; and signifiers, 156–57, 306n. 6; and universal signifieds, 186; *Mythologies*, 16, 25, 48–49, 89–90, 93, 106, 149, 151–52, 154–58, 160–61, 166, 168–70, 186, 271–72, 302n. 13,